MW01047142

Silk

Caroline's Story

SOPHIA ALEXANDER

ONALEX BOOKS
Savannah, GA

The Silk Trilogy

Silk: Caroline's Story

Tapestry: A Lowcountry Rapunzel

Homespun

To those who unravel life's mysteries with open, discerning minds and kindly, passionate hearts.

May you always be equipped for your journey with a sense of humor, a healthy appreciation for irony and, most especially, a knack for finding that silver lining.

The serpent that did sting thy father's life
Now wears his crown.
-Ghost, Scene V, *Hamlet*

ISBN: 978-1-955444-28-6

Library of Congress Control Number: 2021910146

This book contains an excerpt from *Tapestry: A Lowcountry Rapunzel* by Sophia Alexander. This excerpt may not reflect the final content of the forthcoming edition from Onalex Books.

CONTENTS

1• Stowaway.. 1
2• Kingstree Invitation........................ 10
3• The Sewing Factory......................... 18
4• Dime Novel.. 30
5• Meeting Clay.................................... 39
6• Meeting Stephen.............................. 51
7• Sunday Guest.................................. 57
8• Disparaging Shakespeare............... 71
9• Jessie Skulks.................................... 83
10• Christmas Eve.............................. 90
11• Christmas Day.............................. 97
12• Romantic Supper.......................... 107
13• Excursion To Charleston............. 112
14• A Possessive Husband.................. 130
15• School Dramas.............................. 136
16• A Porcelain Life............................ 143
17• Saving Julep.................................. 150
18• The Man On The Premises........... 167
19• The Designer................................. 174
20• New Abodes.................................. 188
21• It's Not The Horses....................... 202
22• Jessie Visits Greeleyville............. 212
23• A Choice At The Creek.................. 219
24• Night Of Sorrow............................ 230
25• Square Root.................................. 240
26• The Anvil....................................... 244
27• Her Condition, His Purgatory....... 250

28• Proposal... 257
29• A New Family.................................. 264
30• Pie-In-The-Sky Offer..................... 276
31• The Birth.. 289
32• Meeting Vivian.............................. 294
33• Anne's Wedding............................. 314
34• Caroline's Fate............................... 331
35• Ruins... 342
36• Assuming The Mantle.................... 347
Epilogue.. 351
Acknowledgments.............................. 354
Tapestry Excerpt................................ 357

1• Stowaway

October 1899, en route to Charleston, SC

GASPING, JESSIE INCHED from under the stifling canvas as if vacating a cocoon. She emerged from between stacks of cotton bales just enough to peek over the edge of the jostling wagon and gulp in the mercifully fresh air. Eagerly, she scanned the terrain.

Alders, sweetgums, and water oaks trailed behind them in an interminable swath of greens, browns, and russets, not much more exciting than the underside of the canvas. She tugged cotton neps from her limp, dark hair and searched the road for something new, for a sign they'd left Kingstree far behind. The banks were overgrown with weeds. A rusty pail lay in a ditch. Dull-brown squirrels chased each other up the trunk of a tree. Nothing seemed new or different. Not yet.

Sighing, Jessie pushed the canvas up and towards the front of the wagon, over the stacks that had nearly suffocated her. Wedging a boot in between the bales of one tower, she braced her back against the opposite stack, hoping to somehow wriggle up to the top. From there, she'd be able to see the road ahead.

To her dismay, the uppermost bale began to shift behind her. She twisted, just managing to catch the teetering mass before it fell in the road and gave her away.

Jessie clung to it. She'd had to undo some of the straps Clayton had used to secure the high stacks in order to make herself fit inside the wagon. It wouldn't bode well if she knocked his clean cotton bales onto the dusty road.

Pulling the tower straight, she found herself once again sandwiched within the narrow space. Reaching up with both arms, she worked her fingers around the twine of the highest bales of each tower, then wedged her feet into opposite spaces between the stacks. Like a daddy-longlegs, she crept upwards, not daring to push too much one way or the other, her forces evenly distributed. Raising one leg at a time, she scrambled onto a high bale, her hand secured through the twine so as not to fall off. It was soft beneath her.

She lay still, panting. Her head settled onto a makeshift pillow, the rough canvas now bunched-up towards the front of the wagon. Wind billowed her dress away from her skin. The autumn sun was warm. Her still-cramped toes wriggled in protest, and she wondered why she hadn't taken off her boots as soon as she'd stowed away. *I could've come up here hours ago. Clay's too busy drivin' to notice me.* Keeping a tight grip on the twine, Jessie twisted onto her stomach and looked down at him. If she scooched forward just a few inches, she'd be able to touch his hat. A thrill of elation trickled up her spine. *So far, so good. He has no idea I'm here.*

Cautiously, she flipped onto her back, one hand still grasping the twine—as if she wouldn't simply take the bale with her if she toppled over. With the other hand, she worked off her worn, tight boots, shoving them back into the space between the bales. A rank whiff assaulted her nose, dissipating just as quickly as the breeze licked her feet.

Stretching luxuriously, she leaned back and examined the cotton puffs peppering the azure sky. A murder of crows flew overhead, gravitating towards her. *So long as they don't mess on me.* Regretting that the boots were out of reach, she glanced around for something to throw.

The crows erupted into a flurry of sharp, raucous cries. Her bale jerked forward as the wagon came to an abrupt halt. Clayton must have drawn up the mule, no doubt straining to see the commotion above. Jessie froze, lying perfectly still, hardly daring to breathe. She prayed the unsecured cotton hadn't brushed against his head. Her pulse pounded in her ears as she waited for Clayton to push the bale back, to climb down and discover her as he tried to secure the cotton again. When the dark birds veered away at last, however, the wagon started up again. Jessie breathed another shaky sigh of relief.

Settling back on the tarp, she began to relax. Soon she was interpreting the cloud plumes above. *Lilies for our wedding. A paddle. A pocket watch. Oh, a snake.* At the memory of the garter snake she'd put in Aunt Sally's pantry only days before, she caught herself mid-laugh. Twisting forward, she was relieved to see that Clayton was still driving as normal; of course he was, she would have felt him drawing up again if he'd heard her, which he clearly hadn't.

Her gaze lingered on his profile, and she gave a delighted shiver. Clayton Bell was the love of her life, though he didn't know it yet. He regarded her merely as a pauper cousin, someone to ignore unless pressed. And she was still only twelve. Nevertheless, she had swiftly and irrevocably fallen for him.

Most girls pass through their crushes and move on, but Jessie was far from ordinary—her intensity funneled every effort into purposeful direction. So when she gazed into Clayton's laughing blue eyes for the first time and felt her insides squeeze into knots and her breath choke away, she took her reaction quite seriously. When he teased her about the gap between her front teeth without incurring a drop of bloodlust, she knew that she must be in love.

That settled, there was only the annoying age difference with which to deal—and to her great frustration, the only answer to that seemed to be the creeping, slothful hands of time.

Clayton coughed, and Jessie rolled onto her stomach, propping herself to study his godlike form from behind. His blond hair was carelessly overgrown, and muscular, broad shoulders sloped towards a trim waist. The next several hours were passed staring at him from this vantage point, slipping between the bales only during Clayton's occasional stops to eat or tend to the mule. When he resumed, she'd straighten the stacks out again before shimmying back up.

Clayton was concerned not to strain Button, never having traveled so far before. After young Jessie had hounded him with questions about his life experiences during one of his regular visits with his aunt and uncle, he'd been struck by how little he had traveled. Seized with an inspiration to extend his break from his mother and see the old state capital, he and Button were carrying his harvest of Sea Island cotton to the Holy City themselves, instead of sending it by railcar.

As the brilliance of the just-turning autumn foliage began to grow dim with the arrival of dusk, Clayton arrived at one of the few inns along the way. Most of the faded plantation house's shutters were closed. It looked like a shedding creature, sleeping with just one eye open. He would have passed it by but for the assortment of buggies outside and the hand-carved sign above the door. Pent-up tension released from his shoulders as he pulled over; he'd been worried that he might travel too slowly and end up sleeping in the elements.

He nodded, pleased that the first day of his trip was ending well. Being no sort of traveler, he had begun to doubt the wisdom of this journey. Yet here he was, bracing himself for the modest expense of supper and the cost of laying out his Spanish-moss-filled bedroll in the common room. He was saving on the cost of the railcar, but the difference wouldn't cover his travel expenses.

Once Button was settled in the stable, Clayton came back to secure the wagon, now devoid of any trace of Jessie.

Wafting aromas of savory home-cooking had undone her reserves. She stood by the inn door, slipping inside after Clayton when he was finished with the wagon and Button.

He took a seat on the bench at the already laid-out, immense dining table, next to one family and a dozen or so other travelers, a handful of students, and a few workmen. As he scooped fried okra and oil-flecked squash casserole onto his plate, a clear, familiar voice said, "Looks good."

He looked up in surprise, speechless.

"Well, it does." Jessie smiled at him from the end of the table. Her straight black hair bobbed like fishing line as she nodded encouragingly.

He could only nod back at her.

With a smirk, Jessie slid onto the bench next to him and began to pile her own plate high. "I'm starvin'!"

His appetite abruptly gone, Clayton stared at the girl with open-mouthed incredulity.

Jessie loved the rush of exhilaration that came from surprising someone. Now she had outdone herself. This trip was not about shocking Clayton, however. No, she just wanted to be with him. And perhaps to find out how much she could get away with—how audacious she could actually be. That elusive upper hand had always evaded her, and something needed to change in her life. Within the previous year, her mother had passed away and her stepfather had abandoned her. She had no friends, was stuck with an old couple who had never asked for her, and was in love with someone who thought of her as a pest, if at all.

"What on God's green earth are you doin' here?" Clayton asked, finally regaining his voice.

Ignoring the looks of the other guests, she met his eyes. "I wanted to see Charleston, too. I knew better than to ask, so I just caught a ride."

"What in tarnation? Where were you? In the back of my wagon?"

"No, on a heron." At his scowl, she added quickly, "But don't worry, I won't do it again. That gin ain't got out all them cotton seeds. They aggravatin' as burrs."

He frowned, vertical lines of worry forming between his eyebrows.

"Burrs in the grass. You know."

"I don't have time to take you back to Uncle Joe's."

"That's alright." Subduing a triumphant smile, she lifted a forkful of barbeque to her mouth and chewed resolutely, meeting the curious gazes of some of the folks around them.

"I don't have money to be payin' for rooms and…" he waved at her plate, "and food for you."

She determinedly chewed another mouthful—a mouthful that must have been too spicy, as her eyes began to water. After swallowing, she said, "Well, I don't take up much space. And maybe you could just sneak me a li'l bit o' food. I really won't need much. I can prob'ly go days." She rubbed at her eyes and dug into the hearty mound again, determined to make the most of it.

Clayton sat and watched her eat for a time. At last, he said, "You can't be sleepin' in the common room with the menfolk, and I can't afford no room."

Jessie pushed a limp, dark lock of hair behind her ear. "No need to make a fuss. I'm gonna sleep in the wagon."

He clenched his head in his hands, murmuring, "This is all I need."

"I can help you." Her voice was suddenly bright and assured. "I can drive the wagon sometimes if the road is gonna be straight for a long time. I can help feed Button. And shave your face. And keep you company."

His buried scowl transformed into a look of perplexity.

"It'll be fun," she added hopefully.

At this, he threw up his hands. "You are one helluva mess, Jessie Bell."

The entire table turned towards him this time, but Clayton was too overcome to notice. He was staring at the girl who had just transformed his adventure into a childrearing exercise.

Jessie shook her head at the onlookers, shrugging as if she had no idea what the fuss was about.

"Well, can't see as how I can get you back home," he said flatly. "Now both of us is gonna have to sleep in that wagon, cuz I can't afford to be rentin' rooms. I ain't made o' money."

Jessie nodded, weak with relief. "Ain't so bad back there. Lots o' cushion, like the tallest mattress in kingdom-come."

At this, the corners of his mouth twitched upwards. He said gruffly, "Guess I better send a telegram lettin' Uncle Joe and Aunt Sally know where you're at."

"Oh, don't worry." She grinned slyly. "I left them a note already."

That night, Jessie lay under Clayton's bedroll next to his warm, formidable figure. He'd pushed the bale stacks together and fastened them in place again. They were on top of the rough tarp—he insisted it had to stay in place to protect the cotton—with nothing over their heads but a sliver of moon and a canopy of brilliant stars. Cicadas buzzed so loudly that they would have wakened her if she hadn't already been unable to sleep for excitement.

She sat up next to Clayton, watching him, her beloved, as he slept. After a while, she eased her hand into his rough, large one. Her chest teemed with the closest emotion she had ever felt to bliss.

Jessie swore then that this was only the first of countless nights they would be together.

2• Kingstree Invitation

October 1899, Beaufort, SC

"I'M GONNA LEAVE IT ALL BEHIND," Caroline swore. She clung to his broad, warm neck and pressed her cheek into his steady pulse. "I love you, and I'm comin' with you."

Her heart felt as though it might burst. He had turned her world upside-down. Though she had known him only two short weeks, she could not fathom being without him. He would leave for Kingstree the day after tomorrow, and she was determined to join him.

Her parents were unaware of the passion she had discovered. Their dry, lackluster lives had surely never known this sort of infatuation.

She ran her fingers through his long, silky hair and settled against him, murmuring tender, heartfelt endearments into his velvet coat.

With a soft snort, he began prodding her skirt in search of the crisp pear he'd come to expect from her visits.

"Here you are." She laughed and fished the treat from her pocket. He nipped at it, dribbling juice onto her palm. The aroma of fresh pear filled the stall. "But you have to swear not to leave without me. Okay, Julep. You promised."

Sam Swann stroked his thick, blond sideburns as his niece approached on his favorite thoroughbred, the clang of iron-shod hooves slowing against the cobblestones. Caroline looked wind-blown. Enough pine needles stuck out from the wide brim of her straw hat to make a whisk-broom. *She's paid about as much heed to my warnings about Julep throwin' riders as to a preacher with laryngitis.*

"He's been an absolute angel, Uncle Sam—just like always." Her words tumbled out in a rush as they pulled up in front of him. A profusion of blond curls had bounced loose from the bun at the nape of her neck. "You don't mind if we take just one more little trip down the road, do you?"

Sam shook his head. He patted Julep, searching for tell-tale flecks of lather. "That's 'bout enough of these roads."

"Oh, we didn't stay on the roads. I took him out of town." Gingerly picking up a fold of her dust-laden riding skirt with her fingertips, Caroline made a rueful face. "As you can see."

He laughed. "I guess you two can go for a little while longer then. Be careful."

Almost before the words were out of his mouth, she'd clicked her tongue and was setting off, clattering rhythmically down the street.

Turning back in the direction of the Corbetts' green-shuttered Federal-style home, Sam decided that he might as well accept his nephew John's challenge to play chess while he waited.

Caroline's older brother was perched on a stool at a high table, bent over his work, scribbling in a tall, cloth-bound ledger. His lips were set in a fine line under a thin moustache, and wire-rimmed spectacles perched on his nose.

Sam leaned against the edge of the large oak table that smelled strongly of pine oil. "Got time for me to whoop you at a game?"

Still immersed in his own world of heavy tomes, precise figures, and ink-filled fountain pens, John looked up distractedly. "Hmm? Oh, sure. I'm almost done here." He stared at Sam for a moment, processing what he'd just agreed to, then ran a hand through ash-brown hair. "I'll be with you in a minute." He grinned. "Maybe you'll get to keep your queen a while longer this time."

"Best worry about your own queen, whippersnapper," Sam laughed. He'd taught John the game of chess when the boy was small, and he felt an avuncular welling of pride each time the young man defeated him. On the rare occasion that Sam still managed to win, however, he made the most of it.

John was naturally reticent, but he opened up with his easy-going uncle, enjoying their verbal jousts and chess games. He'd taken to Julep as well, though he didn't tend to disappear with the creature like his sister did.

Sam admired his two young protégés, as he had begun to consider them, but reassured himself that neither could equal his prowess in the thoroughbred's saddle. During his rides with Julep, he joined into a single consciousness with the beast. Each was attuned to the other's slightest pauses and mildest shifts. Senses amplified, their responses seemed as instinctual as a mare's awareness of her foal underfoot.

Ever since he'd bought the horse, Sam had been trying to prove to his wife that he was at no risk from the temperamental stallion, whose previous owner had sold him for a few pennies and a stiff drink. The man's reckless, headstrong son had pitted his will against Julep's, gaining only a broken pelvis for his efforts.

A wiser and gentler man, Sam had waited to saddle Julep, first cajoling him with kind words, treats, and affectionate grooming. Only when he'd been certain that Julep considered him a friend—when the horse showed no trace of fear and no skittishness at his approach—did Sam attempt to mount him. Once granted this privilege, Sam never pushed him beyond his willingness, and Julep came to trust him.

Julep is takin' to Carrie and John easy enough. The bitter taste of jealousy cloyed in his mouth, surprising him. He tapped his foot, impatient with himself. *Maybe he knows I trust them, too. Besides, Carrie kinda favors me.*

Years ago, Sam had lived next door to his sister and her family; he'd been a gangly, bedbug-bitten adolescent with toddlers at his heels. Then James Corbett had decided to set up shop in Beaufort. Since that time, Sam had made it a point to visit every year or so, despite now having a family of his own and a plantation to run. He anticipated his upcoming departure with reluctance. *Wish I could take them back with me. We have that open cottage, and I certainly could use a hand runnin' the place.*

Sam's foot slowed its relentless tapping as he resolved to speak with his sister and her husband.

To his surprise, Sarah and James seemed open to the idea.

"With five more children here at home, growin' all the time, I'd be grateful for the extra space," the storekeeper granted, pulling at his beard. He eyed the dining room table, which only seated six comfortably. "But what about Mary? Don't you need to run this by your wife?"

"She'd love their company." Sam waved a palm dismissively.

"She *is* always suggestin' they come for a visit," Sarah confirmed, touching the sleeve of her husband's old-fashioned frock coat.

"There's a new sewing plant in Kingstree, did you say?" James rubbed his temple. "Carrie keeps mentionin' how she'd like to try her hand at workin' in a factory. I'd sure feel better knowin' she's livin' there with you than movin' off to God-knows-where like Vivian. Vivian's just too wild, off dancin' that ragtime with sailors and heaven-knows-who-all. She'll never land herself a decent husband."

"Don't say that," Sarah protested.

"Well, I sure don't want Carrie followin' in her dance-steps. It'd be better if you keep an eye on her," James decided, nodding at Sam. "I really hate to lose John, though. He takes care of a passel o' business for me."

James frowned as if tallying the benefits of one less mouth to feed and extra space gained. "But Eli *has* been learnin' the books—maybe he'll be able to manage. I s'pose if John wants to go for a time, that's fine by me, if it's alright with Sarah." The surly shopkeeper turned towards his wife.

She placed a soft, plump hand on Sam's arm. "To tell the truth, I'd rather keep her here, 'cept we're startin' to become a little concerned at Carrie's lack of beaus. She's nineteen now, with no real prospects. Do you think you and Mary might be able to introduce her to a few nice gentlemen in Kingstree?" Sarah patted her graying hair and blinked hopefully at him.

He stared in surprise. "No one's come callin' on her here?"

"Well," she shifted uncomfortably before admitting, "it's not that no one's been interested. She's just not interested in any of them. Her head's in the clouds, but maybe she'll meet someone she likes better where y'all live." Sarah squeezed his arm then added with a hint of exasperation, "Perhaps she'll listen to you and Mary more than she does to us."

Caroline gaped, so surprised at the invitation that her glass of sweet tea slipped right out of her hand. It clanked down, tea sloshing onto the white lace tablecloth. She dabbed at it with her napkin as she gazed up at Sam with shining eyes. "Do you mean it? Really?"

Sarah blinked worriedly from the end of the table. "Don't feel like you have to go, honey. I thought you might meet a nice young man there, but there are plenty here."

"No, ma'am, I don't feel like I have to go, but yes, ma'am, I'd love to." Caroline nodded eagerly, yet at the bereaved droop of her mother's face added, "I'll miss you, of course, but I'll be with Aunt Mary and the girls. And with Uncle Sam. And I can spend more time with Julep." She paused then flicked her fingers. "I prob'ly won't stay that long."

"Well, we'll just have to see about that," Sam interjected. "You might like it there."

"Or like Mama said, you might like *someone* there," snickered Eli. Though taller than John, the sandy-haired youth was as immature as the younger children, who were tittering in the doorway behind him.

"Or she might get a job there," James put in, rising to close the door against curious, hungry young Corbetts.

Sam chuckled. "What about you, John?"

"He can't go," put in Eli quickly. "He's gotta help Pa."

John studiously rearranged the butterbeans on his plate. "I've got the rest of the inventory to finish up, and we're due to process the new shipments any day now. Those are just sittin' in the warehouse."

Nodding thoughtfully, James tugged at his beard. "It sure would be easier to have you here to handle those arrivals, son."

Sarah sighed and gave Caroline a sympathetic look before standing to clear the table.

"I was gonna suggest y'all wait a week or two before comin', anyhow," Sam said quickly. "Y'all can take the train up through Charleston. Transfer at Yemassee, then the line stops right in Kingstree. That would give me a few days to get home and put things in order."

Caroline tugged on a lock of hair, unconsciously reflecting her father's habit. "Can't Eli help Pa with the inventory? You should come with me, John." As her brother turned to regard her, she grinned and batted her eyelashes. "After all, how else in the world am I gonna meet all those eligible young men?"

John's serious expression transformed into one of amusement, and he adjusted his spectacles. His reserved nature and constant companionship would undoubtedly lead to the opposite effect of keeping them more, rather than less, secluded.

Sarah resolutely seized on Caroline's remark, however. She nodded effusively. "Yes, honey, your sister needs you there to make introductions. And Sam says he could use your help on the farm."

John glanced dubiously around the table—at his mother, still nodding her head; at his father, stoically inexpressive; at Uncle Sam, an eyebrow cocked as he waited for John's response; at Eli, balancing his butter knife on its edge; and finally back at Caroline, who was biting her lip. John felt a surprising urge to laugh. *Look at her holdin' back. She usually just blurts out whatever's on the tip of her tongue. Too often.* He hesitated, glancing at Eli. *Maybe Eli will finally grow up a bit if he's pressed into it. And maybe if he thinks he's needed 'round here he won't run off to the Klondike like he keeps sayin' he's gonna.* John took a deep breath. "Fine. If you can spare me here, I'll go. In fact, I can't wait to see those stables."

Sam rubbed his hands together. "We'll keep those horses well-exercised. You might can skunk me at chess, but you can't keep up with this old man in the saddle."

3• The Sewing Factory

LOOKS 'BOUT BIG ENOUGH *for a pair o' circus mice.* Caroline leaned out the carriage to get a better look at the cottage. After passing through miles of swamp, they'd finally reached her uncle's cotton fields, where a dozen or so dark-skinned workers filled earth-colored sacks with heavenly-looking, white fluff that Sam assured them was not so heavenly until it passed through the gin—embedded seeds tore at even the most calloused fingers after a time. Small, shotgun-style houses, each with its own porch, faced each other down a lane to their right. Just ahead, ancient live oaks shaded the avenue leading to the rear of the Swann plantation house. It sat in slightly-faded antebellum glory some distance from the sizeable stables.

They bumped steadily closer. The cottage was as yet just a shell-colored speck between them, its yard a scenic panorama of flowering gardenias, oaks, and grand magnolias, beyond which rays of subdued, dappled light reflected in the tannin-stained waters of the Black River.

The siblings soon found the tabby cottage complete with two small bedrooms and a modest front room. Meant for seasonal help, it lacked a fireplace but did have a small wood-burning oven. Within hours, they settled in. Within days, they rambled about the plantation as easily as if they'd always lived there. Within a week, Caroline woke in nervous anticipation—the time to join the ranks of modern, working women had arrived. John had already begun his duties assisting Sam with the farm, and her uncle had pointed out the way to the sewing factory on their return from church the day before.

Caroline set out for town on foot, dressed in her plainest, hopefully suitable, working-girl attire. She waved at the field workers, grateful that she didn't have to do their jobs. Their soulful, call-and-response songs made her want to stay and listen, however. About a half-hour after their last notes faded from her hearing, the harsh silhouette of the hulking brick factory came into view, and her initial pluck began to waver. Across the river stood a formidable wall—the dam housing turbines to generate electricity for the sewing machines, she supposed. Squaring her shoulders, she approached the massive front door and pulled it open. Inside, her head swam with the musky odor of sweat and the high-pitched hum of sewing machines.

Harsh light from electric bulbs shone on a stout woman leaning over paperwork at a desk. The woman disregarded her presence entirely. At Caroline's timid request for an application, the receptionist shoved a form at her and pointed to a pen and inkwell on the counter. When Caroline returned the completed form, the woman gave it a cursory once-over, rang a large brass bell, and resumed ignoring her.

Caroline sat down on a bench. Her hands clenched together. At length, an elderly, irritable-looking man with a red-tipped nose and a short white beard burst through the door to the workroom. He hardly bothered to look up from his clipboard.

Finally, he picked up her application from the counter. Turning to squint at her, he frowned. "Can you operate a sewing machine?"

Her heart sank as she stood. "No, sir, but I learn qu—"

"Alright, follow me," he said, patting his watch-chain.

Bewildered, she trailed after the man into the noisy workroom. Each time she gathered the courage to speak, he would stop and finger a pile of garments, check off more items on his clipboard, or bark instructions at a seamstress. Resigning herself to meekly following him, she tried to stay within hearing range as he paced through the cramped aisles.

She had been trailing him for more than a quarter of an hour when he stopped abruptly. She bumped into him then scrambled backwards, apologizing in a voice that came out as a squeak.

Lifting his head from his clipboard, he blinked in consternation. "Ah, right," he mumbled, pivoting to the right. "Come along," he snapped, resuming his pace.

She followed a little less closely.

The supervisor paused at an unoccupied sewing machine. "This will be your station. Stay and watch Fletcher today. Break anythin' and it comes out of your pay. That starts tomorrow if you think you can work the machine. Be here at eight sharp."

As the supervisor walked away, staring at his clipboard again, Fletcher said in a gravelly voice, "Might as well close your mouth and pull your chair closer. Ain't gonna waste a bunch o' time repeatin' myself. I don't get paid extra to teach ya. Hate wastin' my time on little rich girls playin' 'round. Some of us really need this here work."

Caroline frowned but self-consciously obeyed, wondering how many 'little rich girls' the woman had taught to sew. Though Caroline had tried to dress appropriately, wearing her plainest white shirtwaist with her dark skirt, she could readily see the difference between her ironed, corseted outfit and Fletcher's worn, slightly-stained garments. While Caroline had conscientiously pulled her thick blond waves into a neat, no-nonsense bun, her co-worker's stringy, dull-brown hair was covered with a sweat-stained kerchief knotted about her head. They did seem to be from different worlds. Caroline was invading Fletcher's realm, but she would prove that she wasn't wasting the woman's time.

To Fletcher's surprise over the next few weeks, the 'little rich girl' did learn to operate the sewing machine efficiently. Though the veteran seamstress had openly suggested she'd have to tolerate Caroline's whining just long enough for the young woman to realize the job wasn't for her, Caroline proved adept and managed to keep her fingers from under the whirring needle. Her determination to work hard and curry favor soon won Fletcher over.

Upon learning of Fletcher's brood of children and shiftless husband, Caroline ceased to wonder at how a woman who sewed new clothing for a living could have such disregard for her own appearance. She began to pack treats with her own dinner for Fletcher to take home to her offspring. At first she solicited homemade goodies from Ettie, though she didn't mention the housekeeper to Fletcher for fear of derision. In short order, however, Caroline spent her own earnings on mouthwatering caramels and eye-opening peppermints at Hammond's Grocery—and not only for her co-worker's little ones but for her own pockets as well as those of her young Swann cousins. Best of all, she could buy dime novels without having to consult anyone first. The meager income felt liberating.

She was so full of enthusiasm that Aunt Mary wrote to suggest the job to her own unmarried sister, who loved to sew. Soon willowy, dark-haired Anne Brighton arrived on the train. After settling into the main house, she joined Caroline at the factory. The machine next to Fletcher was assigned to Anne, while Caroline was moved one station away. Fletcher welcomed the newcomer with all the warmth she had developed for Caroline.

"Why, you done picked up how to use this sewin' machine near as fast as Carrie," Fletcher approved, only days after Anne had begun. Leaning close, she murmured, "Carrie might still be a little faster, but you're a mite more particular."

"I can hear you!" Caroline called from Anne's other side.

To their supervisor, Fletcher recommended matter-of-factly, "You should hire more of these rich girls, Mr. Mouzon."

He rubbed his red-tipped nose and resumed his rounds.

"Oh, y'all might not think he's payin' attention." Fletcher handed them each a stack of the mandarin-orange satin cloth he'd just delivered from the cutting room. "But somewhere in that head o' his Mr. Mouzon stashes away everythin' that goes on in here."

The girls worked lengthy shifts at the factory, their hands kept busy with what was fast-becoming routine drudgery. Once it had become second-nature, they bantered over the din of the machines about their families and about the dime novels Caroline was reading. They discussed dress-pattern variations, and Fletcher told them about some of the more unique designs she'd sewn since the factory's opening a year-and-a-half earlier. Anne eagerly contrasted them with what she'd seen in the pages of *Harper's Bazar.*

When they fell silent at times, the hum of the sewing machines would lull Caroline into her own private musings. As the needle pumped up and down to join the edges of freshly-cut fabric, she thought about how her own life's adventures were finally beginning to unfold. Newfound friends and family, even a career and residence—her life was utterly different than just a couple of months before. Unlike the heroines in so many of her novels, however, she already knew with certainty that she would not be meeting her future husband in her workplace.

At the idea of romance within such dreary walls, Caroline coughed aloud to cover an escaped laugh. Besides Mr. Mouzon, only one other man consistently inhabited their workplace. The paunchy co-owner, Mr. Nesmith, was a middle-aged, married man who spent most of his time in his office, ever busy corresponding with the outside world.

Then there was Mr. Sanders, a more silent co-owner who rarely came into the factory workroom but met with

Mr. Nesmith and Mr. Mouzon on occasion. Each time she saw Mr. Sanders, she had to remind herself who the gentleman with the graying hair and long moustache was. He wore a top hat and nice suits with creased trouser-legs. His reserved manner paled next to Mr. Nesmith's blustery comportment—an unfortunate, continual reminder of the latter's very-present role as owner.

Her thoughts circled back to Mr. Mouzon, and she gave a small shake of her head. *Just imagine that old taskmaster tryin' to make a romantic overture to anyone. I'm fairly certain the only distinctions he makes between us workers are based on productivity.* Proudly, Caroline thought, *Well, if that were the basis for choosing, he might select me at that.* Her sewing machine had indeed earned pats of distracted approval from the supervisor, and she hoped that he would remember her commendable work today—as she had a request to make.

When Anne and Fletcher rose after the peal of the dinner bell, Caroline waved them on, saying, "I need to speak with Mr. Mouzon." She remained seated until the workroom cleared, then fished under her chair for the satchel she had brought to work with her. Picking it up, she tentatively made her way towards the supervisor, who was intently inspecting the morning's batch of wasp-waist dresses with bell skirts.

Waiting for him to finish making a mark on his clipboard, she interrupted before he could resume counting. "Mr. Mouzon?"

The supervisor turned towards a second batch of dresses, and she dared to tap the table next to him.

He blinked up at her. "Ah, yes, Miss… my dear, what do you need?"

Realizing he'd forgotten her name, her confidence wavered, but she went ahead and pressed her question. "Mr. Mouzon, I've brought a few of my personal clothing items from home, and I was wonderin' if I might use the machine during dinner hour to make some alterations."

Mr. Mouzon rubbed his nose. "No, ma'am. Afraid not. Can't have you missin' dinner. Productivity and all that." He turned back to count dresses.

"But Mr. Mouzon, you've said yourself my productivity is exemplary. Perhaps you could allow it this once, and if my productivity doesn't keep up to your standard, then I wouldn't do it again. Please?" She cast him her most winsome smile.

"No, I'm sorry. If I let you, then the whole factory would be full of women makin' personal alterations on company machines." His eyes widened as though he were imagining a wake of vultures.

"I understand," she murmured, shoulders sagging. In a final, dispirited effort, she added, "I'm Caroline Corbett, sir. I sit in the back of the workroom next to Fletcher, just in case you change your mind."

He had already resumed counting, so she made her way fretfully back to her station, stowing away her satchel and joining the other women outside for their meal.

When the workroom emptied, Mr. Mouzon exhaled in appreciation at the welcome silence. He counted on this dinner hour to finish the morning tallies. *How irksome it would be to have a horde of chattering women spoilin' my only—my sacred—hour of focus.* A shudder coursed through him. *That young seamstress had better not hold her stitches waitin' for me to 'change my mind,' for that is surely not gonna happen.*

Just as the supervisor resumed his enumerations, a resounding voice interrupted him.

"Ho there, Mouzon! Are we at quota?" Mr. Nesmith bustled up to a table of finished shirtwaists, his girth unbalancing a carefully-lined-up cartful.

Mr. Mouzon sighed. "I don't know yet. I haven't finished my reckonings."

"Ah, I *reckon* we're doin' alright." Mr. Nesmith chuckled, seeming not to notice his supervisor's pinched expression. "Actually, just wanted to check in with you, cuz I had a most remarkable idea. Y'know how that fancy fashion-agent associate of mine was so sore with me over that disaster with the wool patterns last winter? Well, I was thinkin' maybe I could score some points with the old goat by helpin' him find some new talent. He's always scoutin' around for new potential, runnin' from this city to that city, and he's lost a few designers lately. Anyhow, I got to thinkin', 'Who knows fashion and patterns better than a bunch o' women who do nothin' but sew the latest styles all day?'"

"You think you might find a fashion designer for him *here*?" Mr. Mouzon blinked in amazement.

"I know, I know. I'm 'bout as likely to pull one outta Hellhole Swamp on my fishin' line. But keep in mind she only needs to have the potential, and it makes a certain kinda sense, don't it?" Leaning in more closely and planting his hands on the table, Mr. Nesmith's ruddy, bloated cheeks quivered with enthusiasm. "I'm an eternal optimist. Lot more good things happen that way. Does anyone stand out? Maybe somebody who's real excited by the new patterns or shows creative flair with her own clothing?"

Irritably, Mr. Mouzon silently tugged at a stack of blouses that were being crumpled. Then he took a step back from his boss, who was still regarding him expectantly. *Why can't they just let me do my job? Why must everyone bother me with everythin'? Don't they have their own work to think about?* Closing his eyes, he tried to consider Mr. Nesmith's request, but the only employee who sprang to mind was Caroline Corbett, the annoying but purportedly 'exemplary' seamstress who was so eager to alter her own clothing. Though he couldn't even recall what she had worn, he said dismally, "There's a new girl who might show some promise, but she's fairly inexperienced. Caroline Corbett's the name."

Mr. Nesmith clapped the supervisor on his stiff shoulder. "I knew you were the man to ask! Well, I don't wanna rush into anythin' and put my foot in my proverbial mouth, as they say, so you just keep an eye on Miss Corbett 'til we're sure of her talent. If there's anythin' she needs, take a few extra pains to humor her, why don'tcha?" He winked. "We wanna foster all the positive public relations that we can. Success for our employees and partners leads to good things for us. Catch my drift?" The rotund executive eyeballed the supervisor with bobbing eyebrows until Mr. Mouzon reluctantly acknowledged him.

"Yes, sir. I will watch Miss Corbett's performance and foster her growth here, sir." Mr. Mouzon's lips puckered as if he'd just sucked on a sour lemon.

"Good man! Good man!" At a final slap to the harried supervisor's shoulder, the factory owner waddled back towards his office, pleased with the successful meeting and hoping to soon surprise his associate with a new talent from amongst their very own seamstresses.

Caroline was mystified at Mr. Mouzon's sudden reversal. Though he had not agreed to allow her to sew during dinner hour, he had spontaneously suggested that she stay in the evening after the other workers had gone home. In fact, he'd welcomed her to do so regularly.

"Yes, yes, you may bring your friend—only please don't mention this to the other workers." He sighed dismally while agreeing to the additional request.

Caroline was delighted at her supervisor's newfound indulgence. *Why, I'm gonna have to learn to ask for what I want more often.* She beamed at the old man, who only grimaced and turned away. *Oh well, I s'pose he's just shy. Not everyone is people-oriented. Regardless, my prepossessin' charms must have been irresistible.*

Soon, Caroline and Anne developed the routine of returning to the deserted factory after supper to use the machines for their own personal alterations—and eventually for new creations, at Mr. Mouzon's unexpected suggestion. Only a short stroll from his onsite residence, he would appear at the night's end to lock up after the women. To their surprise, he showed increasing interest in their personal work, inquiring about their sewing plans so regularly that they decided his acrimonious exterior was merely a front; he must be truly fond of them to display such interest in their work and take such pains to continue allowing them the confidential privilege.

In short time, the young women had modified their own dresses to modern styles, had sewn a sailor suit for Anne's niece Emma, and now eagerly anticipated the arrival of silk at the factory, as there was a very real possibility that they would be allowed to buy the remnants at cost to create their own evening wear. Mr. Mouzon assured them that they would get first choice of any extra material.

Caroline's heart was content for the time being. She was absorbed in her new work, and her affections were occupied by Julep and family. She was especially thrilled with her budding friendship with Anne, a newfound kindred spirit, and she hoped their ongoing presence wasn't too much of a burden on Aunt Mary.

4• Dime Novel

AN EARLY-MORNING FOG DRIFTED over Swann plantation, coating it with dew. Mary Swann reclined in her rocker with her gray shawl around her shoulders, creaking back-and-forth as she shelled butterbeans, dropping the speckled ovals back into the bowl on her lap and disposing of the hulls in a bushel basket by her feet.

"Lord have mercy!" A crashing noise in the nearby underbrush caused Mary to snatch the butterbean bowl to her chest as though it were a child to protect. Meanwhile her daughter sat exposed in the grass only yards from where Sam galloped his favorite stallion full-tilt onto the oak-lined road.

"Go Papa!" Emma cheered.

A hatless John followed seconds later on Maritime, riding in Julep's wake like a lunatic mockingbird after a hawk.

"Be careful!" Mary shouted, her own heart galloping as they disappeared into the mist. Releasing the bowl back onto her lap, she shook her head and fished in her bodice for stray butterbeans. *That damn horse. Ever since Sam got him, he's lost all common sense. Doesn't care how many times he gets thrown. Now that his nephew's workin' with him, he should be settin' an example. Instead he's even worse. Showin' off, that's what he's doin'.* She sighed in one long exhalation. *But no wonder I fell in love with him… has it been fifteen years already? Hard to believe he still lives life with that same wild energy and lives to tell the tale. Marriage hasn't changed him one iota.*

As her thoughts shifted to reminiscences about their wedding, she absently seized another pod and snapped it open. A couple of legumes flew to their freedom in the yard, near Emma, and Mary laughed at her own distracted enthusiasm.

"How many toad homes do you have so far, sweetie?" she called to the mud-caked little girl, who had plunked right down on her bottom in the middle of the yard with her bucket of water in tow.

"Eight," Emma counted, surveying her labor with a satisfied eye, "but I'm pretty sure each one is big enough for a whole bunch of toads. How big are toad families, Mommy?"

"I couldn't say, dear." Mary shrugged.

The rosy-cheeked, brunette girl was building elaborate toad dwellings with a purpose she had yet to apply to the lessons her mother devised for her. Emma was supposed to be learning simple household tasks such as setting the table, pulling weeds from the flower bed, and basic stitching—skills that her older sister, Lenora, had easily mastered before entering school.

"Five more minutes, darlin', and then it's washin'-up-time for you." Mary was reluctant to impose structure on her untamed daughter, but it did seem her motherly duty. "You're gonna learn an overhand stitch today if it takes all afternoon."

Studious, responsible Lenora had left for school over an hour ago. Already twelve, Lenora was fast becoming a young lady, and Mary felt it keenly. *I've already got my hands full of young ladies, what with my sister and Carrie.* Mary shook her head and sighed. *It's a wonder neither girl is married yet, but that suits me fine, leastways for the time being. I'm just glad to have Anna here, and Sam couldn't be happier to have John and Carrie's company.*

Far from resenting his distracted attentions, Mary was relieved at how the young pair kept Sam from the horse-races, whose bawdy crowds loved gambling and booze as much as they loved their horses. In contrast, John and Caroline were innocent, sanguine spirits, and Mary felt increasingly secure in their own private Swann plantation world.

She hoped Caroline and John would choose to stay on. Increased household responsibilities were outweighed by the benefits of having them there, and she enjoyed being the family puppeteer, of sorts. *At least I have some help around here. Good old Ettie doesn't seem to mind the additional work since I hired that new girl in the evenings.*

And it's not like I have to sew anymore. Mary touched the stylish ruffles that Anne had recently added to the shoulders of her day dress; the bodice and sleeves had been taken-in at the same time for a more fitted look. *I rather like the new styles, even if I'm no longer nineteen. Actually, I wear them more than they do, since they're always dressin' down in those plain shirtwaists and skirts even when they're not workin', for all their supposed interest in fashion. Next they'll be wearin' slacks and suits like the men.*

Mary shook her head, though Caroline and Anne were only following the current trend, just as she would have done at their age. A decade certainly changed things, but Sam's attentions towards her seemed as amorous as always, despite the presence of the beautiful young women. She felt secure in his avuncular affection for them.

Wouldn't it be nice if things could just stay this way? We can't horde the girls here forever, but only a handful of men in this town are worth their time. Frowning as she remembered Sarah's request to introduce Caroline to eligible local men, Mary picked up the last pod. *I could host a supper party. Invite a few decent fellows. Keep it small. Least that way Sam and I can hand-pick those we wouldn't mind joinin' the family fold. After all, we can't expect such pretty girls to become spinsters. A Christmas party would be just the thing…*

Satisfied, Mary stood up with her bowl of freshly-shelled butterbeans and called to Emma, "That's it, little Miss Messy. Put that bucket away and come on in the house!"

"Is that the end of the chapter?" Anne pulled a toasty cobbler from the oven of the cast-iron woodstove, its filling bubbling up around the crust. The fragrant aroma of baked peaches filled the detached kitchen, located just behind the main house.

Caroline folded *Willful Gaynell* to her chest, overcome with dreamy enthusiasm. She'd first read Laura Jean Libbey's sensational novel almost eight years before, but in sharing the tale with Anne, she was once again swept up by the wild escapades and the sheer romance. Clutching the book more tightly, she confided, "Honestly, Anna, no flesh-and-blood man will ever do for me now. I'm smitten with Percy Granville. Always have been and always will be."

Anne nudged Caroline aside so she could set down the steaming cobbler on the metal trivet centered on a sturdy pine table. "A handsome beau with a fat wallet? Can't imagine why you'd be taken with the idea."

"He's more than that."

"So we just need to find some rich man who looks like Percy." Anne closed the oven door, took off her mitt, and brushed flour from her apron. "Thick, wavy hair? Intense eyes? Would that do?"

"And a chiseled jaw. Oh, and a broad, muscular chest." Caroline edged forward and began picking at the flaky crust.

"I'm not sure Libbey specified all that." Anne swatted at Caroline's hand.

"You haven't finished the book."

"Then should we keep readin'? I was hopin' to finish this weekend. I've never heard such…"

"An adventure? I know."

"I was gonna say such a load of nonsense."

"Mmm, that crust." Caroline reached for the cobbler again.

"Let it cool," Anne ordered, tugging at her elbow. "Come with me into the house."

Wiping her shoes on the mat before stepping into the house and onto the parlor's faded Persian carpet, Anne gave a small, stilted laugh. "You know, Percy sounds a bit like Mr. Sanders."

"Mr. Sanders from work?" Caroline was already shaking her head. "With the gray hair and droopy moustache?"

Anne blinked defensively. "So he's not a boy. He's distinguished. And handsome. Not only that, but Mr. Sanders is exactly the sort of hero that Percy is. I've seen him rescue Lenora and Emma from those hooligans in town, and he donates money to the ladies' auxiliary. He is kind and generous… and has that terrible tragedy."

"What tragedy?"

"His wife died of tuberculosis." Anne sank into a gold-striped, cushioned armchair. "About three years ago. Honestly, Carrie, if you'd known him before then you'd know what I mean. He went to church same as now, except his hair didn't have so much gray in it then—and he was more cheerful." She paused for a moment before continuing softly, "Eleanor must have been the love of his life. He has eyes for no one else."

I can't believe she wants an old, broken-hearted man. Caroline plunked onto the cream-colored sofa across from Anne, surprised at this insight into her friend's heart. *Well, at least we shouldn't have any jealous struggles. I'd rather have someone my own age—and in love with me, not the ghost of his old, dead wife.*

With a long sigh, she smiled. A glimmer of sympathy for her friend's melancholic romantic inclinations was forming despite herself. She grudgingly admitted, "Mr.

Sanders would make a fine husband. He's certainly well-mannered, and he owns that beautiful home." At Anne's relieved nod, she remarked thoughtfully, "And now that you mention it, I've noticed those sad eyes. Rather pathetic, aren't they?"

Anne scowled, but Caroline was warming to the tragic romance. She leaned over to pat Anne's hand. "Well, if anyone can rekindle Mr. Sanders' ability to love, I don't see why it shouldn't be you." After a pause, she added, "Except that he's twice your age. But other than that, I don't see why not."

On the appointed day, the new silks arrived at the sewing factory. The shipment included sapphire-blue, chartreuse, and pale-rose floral patterns.

"Carrie, the sapphire would go with your eyes, and I'll have the rose," Anne suggested, even though their choice of fabric was going to be limited to leftovers after the factory's completion of dress orders.

"My eyes are gray, but I like the blue," Caroline agreed.

The young women bided their time as the enormous bolts of silk gradually diminished. For the next three weeks, the factory workers pumped out their quota of ready-made, identical dresses with tucked bodices, lace trim, front pleats, and skirts pulled back to create a full gathering in the rear. Racks throughout the warehouse were overflowing. While Caroline appreciated why the dresses were popular for the holiday season, Anne cast a measured, critical eye and quietly suggested that their own gowns would be finer.

In the end, however, the eager young women were left with only the chartreuse silk. Anne's disappointment was bitter, but Caroline was cheerful as they entered the cutting room after work that evening.

"Oh, all the other women will be in pinks and blues. The chartreuse will be more distinctive. And festive. And we'll match." Ignoring Anne's baleful glance, Caroline unrolled the under-appreciated silk and blithely continued, "Remember those puffed elbow-length sleeves? Why don't we gather the puffs at the top of the sleeve with some Kelly-green ribbons? We can trim the dresses entirely in green. Can't you just envision it? Imagine, when we're old and gray like Mr. Sanders, we'll recall our chartreuse dresses and how we caught our husbands with them at that Christmas ball."

At her grin, Anne returned a wan smile.

Caroline waved a swath of silk at her. "Behold the future Mrs. Sanders, of chartreuse notoriety."

"Carrie…" Anne rolled her eyes.

"No one's here but us," Caroline smoothed out the fine material and began to pin it. "You can spill your hopes and dreams."

Anne pulled out a pin, repositioning it in the yellow-green silk folds. "I'm not that keen on him. I just respect him."

"Too late. Your poor, lovesick heart has already been revealed," Caroline tutted, silently congratulating herself on distracting Anne from her disappointment about the fabric.

Anne blew out an impatient breath. "Mary said Mr. Taylor's going to be there. He's filthy-rich. And the Bells will no doubt be bringin' along their nephew from out o' town. Molly says he's real handsome." Tossing her head in an uncharacteristic manner, she added, "I fully intend to inspect this new arrival and keep open to all possibilities."

"Of course you will, honey. Keep tellin' yourself that. But it's too late to hide your heart." Caroline waved a dismissive hand, knocking a containerful of cloth chalk off the overhead shelf and onto the silk, dusting it like powdery snow.

"Watch yourself, Carrie. Don't humiliate me at this supper. You're gonna be just as vulnerable."

"Oh, Anna." Caroline sighed as she crammed the chalk back into its box and brushed away the powder. "You're right. I'll prob'ly embarrass us both."

Setting the box back up on the shelf, she added more lightly, "I don't really plan to settle on a husband there, y'know. I'm jus' gonna make the whole town fall in love with me—except for Mr. Sanders, of course—then take my own sweet time choosin' who suits me best."

5• Meeting Clay

THE NIGHT OF THE CHRISTMAS PARTY was a spectacle of holiday gowns. The younger girls wore dresses altered and updated at the factory, and Mary looked elegant in bright-pink chiffon that the young women had never seen on her before.

Caroline and Anne were positioned on the porch in their new silk finery, waiting to greet the arriving guests. Their chartreuse gowns displayed rows of fine stitches on the bodices and boasted the promised Kelly-green trim. Anne had simplified her dress by dispensing with lace, and her hair was piled in a glossy dark cascade; a simple pearl pendant lay at the hollow of her throat.

Caroline's own blond curls were gathered into a low pompadour, and Anne's forgone lace seemed to have found its way onto her own gown, trimming the collar, cuffs, and hem. Even her sleeve puffs were bigger than Anne's. Caroline's face was radiant with excitement as she chattered with her tall, graceful friend, flicking her floral-painted fan to keep from sweating on this still-balmy evening.

Frothy eggnog kept the young women drifting back into the house. They sipped on it between the arrival of guests and every few minutes swiped another delicacy from the elaborate array on the much-extended table, to Ettie's consternation.

"Lands' sakes! Won't you leave my table be?" fussed the round-cheeked, ample housekeeper.

As she approached, Caroline hastily spread open her fan to conceal the jiggling blancmange they'd scooped into their empty eggnog cups.

"Ladies, you won't be able to dance after eatin' all this and supper, too. You'll be too full—not to mention tipsy from the eggnog. And then what would Mr. Sanders think?" As she scolded an impenitent Caroline and a now-stricken Anne, Ettie turned the blancmange dish so that its excavated side faced the pineapple centerpiece, a symbol of welcome. Then she shooed them back onto the porch, where a guest was mounting the stairs. She shook her head as she turned away, tutting and muttering, "Done ruint that perfect ring mold afore all the guests got here."

The new arrival was, unfortunately, Mr. Sanders. Anne averted her blood-tinged face as he greeted them.

"Mr. Sanders!" Caroline bubbled, casting him a welcoming smile. "What a delight to have you here. I have heard so very much about you from dear Anna. We're so grateful for the kindnesses you've shown to my little cousins."

Smiling politely, Mr. Sanders tilted his head and extended a hand. "I'm not sure I've had the pleasure of making your acquaintance, though I remember Miss Brighton here from her visits to Kingstree over the years."

"Oh, I'm Caroline Corbett. I work for you in the sewing factory, as does Anna here." Determined not to let him pass without taking an interest in her friend, she batted her lashes and said, "Anna tells me you're the finest gentleman in this town. You've made quite the impression on her. You must have the most upstandin' moral character of anyone she knows." She laughed and added, "Sounds as if I'd benefit from your example."

His eyes twinkled. Straightening his bow tie, he turned towards Anne. "Miss Brighton, you have apparently been spreadin' ridiculous tales about me. I am forever in your debt." Just as Caroline bobbed onto her toes with satisfaction, he added, "Miss Corbett, I'd be honored if you would sit next to me at supper. I have a feelin' that your zest is just the condiment I need for a perfect evening."

Caroline's face fell. She stammered, "Oh, Mr. Sanders… I'd be delighted, but *Anna* would truly be the perfect companion."

As she gestured towards Anne, he graciously responded, "Your friend should sit with you as well, of course. Those beautiful gowns do complement each other magnificently. I would be honored to dine in the presence of two such lovely, creative, and entertainin' young women." With that, he bowed and excused himself to find the hosts of the party.

Anne stood mutely, eyes glossy and lips tightly pursed.

Caroline bit her lip. "Well, at least he's—"

"I have never been so humiliated," Anne interrupted in a vehement whisper, "and I certainly do not need to be a third wheel to you and Mr. Sanders." She turned on her heel and stalked into the house.

Caroline's eyes pricked with hot tears as she stared after Anne. Turning to flee to the safety of the yard, she immediately ran into another approaching supper guest.

A strong grip steadied her as a rich, resonant voice said, "Whoa! Gotcha!"

She looked up into the smiling face of a towering, fair-haired man with crinkled, light-blue eyes and a dimpled chin. "I am so sorry, sir. I tripped on the step and fell." Blinking away her tears, she resisted the urge to pelt away.

"No harm, no foul. My name's Clayton Bell. Folks just call me Clay." He waited expectantly as she straightened herself.

"I'm Carrie, I mean Caroline. My close friends call me Carrie sometimes, that is. I'm Caroline Corbett." *Goodness, what I am is incoherent.*

Clayton stepped into the yard to let another guest pass, and Caroline followed suit, resisting the urge to hide behind her fan.

"Okay, Miss Carrie Caroline Corbett," he said. "You must be the niece visitin' Mr. Swann."

"And you must be the nephew visitin' Sheriff Bell," she rejoined. "I heard you were visitin'. You are just visitin', right? Oh, but I'm not just—" she halted abruptly, realizing that she was once again about to repeat herself.

He prompted, "You're not just?"

She took a deep breath. "I was just gonna say that I'm not just visitin'. I moved down here with my brother John, and I'm workin' at the sewing factory like one of those worker bees—all the time. But only because I think it's a useful experience—and I'm determined to truly experience life, y'know? All of it." At his encouraging nod, she explained, "My family is supportive—but not smotherin', of course. They say I'm incurably headstrong, so when I decided to move here, they were just relieved I'd be with family, and now I'm a bonafide resident of Swann plantation."

Under his amused gaze, her cheeks were growing warm. *Who on earth is in charge of my babblin' tongue? Did I really just say all that?* Flustered, she focused her gaze on his chin dimple, a little above her eye level. The Teutonic feature seemed suddenly riveting—far more pleasant to ponder than her mishaps. *Practically a cleft in his chin, but I like it. Anne's right about the Bell good looks. Rugged… but sorta boyish, too.* She glanced back up at his sparkling eyes, and her stomach somersaulted at his broad grin.

Clayton laughed out loud at her expression. "Well, it's an honor, Miss Carrie."

Ivory place cards adorned each setting, and Caroline gave a sigh of relief as she realized that Mary had created a seating arrangement for supper. Mr. Sanders was positioned next to Anne, and they were already engaged in conversation. *Blessings on Mary!*

After finding her seat between two unfamiliar gentlemen from town, Caroline draped her fan on the back of her chair and tried to slide into it as inconspicuously as possible. Dutifully, she turned towards the supper companion on her right to make her introduction. "Hello, I'm Caroline Corbett."

Narrowed, rheumy eyes met hers. The heavily-whiskered man mumbled, "Yes, I know. Wayne Taylor." He shot her a quick, flat smile, then turned pointedly to listen to what Sam was saying at the head of the table about hiring workers for the new church roof.

She shrugged and followed his gaze, noting that Sheriff and Mrs. Bell, Reverend Scott, and the Alsbrooks were seated near the head of the table, near her aunt and uncle. Except for the Bells, she had met all of them at church, though never before in a social gathering. As she glanced curiously down the rest of the table, a slow realization began to dawn. *For heaven's sakes! Aside from myself and Anna, there are no other single ladies here. But there are—let's see—seven seemingly eligible bachelors.* Her mouth felt dry as she remembered how she and Anne had jested about finding their husbands at the Christmas party. *I s'pose they'll introduce us to them one-by-one over the course of the night?*

At least Anne was already engaged with Mr. Sanders. *If only in conversation—for now,* Caroline thought with a smile. Though Anne was nervously plucking at tendrils of her hair, she, at least, seemed coherent enough.

When Caroline's wandering gaze came to Clayton, he caught her eyes and flashed another broad smile. For some reason, he was seated at the distant end of the table with the children, including Emma, Lenora, and a raven-haired, solemn girl about Lenora's age.

Caroline nodded awkwardly and averted her gaze towards her newly-arrived soup. *Oh gracious, he's watchin' me. What should I do? Just act natural.* She picked up her spoon and dipped it into her bowl with her best manners, making sure to scoop outwards rather than shoveling it towards herself.

"You are a vision of spring," a reedy voice rasped near her ear.

Drawing back in alarm, she splashed the spoonful of soup directly onto the dinner jacket of Wayne Taylor, who exclaimed in disgust. Snatching her napkin from her lap, she began dabbing at the spots on his jacket, saying, "I'm so sorry."

"Of all the clumsy… Just leave it. Unbelievable…" he huffed, rising to his feet. He strode out of the room, muttering, "The very last time I suffer through one of these ludicrous supper parties."

Mortified, Caroline lifted her hand to her mouth. She skimmed the table to see who had noticed. Instantly, she met the earnest, unfaltering gaze of the poetic speaker—a pasty young man hovering to her left with a skinny, dark goatee; his vast bowtie stretched well past his ears. Forcing her hand down and drawing in a deep breath to compose herself, she smiled politely while trying to tactfully withdraw from his looming face.

Straightening his bowtie, the thin young man resumed his address. "I am so glad to finally meet you, Miss Caroline. I am Robert Keels, manager of the Kingstree Feed & Seed. We provide the very best service that we can to your uncle. I must admit I'm flattered he asked me to this Christmas supper and dance."

Mr. Keels paused expectantly, but at her polite, "Oh, of course, how nice," and wavering smile, he forged ahead.

"May I have the honor of the first dance with you?"

She glanced wistfully at Clayton, reluctantly preparing to accept.

To her surprise, he was shaking his head. Pointing to his chest, he gave her a meaningful look. A grin played around the corners of his mouth, and she suspected that he had not only guessed the gist of her conversation with Mr. Keels but had witnessed the entire soup debacle. The mirth emanating from his eyes made it all seem suddenly amusing, and she repressed a burble of laughter as she replied to Mr. Keels, "I'm sorry, but I've already promised the first dance to someone else… perhaps the second?"

He beamed delightedly. "The second it is."

She spent the rest of the supper feigning interest in Mr. Keels' detailed itemization of his apparently large store inventory. Throughout his monologue, she was distracted by Clayton, visible past the spindly manager's shoulder. He was entertaining the giggling younger girls—and, Caroline suspected, herself.

Clueless and confident, Mr. Keels did manage to briefly engage her attention when he described the newly-arrived saddles with braided etchings in the leather.

"They sound lovely, Mr. Keels. I would like to see them sometime," she said with sincerity.

He sat up even straighter. "That would be wonderful. What day would suit you best? Your uncle tells me that you work at the sewing plant, so I would be more than happy to arrange for an after-hours meeting."

Caroline hid a grimace by lifting her wine glass to her lips. "Oh, I don't think that will be necessary. I can stop by on my dinner hour one day."

"And I will look forward to seeing you then, my dear Miss Corbett."

After supper, Reverend Scott bid the Swanns a good night and took his leave. As he exited the front door, several black musicians were just entering through the back of the house. They filed in, and an excited murmur of approval arose from the guests. Mary had hired the best performers in the region, descendants of the Bell and Snowden plantations. The night was sure to be memorable.

As the guests straggled after them across the large parlor, Clayton made his way to Caroline's shoulder. The lilting strains of a waltz began, and he extended a hand. "May I have this dance, Miss Carrie Caroline Corbett?"

Biting her lower lip to prevent further prattling, she took his hand. The simple waltz was a relief; she automatically performed the steps, her eyes fixed safely on his dimpled chin. She was acutely aware of the feel of their hands together, of their bodies brushing.

Too soon, the waltz was over. She reluctantly withdrew her hand. Forcing her dry lips to part, she murmured, "Thank you, Clay, for the dance."

Before he could reply, Mr. Keels swooped in front of him and whisked Caroline into the second dance. While the storeowner whirled her about the room, he regaled her with his plans for the construction of a new two-story home.

Contrary to her expectations, this second dance was no less thrilling than the first. Clayton was brazenly moving along the room with them. Each time she faced in his direction, their eyes locked audaciously. Before long, she could hardly breathe for the audible pounding of her heart. When the music ended, she averted her gaze and mumbled a polite word of thanks, then escaped to the edge of the room to gather herself—not daring to look up, overwhelmed at the thought of talking with Clayton after such outrageous flirting.

"Carrie, may I speak with you?" Mary was at her elbow.

"Yes, ma'am, of course. What is it?" Caroline looked up, blinking with what she hoped looked like innocence.

"Let's step out on the porch for a moment, honey." Mary guided her outside. "Alright, that's better. You look beautiful, dear."

Caroline smiled self-consciously and touched her hair. "Thank you."

"I do have a concern, however."

"What is it?" Caroline smiled, but her stomach tightened.

"I would like for you to avoid that Clayton Bell character, darlin'. I saw that you danced together, which is fine, but he is not the sort with whom I would like to see you associate. He's only here because we wanted to invite Sally and Sheriff Joe, our dear friends. Clayton is visitin' his Uncle Joe, so any attention that you give him tonight will frankly be wasted. He's leavin' town in a fortnight, I believe." Mary paused for a moment before adding affectionately, "But I have it on solemn authority that you have charmed Mr. Keels thoroughly. We couldn't help but notice that he seemed to have quite an effect on you during your dance. He's gonna make some girl a wonderful husband. Such a kind and reliable man. He attends church regularly and is always well-mannered. A young lady would be lucky indeed to be settled with him."

Caroline stared at her. "I was just bein' polite to Mr. Keels, Aunt Mary. Please don't try to marry me off to him. There's nothin' truly wrong with Clayton Bell, is there?"

Sighing as though completing an unpleasant task, Mary said, "Oh, Carrie. He's just a sharecropper, dear."

Aghast, Caroline watched her retreating back. Then, in frustration, she turned towards the porch rails to look out over the grounds. Though she valued Mary's opinions, she wished Mary had kept this particular one to herself.

As the music from inside the parlor died down, a barred owl hooted in the distance. A moment later, it received a response. Then Clayton's whimsical voice chimed in from behind her.

"You do look a vision of Spring."

At the taunt, she laughed unwillingly and turned to face him.

"I've been wanderin' the dance floor lookin' for you," he admitted, smiling and extending a hand as he closed the gap between them. "May I have this next dance?"

Uncertainly, Caroline took his hand. He led her across the porch in a slow dance. As she glided effortlessly in his arms, she noticed that the dress coat he was wearing hung loosely on him. Frowning slightly, she wondered if he had to borrow it from his broad-framed uncle.

Mary's words swirled in her mind as she moved with him. *A sharecropper? How awful. What sorta future would we have? He's leavin', too...* The protests dimmed, however, as she became increasingly aware of his warm breath on her cheek and his calloused palm against hers. Her skin tingled at the brush of his hand against her waist. Troubled thoughts dissolved away as a pure, breathtaking awareness of his body, of his musky scent possessed her.

The song ended, and Caroline felt herself melt against Clayton. Her breath caught as his arms crept around her. Overwhelmed, she was unable to think past the present—past this exquisite moment with this stranger, her one forbidden choice.

As they embraced, a familiar tune began—a unique, undulating rhythm known widely as 'Snowden's Jig'. Far from a jig, the erotic stanzas brought exotic Arabian bellydancers to mind. Her stodgy father had once even declared the tune 'disgraceful'.

Still melded to Clayton, she began to rock to the irresistible rhythm.

His hands spread across her back, pulling her even closer as he began to move in unison with her. Slow at first, their movements gained intensity as they kept in time with the pulsating music. The cyclical melodic patterns gradually increased in fervor until achieving a tempestuous climax.

As they rocked together, Caroline was oblivious to everything but an indefinable, primal urge guiding her dance with Clayton. Her consciousness returned only slowly as enthusiastic cheers clamored from inside the house. Dazedly, she became aware of Clayton abruptly stiffening.

His hoarse voice whispered in her ear, "I've gotta cool off, Carrie."

To her dismay, he broke away from her, rushing off the porch and across the lawn. When he reached the water's edge, Clayton plunged straight into the Black River.

6• Meeting Stephen

CAROLINE STARED AFTER CLAYTON, MOUTH AGAPE. When Anne's voice called from the doorway, she turned rounded eyes upon her friend, who stood with arms folded, an expression of mildly-amused reproof on her face.

"Okay, Carrie, come on back inside. I know you feel guilty for embarrassin' me earlier, but you can't stand out here in the cold and miss the party."

"I wasn't," Caroline stammered. "I just—"

"Besides," Anne admitted with a dreamy smile, fingering her pearl pendant, "the situation seems to be salvaged. Mr. Sanders has been my dance partner twice already, and we had a lovely conversation."

"But Anna, you have no idea—"

"All is forgiven, dear. Now pull yourself together and get back in here before you catch your death of cold."

Closing her jaw, Caroline didn't argue that it was a warm, downright balmy evening for December, much warmer than it had been in the preceding weeks. She let herself be guided into the house by a radiant Anne, who leaned close to whisper, "Here comes your angel John. He's such a gentleman, askin' me to dance any time I seem without a partner."

"Does he?"

"Mary put him up to it, I'm sure. I'll never be a wallflower with him around. They're sweet to look out for me, but I'm afraid he's so avid about it that he's discouragin' anyone else from approachin' me."

As John advanced with a request in his eye, Anne sighed tolerantly. She beamed an amused smile at Caroline as he led her into another dance.

Caroline was just wondering if she should go back outside to look for Clayton when she felt a tug on her sleeve. She looked down to see the solemn child who had been seated with her cousins.

The girl tucked a black strand of hair behind an ear and met her gaze evenly. Her eyes were wide and disquieting. She spoke in a low, serious tone of voice. "He isn't meant for you."

Caroline raised her eyebrows.

"He's not your sort. He doesn't belong here—neither of us does. We belong together. He's like me." The girl's words were adamant and clear.

"Whatever do you mean, honey?" Caroline gave a baffled laugh.

"You're confusin' him. Stay away from him." A flush overtook the girl's pale countenance. She whipped around and rushed from the room in the direction of the nursery.

Caroline stared after her in bewilderment, but just as she made to follow, she was waylaid by Mary with yet another gentleman at her side.

"Carrie, I would like to introduce Dr. Stephen Connor. Stephen, this is Caroline Corbett."

"Oh, hello," Caroline murmured, gazing in the direction the girl had gone. "I just need to—"

"I've promised Dr. Connor that you'll tell him all about the stables here, dear. You know far more about them than I do. Apparently Dr. Connor shares your penchant for those troublesome beasts." The words came out in one fluid breath, and Mary's laugh tinkled as she adroitly slipped away before Caroline could respond.

Frustrated by yet another distraction, Caroline fumed inwardly even as she admired Mary's ploy. John or Sam could have described the stables with at least as much enthusiasm and knowledge as herself.

Remembering to be gracious, however, she dutifully turned her attention to the gentleman in tails and realized how handsome he was. *Thick, wavy hair, chiseled chin, intense eyes… Well, here's a manifestation—on tonight, of all nights.* "Pleased to meet you, Dr. Connor."

"It's my pleasure entirely, Miss Corbett." He gave a small bow, blinking friendly, dark eyes at her.

Caroline could barely process Stephen's greeting. *Damn that Clayton Bell. And that strange girl. I'm so muddled. Here this gentleman could be my very own storybook prince, in the flesh, but I'm completely distracted.*

Conscientiously studying Stephen's clean-shaven profile, she willed herself to imprint *his* facial structure on her mind. Looking away, she mentally retraced the lines of his countenance to be sure she had them, but those lines morphed to create a chin dimple. The intense eyes lightened and glinted, and Caroline knew that tonight was hopeless for connecting with the physician, however handsome he might be. Clayton was still occupying her thoughts.

"I'm so sorry, Dr. Connor, would you excuse me? I'll be right back." Without waiting for his reply, she spun around and dashed towards the door. As she exited the house, she scanned the moonlit yard and ran towards the river.

There was no sign of Clayton along the riverbank—no floating masses in the water, no suspect movements, nothing at all. She anxiously walked the length of the embankment. *What did I expect? That he'd be sittin' on a log, whistlin' Dixie—idly waitin' for me to come lookin' for him?*

When her foot sank into riverbank mud, she felt suddenly foolish. She'd been negligent in her duties towards the guest Mary had asked her to attend—and for no good reason. Clayton was probably fine, and he certainly wasn't her responsibility.

As she returned to the porch, she found the magnanimous doctor leaning against the railing, humming a Christmas tune.

He smiled sheepishly as she approached. "I hope you don't mind that I followed you out here. Mary was eyein' me from across the room, so I figured I'd make myself scarce."

Trying to inconspicuously scrape mud from her shoe, Caroline was grateful for the dark of the night. A rush of heat radiated from her cheeks. "Not at all, Dr. Connor. I apologize for my rudeness, but I'm at your disposal now."

"You've been fine. Just fine. And please call me Stephen."

Searching for a topic of conversation, she asked, "Did Mary say you're familiar with horses?"

"I am. I breed quarter horses, actually."

"Then you're into the racing circuit? I hear it's rather… racy." She laughed and ran one hand nervously along the porch railing, grateful he still seemed friendly.

Stephen shrugged. "I don't have much time away from my medical practice, but I try to watch out for strong breeding candidates. I'm curious about the Swann horses."

At once she began describing each of the stables' beloved residents, struggling to answer his queries about their pedigrees but responding with authority regarding their temperaments.

"…and Julep's completely sweet, so long as he's not startled. He's my darlin'." Caroline smiled sentimentally, beginning to relax.

"Hearing about Julep almost makes me wish I had a thoroughbred mare to pair with him, but I'll definitely have a talk with Sam about Maritime. Real potential for my Pegasus there, sounds like." He nodded thoughtfully then glanced towards the house as the first notes of a lively polka began. "Would you like to dance, Miss Caroline?"

As the pair re-entered the parlor, she found herself surprisingly lighthearted. They laughingly engaged in the rollicking steps, conversation sidelined. When the dance concluded, she hailed her brother, who had just finished the polka with Anne. "I have someone here that you should meet."

Anne mouthed, "Thank you!" as John left her side at last, and Caroline gave an almost imperceptible nod.

Within moments, John and Stephen were raptly absorbed in conversation, and Caroline escaped to the porch again, eyeing the pineapple centerpiece that still graced the table on her way out. *I should just grab it so they'll all go home. I can't handle meetin' even one more man tonight. And what would be the point? Stephen seems impossibly perfect.* Glancing across the yard towards the Black River, she admitted, *And I'm far too taken with Clay.*

Sighing, she found herself strolling once again towards the river's edge, vainly searching for signs of Clayton. *Stephen may be wonderful, but my Don Juan has vanished, and he's apparently taken my heart with him.*

7• Sunday Guest

SUNDAY MORNING DAWNED BRIGHT and found Caroline more cheerful, with a lucid head and a growling stomach. She buttoned her calico dress and pulled her thick hair into a bun, smoothing strays with lavender-scented pomatum. Gray eyes reflected back at her from the mirror mounted behind her dressing table; the blue in the print of the dress made them appear more blue today—not cerulean or even remotely pastel, just a sort of steely blue. She smoothed her eyebrows into place.

As a blonde, she was grateful to have darker, defined eyebrows, some compensation for the scattering of freckles that got worse every summer. Frowning, she inspected them, wondering if she was spending too much time in the sun.

"Ready for breakfast?" John stood in her bedroom doorway, already dressed and wearing his newsboy cap. She braced herself for one of his well-aimed remarks about her narcissism, but his expression was somber, and he only fiddled with his spectacles, not seeming to notice her preening this morning.

They sidled into the kitchen just as the family was sitting down to the table. Anne also wore a preoccupied but pleased expression, nearly as smug as Mr. Mouzon when they met quota.

I wonder what she and Mr. Sanders talked about last night? Caroline guessed Anne would prefer to share in private, so she merely eyed her friend curiously until John caught her attention by saying, "I invited Dr. Connor over this afternoon."

"Did you?" Mary filled his glass with sweet tea. "That's wonderful, honey. He'll be a good friend to have, even if Carrie doesn't fancy him."

"Aunt Mary!" Caroline protested, holding out her own glass. "Why would you think I'm not interested in him? There's nothing not to like about Dr. Connor."

"Oh, my mistake then. I assumed you weren't interested because you ran off soon as you met him." Mary gave her a pointed look as she topped off the glass.

Caroline waited for Mary to take her seat before explaining, "Stephen and I took our conversation to the porch, actually, and later we danced the polka together inside. Didn't you see us?"

Mary shrugged, clearly of the opinion that this didn't make up for her initial behavior.

Caroline persisted. "Thank you very much for introducin' him to me. I'm delighted that he's callin' this afternoon." Her chin set stubbornly. *She'll see. I'm not gonna throw away this opportunity with Stephen Connor. Clay was distractin', but he—*

"Remember when Mr. Clay stuffed the whole apple in his mouth?" Lenora's voice rang out from the nearby hallway.

"Yeah. And that weird girl said he'd better not let Ettie catch him, or she might throw him in the oven like a roast pig!" Emma squealed.

Caroline smiled to herself as the girls laughed.

"I wish she hadn't been there, though," Lenora sighed, her voice becoming inaudible as the girls clattered up the stairs.

Pursing her lips thoughtfully, Caroline resolved to ask Lenora about the girl at the first opportunity.

Later that morning at the Williamsburg Presbyterian Church, Reverend Scott cheerfully greeted his congregation, including some bleary-eyed Christmas party attendees. With seeming guilelessness, he delivered a thinly-veiled sermon on the merits of temperance, softening his message with fatherly, indulgent smiles.

As Caroline shook the reverend's warm hand after the service, he beamed at her, saying, "I am so proud that you have decided to join our congregation, young lady. Your voice is a real blessin' during our hymns of praise. I'm glad y'all were able to make it to church this mornin'."

Caroline flushed both with pleasure at his compliment and guilt about her somewhat-less-than-pious behavior of the night before. As she thanked him, she spotted Lenora outside. She was standing alone under a live oak, rummaging through her chatelaine purse.

Swiftly catching up to her, Caroline tried to sound nonchalant. "Who was that strange girl with straight black hair at the party last night? I didn't see her at church this mornin'."

Lenora wrinkled her nose as she drew a piece of paper and a pencil out of her bag. Pressing the paper against her palm, she began to write, distracted as she answered, "Her name's Jessie… but she's kinda cracked. Please… don't invite her over anymore."

"Who are her people?"

"Can't rightly say." Lenora shook her blond braids, frowning as she refolded the paper. She brandished it, explaining, "I was writin' down the date for the church bazaar. I'm makin' potholders for it."

"She didn't tell you anythin' at all about herself?"

"Not much. But I think she's stayin' with the Bells. She seems to know Mr. Clay pretty well. Everythin' outta her mouth was 'Clay this, Clay that'."

"Was it, now?"

Lenora nodded as she tucked the paper back in her purse. "I was so glad when Mrs. Bell came to get her last night. Guess she prob'ly goes to First Baptist with them. Sure hope she never comes here."

Caroline's eyebrows shot up. "How is she cracked?"

"Well, for one thing, she didn't play with us." Lenora began ticking off on her fingers. "She refused to look at our books, turned up her stupid nose at Victoria, and fussed at every little noise. Couldn't hear, she said. She just kept peekin' at you adults and askin' questions about everyone." At this, Lenora abruptly clasped her hands and began to study her toes.

"Did she ask about me? What did you tell her? And… who is Victoria?"

"My porcelain doll." Lenora looked up at this last question and tilted her head proudly. "The prettiest doll of anyone I know. I sewed her a quilted underpetticoat and a silk petticoat, and she even has drawers."

"Mommy's waitin' for y'all. She says to hurry up!" Emma shouted from across the church yard.

With a shrug, Lenora ran to catch up with her beckoning mother.

At home that afternoon, Caroline plumped the decorative pillows on the loveseat as she waited for Stephen's arrival.

John watched her with a bemused expression, folding his newspaper onto his knees. "I'm glad you're doin' that. I'm sure Dr. Connor will appreciate the peacocks facin' in the right direction."

She sighed and flopped on the pillow, exclaiming, "But what am I s'posed to do with myself? I have Ettie's pecan pie, and I don't wanna put water on to boil for tea until he arrives. And when he does, I have no earthly idea what to talk about."

"You? I've never yet seen *you* at a loss for words."

"Hah. So funny."

"But I imagine he'd like a stroll down to the stables if he's half as interested in horses as he seemed to be last night."

Just then, a knock sounded at the door. Jumping up, she hastily composed herself before answering it.

Stephen Connor doffed his derby hat. "Miss Caroline, it is a pleasure to see you again."

"Likewise, Dr. Connor." Caroline offered her hand with a small curtsy. *Yes, I did remember correctly,* she thought as his lips brushed her skin. *Dr. Connor is a most handsome and charmin' man.*

After seating their guest, Caroline was surprised to see her generally-laconic brother fall immediately at ease, chatting amiably with Stephen. The men dove straight into politics, and she contented herself with studying Stephen's perfect profile, only vaguely listening as they debated international European conflicts such as the Boer War in Africa and the Boxer Rebellion in China. When their discussion turned towards the morality of the Open Door Policy, she finally remembered to put on the water for tea. As she waited for it to boil, she stifled a yawn. The conversation had shifted to American concerns such as the takeover of Cuba and Guam as well as the ongoing Philippine-American War.

"We did pay for it. Twenty million," John was saying.

"To Spain, not to the Filipino natives. Spain invaded 'em jus' like we're doin' now."

"Not the same at all. The Spanish are so much worse than us."

"How so?"

"Starvin' thousands of Cubans and blowin' up our battleship in Havana, for starters. I don't know as much about the Philippines," John admitted, "but I have faith we're better than that."

"There's no proof the Spanish blew up the *Maine*. And I'm not convinced we're so much better. Over a hundred thousand native Filipinos killed so far in our takeover of *their* islands, whereas Spain's gone home."

"Lickin' its wounds, thanks to us."

"Well, I suppose we can all be grateful the Spanish-American War is over, at least," Stephen offered with a wry twist to his mouth.

Just as Caroline was beginning to listen with a bit more interest from her position next to the woodstove, the kettle began to whistle. At once, the men shot to their feet as if it were a signal. When they announced their intention to take a stroll down to the stables, she sighed and set the kettle aside.

"Do you mind?" Stephen asked, briefly turning his attention to her.

"Of course not." She smiled. "I was expectin' it."

On their way out the door, John asked, "Oh, would you like to come along?"

"I generally do, don't I?" Though she hadn't been thinking about it and wasn't dressed for riding, she grabbed a sun hat and an apple out of the fruit bowl, then hurried after them, not about to leave herself open for more of Mary's criticism.

While John gave Stephen a tour of the stables, she wandered over to visit with Julep. Approaching his stall, she pulled the apple out of her pocket. His wet lips brushed her palm as he nabbed it.

"Hey there, sweet Julep. We brought company today." Embracing his neck, she inhaled the warm horse smell of the stalls. "He likes to talk politics."

Julep shifted back and forth impatiently.

As the men rattled on, she began to saddle Julep, this time with the side-saddle. After all, she couldn't always wear her practical split-skirt riding habit, and this was good practice. Cinching the saddle tight, she called out, "I'm goin' for a ride. Y'all wanna join me?"

The men chorused their enthusiasm, and by the time she led Julep from the stall, John was pointing out a handsome roan gelding named Hurricane to Stephen. For himself, John held the reins of his favorite, Maritime.

Caroline flounced her skirt at them. "See you boys at the river."

At their good-natured laughter, she grinned and left the stables, mounting Julep at the block and heading out at an easy trot.

This was another of the balmy, sunny days that often grace the Lowcountry throughout even the winter. Although the grass was brown and brittle and many trees had lost their leaves, Caroline gazed at the panorama appreciatively. She began to circle the plantation on an old riding path, inhaling the fresh air but not quite daring to throw her head back as she would sitting astride. Soon, the faint hoofbeats of the men's horses were behind her, and she leaned forward, clicking her tongue, spurring Julep to go a little faster.

Julep fell into a rolling canter over the open lane and set her bouncing precariously.

She dared not ask Julep to go any faster, even though she could hear the pounding of hoofs gaining on her. The men waved their hats as they passed her, and with a twinge of regret, she resisted digging a heel into Julep's side. He leapt forward, regardless. She drew back on the reins with alarm, gasping as he reared. He soon settled, and she laughed with exhilaration at managing to keep her seat—and at his momentary competitiveness.

A few minutes later, they were taking their time in the final stretch. Gnarled branches of nearly a hundred live oaks formed a majestic, emerald arch over the dirt road, eventually leading past the stables and Swann plantation home down to the Black River, where nearly all traffic had occurred a mere half-century before. The growth of the railroads, along with the War Between the States, had changed plantation life forever. The farm was now relatively secluded, but she relished the privacy of the estate.

When she arrived at the river, John and Stephen were skimming rocks across the surface of the water.

Caroline slipped down from Julep and led him to where the other horses were tied. Noticing Stephen watching her, she asked brightly, "Did you enjoy the ride?"

As he smiled, a skipping rock fell from his hand. "I did."

"If we'd planned this better, we could've brought a picnic to the river with us," she remarked, tying Julep's reins to a limb.

"Maybe next time." John flicked another rock across the river's surface, bobbing his head each time it bounced. Then he jogged over to Maritime's saddle and untied a blanket from behind it. With a flourish, he spread it out on the ground nearby over a bed of dry leaves. Then he threw himself down as if tackling it.

Stephen tumbled easily beside him, but Caroline only perched primly on the edge. She would have sprawled next to John if it had been just the two of them, but now she spread out her skirts carefully. Surreptitiously, she scanned the river for any tell-tale reminders of Clayton. Crickets chirred, and a box-turtle slid into the water with a small splash. Mosquitoes were blessedly absent due to a recent cold snap, making it the most pleasant of days for being outside. She shook her head and tried to redirect her attention. "So, Dr. Connor, tell us about your medical practice. You must be terribly clever to make sense of all those patent formulas."

With a sigh, Stephen put his arms behind his head, staring up at brown water-oak leaves rustling overhead. "There's still so much for me to learn. I wish I could personally follow up on all my patients to find out how their prescriptions worked, but I don't have time for that."

"Won't folks just tell you?" John asked.

"Not unless we have a follow-up appointment scheduled. So I'm still tryin' to figure out which patent medicines I can rely on. These new pharmaceutical companies would push snake oil on us if they could. Many of their remedies are no better."

Caroline raised her eyebrows. "I've heard such good things."

"Well…" Stephen sat up to meet her gaze. "What the companies are sellin' more than anything is an idea. Marketing is not always based on the facts, even in the world of medicine. Most patients are gonna get better, no matter what you give them."

"Most of them?" Caroline plucked a blade of dry grass.

Stephen nodded. "The human body is an amazin' thing. Most would get better without any treatment, while others won't get better, no matter what. Then there are those who need something, anything to believe in. Sometimes, if a patient believes a drug will cure them, it will."

John laughed. "You forgot to mention that some folks are actually cured by those drugs."

"You're right," Stephen chuckled. "Don't tell my patients."

Caroline studied him. "Mary tells me that she counts on her Hood's Sarsaparilla… and that Bayer aspirin. She seems to believe they work."

"Sure do." Stephen leaned back onto his elbows. "She's got herself a great blood purifier and pain killer. Those are easy. There are so many others, though. And then I have this huge set of homeopathic remedies. Even less predictable, but often the first thing I try. Remarkable results sometimes, and I don't have to worry about them hurtin' folks. Kids like 'em, too."

"Must be hard to figure it all out on your own," Caroline sympathized, eyeing the water's edge wistfully. She was tempted to take off her boots, despite their company.

"Hopefully I'll have help soon," Stephen continued. "There's a young doctor who's supposed to join my practice here in a few weeks. Dr. Davis. It'll be nice to have someone to consult with."

"How long you been practicin' by yourself?" asked John.

Stephen eyed them for a moment then smiled conspiratorially. "Truth be told, I'm not completely alone out here. If I'm desperate, I send folks over to Doc Thomas."

"Doc Thomas?" they echoed.

"The Negro root doctor. Heck, sometimes I send 'em if I'm just busy."

"What does he do?" Caroline asked.

"He uses native herbs and much more than that, from what I understand. Real eclectic-type, pullin' from many traditions."

"You're sendin' folks to a witch doctor?" John's brow creased, and in the distance a bobwhite trilled.

Stephen laughed. "I wouldn't call him that."

Caroline frowned. "How can you be sure it's not just superstitious, backwoods nonsense?"

"Some of the herbs he uses are the main ingredients in my most reliable patent medicines—including the ones you mentioned. Remember that when remedies are handed down over centuries, there's generally good reason for it. He's cured at least six cases this year that I couldn't get a handle on."

John whistled. "For centuries, hmm? Do you think?"

"So you're tellin' us," Caroline laughed, "that we might be better off callin' for Doc Thomas than callin' for you, Dr. Connor?"

"Way I see it, health is like a jigsaw puzzle. Sometimes you've gotta look around to find the right treatment. Doc Thomas could just save your life with his root medicine."

"Well," said John, climbing to his feet somewhat awkwardly. "I'm gettin' hungry with all this talk about roots. Sweet potatoes don't sound half bad right now. Shall we head back?"

When the companions arrived back at the cottage, Caroline said, "I've got the pie, but it's gettin' time for supper. Ettie said last night's leftovers would be in the icebox." Stoking the small wood stove, she added, "I'll go over to the kitchen after we have some tea. The water should be boilin' in just a few minutes."

"Or I can just go fetch them right now." John was already at the door. "I'll be back in a jiffy."

Realizing she was alone with Stephen, Caroline busied herself with the tea service, dispensing orange-pekoe tea leaves into a bone-china teapot. Matching teacups and saucers were soon set out for the three of them and boiling water transferred into the teapot.

"Here's the sugar bowl, and I should've asked John to bring some milk. Do you take milk with your tea?" Caroline placed a spoon in the sugar bowl.

"I like mine plain, but thank you." He fingered the edge of his teacup. "I hope I haven't overstayed my welcome, Carrie. I'm havin' trouble tearing myself away."

"Not at all." She waved a hand as she sank down across from him. "We're delighted to have you here."

"It's been a long time since I've felt so at ease," he admitted, "and I'm afraid I let myself go this afternoon. I talked so much you must've been about ready to jump in the river. I noticed you eyein' it."

She laughed, caught off guard. "Not at all. We were real interested. Maybe you can show us your office sometime, tell us what everything's for."

He shrugged. "If you like. I live above my office, but I already feel at home here with you and John. Your little cottage is cozy and… happy."

Smiling awkwardly, she stared down at her teacup. He seemed surprisingly trusting of her—especially given her behavior of the night before. Swallowing, she managed to say, "I'm glad you like it here. Truly. We're pleased you've come."

Reaching tentatively across the table, he touched her hand with his fingertips.

For a suspended moment, she found herself gazing at his perfect face. Their eyes locked, and she sensed a subtle shift, as if she were somehow falling into sync with him, bonding in a mere instant. Somehow, inexplicably, ageless invisible strands of connectivity were forming between herself and this incarnate man of her dreams.

The door creaked open, and John stepped inside with his icebox finds. "I've got butterbeans and rice, cornbread and collards, but not a single root. Sorry 'bout the delay, but Uncle Sam was talkin' with me about work tomorrow."

Caroline's gaze dropped to her empty cup, and she busied herself with the tea again, hoping that John wouldn't notice the twin spots of heat rising to her cheeks. As John engaged Stephen again about the stables, she silently blew on her tea and listened to them converse, only occasionally adding a word here or there between sips.

Finally, Stephen stood to take his leave. He shook John's hand. "Thank you for the wonderful afternoon. I hope I will have the pleasure of spending many more with you and your lovely sister."

John clapped the doctor on the shoulder in uncharacteristic camaraderie. "As do I, my friend."

Turning to Caroline, Stephen asked, "May I call next Sunday?"

Her breath caught. He'd directed the question to her, not to her brother. She could only nod her acceptance.

John answered for her. "We'd love to have you, and this time maybe we'll plan our meal a little more thoughtfully."

8• Disparaging Shakespeare

THE NEXT MORNING GREETED THEM with more traditional winter weather. It was cold and dreary, the sky a suspended sheet of iron-gray. The usual stray creatures were out of sight, no doubt huddled under houses, in coops, and in trees. The young women were walking to work, well-insulated in coats and quilted flannel petticoats.

Anne had unburied her face from her broadcloth scarf to tell Caroline about her evening with Mr. Sanders at the party. Her breaths were creating a white mist. "He's not only nice to talk to, but real witty."

"Mark-Twain witty?"

"Maybe not quite," she admitted, "but I was surprised. I mean, I knew how thoughtful he was, but I didn't expect him to make me laugh so much. And he wanted to know all about me. He seemed… spellbound, askin' about my life and what I'm interested in. We share a love of art and design and, well, you'll never guess." Anne took a satisfied breath before turning to face Caroline, stopping them in their tracks.

"What?" Caroline lifted numb fingers to her mouth to puff on them.

"He wants me to join him on his next business trip to Charleston."

"Really? Already?" Caroline gaped.

"Well, Dr. Connor invited you to his office," Anne pointed out, rubbing the tip of her frozen nose.

"Hardly the same thing. I don't have to travel off to the hinterlands with him to get there."

Anne shrugged. "He promised to take me to a concert. He has tickets to see some world-famous prima-donna opera singer. Can you imagine?" Her eyes sparkled.

"You can't go, Anna. Not by yourself."

"Maybe Mary will be my chaperone."

"When is it?" Caroline tugged Anne's arm for them to resume their walk to work. Gravel again crunched beneath their feet. "The new satin fabrics arrive this week, along with the latest patterns. We may have time to make you a new dress." Her nose crinkled. "One that is not chartreuse."

Anne looked at her hopefully. "Oh Carrie, you're right. It wouldn't be too extravagant, would it? After all, what if it affects my future? And I wouldn't want to embarrass Mr. Sanders in front of his business associates."

"Absolutely not, honey." Caroline patted her arm. "A new dress is critical to your future as Mrs. Sanders."

"He did compliment my silk dress, the chartreuse. He even asked me to bring it along," Anne said thoughtfully, too preoccupied to react.

During dinner hour, Anne and Caroline huddled together on a bench outside the sewing plant.

"He just jumped into the river, and you haven't heard from him since?"

"Not a peep." Caroline grimaced as she stowed the remains of her meal. "Guess he's alright, since we haven't had any news, but I'd like to know for sure. I'd feel better if I could see him again."

"But only because you're worried about his well-being, right? That handsome Dr. Connor is your new beau, of course." When Caroline delayed her reply for a moment too long, Anne added, "You don't mean that you like both of them?"

"Don't be silly. Stephen is the obvious choice."

"Agreed."

Caroline hesitated, then looked down. "I'm just not sure my heart knows that."

"Explain." Anne folded her hands into her lap. "You're not going back inside until I understand."

"Clay is just excitin'," Caroline mumbled, smoothing her dark skirt. "I've never met anyone like him. He's so unpredictable, so… spontaneous. I feel happy with him, like I can breathe. With Stephen it's a bit like a… a scarf is over my face."

At Anne's thoughtful frown, Caroline continued in a rush, "I don't understand it either. I thought that the darkly handsome, serious type of suitor would be the most thrillin' in the world. Stephen's perfect, all those things and more, and I do feel drawn to him, but next to Clay he seems… more like a new friend than any sort of lover."

"That's because he is—and he's supposed to be." Anne shook her head. "You barely know Clay, but it sounds like you're ready to roll into bed with him already. I hope you don't throw away the perfect man for a bit of passion. You'll end up a penniless pauper with a brood of children and a truant husband."

"That's hardly fair—"

"For goodness sakes, Carrie, Clay has already disappeared on you. Listen to me. Stephen is predictable, handsome, and financially secure."

"I barely know Stephen, either."

"Which is why he shouldn't yet be your lover. And neither should Clay." A small group of coworkers bustled by, and Anne paused, her face softening. "Besides, I have a personal interest in seeing you marry well. When we're all settled with our husbands, I want you to accompany me to Charleston and, well, wherever we wanna go. Dressed in your own latest fashions, of course. We'll replace that Gibson Girl ourselves."

Caroline sighed.

Placing a hand on her arm, Anne said meaningfully, "Besides, Dr. Connor just hasn't become your lover *yet*. I'm glad he's a gentleman, but when he warms up, I can't imagine you're gonna have any complaints. He's an absolute Adonis. Did you look at him?"

"Anna!" Caroline grinned at last and nudged her friend. "Were *you* looking at him?"

Anne gave a cryptic shrug as the bell rang for their return to work.

That evening at home, Caroline sidled up to John. She'd been noting gray shadows beneath his eyes.

"Dear me, *Hamlet* again? If it's not the newspapers, it's Shakespeare? Must you always read such tragic stuff?"

He closed the leather-bound book, more disconcerted at the interruption than she had expected. This only confirmed the need to intervene, to distract him from such tragedy with a mission.

"John, would you do me an oh-so-tiny favor?"

He managed a small smile. "What is it?"

"Well, I thought you might take the fig jelly roll that Ettie made over to Sheriff Bell's house."

"Why don't you send Molly?" He slid the book onto an end table.

"She's busy helpin' Ettie. Besides, I need *you* to find out some information for me."

"What kind of information?"

She picked up a peacock-bedecked cushion and clutched it. "Remember Clayton Bell from Saturday? Well, he disappeared that night, and I won't feel settled until I know that he didn't get lost in the woods or drowned in the river."

John looked at her curiously. "Didn't I see you dancin' with him?"

"Well, yes. That's partly why I'm in a state about it. My dance partner went and jumped in the river. I can't go seekin' him out myself or he might… get ideas. Please, would you?"

"He jumped in the river?" John ran a finger reflexively over his thin moustache.

She nodded with a small grimace. A moment later, she gave a light laugh and added, "Oh, I was wonderin' about that strange child they brought along, too. Jessie's her name, I think. If you mention her to Mrs. Bell, she'll prob'ly tell you all about her."

His brows knit as he pulled on his tweed overcoat and newsboy cap. Heading towards the Bells, jelly roll in tow, he wondered when he would learn to draw the line. As if being delivery boy were not enough, he was also to be his sister's snoop regarding a family in whom he had not the slightest personal interest whatsoever.

Once the door closed behind him, Caroline sank to the loveseat, relieved that he had complied. Resolution about Clayton's fate—and a bit more information about the girl Jessie—would help to settle her mind about the sharecropper. Then she could move on.

Absentmindedly picking up *Hamlet*, she opened it to where John had marked the page with a handwritten note from Anne. She smiled as she reread the memo, noting Anne's ornamental 'A' and flourish under her surname. *Such artistry, like with our dresses. What amazingly good taste she has—and she's so proliferative with her ideas. I, on the other hand, am merely proliferative with my sewing labor.*

Somewhat disheartened, Caroline transferred her attention to the book at hand. She began to scan the stanzas, but they weren't of much interest to her. The antiquated Elizabethan prose and utterly hopeless, depressed, and irredeemable characters wore her patience as thin as the book's brittle pages. It even smelled dusty.

Her own 'dime novel trash,' as John disparagingly referred to her books, took her to a realm full of hope and satisfying romance. *The characters in my novels are modern women full of new ideas—women with whom I can identify.* Caroline felt herself cheering, warming up in defense of her own literary preferences. She'd never been sure what there was to learn from men who wrote plays centuries ago. Shakespeare had a nasty habit of disposing of his main characters, so tragic when real life seemed hard enough already. *If there has to be a tragedy, then perseverance and optimism should still win out in the end. Sadness must be overcome.* Her eyebrows knit in sudden conviction. *Shakespeare's pleasure in tormentin' readers is not so mystifyin' as is his popularity. I just can't fathom John's high-brow, afflicted preferences.*

Exhilarated, Caroline began perusing the gloomy book with a different intent—to condemn the questionably great poet. She was in the midst of trying to decipher a stanza when a knock sounded at the door. With four lines remaining, she called from the loveseat, "Come in!"

A few footsteps were followed by silence. As she finished reciting the last line to herself, she looked up to see Clayton Bell standing there, a sprig of mistletoe in hand.

Looming huge above her, he smiled impishly, eyes twinkling and chin dimpling. "Hey, Miss Carrie Caroline Corbett. Nice to see you again."

Eyes wide, she stammered, "Clay! Hello. Why are you..." Diverting her eyes, she quickly collected herself. "What can I do for you, Mr. Bell?"

His smile broadened as he presented her with the mistletoe. "My apologies, but this is hardly the season for flowers, so I brought this pitiful bouquet instead."

Standing up, she took the mistletoe and laughed. "I s'pose I could put it above the door there. That's where it goes, right?"

"Allow me." He took it back from her and hung it on a protruding nail above the doorway, within easy reach for him.

As he fastened the bough in place, she said in as flippant a tone as she could muster, "I hear you'll be headed out of town soon, that you're just here for a visit."

He glanced over his shoulder, adjusting the mistletoe. "Well, that's true, I s'pose, though I tend to visit fairly often. I live over in Greeleyville, just down the main road on the left as you're headed towards town. Little white clapboard house on a farm across from the New Market Cemetery. Not but just a couple of hours or so to get here on a decent horse." He paused. "Takes me a little bit longer than that."

Caroline bit her lip, mulling this over. Unconsciously, she brought the Shakespearean volume to her chest.

Clayton glanced at the book in her hands. "So you're the literary sort, eh?"

Surprised, she looked down and shrugged with distaste. "Well, I do enjoy a good novel, but this stuffy, miserable old tragedy? Land's sakes, no."

His laugh suffused the room.

She countered, "And are you the literary sort, Mr. Clayton?"

"God no… I'm not sure the last time I picked up a book—but I do know how to read," he added, as though to assure her that he had some vestige of culture.

Grinning, she challenged, "Alright then, Mr. Bell… read to me from this dreadful play. You can't make it any worse."

Taking the book from her hand, Clayton flipped through, pausing occasionally to scan a section.

"Alright, here's one," he finally said. In a serious and resonant voice, he intoned,

He is dead and gone, lady
He is dead and gone;
At his head a green-grass turf,
At his heels a stone.

Wide-eyed, Caroline remarked, "Just in case I wasn't sure he was dead…"

Clayton chuckled as she repeated the stanza then demanded, "Read another."

He flushed and admitted, "To be honest, Carrie, I picked that more because I could actually read it than because of the humor. Most of this book is Greek to me."

"Just try," she urged, still tickled by the verse.

Shifting from one foot to the other, he opened the volume, again towards the beginning, and read a marked passage. His vibrant voice hesitantly intoned,

I could a tale unfold whose lightest word
Would harrow up thy soul, freeze thy young blood,
Make thy two eyes, like stars, start from their spheres…

"Terrifying!" Caroline declared, clutching a sofa cushion over her face momentarily in mock fear. In truth, a shiver had travelled down her spine.

As he closed the book, she suggested, "Just one more."

He handed it to her and gazed around curiously. "Where's your brother?"

Caroline stood abruptly and began adjusting the cushions. "Well, actually, he's over at your place, the sheriff's house."

"My uncle's house?" His eyebrows lifted in surprise.

"I asked him to go by to make sure that you were… alive. It wasn't his idea, obviously. He's deliverin' a jelly roll so they won't know he's really there to check on you," Caroline explained, a flush creeping into her cheeks.

"You were worried 'bout me? Why?" Clayton gave a perplexed smile.

Indignant at her own embarrassment and his seeming pleasure in the situation, she retorted, "Why, Mr. Bell, you disappeared straight into the river in the dark of night. You never came back. I didn't know if you had been drowned or devoured by alligators… or if you'd gone mad, for all that." She glared at his palms, which had flown outwards as if to stop the onslaught.

"Carrie, be reasonable… I told you why I went in the river. And I could hardly have walked back into the party a soppin' mess, now could I?"

"Well… your behavior was highly irregular," she murmured, eyes still fixed on his broad hands.

"—but necessary." He tilted her chin and locked eyes with her for a heart-stopping moment. Then his glance shifted downwards to where he touched her face. Exhaling, he began to trace her jaw line with his fingertips, almost contemplatively.

He continued to study her until his gaze locked on a glossy blond strand that had escaped the red silk ribbon holding back her hair. It lay on the exposed skin above her bosom. As her hand reached up to adjust it, he murmured, "I'll do it." His fingers traveled down her neck and unhurriedly caressed her skin as he slid the tress back, his contact lingering on the nape of her neck.

Tremors ran through her body. Her knees went weak. A palpable awareness of his touch consumed her, even as a distant voice in her mind called for caution.

Gathering her reserves, she compelled herself to say, "Mr. Bell, this is a precarious situation. I shouldn't be alone with you. Others may get the impression—"

Clayton turned glazed eyes onto Caroline's mouth. Deaf to thought or reason, his burning lips descended on her trembling ones.

She gave no protest as they slid down onto the loveseat, his hands sliding down her back and pulling her to him urgently. Her own skin seared with desire where he touched her. Her hands hesitantly embraced his broad shoulders, and her lips returned his ardent kisses, uncertainly at first and then with increasing fervor.

Caroline blinked, catching her breath when he finally pulled back from her. With alarm, she realized that he was unfastening his belt buckle. Aghast, she seamlessly withdrew and rose to her feet.

"I think you have the wrong idea!" she exclaimed in alarm.

"Carrie," he groaned. He stood and stepped towards her, but she fled to the front door.

Flinging it open, she pointed outwards with a tremulous finger. "The river is that way, Mr. Bell."

Clayton's face slowly gained comprehension, and his eyes cleared. He began to chortle and then to laugh out loud. Gathering himself, he stepped towards the door, shaking his head. "I have no excuse except that I'm mad about you, Carrie."

As he moved past her, Caroline felt her heart tug.

He was already through the door when she murmured, "Mr. Bell?"

As he turned back towards her, she touched his sleeve, almost inaudibly reminding him, "I s'pose just one for the mistletoe."

He leaned forward and gently grazed her lips. Brushing his thumb over her cheek, he promised, "I'll see you soon."

9• Jessie Skulks

A SLIGHT, SILENT FIGURE slid from behind the aging cypress tree. Her dark eyes were dry, but a painful, gnawing sensation twisted in her stomach. Clayton had been in the small cottage for several never-ending minutes, and Jessie felt an abdominal stab each time she heard the obnoxious, tinkling laughter of the teasing seductress.

The hollow-eyed girl ignored not only the gripping pains but the stings of fire ants. She stood motionless, waiting until the wooden door burst open. Caroline was standing there, pointing outside. Clayton's rich laughter emanated from the house, and Jessie watched raptly as he momentarily emerged. She hissed aloud when the blond temptress stopped him for a kiss.

Waves of revulsion threatened as Jessie waited for Clayton to pass her. Once she was sure he was gone, she slipped away using an old Indian trail as a shortcut back to the Bells' home. She hurried along, whispering furiously, "One day I'll be Mrs. Clayton Bell, I will," repeated between chants of, "She doesn't matter, she doesn't matter."

A sigh of relief punctuated her recitations as she arrived back at the Bell homestead. She slumped safely against the porch railing, no inquisitive relatives yet in sight. *There's nothin' I can do about it. I can't play the coquette, but my turn will come. It will.*

Caroline crumpled onto the loveseat. She took a few deep breaths and then threw herself back, flinging her arms wide. For the moment, she would refuse to think. She preferred to simply relive the ecstasy of his touch. Her eyes closed as she recalled the burning trail that his fingers had etched into her skin. She vividly remembered his lips on hers and his arms pulling her towards him. Desire still felt palpable in the air.

A clatter at the door startled her, and she sat upright quickly, smoothing her hair and trying to regain her composure.

John stepped into the room with a preoccupied air.

"Hey, how'd it go?" she asked brightly.

"Hello, sister." He gave an exaggerated bow, though he still looked somewhat distracted. "Your bidding has been accomplished."

"Oh, thank you. You are a darlin'. Pray tell what you have sleuthed out for me."

"Very well," he began, blinking as if emerging from a reverie. "It all seemed pretty peaceful when I first arrived at the sheriff's home. Mrs. Bell graciously invited me in, but I paused when I crossed the threshold. There seemed to be an… unnatural energy."

"Unnatural? How?"

"I wasn't sure at first. I was still standin' in the foyer when this blindin' pain shot through my ankle."

"What happened?" She leaned forward to look at his trouser-covered ankles.

"A gray, scaly water moccasin had its fangs in me like it had latched onto a fish."

"What? In the house?" She jumped to her feet.

"Wait. Let me finish." He adjusted his spectacles. "It was then that Mrs. Bell started cacklin' and the moccasin transformed into that strange child—" He broke off as Caroline began pummeling him with a sofa pillow.

She giggled helplessly. "John! You are wicked!"

"Wait. You need to hear this before the poison sets in." He held up a hand with a small frown. "Jessie is a shape shifter. That's why she's so peculiar.

"Mrs. Bell offered me a cordial to delay the poison's effects while they prepared their ritual sacrifice to Hades. So I took it. I figured matters couldn't get much worse. After a bit, Clay entered the room in this dark, floor-length robe lined with red silk—so the blood doesn't show so much, I'm guessin'. He was chanting ancient Greek verse."

Caroline touched her hair ribbon, unnerved at the mention of red silk—and of Clayton reciting verse. "What then?"

"I did the only thing I could think to do. I took the jelly roll from under my arm and offered it as a sacrifice in place of me."

She nodded slowly. "Quite sensible. I'd have done the same thing."

"I've taught you well." John patted her shoulder. "So, after consultin' with each other, they decided that the jelly roll would be an adequate substitute. Not real flatterin', but they let me go. It was a narrow escape."

"Mm-hmm."

"They tell me that, in the future, I should present the offerings *before* I enter the sanctified dwelling."

"Thank goodness they let you go." Caroline wiped her forehead with mock relief. "But now we need an antidote. I've heard tell that a snifter of bourbon can cure the venom of a shape shifter."

"Then I will surrender to your tender ministrations." He staggered to a chair and sank into it. Moments later, as he was relaxing with his bourbon, Caroline pulled up a seat.

"Did you find out anythin' else while you were over there?"

"Well, I did chat a bit with old Mrs. Singletary. That's Mrs. Bell's widowed mother. She seemed to be the only one there. I listened to her ramble on for ages about the Christmas bazaar they're havin' at her church. That's why it took so long. Oh, and by the way, are you and Anne still singin' at our candlelight service? We need to practice."

"Of course. We will." Caroline nodded, though she had forgotten about it entirely. "But tell me about their visitors."

"Clay and Jessie? Alright." His hands spread out as if smoothing a pie crust. "Mrs. Singletary says Clay has been helpin' the last few days with building a new barn on his cousin's farm. The youngest Joseph Bell—the third, I think she said—recently got married, and he and his wife Lizzie are livin' out at the sheriff's old place."

"Did she say anythin' else about Clay?" Caroline's eyebrows knit together.

"And back to the subjects of our investigation…" John sighed. "Mrs. Singletary tells me that Clay isn't keen to go home. Never is. Did you know his mama lives with him? A horrid woman, apparently, but he's her only child. He occasionally visits here to 'help out', but it's really to get a break from his mama."

Caroline was now perched on the edge of her seat. "John, you are practically Sherlock Holmes himself. I'd never have known."

"Ah, but I saved the best for last. I'm afraid, though, that the lingering after-effects of the poison have exhausted me." He feigned a swoon.

"Would you like some tea? Some sweet potato pone?" Caroline asked in a syrupy voice.

"Both should help," John admitted from his sprawled posture. He grinned and continued, "That girl Jessie sounds like a piece of work, maybe touched in the head. Mrs. Singletary feels protective of her, seems like, because she's an orphan—but Jessie's from the Bell side of the family, so she's not actually blood kin to the girl. She's tryin' to help Jessie feel at home here, though—even asked the girl to call her Granny."

"Well, Mrs. Singletary's not related to Clay, either, is she? She's the sheriff's mother-in-law, right?"

John nodded.

Caroline pursed her lips. "So maybe we shouldn't listen to all that talk about Jessie bein' cracked—and Clay's mother bein' horrid. I'm not sure we should always take in-laws at their word."

John shrugged. "Well, old Mrs. Singletary seemed defensive of the girl. But maybe you're right."

Caroline nodded, handing him a slice of pone on a saucer. "Anythin' else about Jessie?"

"A bit, actually. Seems Jessie's mother recently passed away, but the girl's real quiet about it. Her father died when she was little—that was Sheriff Bell's brother, so the Bells hadn't so much as seen the child since the mother remarried."

"So how'd she come to live with them?"

John took a bite of his dark-orange treat, shaking his head. "It was somethin' else. One day a few months ago her stepfather—a Hawkins fellow, I believe Mrs. Singletary said—drove up in his buggy and dropped Jessie off just like he was deliverin' a package. And he didn't mince words."

"What did he say?" Caroline frowned.

"Told the family in no uncertain terms that he didn't wanna raise the child." John rose to his feet and gesticulated as he pronounced in an exaggerated drawl, *"She's an unnatural critter what ain't shed a tear since her own mama's death. And she's always skulkin' about so's a man can't sleep easy in his own bed. All I can say is good riddance."* John leaned towards his sister, sharing in a conspiratorial tone as he took his seat, "Somethin' like that, from what I understand. Then he announced that he'd keep the other children unless they became cracked like Jessie. He left immediately. Didn't even go in the house or water his horses."

"How strange," she murmured.

"Does a stepfather count as an in-law? He seemed to think she's cracked, too."

"Well, maybe that's why Mrs. Bell thinks so."

He gave her a doubtful look. "Mrs. Singletary says Jessie runs around on her own most of the time and can't be bothered with other children. She seems to have taken a shine to her cousin Clay, though. Even went on some sorta trip with him. The Bells wanna put her in school, but she doesn't wanna go. They'll make her after Christmas break, but for now they're just takin' her to church."

Caroline clasped her hands to her chest sympathetically. "The poor girl. I'm sure this is all real difficult. Her whole life sounds like one long tragedy."

"What we know of it, anyhow." John nodded with a bit more pragmatism. "I'd say we should stay as far away from the creature as possible. No need to become part of that tragedy."

10• Christmas Eve

DR. STEPHEN CONNOR CHECKED his pocket watch as he exited the black buggy. After a long day of making house calls, he was to accompany the Corbetts to the Christmas Eve candlelight service at church, but he was running late.

He shook his head as he approached the steps of the tabby cottage. His last patient, Mr. Carter, should have been a quick follow-up, but the old fellow's wife had retained him with her chatter for over an hour. Between "Yes, ma'am"s, he kept telling her that he had to go. The nimble lady had followed him across the foyer, onto the porch, and all the way to his carriage, delaying his periodic advances with a staying hand on his arm. Even after he was in his carriage, she stood next to it and continued talking. Stephen was at his wit's ends. *This business of extractin' myself from patients' homes is gonna be the end of me. But it's sometimes even trickier to convince them to leave my office.*

As Stephen knocked on the cottage door, the lilting notes of a soprano voice and a violin twined through the illuminated windows. Relaxation began to seep through his body despite the cool night air. He edged open the door, revealing the siblings practicing for the service.

Caroline looked up in surprise. "Why, Stephen! We didn't hear you." Impulsively, she ran forward to give him a hug. "Merry Christmas Eve! Anne left with the family already, so John was just rehearsin' her part with me."

Pleasantly surprised, Stephen nodded. "I apologize for holdin' y'all up, but hopefully we can make it on time."

They arrived just as the hour struck. Caroline slid onto the front pew next to Anne, and Stephen followed John into the Swann's regular pew behind them.

The special service was dedicated to Christmas hymns with the young women's duet near the end of the service. They sang 'Silent Night' *a capella.* As their harmony swelled, candles glowed brightly around them, silhouetting their figures and shining on Caroline's golden hair.

Stephen gazed at the lovely angel before him. The contentment he felt here was the same as that he'd felt at her cottage. His heart expanded with the conviction that he had found the woman with whom he could spend his life.

After the ceremony, the congregation exited in procession with their candles. Anne's cape slipped from her arm as she left her pew, and John smoothly nabbed it, not even spilling the wax from his candle. He followed her down the aisle.

Once outside, families and neighbors gathered together in groups for the trek home. As Caroline and Stephen headed to the parked buggy towards the rear of the church, John excused himself to deliver the cape.

Stephen assisted Caroline into the buggy then settled next to her. He felt secure and protective, comforted and attracted all at once. He couldn't recall having ever felt so love-inspired. Turning to face her, he said earnestly, "I know our courtship is only beginnin', but I have hopes for a future together."

"I'm lookin' forward to spendin' more time with you, too." Her hands twisted together as she sought for the right words to encourage him. Before she could say more, however, his dark eyes had moved to her mouth.

"May I kiss you, Carrie?"

She smiled, tickled at his formality, then mirrored his ceremoniousness by straightening her face. Solemnly, she answered, "Yes, you may, Dr. Connor."

As his warm, soft lips pressed against hers, she inhaled the clean scent of castile soap. His arms drew her to him as their kiss deepened.

Her heart quickened. Anne had been right, after all. As exciting as Clayton might be, she was already more than satisfied with kissing Dr. Stephen Connor.

Across the churchyard, John briskly strode through the damp grass towards Anne. As his mouth opened to greet her, he came to an abrupt standstill. She was conversing with Mr. Sanders, her eyes transfixed on a book-sized gift box tied with a dark-green velvet bow.

John watched as Anne pulled away the ribbon and gingerly opened the box. Her face lit up, and she stammered her appreciation.

Mr. Sanders' self-satisfied reply was more audible. "Yes, ma'am, I knew you'd enjoy these pastel sticks. I ordered them directly from Charleston. Thought you might use them to sketch your dress designs."

How patronizin'. John scowled with annoyance, but Anne's eyes were shining as if Mr. Sanders were Santa Claus himself. *If only that were the case.*

The older fellow was continuing even more smugly, "Pastel sticks have been used by artists since Leonardo da Vinci. S'posed to be a favorite medium of that Impressionist artist, Edgar Degas. I don't care for his work personally, but you ladies seem to appreciate his depictions of ballet dancers."

John rolled his eyes, but Anne still beamed with gratitude and interest.

Mr. Sanders doffed his top hat and set off, calling jauntily, "Until the weekend, then, Miss Brighton. Have a wonderful Christmas."

John waited another moment to allow Anne's starry-eyed naïveté to settle before approaching her. "You dropped your cape, Anna."

She accepted it with an absent-minded smile and looked towards the rest of the family. They were already a short distance down the road, walking with their still-lit candles, singing carols.

Anne turned to join them, seemingly unmindful of John, when she spun back and implored with a cheery smile, "Go carolin' with us. It's a beautiful Christmas Eve."

Hesitating, John glanced back towards Stephen and Caroline. He was startled to see them embracing. Opting not to interrupt, he linked arms with Anne. His spirits began to rise as his tenor voice melded with her alto in a chorus of 'Hark! The Herald Angels Sing'.

Jessie shivered with the pleasure of a new discovery. She normally disdained the simpletons who touted a mysterious, generous stranger in red garments to her. She knew better. She had watched through neighbors' windows as parents lay presents out for their children late in the night, and she had seen her own mother prepare some of the meager presents she and her siblings had received so sporadically over the past few years.

Tonight was Christmas Eve, and it was a wonderful night. Not because her obtuse uncle and aunt plied her with ludicrous Christmas tales and eggnog, and not only because she had spent much of the night with Clayton—even holding his hand as they walked to the Baptist church, where she had sat next to Clayton and had been surprised to discover that the preacher's words held a new thrill for her. As he spoke of God's omniscience, of the goodwill and benevolence we have to trust in even through our darkest hours, pins had pricked down her spine. *God brought me here somehow, didn't he? If all those terrible things hadn't happened with my mama dyin' and Hawkins throwin' me out, I wouldn't be sittin' next to Clay now, would I?*

The joy of being with Clayton made it more tolerable to join her guardians in trite holiday customs at home as they sat by the woodstove. She even smiled graciously when they shoved a limp rag doll at her, embracing it as she had observed that insipid Lenora Swann do to her own doll.

"I'll name her Caroline," she said, thinking to dismember the thing and toss it into the Black River.

This notion caused a small laugh to escape her, and Granny Singletary smiled in delight, warmly mentioning, "I made her just for you, dearie. I knit the trim on her dress myself."

"Speakin' of Caroline," Aunt Sally remarked to Uncle Joe as they rocked perfectly out-of-sync in adjacent rocking chairs, "I saw her with Dr. Connor tonight. They were ridin' through the middle of town *unchaperoned*, if you please, and just as brazen about it. She was leanin' against him, and he had an arm wrapped around her, like they were tryin' to display themselves to the whole town. Frankly, I'm surprised Mary isn't keepin' a better eye on her."

Jessie's heart leapt at her aunt's words, and she quickly glanced at Clayton, whose firm lips were drawn in a tight line. His knuckles whitened as they clutched the armrest.

Aunt Sally blithely continued, "But my, what a handsome couple they make. His dark good looks and her blond beauty. Wonder how long they been courtin'?"

"They were dancin' together at the Christmas party. I know that much," replied Uncle Joe.

As they spoke, an unaccustomed sense of relief flooded through Jessie's body. Soon she was as drowsy as a cat with a full belly. When she yawned for the second time, Clayton pointed out that it was late, that she was tired, and that perhaps they should all head to bed. His voice was even deeper and slower than usual. His whole body slumped as he stood and excused himself.

Jessie considered staying up to watch him—seeing him settled in tended to ease that constricted feeling around her chest—but tonight her eyelids were lead sheets. It was all she could do to keep them open, just tiny slits that allowed her to make her way to bed. It helped that tonight she didn't feel that constricting sensation, for some reason. After changing into her nightgown, Jessie let herself go straight to sleep. It was a deep, dreamless slumber, the first since her mother's death.

11• Christmas Day

CLAYTON BELL KNEW HIMSELF. He knew his faults and he knew his strengths. He was reasonably quick to form opinions, and thus he knew pretty clearly what he liked and what he didn't like.

He was a passionate man, but he wasn't obstinate. He admitted fault when he deemed it appropriate, and he had no problem standing up for himself, either.

Life seemed straightforward most of the time. What Clayton did have trouble fathoming, though, was Miss

Caroline Corbett, so he knocked on her cottage door with a mission to figure her out.

Instead of calling for him to come inside as she had at his last visit, she creaked open the door and peered out at him, blinking in a furtive manner.

Glancing past her, Clayton could see John and a tall, dark stranger peering back at him curiously.

"Hey Carrie. Hope I'm not disturbin' you," he said tentatively.

"Oh, Mr. Bell, it's no trouble." Her cheeks instantly flared. She still didn't invite him inside. "How can I help you?"

He already knew what he'd aimed to find out. She obviously did not intend to pursue their relationship. Willing his suddenly-aching heart to harden, he said brusquely, "Just wanted to come by to wish you and your family a merry Christmas. I'm headin' back to Greeleyville, as it's 'bout time I tend to things over there. Hope y'all have a nice day."

His heart twisted at her look of relief.

She beamed at him. "Best of luck to you, Mr. Bell. I'm sure we'll see you again soon. Have a merry Christmas."

At this, he'd had enough. Nodding politely, he turned on his heel and headed to pack his things. He would be home by nightfall.

Caroline turned to face John and Stephen. Their quizzical expressions demanded an explanation.

"That was Mr. Bell sayin' good-bye," she said with a shrug.

Nodding, John remarked, "Prob'ly a good thing."

She darted a glance at Stephen, who was observing quietly, forehead slightly furrowed.

"So… isn't this the fellow I had to wait on at the dance, before I had the chance to meet you? I'm rather jealous that he's poppin' by to see you."

Caroline frowned, but before she could respond, Stephen stepped behind her and wrapped his arms firmly around her waist. Clearing his throat, he announced as if to the whole world, "Hear! Hear! I hereby designate Miss Caroline Corbett off-limits to all other potential suitors. That is," he added, twirling her around to face him, "if you'll agree to be my wife."

Gasping, Caroline speechlessly nodded her assent.

Stephen smiled and drew her into an embrace.

John tactfully withdrew from the room as his sister once again confirmed the enjoyment of kissing Dr. Stephen Connor.

Her thoughts were an elated whirl. *I'm to become Mrs. Caroline Connor… Mrs. Caroline Allie Corbett Connor… Carrie Connor… Mrs. Stephen Connor.* Her new names swirled about her mind in an enchanting dance, and she brushed nagging thoughts of Clayton away as best she could.

Mary sighed with contentment and rolled to her side. "Happy birthday, honey..." she murmured, kissing Sam's muscular shoulder. His birthday fell on Christmas day, easy to remember but sometimes too much for her—especially since the girls were born, what with so many celebrations at the same time.

Sam grinned and murmured appreciatively, "Yes, ma'am, it has been so far."

He reached to stroke the smooth skin of her heart-shaped face. "How is it, Mary, that you are as beautiful as the day we met? Farm life and children are s'posed to age you."

She smiled. "I'm not exactly a field hand, darlin'… and I certainly don't look sixteen anymore." Running a finger along the furrows of his sun-kissed face, she added, "I don't mind a few well-deserved lines. They are a record of our lives together. See, this line is for me… this one for Lenora… this one for Emma… and, I think, this and this and this line are for Julep."

He chuckled. "Speakin' of the girls, we'd better get downstairs. I hear them up already."

They were sorting through their Christmas stockings when their parents arrived. Lenora was delighted with a pair of white leather gloves, and Emma hugged a new wax doll to her chest.

Anne looked up from her perch near the crackling hearth, admitting sheepishly, "It's my fault, Mary. I couldn't wait to give the girls the presents I got them, and I didn't wanna wake you."

"You're gonna spoil these girls," Mary warned before leaning down to whisper to them.

"Happy birthday, Papa!" they chorused, rushing to hug him. Then they rushed just as quickly towards the tree, clamoring for the tiny boxes that had appeared overnight.

"What is it?" Emma asked in wonder as she held up what seemed to be a miniature tin pail like the one Lenora carried to school—the one she admired so much. It hung from a chain and a clip.

"A thimble. You attach it to your skirt." Lenora indicated the small purse dangling at her own waist and the tiny, chained sewing implements hooked together on Anne's chatelaine.

Mary's brows narrowed as she noticed Emma eyeing the yard. "Do *not* use it for diggin'," she said firmly, shaking her head. "Or buildin'. Or toad furniture. No dirt."

Emma's face fell.

"Lenora," Mary said, "perhaps tomorrow you can show Emma how to use her thimble. Try it on the heavy cloth we bought for curtains."

Pulling a tiny pencil from its slot on the side of the brass-covered memo pad newly attached to her own chatelaine, Lenora marked down her first reminder.

The aroma of freshly-baked biscuits soon called them to breakfast. Just as the family finished up, John, Caroline, and Stephen clattered through the door, carrying a new bundle of gifts for the family.

"You missed breakfast. You never miss breakfast," Emma said with a scowl. "And it's Christmas!"

"They had company, dear," Mary explained.

"And they have presents, silly," Lenora pointed out.

After another flurry of gift-opening, the girls exclaimed that it was the best Christmas ever.

Mary assured everyone that the girls were ruint forever.

Caroline took her arm and led her onto the porch, despite the brisk air. There she shared about her engagement.

Mary clasped her hands together in front of her lips, her smile wide.

"But you don't seem surprised," Caroline noted, raising her eyebrows.

Laughing, Mary wrapped her arms around herself for warmth. "Stephen asked Sam's blessing last night, after he dropped you off." Seizing hold of her astounded niece's hand, Mary pulled her back towards the front door. "Come on inside. We have to tell Sam. He will be beside himself."

Upon hearing the news, Sam burst out with a shout of joy and gave Caroline a brawny hug. He then shook Stephen's hand heartily. Soon the entire family was abuzz with the engagement. Anne shrieked with joy, and the girls jumped up and down with her, shouting "Best Christmas ever!"

Mary watched them, more content than she could ever remember feeling. Her girls had so many presents that the wrapping paper was now a mountainous hazard next to the fireplace. Caroline had matched up with a handsome, local doctor, and Anne seemed well on her way towards a sound marriage—Mr. Sanders had also approached them the night before, in his case to ask for Anne's company on a certain February venture to Charleston, for which Mary had agreed to serve as chaperone. Though Anne had discussed the trip with a demure, calm demeanor while in his presence, she'd later rushed from room to room, surveying their closets for what to bring. With garments in either hand, she'd excitedly told Mary about the factory's new shipment of satins and her plans to buy remnants to sew new dresses for them.

Remnants would not do for Caroline's wedding dress, Mary decided. White silk and lace would be specially ordered within the next month so Caroline could represent the Swanns with utmost class at their first-ever Kingstree wedding.

After dispensing hearty congratulations several times over, Sam suggested that the newly-engaged couple join him on a midday ride. Just as they were agreeing, the clatter of a rapidly-approaching carriage came from outside. Everyone fell silent as it drew to a halt and a frantic voice called, "Dr. Connor! We need Dr. Connor!"

Stephen hurriedly grabbed his topcoat and dashed out, murmuring a brief apology.

Caroline stood in bewildered disappointment. The grandfather clock ticking in the corner said it was not yet eleven o'clock—the holiday had hardly begun. She bit her lip. *If I'm gonna marry a doctor, special occasions are gonna be disrupted. It's that simple.* She sighed, feeling selfish to be so bothered. *He's the one who has to leave, not me. I'll just have to adjust to this sort of thing, I s'pose. Hardly a sacrifice on my part, but I wish we could've been engaged for more than a few minutes before he had to dash off.* She took a deep breath and then smiled in wonder. *I'm gonna be a doctor's wife.*

With that in mind, Caroline turned to Sam. "Well then, how about that ride, Uncle Sam? John? Anne, how about helping me balance out these here menfolk?"

Jessie had woken unusually refreshed that Christmas morning. She stretched lazily in her bed, appreciating for the first time the comfort and quiet of a cotton-filled mattress so much better than the crackling, lumpy cornhusk one she'd shared with her siblings. Remembering the inspiring sermon of the night before, she thought, *Another sign that livin' here is God's blessing, not a curse.* Glancing over at the new doll, she climbed out of bed to set it on her bureau with approval. *Perhaps I'll keep her, after all.*

Pulling on a gray frock and pinafore over her cotton chemise, the girl ran a comb through her limp hair before heading to the living room, where the full-bearded sheriff and his wife were still in their night caps, seated in their rocking chairs and engaged in a low discussion.

"Good mornin', honey," Aunt Sally said, breaking off from their conversation.

Granny Singletary stepped in from the kitchen and gestured at the tree. "Look-y what Santa brought you!"

Jessie glanced under the tree with mild curiosity. She picked up the smaller of two packages first.

"Go on, they're for you, darlin'," Granny Singletary encouraged.

Jessie opened the present to reveal an assortment of hair ribbons, which she fingered slowly. *Carrie wears this sort of thing. Maybe I should try lookin' prissy, too. Clay seems to like it.*

With honest feeling, Jessie remarked, "I've never had anythin' like these. Thank you."

Granny Singletary beamed, apparently forgetting the Santa charade.

Jessie picked up the larger package, in which she found a slate, a slate pencil, and a primer for school—gifts from her aunt and uncle. She set them down, irritated at the reminder that she would soon be spending her days cooped up with other children.

Clayton's absence struck her only then. Her body tensed as she swiveled to look around the room, searching for him. A pang of panic wrenched at her gut as she wondered if he'd left, if the previous night's news had driven him away.

In a mere moment, the fleeting aura of wellness that had blanketed her since the night before slipped away.

Granny Singletary had seized on this glimmer of hope for Jessie's emotional convalescence but now watched with confused apprehension as the girl began murmuring soft reproaches to herself while gathering her things. The elderly woman gazed after Jessie as the child carried the gifts towards her room without a backwards glance.

Jessie paused at Clayton's sleeping quarters in the wide hallway and sank to his bedroll in relief. His few possessions—some clothes and a comb—were still there. She'd been dreading his departure for some time, and since he did not seem inclined to share his plans with her, she watched daily for signs that he was leaving.

After depositing the gifts in her room, Jessie exited the back door and instinctively headed towards the Swann plantation. En route to the old Indian trail, she spied Clayton returning with a determined frown on his face. Forgetting stealth, she ran across the yard directly to him and stood pointedly in his path.

He stopped with a preoccupied, impatient glare.

She clutched at his rough cotton sleeve and gazed back unblinkingly. "When?"

"Today… now," he responded, as though he, too, desired brevity.

"I can help you. You should take me."

"No."

"I can help with your mother."

"No."

Jessie's eyes narrowed, but her throat constricted with the realization that she would not be able to sway him.

He strode past her, soon vanishing into the house. She followed.

Inside the hallway, Granny Singletary stood near Clayton, wringing her hands as he packed.

He was making a dismal attempt to sound and look natural. Smiling stiffly, he reassured her, "Of course I've had a pleasant stay. I just need to get home."

"But honey, it's Christmas day. What's goin' on?" Granny Singletary was not normally so perturbed at his departures, but she could sense his pent-up fury.

"Just thinkin' I oughta spend part of the day with Mama," he answered, refusing to meet her eyes.

Jessie bolted into her own room and picked up the doll from her bureau. One by one, she began pulling off the soft appendages and dropping them onto the cold wooden floor.

Granny Singletary, in her consternation, moved to the doorway of Jessie's room. A hand trembled on her papery cheek at the sight of Jessie mutilating the doll she had so carefully and lovingly sewn.

Repulsed, she began to wordlessly retreat towards her daughter and son-in-law, who still sat contentedly in their living area. She turned and stumbled through the corridor, but before she reached them, she clutched her chest and collapsed, unconscious, to the hardwood floor.

Clayton rushed to her side, shouting for the sheriff to fetch the doctor from the Swann plantation.

As Sally ran forward to tend her mother, Jessie stood transfixed in the doorway of her room, experiencing a sudden thrill of fascination and a swell of newly-discovered power.

12• Romantic Supper

GRAY SKIES AND DANK WINDS heralded the new year, as if even the heavens were still mourning the widely-beloved Mrs. Singletary. Celebrations of the arrival of the twentieth century were subdued, and Caroline and Anne were soon marching back to the sewing factory like well-dressed worker ants.

Within a few short weeks, the young women produced the satin gowns planned for the Charleston trip. Anne's sequined mauve gown and Mary's pale taupe one both featured small bouffant sleeves and ruffled bodices that covered the pleats of narrow, trumpet skirts. Discreet slits at the ankle allowed them to walk with ease.

Caroline was delighted with the trendy, fitted skirts, waving away Anne's belated concerns about the more daring fashion. "They're fine. You and Aunt Mary will be the most stylish women at the show—includin' that prima donna—and Mr. Sanders will have eyes for no one but you."

When they brought the gowns home for their final fittings, Mary twirled around in hers, speechlessly running her fingers down the smooth material that clung to her legs.

Seeing her delight, Caroline spontaneously suggested, "Aunt Mary, let's fix up your hair. Uncle Sam will be home soon, and I do believe Anna and I should take the girls to the stables for a ride this evening." With a wink at the clamoring girls, she shunted a mildly-protesting Mary to her dressing table and directed Lenora and Emma to pull on their riding skirts.

Meanwhile, Anne spoke with Ettie about an impromptu alteration of the supper menu; seized with the spirit, Ettie pulled out the china and silver candlesticks. Anne then put on her own riding attire and furtively collected Sam's three-piece gray woolen suit.

Caroline arranged Mary's hair and smoothed it perfectly into place with pomade. After dabbing geranium-scented cologne behind her ear, Caroline inhaled the sweet, floral fragrance appreciatively then pronounced her 'perfect'. Leaving Mary to finish her own preparations, she hurried towards the stables with the girls. There she pulled John aside to enlist his aid in preparing Sam for the evening.

John listened with interest and suggested that he could provide a supper accompaniment on his violin. At Caroline's enthusiastic agreement, he set out to waylay Sam at the cottage.

When a besuited Sam Swann finally entered his home, he forgot his rumbling stomach. Mary had stepped into the foyer to greet him. His breath caught at the sight of her.

She smiled and awkwardly touched a ruffle on her bodice. "Good evenin', Sam. The girls finished my gown, and they wanted to consecrate it with this ridiculous supper. I'm not so sure it's a good idea. I'm terrified of ruinin' this dress."

"I'm glad they did," Sam said with a smile. "You are radiant, Mary. I'm the luckiest man in the world."

As they sat down to supper, their minstrel emerged from the kitchen, regaling the surprised pair with dreamy, romantic strains from Bizet's 'Je Crois Entendre', a sentimental and perfectly overdone touch to round out their evening.

As the violin soared, Sam became increasingly thoughtful, and he reached across the table to take Mary's hand. She met his gaze over flickering candles, and their shared look conveyed mutual messages of enduring love that they knew would last a lifetime.

When they finished their meal and rose from the table, John shifted into a popular waltz, 'The Blue Danube'. Pausing in surprise, Sam chuckled and then asked Mary to dance.

"I can only take small steps," she warned, waving a hand at her fitted dress.

"We'll manage somehow," Sam laughed as he stepped into position. The solitary couple spun slowly across the dining room then glided into the parlor, the violin following them. Husband and wife were one, and the world around them continued to dim. John quietly bowed and exited after a time, leaving the happy couple to their privacy.

After taking leave of the cottage, Anne had hurried to the stables despite the heavy, darkening sky. There Caroline and the girls were readying Hurricane and Maritime, the gentler mounts. Caroline merely gave Julep an affectionate pat, as she well knew Mary's rule that her girls were not to ride on the skittish stallion.

Wrapped in woolen cloaks, each young woman soon had a girl riding pillion behind her, all securely astride in their split skirts. They ventured out into chill winds under the gray sky and continued until well past dark, Caroline leading them on paths she knew to be safe.

When the horses finally arrived back at the stables, Anne and Lenora dismounted from Maritime. Anne patted windswept, wayward strands of hair as she went to help Emma down from behind Caroline. The warm weight of the child filled her arms. She shook her head. "Why, I do believe I'm falling prey to your rash mind, Carrie. What in heaven's name are we doin' out here in the middle of the night, when the girls and all manner of reasonable folks, including yours truly, should be tucked into their beds?"

Slipping off of Hurricane, Caroline smoothed his withers. She replied warmly, as though to herself, "Anna, girls, we have just created a memory." She looked up, as if struck with a premonition, and said with sudden inspiration, "Let's promise to never stop makin' memories—no matter what. As long as we have breath, we will *live*. Agreed?"

Impressed with Caroline's suddenly profound and fiercely-determined expression, Anne and the girls solemnly swore on that overcast, moonlit night their commitment to living life in the moment. They never forgot that oath.

13• Excursion to Charleston

THE SISTERS' TRUNKS WERE PACKED and all in a row on the Turbeville porch like heavy-laden box cars waiting on a sideline. Mary was generally pleased with their contents. An ivory cashmere shawl that she'd had since her wedding still looked soft and smooth, and her new satin gown had survived their romantic evening without mishap. Still, she kept dashing from the porch to her bedroom or the kitchen, afraid she might be forgetting some essential, even retrieving items she rarely used at home. She'd given little thought to fashion in her years on the Swann plantation, but now she wanted to have just-the-right sort of hat or hairpin if it were at all possible.

She had been on annual trips to visit her parents, some without Sam, but this one to Charleston was a rare excursion bent on leisure, an indulgence, something she'd not done since her bridal trip. They would dine in restaurants and tour the battery, visit the old slave market and attend a concert.

She would fret about the children, though. Although Lenora and Emma would be well-cared for by day with Ettie and would be checked on regularly and tucked in at night by Sam, Mary was still unsettled about leaving them, perhaps in part because Emma was clinging to her waist, wailing, "Don't go, Mommy!"

"Oh, come here, sweetie." Mary pulled the child onto the lap of her recently-modified chambray traveling suit. She sank back onto the joggling board and wrapped the child in her arms. Emma's nose was red from crying.

Lenora stood by the door, drooping like a forgotten house plant.

Mary called to her and soon had them both close. "Girls, you know I'll be back in a fortnight. That's only two weeks. If I don't go, then Aunt Anna can't see Charleston. We've even got tickets to hear a famous singer trained in Europe. She's named Emma, just like you. Wouldn't you like to attend her concert, if you had the chance?"

"No, ma'am." Emma buried her face against the soft wool of Mary's shawl, inhaling her mother's scent. "Not if I couldn't be with you."

Mary hugged the girl close. "Well, when you're older, maybe you'll wanna go. And then maybe I'll go with you. But right now, Aunt Anna needs me to be with her."

Lenora wistfully repeated, "Aunt Anna needs you to be with her, I know… but we'll still miss you, Mommy." Her eyes filled with unshed tears.

Mary closed her own eyes, her heart aching from what she knew should be dismissed as sentimental, illogical guilt. She sat with the girls until Mr. Sanders arrived. Even then, Sam had to pry Emma off of her.

Sam stood holding Emma as the carriage drove away. An unfamiliar pang of apprehension pierced his chest—no doubt induced by Emma's sniffles.

Setting Emma next to Lenora on the joggling board, he said gruffly, "Take your sister and find Ettie. See if she needs y'all to do anything. You're responsible for runnin' the house while your mama's gone."

"Yes, sir." Lenora wiped her eyes as Sam ran down the porch steps. She cast a reproachful glance after him and then at the too-empty dirt road down which her mother had just disappeared in Mr. Sanders' carriage. She tugged on Emma's hand. "Come on."

Entering the spacious stables, Sam sighed as if exhaling an entire cache of anxiety. He stopped abruptly, however, at finding Caroline already in the stall with Julep. She was grooming the thoroughbred and humming to herself, oblivious to her uncle's presence.

Sam watched for a moment before greeting her. "Mornin', Carrie."

"Oh, Uncle Sam." She looked up. "I didn't hear you come in."

"Just thinkin' of taking a ride on Julep."

She paused, short-bristled brush in hand. "I've just gotten back from ridin' him myself. I came here since Anna and Aunt Mary were leavin' for Charleston without me."

"Well, I suppose I should ride Hurricane, then, since Julep has already been out."

"I'm sorry." She gave a little frown. "I know he's your favorite."

"Not at all. I'm glad you spend time with him. Nice to know someone else appreciates and looks after him like I do."

"Well, he is the most beautiful creature on earth." Her gray eyes were wide with conviction as she hung the brush back on the wall.

Sam gazed approvingly at his niece, who turned to stroke the stallion's muzzle. "Julep sure favors spendin' time with you, too. I've been thinkin' that I should give him to you one day, but…" he winked, "I doubt I ever let go of him myself."

When Mr. Sanders called the sisters' attention to the church steeples dotting Charleston's skyline, Mary breathed, "I see why they call it the Holy City."

Nodding proudly, he settled back into his seat across from the women. He always enjoyed introducing folks to Charleston, appreciating his favorite city more each time—despite the inevitable stench of coal smoke that pervaded the coach as they rolled past well-shaded homes towards their hotel, slowing to a crawl behind other carriages. Meanwhile, derbies and ladies' hats piled with bright, artificial flowers wound between horses and buggies. Mary was impressed with how well the enormous hat brims protected the ladies' faces—much better than the ones she'd brought along.

Anne craned out the window to see a well-dressed couple pushing bicycles onto the cobblestones from the narrow, street-side end of a long porch running the depth of a house. As the man mounted the huge-wheeled ordinary and the couple cycled away, passing the carriages, Anne asked, "Are all the porches on the sides of the houses?"

"Almost all of them." Mr. Sanders glanced out of the window appraisingly. "Most homes are only a single-room's width but several rooms deep, if you'll notice. Side porches provide better ventilation in city quarters. It's a practice brought by early settlers from Barbados to deal with the heat."

"They raise their families in sideways houses?" tutted Mary. "Well, I feel sorry for them. Least with our plantation house—or your Queen Anne—you can actually see the house and there's plenty of room for family." She glanced sideways at Anne, but her sister was gazing out the carriage window again.

"What do the stars on the side of that house mean?" she asked.

Mr. Sanders turned to look at the building. "Special guests have stayed there—like General Lafayette," he began, pressing back against his seat even as Mary leaned to catch a glimpse of the black, iron stars located midway up the side of a house between the upper and lower floors. "Or me."

As their eyes widened, he laughed. "No, no. Those are just the ends of huge bolts that were put in almost all timber-frame houses here after the earthquake of 1886."

He smoothed the legs of his lounge suit. "Do you remember it?"

"I've heard of it," Anne said.

"I remember," Mary murmured.

"Well, some of the bolt plates are stars. Others are crosses, circles, or scrolls. I've always thought of them as ornamental, like most of our clothing fashions, although now you've got me wondering if they have any other meaning." He gave an intrigued smile. Then he glanced forward, and his eyes lit up. "Ah… here we are. Ahead is the seawall. They call it the battery—and this is White Point Gardens. Once we're settled in, we'll spend a bit of time strollin' the promenade. Unfortunately, it replaced a bathhouse that used to be here, or I'd take y'all for ice cream on the water."

The women looked out over the manicured lawn of the gardens. A group of young men were performing calisthenics in the shade of live oaks. Beyond them, a broad walkway bordered the sea wall. A young couple leaned against the fence railings that topped it, gazing out at the endlessly shimmering, sun-dappled waters of the inlet.

"The Ashley and Cooper rivers meet here, flowin' together past our lovely peninsula and on towards the sea," Mr. Sanders said, almost worshipfully. "And I see they've put up some cannons… just for decoration this time, I do hope. Always changin' things."

"They weren't here before?" Anne asked. "Not left behind from the war?"

"Certainly not, certainly not."

They rode in silence past the park and then along a row of palm trees that separated the street from a line of stately mansions. Anne was keeping her eyes peeled for one of the automobiles only rich people could afford, but so far she hadn't spotted a single horseless carriage. Then suddenly she gasped. A train engine looked to be barreling down the street, straight towards them.

"Ahh, the trolley. Never fear. It'll stay on its tracks," Mr. Sanders' voice rose over the rumble as it passed them and the brakes began to screech. "Stops right back there at the gardens. Between the streetcars and the ferries, city-dwellers hardly need a horse at all. We should take a tour on the trolley before we leave. You might find it amusin'."

Soon they arrived at their luxurious, five-story hotel, the St. John, and Mr. Sanders exited the carriage with a sure step, confident that his companions were well on their way to developing a true appreciation for Charleston.

The trip was a whirlwind of activities, and the Brighton sisters delighted in Mr. Sanders' hospitality. While introducing them to the city's architecture on foot, he insisted on protecting them from the sun with a white lace parasol, a novelty to them. He treated them to restaurants, took them to theatres, and regaled them with tales of local ghosts. On occasion, he left them to their own devices as he met with business associates from the textile and fashion industries.

Several afternoons were spent shopping on King Street, though they bought little after a visit to the millinery. Now bedecked in an ornately-garlanded hat with enough shade for an entire family, Mary spent much of her time idling on the cobblestone street, engaged in conversation with Mr. Sanders outside the dress shops in which Anne, wearing an angled toque hat, dallied. Anne deemed the small hat ideal for exploring the streets of

Charleston whilst under the shade of Mr. Sanders' parasol. From his side, she could observe the newer styles being worn across the city perfectly well, marveling when she recognized fashions she'd only seen in pattern books at the factory.

Charleston's more stylish citizens were bringing to life for Anne the simpler elegance of the new century. Narrow trumpet skirts and slimmer, more fitted sleeves were replacing the wide skirts and beloved sleeve puffs that lingered from the Gilded Age. At the same time, throwback elements sometimes graced the new styles, like tiny ruffs around standing collars, reminiscent of the sixteenth century.

In one shop, Mr. Sanders pointed out a rack of mandarin-orange dresses that had been made in their very own factory, and Anne laughed in astonishment. The price tags impressed her, and she felt prouder than ever of the personalized gowns she and Mary had brought along to wear to the concert. Some of the fancier dresses had sequins, and Anne blinked enthusiastically at seeing her gowns' painstaking embellishments in the stores already. With those sequins, she had defied her own tendency to simplify designs, but now she felt validated after seeing that patterns of sequins had been added by paid, professional designers. She glanced at the price tags again, curious as to the added value.

"Your sister has quite the passion for clothing, doesn't she?" Mr. Sanders remarked, smoothing his moustache as he and Mary went outside once more to wait for Anne.

"Oh, she certainly does," Mary agreed. "Our mother used to tell me that she spent all her pin money on magazines just so she could study the fashion plates."

"It's what the girls do," he chuckled.

"Oh, not like her. When she was little, she was obsessed with raidin' closets and playin' dress up. I remember this one time she made me wear one of our mother's dresses with a huge bustle—the kind that sticks straight back like a shelf. Can you imagine?"

"Those were magnificent days."

"More ridiculous than magnificent. The looks I got!"

"You wore it out of the house?" His eyebrow quirked up.

Mary shrugged. "It was her birthday. I had to. But I drew the line at the huge straw bonnet."

"All the ladies wore them when I was young."

"Then you know how they were. I felt like a horse wearin' blinders."

He laughed aloud.

"And now she's dressin' me again." Mary indicated the streamlined outfit she was wearing.

"You have infinite patience."

"Hmm. I don't know. Seems I was rather ignorant of fashion before she came to stay with us. Believe you me, you wouldn't have recognized these clothes just a few months ago."

He cast her dress an appraising glance. "Then perhaps your patience is payin' off. She's done a nice job."

"I think so," Mary enthused. "I have to admit I was rather skeptical about some of her ideas at first, but she and Carrie have been a blessing to my wardrobe. I'm becomin' quite spoilt, as a matter of fact."

That evening at supper, Mr. Sanders asked Anne, "Have you had the opportunity to try out those pastel sticks yet?"

Anne rubbed at a spot on her tea glass. "I used them a bit when I drew the designs for the gowns we brought with us—the ones for the concert."

"Did you find them to be useful?"

"They are so nice, Mr. Sanders." Anne took a sip of sweet tea and fiddled with the remains of her crab cake. "But the truth is that these past few weeks have been so busy that I've hardly worked with them at all." Her cheeks grew rosy. "I mean, they've already been helpful, but I hope to do a lot more with them."

He waved a nonchalant hand as their server brought dessert. "Never fear, Miss Brighton. I have no doubt you'll find ample time soon enough to pursue your creative endeavors. But for now, *I* am gonna pursue the fine art of appreciating this caramel custard."

Anne's eyes widened at the implication of his remark, and Mary slipped a hand over hers to give an exultant squeeze. Meanwhile, Mr. Sanders sank a spoon into his dessert.

That night, as they settled down to bed, Mary said, "It's goin' well, dear."

Anne smiled sleepily, closing her eyes to dreams of being on what seemed to be Mr. Sanders' estate, wandering through room after elegant room until she arrived at one containing a multitude of fabrics and a sewing machine. She ran a familiar hand over the instrument. Then she walked into a bright, circular room in a turret, filled with sketches on tables and walls.

A velvet chair was positioned in front of a window. As she stepped forward to take a seat, the clack of footsteps interrupted her reverie. She turned around to find Mr.

Sanders standing there, pride brimming in his pale eyes. As she reached for his hand, he said, "Scoot over, Anna. Stop stealin' the blanket."

Anne blinked then moved over for her sister. Mary grew quiet again, but Anne was now fully awake, remembering how right her dream had felt. Life seemed sweet and promising as she lay snug on the hotel's feather mattress. When she finally went back to sleep, it was to thoughts of a certain doting, refined husband, and she burrowed contentedly under the down quilt.

The next evening, Anne and Mary excitedly prepared for the concert. They had never looked more like sisters. Their elegant satin gowns were cut from the same pattern, and they wore similarly-styled upswept hair, loose brown tendrils cascading in careful curls down their uniquely adorned necks; Anne again had on her pearl pendant while Mary graced a seldom-worn wedding present from her husband—a cameo brooch with matching earbobs.

When they emerged from their rooms to meet Mr. Sanders, he stood in silent admiration, touching his gold paisley ascot for a long moment before bowing deeply. "I am honored to be accompanied by two such finely-dressed ladies this evenin'." As he straightened, he met Anne's eyes and added reverently, "Your gowns do justice to your beauty."

Anne forgot to reply as she absorbed the sincerity behind his words. *You think I'm beautiful. You think my creation is beautiful.*

Noting Anne's unconscious muteness, Mary answered for her, "The honor is ours, Mr. Sanders. Shall we go?" She placed a hand on Anne's elbow and propelled her towards the door.

As he escorted them towards the theatre, he remarked with sudden playfulness, "Do forgive me if I begin to strut. It's hard not to with such splendid companions at my side, but I'm valiantly fightin' the urge."

Anne smiled as Mary answered, "Strut as you will."

Minutes later, they passed a crowd of carriages waiting outside the theatre to drop off their passengers. Magnificently-clad men and women dashed between vehicles, brushing against muddy wagon wheels, lathered horses, and blustering drivers alike in their rush. Mr. Sanders seemed not to notice the hubbub, only directing his guests into the lobby, where he commenced to procure three glasses of wine.

As they sipped, Mary stared out of the large windows, whispering, "Someone's going to get run over," but Anne was distracted by the profusion of feathered boas and hats. The crowd looked like a gathering of fabulous birds, glittering with rhinestones under the gold-plated, rose-crystal chandelier suspended overhead.

Meanwhile, Mr. Sanders scanned the gathering crowd. "These performances are an occasion for the best society of Charleston to gather, so hopefully we'll… ah, hello Mr. Randolph. A pleasure to see you again."

A medium-built young man with oval spectacles shook hands with him. Mr. Sanders introduced him to the young women as the president of the city's college. "He may be young, but I understand he has grand plans. Was that your team of young men exercisin' out at the battery?"

Mr. Randolph smiled, blinking at them each in turn with his medium-brown eyes. "I hope so. We've got several teams goin' now—fencin', baseball, football."

"Not that education is really about sports," Mr. Sanders asserted.

"It's good for them to try their hands at different endeavors. And athletics are a great draw for prospective students."

"And donors, I suppose."

Mr. Randolph gave a broad grin. "The city supports us, but we *are* acceptin' donations to set up some new scholarships. We're hopin' to start recruitin' gifted young men from all over the state, not just locally."

"Gifted academically, I hope you mean."

"Of course. Academics are very much our focus." Mr. Randolph straightened. "You might recall that we're just about to launch that new Bachelor of Science degree."

"Ah yes." Mr. Sanders turned to the women with a sardonic expression. "As I understand it, the Bachelor of Science degree requires students to take even more classes than are usually required for their majors."

"Hmm…" Anne swallowed a mouthful of wine. "So you're lookin' to grow enrollment in your classes, then?"

Mr. Randolph's head bobbed. "Our new residence halls are almost complete, and we're expectin' to be housing students from all around the state by this comin' fall semester."

"I'm sure that will be lovely," Anne demurred, "but if you allowed women to attend, wouldn't you more immediately boost your enrollment numbers?"

He chuckled but shifted his bowtie as though it were too tight. "Perhaps. I'm not personally opposed to the idea, and South Carolina College has been experimentin' with lettin' women in these past few years, but I jus' don't see it happenin' here anytime soon. Our board members aren't too keen on it."

"I'm sorry to hear that."

"I can recommend a good women's college if you're int—"

"Oh no," Mr. Sanders interjected with a short laugh. "Miss Brighton works for me. Can't have her traipsin' off to some school. Need her too much for that. Too much."

"Of course." Mr. Randolph nodded graciously.

Mary elbowed her sister, going on tiptoes to whisper in her ear, "That's a *good* sign."

Wondering at Mary's insistence, Anne realized her face had puckered into a look of irritation. She tried to clear her expression as Mr. Randolph added, "You're lucky to have her, I'm sure."

"And the College of Charleston is fortunate to have such a motivated leader as you," Mr. Sanders returned, but his attention was already shifting to a pair of gentlemen in tuxedos. He puffed up proudly as they approached. "Do you by chance know Mr. Otis and Mr. Longstreet, our own titans of the fashion industry?"

Beaming at the newcomers, he waved broadly in the direction of his companions. "May I present the Brighton sisters? Miss Anne Brighton made these dresses herself."

"Homemade?" Mr. Otis gave a nod of grudging respect.

"Machine-made. At the factory," Anne corrected, watching as Mr. Randolph slipped away. Heat erupted up her neck, no doubt transforming her coloration into what she hoped seemed a mere reflection of the rose-paned chandelier above.

"She stays after work," Mr. Sanders clarified.

Anne wanted to sink right into the plush red carpet. She had to consciously force herself to stop clenching her skirt.

Mary, however, twirled around for them to inspect her garment, and the men murmured their approval.

Telling herself to trust in her host's judgment, Anne lowered her shoulders and tried to breathe. After all, he was the experienced traveler, the socially-adept and business-savvy Mr. Sanders that she had always admired.

At last it was time to be seated. Mr. Sanders guided Anne and Mary to their seats, whispering as they settled in, "Be sure to take a gander at Madame Nevada's gown—the finest European tailors design her clothes. They keep the lines of her dresses simple so as not to distract from her performance."

Anne was so busy looking around the magnificent theatre that she nearly missed the opening of the curtains. Emma Nevada's expressive voice soon erased all other thoughts, however, and Anne failed to notice for the longest time how diminutive her size was—as the tailors had intended, perhaps.

The prima donna's performance included both operatic and popular songs. Anne was riveted by them all, completely unaware of Mr. Sanders, who was as mesmerized by his companions as by the singer. He smiled at their expressions of incredulity when Madame Nevada majestically completed an aria full of vibrato and then, without hesitation, seamlessly began the pure notes of 'Listen to the Mockingbird'. He chuckled with delight as their eyebrows moved up just a little further with each trill.

Hours later, in their room, Anne confided to Mary, "I'm not half so self-conscious about these trumpet skirts now that we've been in Charleston for a while. They're everywhere."

"Mr. Sanders certainly seemed pleased with our gowns," Mary said with a small smile.

"I just wish he wouldn't go around tellin' everyone they're handmade. Why introduce us to high society if he's gonna do that?"

"He was braggin' about your talent." Mary burst out laughing. "And I don't think he minded your form-fittin' skirt in the slightest."

Anne rolled her eyes then turned to disrobe. She started humming a tune from the show, then paused to remark, "It's strange not to have petticoats, but I imagine it might be nice in the summertime." Unhooking her corset, she began to dance around the room in only her chemise, singing nonsensical syllables to 'The Last Rose of Summer', Madame Nevada's final song.

Mary couldn't help but join in, making up her own words to go along. As she spun, pivoted, and trilled with Anne, Mary felt a far cry from a woman in her last bloom.

Eventually, they collapsed together on the bed in gales of laughter, much to Mr. Sanders' curiosity in the neighboring room.

In the quiet days during Anne's trip, Caroline found her solitary walks to the sewing factory unexpectedly refreshing. She swung her dinner basket and took the opportunity to observe the outskirts of Kingstree. She was generally so absorbed in conversation that she paid little heed to her surroundings, but now she discovered not only individual residences she had missed, but whole areas to which she'd never devoted a single conscious thought. It was growing more familiar, but she might still be lost if someone were to randomly drop her off at certain points en route to her workplace.

She often left earlier now in order to make a diversion to the newsstand in town, taking this opportunity to peruse the dime novels more thoroughly. More than ever, she reveled in her autonomy as a working girl to spend her money as she pleased—and, even better, her time. The latest Laura Jean Libbey tale now lay in her basket. She would eagerly anticipate the story until dinner hour, during which she would devour a chapter or two along with her blackberry-jam-filled biscuits.

She had grown up in a frugal, modest home, ever craving those small extras that make life more colorful and interesting. Novels, silk hair ribbons, and other such extravagances had never been at her disposal until her older sister, Vivian, had left to work at a sewing plant in Georgetown. Then packages with all manner of discarded treasures began to arrive. The dime novels, in particular, had provided a world of fantastical escapism. It had become a familiar world, whether she lived at her parents' home or here in Kingstree, whether she was surrounded with worldly luxuries or spent endless hours in a sweat shop.

As if I need an escape, Caroline mused with a small smile. *My life is fascinatin' enough already. A double life. Workin' factory girl AND privileged fiancée of the town doctor.* A grin flashed across her face as she thought ahead to June. *My dual existence isn't long for this world. It'll be over when I move into Stephen's apartment after our wedding, and then we'll build a home together.*

Her days were spent working, daydreaming about the future, and inhabiting dime novel storyland; evenings were dedicated to her family and to Stephen, who was usually present unless he was with patients or attending the horse races. He assured her that he would soon become more available once the newly-arrived Dr. Davis became accustomed to their practice.

As for the races, Caroline, John, nor Sam cared to attend—they preferred riding their own horses. When not riding, they generally amused themselves with games, singing, or reading books in front of the crackling fire.

Stephen was unfailingly a gentleman with her, but she felt an inner fire beginning to burn, her ardor at the ready for his slightest touch. Their kisses had begun to ripen her body's readiness for him, and June seemed an eternity away.

Caroline still thought of Clayton with an occasional wistful pang but was well-content in her love and respect for Stephen. She felt immensely thankful that Anne's and Mary's influence had prevailed.

14• A Possessive Husband

ON A COOL EVENING IN EARLY MARCH, a handsome carriage clattered up the dusty driveway to the Swann plantation home.

From the remote steps of the tabby cottage, Caroline and Stephen observed two ladies with floral hats of different sizes and a gentleman in a top hat emerge from the gray cab. They ascended onto the porch while the driver unloaded luggage from the rear of the carriage. The illusion of sophisticated dignity was shattered by Emma bursting through the front door and throwing herself onto one of the women, screeching "Mommy, Mommy!" at the top of her lungs. Quietly, Lenora joined the happy tangle.

Caroline laughed with delight, suspecting she'd have thrown herself on the new arrivals with equal zeal if she'd been close enough.

Smiling at the display, Stephen put an arm around Caroline. "I wonder if we'll be blessed with such lovin' children one day."

A warm glow pricked Caroline's skin at the thought, and she nestled contentedly against him. *Children. We haven't discussed children yet… Of course we'll have children. Maybe two wonderful girls like Emma and Lenora or perhaps a handsome little boy to carry on the Connor name… but Stephen won't be attached to that. Other men are all caught up on havin' a son, but not Stephen. He'll be a wonderful father, no matter what.* Her eyes glistened as she realized with certainty, *I love him.*

Sam emerged from the house to greet the travelers. He cordially shook Mr. Sanders' hand and invited him in for a drink, but the older gentleman begged off, pleading weariness from travel.

"I am lookin' forward to a long soak and then bed, Mr. Swann."

"Of course." Sam turned to embrace Mary.

She whispered in an awe-tinged voice, "He has a porcelain bathtub inside his house, just like at the hotel we stayed at."

Sam shrugged and gave her a squeeze as he whispered back, "I'm happy with what I've got."

When the trunks were unloaded and Mr. Sanders had departed, the women began what promised to be a nonstop deluge of chatter about their trip.

Sam laughed and caught Mary's hands. "Hold on now. I'm more than happy to hear y'all's stories, but first I need to kiss my wife. I've missed you so much." He pulled Mary towards him, ignoring his daughters' protests.

Mary's flood of words were silenced as she kissed him. It was good to be with Sam again, but just as she felt a flicker of unbidden desire to be alone with him, a small hand yanked on her skirt.

"Mommy, did you see my scab?" Emma thrust out an arm to show her elbow half-caked in an impressive brown crust.

"What happened, sweetie?" Mary's face pinched with concern. Though still in Sam's arms, she was already oblivious to her husband.

Recognizing that he could not compete with his daughters, he took a deep, frustrated breath. A new scent on Mary filled his nostrils. He wanted to draw her close and keep inhaling her fragrance, but he'd allow the children their time with her first.

"I fell down," Emma announced proudly.

"Did you get that hat in Charleston?" wondered Lenora, ignoring her younger sister.

"Did you bring back anythin' for me?" Emma added.

"Don't be greedy," Lenora chided. "How was the concert?"

Mary laughed at their questions. "Hold on," she pleaded as she unwrapped herself from Sam's arms. "I'll tell y'all all about it, but first we have presents—for *both* of you."

At long last, after the distribution of gifts and a few avid descriptions of the sights and sounds of Charleston, the family retired for the night.

As they climbed into bed and drew the curtains, Sam admitted, "I've been missing you, darlin', countin' down the days until we could be together again." He buried his face in her rich brown hair. Over the last few nights, his need for her had been building. "What is that scent? You smell different. But it's good."

"Vervain. My new cologne from Charleston."

His heart sank as he heard the exhaustion in her voice. Exerting his last shreds of self-restraint, he suggested, "Another night won't kill me. You get some rest, Mary." Although he meant it, he felt a pang of disappointment when she nodded gratefully and sank into the pillow, falling asleep almost immediately.

Sam lay awake for hours, struggling to be patient until the following morning. When he awoke, laughter was ringing up the stairs. Mary was already up.

The children, Caroline, and John were again being regaled with the women's adventures in Charleston. Sam chuckled good-naturedly at the stories as he joined them, but by mid-afternoon, he began to wish things could just return to normal.

That night, Sam followed Mary into their bedroom, anxious to be alone at last. As he closed the door, she began laughing to herself at the dressing table.

"What is it?" He turned towards her, eyebrows knit in perplexity.

"Oh nothin', honey… Just rememberin' Mr. Sanders' outrageous threat to strut all the way to the theatre." Mary smiled with delight as she began unbuttoning her boot. "Oh, take a gander at my new stockings. He pointed these out to me." Slipping off the boot, she pulled back her skirts and extended a foot. Floral embroidery decorated the instep of the cotton stocking. "Isn't it lovely? I'm gonna try to do the same for the girls' stockings."

Sam gazed at her foot in angry disbelief. "And did he pick out your drawers, too?"

Her jaw dropped. She stared at him, speechless.

"You're beginnin' to convince me that I am a fool. I sent you off with another man, lettin' him wine and dine you for weeks on end. Now you can talk of nothin' but Mr. Sanders. I'll be damned if I'm ever so gullible in the future."

"What on earth?" she finally gasped. "Sam, you've lost your mind!"

"No, I haven't. I've been agonizin' over bein' separated from you these past weeks, seein' it as a sacrifice for Anna's sake, when the truth is, you've been gallivantin' all over the state with another man. Oh, he's had a fine time, with two beautiful women at his beck and call. You'll make me the laughin'-stock of the town, if you don't stop carryin' on like that."

"Darlin', be reasonable." Mary stood, frowning.

"I am reasonable. Damn you and damn Sanders!" With that, he yanked open the bedroom door.

"Wait, Sam. Stop, please!" Mary rushed forward, clutching at his sleeve.

Sam snarled a profanity and hurled himself from the room, down the stairs, and out into the night.

A half-hour later, Mary found him in his shirtsleeves at the stables, stonily perched on a scattered pile of hay. Pulling her gray woolen shawl more tightly around her shoulders, she stood in the doorway for a few moments before whispering, "I'm so sorry, Sam."

He sat there mutely.

She cringed and tried again. "Sam, I love you. Please don't be angry. I had no intention of hurtin' you or of bein' unfaithful in any thought or deed."

Still he did not reply.

Tears were now trickling, unheeded, down her face. Never before had she fought with Sam like this. She approached him and lowered herself to her knees, touching his own knees with her soft palms.

He did not protest when she pressed her wet lips onto his hand.

She kissed both hands and sighed with relief when he finally reached for her, pulling her into his arms.

As he kissed her lips, his hands trembled with an overpowering, possessive ferocity that she'd never sensed before.

Mary made no protest as he laid her back in the hay and took her there, asserting his authority as her husband and lover.

15• School Dramas

SAM THAWED OUT SLOWLY over the next couple of weeks. Mary was careful not to mention the trip around him and asked a mystified Anne not to mention it either, only saying that she and Sam had quarreled.

At church, however, Sam's stony glare captured Mr. Sanders' attention. His initial surprise transformed quickly to a decision to steer clear of Sam and his family for a while. With his age and experience, Mr. Sanders knew how unreasonable others could be. He also understood the adaptability of human nature, and he was a patient man.

He would wisely maintain a wide berth from the Swanns for now.

Anne wondered at Mr. Sanders' coolness, but she suspected his distance was related to Mary's request. She was oddly relieved at having life simplified for a time. The stable, regular aspects of her days provided a steadying influence after all the changes of the past months. These included simple walks to work with Caroline, leisurely horseback rides, games of Seven-Up with the family, and time spent with her young nieces, who had their own small dramas to share.

For instance, after her mother had left for Charleston, Emma had decided to attend school with Lenora.

"Because you missed your mommy and wanted to be with your big sister?" Anne sympathized. She and the girls were sitting together on the forest-green joggling board on the front porch.

"Well, I really jus' wanted to carry a shiny dinner pail like Lenora. Only Ettie didn't have another one, so I had to carry a wooden bucket instead," pouted Emma, holding out a mish-mash of practice stitches for Anne's inspection. "Lenora wouldn't share with me."

"Is that the real reason you wanted to go to school?" laughed Anne, eyeing the dubious stitchwork.

"Yes, ma'am, it sure was," Lenora chimed in, "but Papa made her go anyway. Said she was bein' foolish."

"I was not!" Emma protested, then blinked up at Anne. "You don't think I'm foolish, do you?"

"Hmm. Well, we're all foolish at times, but why weren't you in school this week?"

As Anne helped Emma with her overhand stitch, she learned that Emma had been at school for only two days when she became frightened by the teacher's loud scolding of the class and his threat to use the switches. She fled the school building, running as fast as she could towards the Swann plantation. That's when she tripped over a root and busted her elbow.

Sam had found her crumpled at the side of the dusty road during the middle of the school day, sobbing and bloody. He'd picked her up and hugged her close, riding Julep home with her in his arms, for once breaking Mary's mandate to keep the children away from the temperamental creature. Julep remained so docile for the entire ride home, however, that it was as though he, too, wished to soothe little Emma.

Pleased enough to relinquish her sister's company at school, Lenora now heartily reassured Emma, "Don't worry. I'll teach you your letters at home so you won't have to attend school until you wanna." In a conspiratorial whisper, she added, "But the switches are only for the boys."

Emma brightened. "Okay. But I'm gonna play all day at home and won't ever go back to school, anyway."

Soon enough after Emma's troubles, Lenora faced her own school intrigue. The teacher, Mr. Wright, was administering daily drills in preparation for the June spelling bee, and Lenora was locked in mortal combat with tall, lanky Owen Bodiford, the other top student. The winner of the bee was to receive an ebony-and-gold Waterman fountain pen, kept on display at the front of the classroom on the teacher's table.

Jessie Bell was now enrolled in school. Still as strange as she had been at the Christmas party, she generally disappeared during the two-hour dinner breaks and was left alone by the other girls. Though the schoolboys initially picked on her, they soon became wary, too. This seemed to suit her.

Lenora often felt a tingle along her spine during lessons and would turn to find the girl's dark eyes fixed on her. Gathering her courage one morning before class, Lenora adjusted her smocked pinafore and approached Jessie at her desk. "How you likin' school?"

Raising a single thin, dark eyebrow, Jessie replied, "It's what I expected."

Lenora nodded and gestured towards Jessie's slate. "Need any help with your letters or sums or anythin'? Since you're new and all."

Jessie purposefully rubbed her sums from the slate, then answered coolly, "If I did, I wouldn't ask you."

"Isn't that your homework?" Lenora threw up her hands. "Fine. I was just tryin' to be nice. In that case, give somebody else the creeps with your stares."

Jessie flinched but did not reply. The war had begun.

When Lenora went to retrieve her doll Victoria from the nursery that evening, she could not find her. Though Emma dissolved into tears and denied the charge of losing the doll, Lenora angrily refused to play with Emma or teach her letters until the doll was returned to her.

When Lenora complained to their parents at supper, Mary scolded Emma thoroughly. "You know not to touch Lenora's doll, and it's even worse to tell a lie about it. I thought you had learnt to leave Victoria alone by now. Until you find her, give me Martha."

"Martha? But I didn't!" Emma's voice rose hysterically, but Mary was firm, and Lenora retrieved the wax doll for her.

That night, a pitiful Emma made her way to her Aunt Anna's room and fell asleep sobbing into sympathetic arms.

Lenora refused to speak to Emma until the following afternoon, when her forlorn face finally melted Lenora's resolve. "You really don't remember playin' with her?"

Emma sadly shook her head.

At this, Lenora's heart tugged towards her baby sister. She reached out to tuck a strand of Emma's thick brown hair behind her ear and sighed. "I suppose we'll come across her eventually. Here… let's practice our letters for a while."

That night, a forgiving Lenora cuddled with Emma. Emma clung to her big sister in relief, allowing her confusion to sink away as Lenora's arms encircled her securely.

The next Monday, Lenora sat down at dinner hour with her friend Mabel and opened her pail. She pulled out her biscuits and found, wrapped with them, a scrap of velvet material, the same material that Victoria's dress was made of.

Lenora dropped the biscuits.

"What's the matter?" Mabel asked.

Lenora shook her head. "I'm not feelin' well."

Hands shaking, she put her dinner away and lay down on the blanket, her head cradled in her arms. She was beginning to comprehend. *Jessie saw Victoria at the*

Christmas party. I showed her where I keep her. I told her how precious a porcelain doll like her is.

The sick feeling continued squeezing her gut throughout the day. *I can't let her get away with this. She wants to play dirty, so I will, too.*

That night Lenora furtively took some old newspaper and collected a small bundle which she left outside until the morning. At school the next day, she waited for the other children to go inside before proceeding into the coat closet, where she emptied a cow dung patty into Jessie's wooden dinner bucket.

Two pensive days passed, and Lenora began to relax, hoping that Jessie had decided not to pursue their battle. Though Lenora had certainly not repaid Jessie's crime in full, her conscience was punishing her, and Lenora longed to leave her troubles behind.

On Friday, however, during their morning class session, Mr. Wright interrupted class to ask, "Has anyone moved the fountain pen from my desk?"

Lenora gasped as a chorus of murmurs erupted from the students. Owen and Lenora looked at each other in dismay until Lenora turned to narrow her eyes at Jessie—Jessie, who had taken her doll… Jessie, who wouldn't want Lenora to win the much-coveted pen. With outrage, Lenora saw a pleased smirk on the girl's face.

"It's JESSIE!" The words escaped her mouth before she realized they were out.

Mr. Wright looked with surprise at Lenora, always a model student, and asked quite seriously, "Are you accusing Jessie of stealing the fountain pen, Lenora?" He would not normally rely on a student's accusation, but he trusted Lenora implicitly. At her hesitant nod, he barked, "Set everything down at your desk, Jessie. Stand by the window." The determined teacher began to search through her desk, without luck. Finally, he ordered Jessie to turn out her pockets, which revealed nothing.

Jessie endured this invasion with a wry twist of her mouth, but then she suggested, "Perhaps you should check Lenora's desk. She's the one who wants the pen so much."

Rubbing his temple, Mr. Wright turned slowly to Lenora. He asked more kindly, "Do you mind, dear?"

Lenora moved away from her desk with dire anticipation. Only a moment later, Mr. Wright located the pen tucked into her McGuffey Reader.

Aghast, Lenora's heart sank. "She planted it there, Mr. Wright. I would never have done that. You know I wouldn't!"

At this, Owen spoke up, "She's done rotten things to us boys, too, Mr. Wright—puttin' bugs down our shirts, tellin' lies to start fights between us, and… other stuff." He shifted from one foot to the other and looked down at the ground, but then he continued, "There's somethin' not right about that girl. Besides, Lenora wouldn't steal the pen, cuz she wanted to win it fair and square." His cheeks reddened perceptibly as he glanced at Lenora.

Mr. Wright looked from Owen to Lenora and back to Jessie, whose slight smile seemed to mock the other students. He made a poignant decision and picked up a switch. "Step forward, Jessie."

16 • A Porcelain Life

A SUBDUED LENORA WALKED HOME FROM SCHOOL that afternoon. She felt almost contrite, so great was her shock at seeing Jessie beaten in front of the class. Mr. Wright rarely used a switch on even the naughtiest boy—the switches were there more for show than anything else.

Jessie, however, had received a blistering unlike anything Lenora had ever seen. Still, the girl remained dry-eyed and had not cried out. In fact, her face showed no more emotion than if she had been called forward to write a line of grammar on the board. She had not so much as glanced at Lenora or anyone else for the rest of the morning. When she disappeared as usual during dinner hour and did not return, no one remarked upon it.

As Lenora strolled up the dusty driveway to the house, she was aroused from her thoughts at the glint of broken pottery on the lane. She reached to pick it up. When she recognized the hand of her beloved Victoria, she cried out. Breaking into a run towards the house, her horror grew—fragmented bits of the doll littered the driveway. As she approached the porch, she spied the doll's mangled head hanging by its gossamer hair in the azalea next to the steps.

Lenora screamed and began to sob, bringing her mother at a dash through the screen door. A bewildered Mary soon held the hysterical and incoherent girl in her arms.

Hearing the commotion all the way from the stables, Sam quickly directed Julep towards the house. Moments later, he scooped his daughter from his wife's arms, carried her inside, and laid her on the couch. Mary applied cool cloths to Lenora's forehead until her sobs began to settle and she was able to speak. As Lenora related the incidents with Jessie in fits and bursts, their brows creased with concern.

Sam spoke decisively. "Mary, stay with Lenora. I'm gonna pay a visit to Sheriff and Mrs. Bell."

He strode out of the house and directed Julep towards the Bell's home. As he rode, his wrath grew, and he was soon headed there at a full gallop, with fire in his eyes and a wrenching pain in his chest from seeing his little girl in such a state.

In verdant woods near the road to her uncle's farmhouse, Jessie lingered on the old Indian path. Brambles scratched her ankles and gnats flew into her eyes, but she needed this space to herself, away from the school, away from others' eyes. Helter-skelter thoughts collided in her head like billiard balls. She was attempting to regain her composure and formulate a plan before heading to her aunt and uncle's house. Her excuses needed to be ready, just in case.

Her backside throbbed from the switching she had received, but what truly ached was the damage to her self-esteem. She had been proud of her ability to be subtle, to operate on an invisible level.

She had surpassed her normally cautious, self-imposed limits with Lenora, who reminded her too much of Caroline—and not only in her looks. She had the same insufferable mannerisms and seemed likewise to be beloved by all for no apparent reason.

At the sound of swift hoofbeats, Jessie flicked her eyes up the road. After a moment she recognized Mr. Swann, Lenora's father, leaving a trail of dust behind him. With a jolt, Jessie realized he was headed in the direction of her uncle's house. *I'm not ready. There's not enough time.* Unthinkingly, she stepped into the road, willing him to stop.

Swerving, Julep reared at the sudden apparition before him. Sam swayed in the saddle before falling, his head striking the hard-packed road with a sickening thud.

Jessie stood transfixed. Her eyes grew wide and her pulse quickened as the seconds passed. She sensed his death by the odd tilt of his head and the staring blue eyes.

Julep likewise stood still, nuzzling Sam and snorting.

Her mission had been miraculously accomplished, but Jessie lingered for a timeless moment to absorb the scene—the warm horse scent, the rays of sunlight dappling through the trees, the streak of dust on Mr. Swann's forehead. Flies already buzzed around him. Reverently, she stepped forward and leaned down to touch his forehead. Her fingers ran tentatively through his blond hair and sideburns, then lightly over the collar of his linen shirt. Full of awe at God's will, she slowly stepped backwards before turning to glide into the forest.

The day was growing dim, and still Sam did not arrive home. Mary wandered onto the porch again to peer down the lane, her concern mounting. She was sure no dispute had erupted between Sam and their old friends; more likely they were well-past discussing Jessie's conduct and were having supper together.

Lenora was inside the house playing a game of chess with John. She'd settled nicely once he had arrived. He'd come up from the stables a couple of hours before in search of Sam but had stayed to keep Lenora company once he got the gist of matters, allowing Mary to clean up the doll fragments while he sat with Lenora.

Mary spotted a shape in the distance—Julep's unmistakable chestnut sheen and Sam's wide-brimmed hat jostling up and down none-too-fast. *He must really be tired.* Stepping back into the house to tell Ettie that supper could be served, Mary blew out a breath of built-up tension and smiled. *Just in time for supper.*

After setting out the diningware, she was carrying an etched-glass pitcher of tea from the kitchen when a knock sounded at the front door. Mary stopped in her tracks. Sam wouldn't knock on the door.

John answered it, and low voices consulted in the foyer. When John re-entered the living room, his face was pale and solemn. Sheriff Bell strode behind him with a grim frown on his bearded face. He wore a Stetson hat the same brown color as Sam's.

Mary heard a distant shattering of glass as she gazed at them curiously. "Hello, Joe."

The sheriff's boots crunched across the shards and through the spilt tea all over the floor as he hurried to support Mary and lead her to the sofa, instructing, "Have a seat."

She made no protest at being settled onto the sofa and only stared at him with foreboding. Lenora drew close to her mother, clinging to her arm.

"It's Sam. We found him on the road that goes down to my house."

"Is he alright?" Mary's words were a whisper.

"No, Mary." The sheriff's voice was grave. "He apparently fell from his horse. Julep was still with him, but Sam didn't survive the fall."

At this, Lenora let out a piercing cry.

Mary moved to gather her daughter into her arms. She still felt strangely hollow as she gripped Lenora close to her. "Where is he?"

"He was near my home, so we brought him inside. I rode Julep back here. He's just outside."

"I'll go put him away," John offered. Not wanting to cry in front of the others, he was relieved at having something to do.

"No." Mary stood, suddenly decisive, and handed the sobbing child to John. "I'll take care of Julep myself."

She stepped to the wall and removed Sam's Browning double-barrel shotgun from its pegs. The men watched wordlessly as she fished two slugs from the shell pouch and then strode onto the porch.

She had always known that Julep was a danger to her children, but she'd come to consider Sam to be invincible. Julep would not be allowed to hurt anyone else.

Mary opened the breech and loaded the slugs. Closing it, she cocked the hammers and brought the gun to her shoulder, taking aim directly between Julep's warm amber eyes, which were gazing straight at her. She set her jaw and had just begun to squeeze the trigger when a pair of lean arms encircled her from behind, one hand smoothly lowering the barrel.

A gentle voice said, "This can wait, Aunt Mary. Put down the gun."

Beginning to tremble, she relinquished her hold of the firearm, which John awkwardly removed from her grasp.

John leaned the gun against the wall then assisted Mary into the house and up to her bedroom, where he convinced her to lie down.

The trembling escalated as John unbuttoned and removed her boots.

Helplessly, he smoothed her hair for a moment then exited the room at an utter loss. He was standing outside in the hallway rubbing his forehead when the door opened and the cheery voices of Caroline, Anne, and Stephen rang up the stairs.

"Stephen!" He pelted down to meet them. "Could you see to Mary upstairs? She seems to be havin' some sort of nervous breakdown."

"Let me get my kit." Stephen unhesitatingly dashed outside.

The young women cast worried expressions at John, and he reluctantly told them the news. Caroline's eyes instantly filled with tears, and Anne supported her friend, stunned with disbelief.

Returning with his doctor's bag, Stephen noted Caroline's changed demeanor. He paused uncertainly. "What's goin' on?"

"Uncle Sam had an accident," John said. "He didn't make it."

Stephen's lips set in a grim line, and he ran up the flight of stairs two steps at a time.

John gathered Lenora back from the sheriff, who nodded helplessly.

"Let us know if there's anything we can do," Sheriff Bell said. "Perhaps someone can head over to prepare him tomorrow morning, but y'all just don't worry about it tonight."

With a last sad nod, Sheriff Bell took his leave.

Breaking the prolonged silence after his departure, John quietly explained what he knew to the stunned young women.

Pale-faced, Anne stood up and approached the grandfather clock. When she reached for the pendulum and stopped it, an unnatural silence fell over the room. The young people sat without speaking until Lenora finally fell asleep from exhaustion. Anne carried her up to her bedroom, only bothering to remove Lenora's boots and pinafore before snugly tucking her in. Then she gathered Emma's nightclothes to take to Ettie's house, where Emma had spent the day playing with Ettie's grandchildren. Anne gazed for a moment at Lenora sleeping and then at Emma's empty bed. She wondered what Mary and the girls were going to do without Sam.

17• Saving Julep

AFTER A SINGLE ADMINISTRATION OF LAUDANUM, Mary fell into a dark, heavy, dream-filled sleep. She woke the next morning to the rooster's crowing; cheerful songbirds warbled relentlessly from the branches of the nearby yellow poplar, while the sun splayed its bright rays mercilessly through her southerly-exposed window. No one had bothered to draw the bed curtains for her.

The space that Sam normally occupied in their bed seemed too small for him. He was everything to her, but now he was somehow gone. The world seemed cruel in its ability to heartlessly proceed without him.

Mary stiffly arose from bed, feeling a leaden weight inside. She ambled slowly to the windows and pulled the inside shutters closed, latching them with a deep sense of finality. Her aching eyes scanned the room, lingering over Sam's clothes and mementoes. Walking to his bureau, she picked up his mother-of-pearl cufflinks and remembered helping to fasten them before the Christmas party. *Never again*, she realized despairingly.

Numbly donning her mourning black, she spent the next hours latching shutters, shrouding mirrors, and putting away games and instruments.

Over the next few days, Mary was little more than a hollow shell, responding to her surroundings mechanically while Sam's name continued to reverberate through her mind. She operated in a fog, hearing and responding to the sounds of the other family members as though from a great distance. Meanwhile her soul cried out achingly, yearningly for Sam.

Samuel Swann's wake and funeral amassed a large congregation of mourners. He was well-liked by a community that was shocked by his untimely death. Anne and Caroline helped Mary through most of the funeral preparations. Neighbors and friends brought food and quietly tended the children.

Mary dressed Sam in his three-piece woolen suit for the funeral, remembering their special night. She told John, who was of a somewhat slighter build but similar height and bearing, that he should take the rest of Sam's clothes. Reassured by John's presence, she was relieved that he was helping to run the farm.

Reverend Scott provided a benevolent, fatherly presence throughout the ceremonies. Even Sarah and James Corbett made the train journey, staying at the plantation for a few days and helping to deal with the many visitors who came and went in a blur, bringing with them countless casseroles and aspics.

Tongues clicked and unsolicited advice was dispensed, but Mary absorbed none of it. She did understand, however, that she would have to think about the farm and what made sense financially. Her girls were still young and the most important piece of Sam that she had left. Sound decisions needed to be made based upon their best interests.

For now, though, Mary could only grieve. The man she loved more than anyone else in the world was with her no more.

Lenora went back to school after a couple of weeks. Her bright spirit was subdued, but she and Jessie achieved a presumable peace by avoiding each other.

The spelling bee came and went with Owen easily winning. Less than pleased at his victory, he accepted the ebony-and-gold fountain pen with a reluctant politeness. He was distraught at seeing Lenora so different from her usual sanguine and competitive self, but she was distracted and quite unaware of Owen's attentions.

Jessie kept to herself for the rest of the school term. She, too, was impressed at the difference in Lenora and felt a new and unique sensation, perhaps a strange sense of empathy. She remembered her own acute sense of grief at losing her mother, and something deep within her keened sympathetically for Lenora, if only a bit—Jessie had never even been given a black dress to symbolize her mourning, and at least Lenora still had her mother and a home. Nevertheless, this sensation of empathy was novel, and Jessie felt a new layer of caution about her.

She was in awe of the momentous effects of her own actions—and more apprehensive. While she did not precisely regret the death of Mr. Swann, she had not consciously planned it, either. She was willing to be God's instrument, but she rather hoped He would not need her in that way again soon. Her overnight vigil on the night of Mr. Swann's death had been exhausting. Nevertheless, she prayed fervently in hopes of receiving the Lord's directives more clearly. In contrast to her school truancy, she never made any attempt to miss church.

Jessie resolved to show restraint and perhaps a bit of self-denial—to fall dormant until she received clear instructions from God. She would become a purer instrument for his purpose, when and if that time arrived again.

As Jessie stared at the back of Lenora's bent head, she thought, *What does it matter if life seems unfair? For me or for Lenora? We don't understand God's will. Only He does. He brought me here and allowed me to be with Clay. He showed me Clay, showed me that He knows best, and I will prove myself worthy of His gift. I must wait to be with Clay. One day I'll be old enough. God has placed me here in this situation, and this is the trial I am facing now. God wants to see my patience.*

Over the course of the next couple of months, the Swann home returned to a somewhat normal routine. Caroline and Stephen postponed their nuptials until September, and John seamlessly took over the care of farm operations, consulting Mary as needed. Mary tried to bury her grief by throwing herself into the details of farm management and routine housework, struggling to get through each day.

John and Caroline were sad but nostalgic. John thought of Sam each time he used one of Sam's tools or wore another item of inherited clothing. Caroline remembered Sam during her daily rides on Julep. Both were concerned about Mary's eventual decision regarding the horse.

Caroline's excursions with Julep were increasingly spiritual exercises, channeling Sam's love for his horse with her own. She was comforted by the sense that Sam's spirit was at peace, that only fragments of his loving energy remained. She connected not only with Julep, but with that lingering energy from Sam and the universe when she rode—even as the wind in her face, Julep's warm scent, and the hoofbeats pounding the dirt and clattering on the gravel bonded her physically and sensorially to the experience.

On a dry June morning, Mary announced at breakfast, "By the way, Mr. Floyd down the road is comin' to get that horse this weekend."

Caroline's chest constricted as if Mr. Floyd's wagon had just run over it. She did not have to ask which horse. The coffee in her mouth tasted unusually bitter. "Old Man Floyd? Doesn't he supply cart-horses to Georgetown?"

"Fine by me." Mary shrugged and looked away. "We've gotta get rid of him, honey. I can't bear to walk in the stables as it is."

"Can we wait a while longer?" Caroline begged, her voice shaking. "You know I love Julep."

John interjected, "I could prob'ly find another place for him. I'm sure I could. He's gotta be worth more than Mr. Floyd would give you for him."

As Mary began clearing the table, her voice became strident. "I'm gettin' rid of him, and the sooner the better. I saw you ridin' him yesterday, Carrie. You looked just like Sam used to. Absolutely no sense. I'm scared to death of losin' either of you, and I'm not gonna be blamin' myself for not takin' care of him when I had the chance."

Caroline stood to help Mary with the table, taking dishes from her hands. "I'm perfectly safe—"

"Believe me, Carrie," Mary interrupted, her hands on her hips. "I still think I should shoot him, but John's made it clear that you would never forgive me."

Caroline clanked the plates she was holding back onto the table as if too overwhelmed to continue. "Please don't sell him." Her voice was quavering. "Uncle Sam loved Julep."

"And if he hadn't, he'd still be here with us." Tears shone in Mary's sad brown eyes. "Julep will either be sold or shot this weekend. That is final."

Saturday came too swiftly. Caroline woke early and went to the stables in her riding habit. Her aching heart was full as she harnessed and saddled Julep for a final outing. Today she would allow him to journey farther than they had ever ridden before—and she entertained thoughts of not coming back at all. She wanted to savor every moment, but worried speculations consumed her as they began their outing.

Trotting away from Kingstree over the bridge traversing the Black River, she leaned forward, speaking aloud to Julep in a sweet voice that contrasted sharply with her riotous feelings, reminding herself of a mother singing the terrible 'Rock-a-bye Baby' lyrics to her infant.

"Mr. Floyd is horrible," she said pleasantly. "The absolute worst horse caretaker. How could Mary? He's not a caretaker at all. More like a horse consumer. A horse processor. Always replacin' them because they collapse on him. Hodge mules are treated better than his horses."

Julep drew to a halt, as if he could sense something was wrong. Caroline's pulse pounded in her ears, but she clicked her tongue, encouraging him down the unfamiliar road. She tried to relax even as her gentle tirade continued.

"You're a thoroughbred, not some mule. You're too refined, too sensitive to be a cart-horse. How could Aunt Mary do this? What would Uncle Sam say if he knew?" Sam's words to her on the day of Anne's departure for Charleston came back to her then. "He was happy that I look after you. He wanted me to have you. You're my responsibility now. Maybe we should go straight to Beaufort and see what my folks have to say. I should've talked to them about it while they were still here."

Her desperate thoughts continued as the morning wore on, but eventually she lapsed into silence. They'd been traveling along a swampy area, the road rising above endless pools on either side, dotted with cypress knees. She was growing nervous about traveling alone, but at least her horse was faster than almost anyone else's. Nevertheless, when they came to a creek, a tributary of the Black River, she dismounted to allow Julep to graze the few grassy patches in clearings along its banks. Meanwhile, she lolled despondently on a log, tearfully gazing at the beautiful chestnut stallion, trying to etch him into her memory. By the time he began nuzzling her for a treat, she could hardly see. She fished his final pear from her pocket and held it out on her palm, laughing brokenly as his scratchy, wet lips brushed her skin.

Wiping her eyes, Caroline stood and hugged him. At the feel of his wide pulse steady against her cheek, she set her lips. She could not betray him. She wouldn't stand by and let him be ruined. An idea sprang to mind then—a slim hope, but it was the best plan that had yet occurred to her. In fact, she wondered if it hadn't been percolating in the back of her head for some time. When Caroline mounted Julep again, she guided him over the creek, continuing exactly in the direction they'd already been traveling.

The tomatoes had produced well that spring. Bushel baskets of the vermilion fruit filled the kitchen table in the clapboard house that Clayton shared with his mother, waiting for her to stew and can them.

Just the two of them lived there. Visitors, all except for Amarintha's brother Simms, tended to be put off after hearing her cuss and blaspheme through decayed, twisted stumps that used to be teeth. She sniffed snuff like it rivaled with air and smoked a corncob pipe like it was necessary to maintain the peace. Add to that the heat from canning, and folks might think they'd landed in a sort of Lowcountry hell. Even without the canning, Clayton had long ago learned not to invite company over.

Despite her faults, Clayton was fond of his mother. It was no surprise that she had never been married, however. In fact, Amarintha had never even told him who his father was. In her occasional drunken stupors, she would every so often blame Clayton for her unwed state in some variation of the same script.

"It's cuz o' you, my bastard son," she would spit, "no man wanted to marry me and shame his family, but there's plenty who thinks I'm gonna let 'em just have what dey want."

Clayton would try to pretend that he couldn't hear her.

Amarintha would laugh then, "Ha! Dey all gonna be disappointed. Ain't gonna spread my legs for no man, never again. Ain't havin' no more bastard babies to give suck to. No sirree." She would guzzle her moonshine and cackle delightedly at her own cunning. "I don't hafta take care o' no man now, and I got you, my strong, handsome son, to take care o' me. Why would I want some ole fool makin' demands o' me? I got alls I want right here."

Her cackles would eventually turn into sobs, and Clayton would miserably try to ignore the whole tirade, waiting until she fell asleep to move her to her bed. She would unfailingly forget the entire outburst by morning, but he never could.

Lost in morose thoughts about such an incidence the night before, Clayton was standing still in his field, staring into the distance. So far he'd planted only five of the ten rows of okra he had planned. Sweat trickled from under his broad-brimmed straw hat. Absentmindedly reaching up to wipe his face, he noticed a dust cloud on the main road. Squinting, he could make out a single horseman wearing a dark riding hat. The rider was turning onto the lane.

Clayton laid down his hoe and walked forward to meet him. As he drew near, Clayton realized the rider was a *woman*. A moment later, he caught his breath, recognizing Caroline Corbett.

A rush of confusion washed over him as he noted her smart black riding habit and fine chestnut horse. She was already dismounting before he even considered what he must look like. Rubbing dirt-encrusted hands on filthy overalls, he cleared his throat. "Hey there, Carrie. What brings you way over here?"

"I'm so glad I found you." Sliding down from the horse, she faced him with a distraught, pathetic look that instantly garnered his sympathy. "I didn't know where to go. Please forgive me for showin' up like this."

"What's goin' on?"

"Clay, this is Julep." Uncertain how to begin, she presented her horse.

Clayton raised an eyebrow and said to Julep, "Hello there, you're a handsome fella."

"Julep needs a place to stay," Caroline burst out, running a shaky hand over his withers. "I have nowhere else to turn. Please, would you let him stay here until I can get him back? I don't know when that'll be."

Mystified, Clayton asked, "Why?"

She nervously launched into an explanation of the events leading to this desperate maneuver.

"But Carrie, I can't keep Mrs. Swann's horse. She might have me arrested."

"She won't know he's out here," Caroline insisted. "She'll never suspect. I can't keep him anywhere in Kingstree, or word would get back to her. Please say you'll do it, Clay. Julep's life is at stake. Please."

Her imploring face, framed by wisps of blond hair peeking out from under her hat, was too irresistible. "I'm a damn fool," Clayton muttered, rubbing his forehead. "But I s'pose I can keep him with my mule, Button. Let's get Julep watered and settled in the shed."

"You don't know what this means to me..." Caroline's throat became thick with emotion as she tried to thank him. She barely held herself back from throwing grateful arms around him.

Clayton shook his head as he began to lead Julep away. "There's not a lot of room," he warned. "Why don't we just see how he likes it?"

"I'm sure it will be fine," Caroline said quickly. At the shed, she glimpsed tack and grooming equipment hanging on walls lined with bales of hay. A waterer sat nearby. The essentials seemed to be there, even if Julep wouldn't get his own stall. After unsaddling him and taking off his harness, her shoulders and forehead began to relax. As she led him to the fenced area behind the shed to join Button outside, she smiled at last. She had thought Julep deserved a better fate than a mule, but now she was perfectly happy for him to be kept with one.

Only after Julep was contentedly grazing did Caroline's thoughts shift towards the journey home. Inhaling sharply, she lifted horrified eyes to Clayton. "Oh goodness, I don't know how I'm gonna get back."

Clayton uttered a low whistle. "Well, I suppose I'll have to take you," he mused. "I s'pose we can't ride Julep, cuz someone might see him. Button will have to do. She's a good mule. It'll be a lot faster and easier on her without the wagon."

Caroline wanted to sink into the ground. She'd already entangled Clayton in her troubles and complicated his life. Now he would have to spend his entire day transporting her, when he clearly had work to do—and these were only the earliest infringements. Not only did he have the constant care and feeding of Julep before him, but he was at risk of being hung for horse thievery. As she became excruciatingly aware of the position she was placing him in, Caroline fell speechless. She didn't have the words to thank him adequately nor to apologize enough.

Unaware of her revelations, Clayton was distracted with more pragmatic thoughts. "Best if you don't come in the house. No point in Mama seein' you, as she prob'ly shouldn't know who brought this horse over. Wait here while I grab some things."

He took only a few moments in the steam-filled kitchen to scrub his hands and face and pull together an assortment of biscuits, cheese, and figs into a satchel. Filling a canteen with sweet tea, he kissed his mother's sweaty cheek and told her that he needed to run into town for a while. As he let the screen door close behind him, he called, "Prob'ly won't be back until nightfall."

Meanwhile, Caroline said her farewells to Julep. She stroked his glossy neck and gazed at the modest shed. "I'll be back soon, I promise. This is temporary, but you're in good hands. He'll take care of you." As the words fell from her lips, she wondered how she could be so sure. *I have no way of knowin' that he will,* she told herself, but somehow she felt in her gut that she could count on him.

Minutes later, Caroline and Clayton began the journey back to Kingstree on Button, a ride which promised to be inexorably, excruciatingly long. The trip to his farm had been made in only two hours, but it was going to take over twice that time to get home.

Perched behind Clayton, riding pillion, Caroline was all too aware of her proximity to him, of her hands touching his waist and her body brushing against his. He smelled like earth and musk. They rode silently and somewhat stiffly in the uncomfortable midday heat.

After two long hours of mute journey, Clayton pulled in the reins and came to a halt just as they reached the creek she'd stopped at before. He explained in a dry voice, "We're jus' past halfway, and I need to give Button a break."

Caroline nodded, slapping at a mosquito on her cheek. Awkwardly, they dismounted and stepped apart. Button immediately wandered near the bank of the creek to graze.

Clayton fished in his satchel and held out a biscuit. He watched as she bit into it then wordlessly passed the canteen, shaking his head. *Peculiar how everythin' she does is so fascinatin'.*

Taking the canteen back from her, he lifted it to his own parched lips. *Might be close as I ever come to kissin' her again.* After swallowing the mouthful of tea, he finally broke the silence, asking dolefully, "Still with Dr. Connor?"

"Yes." She hesitated, a flush rising from her collar. "Stephen and I are engaged."

Nodding thoughtfully, Clayton pressed his lips together. *Of course. I'll look after a beast that weighs a ton, risk bein' charged with horse thievery, and gladly spend hours in maddenin' closeness to this woman I can't have, simply cuz she asks me to.* No matter how he might call himself crazy, however, he knew he would still do it—and do it again.

Caroline cringed as she watched his thoughts play across his face. *Did I really have to drag him into this? Did I just wanna? How can I be so selfish?*

Noting her look of misery, Clayton regretted mentioning Dr. Connor. He rose from his reverie and waved a hand towards the creek, hoping to distract her. "You know, this stream is awful nice for wadin' in."

She smiled in relieved confusion. He was so kind and wonderfully unpredictable. Taking heart at his look of encouragement, she joined him in pulling off boots and stockings. As she made her way to the stream and slipped her feet into the warm, flowing water, brown with tannins, her worries began to wash away.

Tilting her head back, she allowed the warm rays of the sun to penetrate for several moments until the heat began to demand its due respect. She leaned and dipped a handful of water, splashing her face and cooling her neck.

"Go on and cool off your legs a bit more. You can hike your skirt—of course I'll be a perfect gentleman." Clayton ogled her hem playfully.

Laughing, she cocked a defiant eyebrow. "Why, I think I will, Mr. Bell." Raising her riding habit a mere two inches, she took a step further into the stream while watching his expectant, bright expression. As her foot descended, it failed to meet the expected resistance, and she fell, floundering to regain her footing. She could hear his guffaws as she gasped in shock.

"And here I thought you were a gentleman," she protested, clambering into the shallows. Once upright, she splashed the still-laughing farmer.

He returned her volley with enthusiasm, and the pair continued flinging water and laughing until quite drenched.

"Now, how you gonna explain all this?" Clayton chuckled as they emerged, soaked and bedraggled, from the stream.

She flicked water from her fingertips at him. "You think it's funny, don't you?"

"But of course."

She sighed ruefully. "You should laugh at me. I don't know how I can ask you these huge kinds of favors, Clay."

He mockingly bowed, still in his playful mood. "Cuz you know I'll oblige. I'm at your mercy, milady, and at your beck and call."

Overcome with gratitude and confusion at her feelings, she smiled a bit sadly then returned an awkward curtsy, her riding habit sticking to her legs. As they approached the mule, she suggested, "I think it might be better if I walk for a while to dry off a bit."

"Not a bad idea," he replied, taking Button's reins in hand.

They began to stroll down the uneven road, lapsing again into silence. The day's long tumult of distraught emotions and the unusual demands she'd placed on her body caught up to her as the sun beat through the trees onto her back. Her perspiration drew even more mosquitoes.

Exhausted, Caroline continued plodding along, looking forward to the close of this neverending day, whatever it might bring. She was too tired to continue reflecting on her day's actions. Besides, she would not undo them if she could. She loved Julep too much.

As she continued, the sun became increasingly oppressive until she paused in her tracks, swaying with dizziness.

"Are you alright?" Clayton grasped her elbow.

"Just a bit light-headed."

"Here, drink some more tea." He handed her the canteen again. "Let's ride Button. These wet clothes ain't doin' no harm. They'll jus' help keep us cool. Come on." Before she could reply, he had lifted her onto the mule and climbed astride behind her.

As Caroline sank back against him with relief, her hat fell forward. She barely caught it. His solid presence was comforting, though, and he shaded her from the sun well enough. She turned her face so that her cheek met the refreshing coolness of his shirt. Already she was less nauseated. Her shakiness and vague, overwhelming guilt melted away as she settled her hat around her neck and rested against him.

As they rode, she became aware of his brawny arms braced on either side of her, supporting her as they held Button's reins. She became exquisitely conscious of the broad area of contact between them and of how the wet clothing clung to their bodies. Her contours molded to Clayton, and his sculpted thighs pressed firmly against hers, encircling her. She felt deliciously contained by him.

After a while, Clayton's warm breath began to rustle the hairs of her neck. Her heart began to race as his breath crept gradually closer, so slowly that she thought it might just be due to the jostling of the animal—which also seemed to move his body increasingly closer to hers, if that were possible. She had forgotten how intoxicating it felt to be in his arms.

When his lips brushed her neck, ever so lightly, she struggled to contain her gasp. A shiver of pleasure ran down her spine, and she closed her eyes as she willed him to continue. Her hands released the pummel of the saddle, as if of their own accord, and slipped onto his hands, her fingers sliding tentatively between his. As his lips and warm breath continued to ever-so-lightly explore her neck, Caroline's fingers began to course slowly over and around his hands, the caresses sending jolts of lightning quivering throughout her body. Warm pulsations began to explode inside of her.

Consumed by their subtle lovemaking, Caroline and Clayton continued this way for the last hour and a half of the journey. Finally, throbbing in agony and ecstasy, Caroline became aware that Clayton had reined in Button. Her heart thrilled in sudden panic until she realized that they had stopped in the last stand of woods before crossing the Black River, so near to the Swann plantation.

Dismounting Button together, she drew away from Clayton with agonized reluctance, staring at his dimple as she thickly thanked him.

Clayton wordlessly reached to touch her jaw with his fingertips, allowing his thumb to brush her lips. He ached to kiss them. Finally, with herculean effort, he withdrew from her and climbed astride Button again.

She raised her eyes to meet his smoldering gaze. It threatened to consume her. She returned the look for just a moment before pulling herself back to reality, painfully tearing her eyes away and turning to meet her chosen destiny.

18• The Man on the Premises

AS CAROLINE CROSSED THE LAWN to the Swann house, she met with a rush of concerned faces. Mary, John, and Anne all came outside to meet her as though she were a prodigal child.

John gripped her arm, wide-eyed with relief and concern. "What happened to you, Carrie?"

She shook her head in distraught bewilderment. *Oh gracious, Anne's eyes are all puffy and red. And Mary is practically gray with worry*. Unbidden tears began to trickle down her disheveled, dirty face.

Mary hugged her close. "You've clearly had a hard day, honey. Come on in the house, and let's get you cleaned up. You're home now, so don't you worry 'bout a thing."

She led Caroline into the house and up to her own bedroom, where she helped her to strip off the still-wet riding habit. Wrapping her in a quilt, she led her down to the kitchen, where Ettie was already heating water for a bath. As Caroline lay in a half-stupor in a tub situated perilously close to the warm cookstove, Mary and Ettie washed her hair for her. When the water began to cool, they helped her out and dried her off vigorously, dressing her in one of Mary's nightgowns as though she were a porcelain doll. After getting her to down a warmed-up bowl of soup, they led her to Anne's room and tucked her into bed, with nary another question.

Back downstairs, Mary waved away John's concerns regarding both his sister and Julep, saying firmly, "We have Carrie safe and sound here at home, and all I have to say about that horse is good riddance."

Before going to bed early herself, Mary checked on Caroline one last time, then retired to her own bedroom to shed pent-up tears—the girl's disappearance had freshly exacerbated her anguish over losing Sam, all the more triggered since she'd been with Julep.

When Stephen arrived at the plantation that evening, he was surprised to hear the sketchy details of Caroline's disappearance. Following John to the stables, he re-saddled his own bay colt, Hermes, to help look for the missing horse. Skeptically, he asked, "Do you really think Julep ran off?"

Mary had refused his offer to purchase Julep flatly, saying without apology that she did not want Caroline on the creature again. Then he'd made advance arrangements to buy the thoroughbred from Old Man Floyd directly, keeping it secret from Caroline in case it fell through. That obviously had been a mistake.

"I've never seen Julep even hint at running off," John admitted as they set off. "I don't know what Carrie was up to. She was gone for too long and looked a complete mess, so surely she didn't just ride to a neighbor's farm to hide him, though I guess maybe she could have spent the whole day tryin' to find somewhere to stow him."

"Or perhaps she just rode him way off, slapped his rump, and made her way back home on foot?" Stephen suggested, patting Hermes' withers.

"Wonder what she'll tell us." John scanned the woods dutifully. "Let's have a look around, anyhow."

The next couple of hours were spent circling the perimeter of the property, occasionally calling out for Julep. Eventually, Stephen took his leave.

John returned home to find Anne asleep in the tabby cottage. Caroline's clothes were clasped in her arms, but she had lain down on the loveseat, exhausted from the day's worries. She looked peaceful there with the peacock cushion under her head.

John extracted the clothing from her arms. He touched her cheek and then retrieved a quilt for her, tucking her in right where she was. Cautiously, he bent forward and gave her forehead a butterfly kiss.

Anne sighed and murmured, "Thank you, John..."

He smiled at hearing his name and then stole away to finish Anne's task for her. When he entered the Swann residence, he marveled at the quiet of the household so soon before bedtime. Ettie had apparently already put the younger girls to bed before leaving; despite Molly's presence, she'd taken to once more staying later into the evenings to help with them ever since Sam's passing.

Making his way upstairs, he slipped into Anne's room and laid the clothes on her bureau. Then he turned to regard his sister. Caroline rested quietly, her blond curls splayed out. She looked angelic, though John suspected that her day's activities had not been completely innocent. He touched her cheek before leaving the room.

Feeling particularly sentimental, John checked in on the youngest members of the family. The girls were tucked in together, Emma's arms tightly around her wax doll while Lenora embraced her.

John tiptoed out of the room feeling a warm, paternal sensation. The reality that he was now the only man on the premises had not escaped him, and he felt oddly protective of them all.

He started to bypass Mary's door and then paused in concern. Mary had been visibly shaken the entire afternoon, and he worried about another nervous breakdown. He knocked gently and then peered into the darkness of the room, unsurprised to see her curled into a ball on her bed, still fully clothed.

John approached the four-poster and placed a hand gently on her shoulder. "Mary," he whispered.

She shifted, and large, beseeching eyes glinted in the dark. "I miss Sam," she said hoarsely.

John nodded, blinking away his own sudden tears.

"Would you hold me, John, please?"

Taking off his spectacles, John set them on the dresser and brushed at his eyes. Then he slid behind Mary and cradled her close.

She sighed as the ache in her chest subsided. He felt so comforting. Laying a hand over his, she interlocked fingers with him as she had with Sam for so many years. At last, she fell fast asleep.

She woke at dawn still cradled in his warm embrace. Blinking, she began to recall the night's dreams until she became aware that she was unconsciously rocking—against *John*. One of his hands had drifted to her clothed breast, and she felt an all-too-familiar pressure against her from behind, so close to her own aching need. As this awareness possessed her, she reluctantly pulled away to sit on the edge of the bed.

Mary gazed at his still-sleeping form. John was beautiful, young and innocent. She was widowed and older than him, mother of two girls. She had never been with any man besides Sam, and she didn't intend to start by taking advantage of John. She would get a hold of herself before she hurt John in an attempt to fill the gaping void Sam had left.

Mary fastened the bed curtains back then shook him gently. "Wake up, sweetie," she whispered near his ear.

John opened his eyes and sat up, running a hand through his rumpled hair.

Having gathered herself, Mary's expression now appeared normal as usual, despite her wrinkled clothing and mussed hair. She smiled at him gratefully. "Thank you so much for comfortin' me last night. You are so like my Sam—I'm afraid I'm leanin' on you far too much." She laughed ruefully. "And fallin' asleep like this was definitely… too much." She gestured towards the bed.

John touched her shoulder. "Are you sure you're alright?"

She gave another soft laugh and rolled her eyes. "No, of course not. But, you know," she admitted, "I do feel better, though you should prob'ly get out of here before we generate talk."

As John gazed at her, he found himself thinking of how she had felt in his arms only moments before, lying on this soft feather mattress. The depth in her large eyes compelled him towards her, and he recalled only too well the supple and receptive feel of her body pressed against his. Indeed, he'd woken to their rocking more than once during the night—and had not stopped himself when he realized he was exploring the shape of her body through her clothing. Her moans had invited his touch. Now that she had drawn away, his pressing desire clamored to be fulfilled.

Hesitantly touching her hand, he stated evenly, purposefully, "Mary, I would like to comfort you now, again, more."

She caught her breath at his candor. His message was quite clear, and, despite her resolve to protect his innocence, she felt torn and confused. She struggled to formulate a response. "But John—"

"Listen," he interrupted, "I want you. I need you. You need me, too, I know. Pretend I'm Sam, Mary."

Shocked, Mary could see that he was in earnest. She gazed at his lovely, youthful face—so smooth with its thin moustache—then fingered the black armband he was still wearing to indicate mourning. He was the answer to her problems. John could take care of the plantation, of her, of her girls. As his hand pulsated on hers, desire flickered insistently through her body. A rising sensation of disbelief, excitement, and panic stirred in her as she heard herself ask, "Would this be your first time?"

"Yes." John did not look away.

Mary closed her eyes, appalled at what she was about to do, then stood and crossed the bedroom to bolt the door. She turned back towards John and began to unbutton her black dress, impending pleasure consuming her arguments even as he reached for her.

19• The Designer

ANNE CAREFULLY ROLLED UP THE WHITE SILK and placed it in her carrying-bag. The slippery material was now cut into its wedding dress pattern, but she still held a whole lot of silk. A traditional long train would lift and button to the back of the high waist.

Anne was grateful that Caroline's wedding had been postponed. She'd had far too little enthusiasm for the wedding dress and was only starting it now—in the month of their initial wedding date.

She sighed, not a little discouraged about her own marital prospects. Mr. Sanders had shown proper respects at the funeral but had otherwise been distant and out of touch.

Life at home seemed less rich than it had, as well. She could not quite say why. Perhaps it was because of Sam's glaring absence—each of them had more to do with Sam gone—and because of the impending wedding.

Nevertheless, Caroline's wedding dress would be the forte of all her dress-making efforts. She was determined that her friend would be the most elegant and beautiful bride in the history of Kingstree—but in order for that to happen, she had to actually make the dress.

She glanced out the parlor window, wondering if Caroline and Stephen were back yet. They were out for a walk this evening, as usual. Their routine was to walk for a while and then sometimes go for a ride. The walks seemed to take longer these days, and Anne suspected that the couple dallied in the privacy of the woods or stables.

At that moment, Caroline was pressing herself firmly against Stephen. He returned her kiss but then drew away. Straightening his straw boater, he murmured, "September cannot get here fast enough."

Caroline sighed with frustration. Ever since her journey with Clayton, she had been racked with guilt and felt the need to physically cement her bond with Stephen, but he was just so damned respectable. She feared her status as a lady had already been placed in jeopardy with her ever-more-suggestive and passionate rendezvous with him, though he was simply too much of a gentleman to even recognize, much less allude to, her attempts to seduce him. She stopped short of removing his clothes—except for his linen jackets. Those she had become quite adept at slipping off.

Caroline wondered at her own descent into the eternal land of carnal desire. Stephen was clearly not so depraved. His own passions seemed to find voice in his discussions of herbs and patent medicines, of the Philippine Insurrection and American Imperialism, of the new quarter horses on show at the races, and of other bits of news and philosophy that he related on their walks. Meanwhile, Caroline would simply watch his handsome face, murmuring agreeably while scandalously intent on arriving at a sheltered location where they could kiss. She willed him to explore her body during these private moments, but so far Stephen's hands remained restricted to an appropriate, and therefore quite unsatisfactory, embrace.

Even though Caroline could often only half-listen to his talk, she was awed and humbled by his morality, his empathy, and his avid interest in his work. She had felt proof of his desire as she pressed against him, so took a meager bit of vengeful pleasure in knowing that he, too, was suffering to at least a certain degree from his own stubborn morality. He'd have to be dead to have missed her unspoken invitation.

Riding off her frustrations helped, and the pair spent many long and happy evenings challenging each other to races.

The days of summer passed slowly, with subtle but significant changes on the Swann plantation. Mary's sadness seemed to subside, and she transitioned into the softer grays and purples of mourning sooner than was customary for a widow. John stepped more fully into his own as the farm's caretaker. The younger girls began playing outdoors as usual again, and Lenora regained her bright spirits. When not working, Caroline spent most of her time at the stables, even without Julep's presence; Stephen was there more evenings than not, though he was too frequently called away for medical emergencies.

Meanwhile, Anne grew increasingly preoccupied with her dressmaking. She maintained a dwindling hope in a future with Mr. Sanders. He still looked delighted to see her—even suggesting, with a twinkle in his eye, that he hoped to meet with her very soon. But he had yet to come calling on her.

Anne sorely missed Caroline, who no longer stayed late into the evenings at the factory to work on the sewing machines with her. In fact, Caroline was becoming habitually absent even during normal work hours—usually on Wednesday mornings, it seemed, when her sewing machine at the factory sat unspeakably idle. Such neglect generally signified a worker's death, childbirth, grave illness, or worse—that she'd been fired. But to everyone's surprise and confusion, the productivity-oriented Mr. Mouzon allowed the absences without a fuss.

"He's extra-irritable when you're gone, Carrie. He must be plannin' to fire you privately," Anne predicted as the evening bell clanged and they prepared to leave work one Wednesday. "So you might wanna hurry on outta here."

Glancing in Mr. Mouzon's direction, Caroline shrugged. "I'm not sure how much longer I'm gonna be here, anyhow."

"You plannin' to spend all your time on mysterious 'errands'?" Anne swept the floor around her machine with unprecedented vigor. "Hopefully you'll get married before it becomes your full-time employment."

"Anna! That's not how it is."

"Well then, how is it?"

Caroline massaged her temples as if she had a headache. "You can't breathe a word."

"I'm not the only one who's noticed. It's not such a secret."

"I don't care if I get fired, but what I'm up to *is* a secret. You have to promise not to tell."

"Except for Stephen? Surely he won't mind my knowin'."

"Especially Stephen—and Mary. And swear you won't tell them I've been skippin' work, either," Caroline demanded, gray eyes flashing.

"That isn't a secret," Anne repeated in exasperation, one hand on the broom as she gestured around the emptying factory with the other. "Our coworkers already know—Fletcher even said yesterday that she'd been right about us rich girls, after all—and you should've seen the way she scowled at me like it was my fault. As for Mr. Sanders, he has only to step in here one Wednesday mornin', and he'll know right off you're missin'. Someone is bound to mention it to Mary—or Stephen." Anne's brow crinkled as she realized lovers' trysts were unlikely if Caroline was so worried about Stephen knowing that she'd missed some work.

"If you swear secrecy, I'll tell you—and then you'll understand." Sighing, Caroline turned to close the spool cabinet just as the lights dimmed. "But even if you won't, please don't tell Mary or Stephen that I've missed work. I do have a reason. The best of reasons."

"Very well. I promise." Anne set aside the broom and crossed her arms.

"It's Julep. I take him feed every week."

Mouth agape, Anne started laughing. "That horse? This is about a horse?"

"John takes care of business in town on Wednesdays, so I go to meet Julep then, when he won't notice me goin' back and forth from the stables."

"But Julep's not in the stables."

"Not anymore."

"Then where do you see him?"

"We meet at a creek about midway between us. I take Hurricane."

"Julep keeps a calendar?"

"I—I left him with a friend, of course." Caroline began to inspect the seam of her sleeve.

"A friend?" Anne studied Caroline for a moment then scowled. "Not that sharecropper, the Bells' nephew? What's his name?"

"Clayton." Caroline met her friend's eyes for a brief moment before heading towards the exit, where shafts of light still streamed through the windows.

Anne shoved on a wide-brimmed hat and hurried after her. "What in heaven's name are you thinkin'? He was interested in you!"

Caroline kept her gaze straight ahead as their boots crunched down the gravel road. "He knows I'm engaged. He's so understandin' about it all. I'm givin' him a little sewin' money, but he'll hardly even accept it. It doesn't begin to cover his trouble."

"I don't know. Sounds like he gets a horse and weekly rendezvous with you."

"He didn't ask for this!" Caroline protested, spinning on her heel to face Anne. "I shoved that horse on him. He's doin' me a huge favor. He skips work in his fields most Wednesdays to meet me, and he's riskin' all sorts of trouble. He's the best friend anyone could hope for."

Anne flinched.

"I didn't mean..." Caroline rolled her eyes. "I don't spend that much time with him. Nearly the whole time I'm just travelin' back and forth. When I get there, I give Julep a treat and then ride him a bit. After that Clay chats with me while I groom Julep. He really needs it... I don't think Clay does a whole lot of that."

"Maybe he wants to give you extra reason to meet up with him." Anne's arms crossed.

"I have one. I have to bring feed for Julep. And I wanna see him."

"Julep or Clayton?"

"I'm perfectly happy to see Clay!" Caroline's eyes flashed. "We not only chat while I groom Julep, but then guess what we do? We take off our boots and wade in the stream with our naked feet. We talk. We laugh. I enjoy it. And he never, ever looks at me the way you're doin' right now."

Not only is Carrie angry with me, Anne mused while staying late at the factory the next evening to sew on the wedding gown, *but Mary isn't talkin' much to me, either. And even John—him, too. He hardly seems to notice me anymore, for all that he made me feel so special at first, like I had a new brother.* She pushed a needle into the pincushion with a sigh. *Ever since Sam died, all his attention goes to Mary. I shouldn't be jealous. He feels responsible for her now. Still, I might as well just be a ghost around here, for all they notice me.* Anne sniffled at the selfish, lonely ache that panged inside her chest.

At least I have little Emma and Lenora... at least they never forget me. Anne managed a small smile at how the girls snuggled with her and begged for stories at night—when she was home before their bedtime. A maternal ache rewarded those thoughts, however.

Anne wiped her eyes, chiding her self-pity, but she was having difficulty managing her sadness as she usually did—by throwing herself into dress-making. Working on this wedding gown only reminded her of how she'd pinned her recent hopes and dreams on Caroline and Stephen's engagement. She'd been living vicariously through what seemed the perfect couple—and Caroline was her dearest friend. Now, as she crammed the white silk under the sewing-machine needle, she wondered if Caroline valued her own engagement as much as Anne did herself. She spent countless evenings sewing on this wedding dress after work at the factory. At home on the weekends, she drew designs for the beadwork with her pastels and then sewed them on by hand, often until bleary-eyed. *Meanwhile, Carrie's plannin' rendezvous with Clayton.*

Over the next weeks, the distractions of the workday did nothing to lift Anne's spirits. The dingy conditions of the factory were starting to bother her—conditions which had seemed almost novel at first—and she was spending more evenings working on the gown at home. Now that the basic dress was sewn, much of the rest needed to be done by hand anyways.

Carrie must be feelin' that way about the factory, too. That's why she doesn't care if she's fired and doesn't wanna stay afterwards anymore. Doesn't care that they adore her so much that they let her get by with pretty much anything. Anne threaded another bead as she sat in the gold-striped armchair, heels propped up on a footrest. Across from her, framed tintypes of her parents graced the mantel amidst older daguerrotypes of other family members, all neatly lined up under portraits of Swann forebears who no doubt would have disapproved of Caroline's Wednesday meetings with Clayton, too. Anne's own dismay, however, was slipping away like the silk between her fingers. After all, Caroline had been devastated over Mary's plans for Julep, and she did seem truly attached to Stephen; most of her evenings were still devoted to him.

Anne held up a section of beadwork to examine it, then smiled. *This is beautiful. There's not much I would rather do. It's nice, too, readin' the girls their stories in the evenings and goin' to bed early. We all go to bed early these days—except for maybe John.* Anne bit her lip and laid aside her needlework. She rose to go outside. *Time for some fresh air.*

The night before, Anne had been starting to leave the girls' bedroom after stories, and she'd heard the click of Mary's door. John had passed down the hallway, stealthy as a satiated fox. Her heart pounded as she descended the stairs after him and watched him exit out the back door.

This morning, however, she'd laughed at herself for being suspicious. *Prob'ly just askin' Mary about tomorrow's agenda. Or fixin' something. Didn't she say her bedroom window was stuck?*

Over the next few days, Anne began to hear murmurs coming from Mary's room and to see John upstairs all hours of the night. Finally, she admitted to herself that they must be lovers, disregarding not only God's and man's rules of conduct but hiding it from her. She struggled to conceal her indignation and felt increasingly alienated. Anxiety settled in her gut, sprouting like a seed. Tendrils of blackness writhed all the way down to her feet, rooting her to the ground then doubling back to twine over her shoulders and head like a contorting, relentless cape of gloom.

Depression seized Anne. Lovers were all about her, and even Lenora and Emma had each other. She considered moving back to her parents', but she would hate to give up her sewing job—a distraction, as dismal as it was—and she still cherished a sliver of hope when remembering Mr. Sanders' positive words about her future. Clinging to these shards of light, Anne devoted herself to finishing Caroline's wedding gown, which, given the sinful state of their household, now seemed even more symbolic and important.

On a sultry Friday in early August, Caroline did stay late at work once more; Anne had asked her to remain after for a final fitting of the wedding gown. This time, however, they weren't the only ones to stay late. Over the preceding weeks, word of the dress had somehow seeped out amongst their coworkers, and Mr. Mouzon had agreed that the final fitting should be a planned event.

A roomful of curious, enthusiastic factory employees waited to see the dress. The dark tendrils weighting Anne down retracted for the occasion, and she glowed almost as radiantly as Caroline when the dress was finally donned and fitted to her own critical approval.

Before emerging to display the gown, Caroline regarded it a final time. Countless tiny pearls were sewn into the lace bodice, the skirts billowing out from it so that she didn't even really need her corset. She glanced behind to admire the Watteau back—a swath of silk flowing down from the neckline to join fluidly with the train.

Caroline was preparing for the biggest day of her life, and she could not imagine a finer gown for the occasion. Despite her frustrations with Stephen's conventions, she had grown under his influence to increasingly regard marital vows as sacred. A certain begrudging gratitude towards Stephen filled her. He'd steeped her life in chivalry and honor. She would be his truly pure and virginal bride, despite her attempts to the contrary. Her skin tingled almost magically with anticipation. Soon she would slip from this musky workshop into a fairytale life with him. A modest glow of pride in her purity warmed her, and she loved Stephen for so quaintly prioritizing her chastity.

As Caroline stepped up onto a platform to model the gown, gasps of audible pleasure could be heard from the coworkers, a slow hand-clapping rising above their murmurs. She stood for a long, uncertain moment like a porcelain doll. Then she curtsied.

Her coworkers chuckled.

Catching up the Watteau silk, she slowly twirled in place before slipping an arm behind her to unbutton the train. Anne stepped forward to extend it, and sighs of delight filled the room.

Caroline's breath caught as she discerned the form of Mr. Sanders emerging from the crowd. Turning to Anne with wide eyes, she hissed, "Mr. Sanders is here."

"Congratulations!" His genteel voice carried over the workers scuttling to create a path for his small entourage.

At Caroline's smiling nod of acknowledgment, Mr. Sanders responded, "Oh yes, to you, Miss Corbett, on your impendin' wedding, of course. But I was actually complimentin' Miss Brighton, our own designer extraordinaire."

Teetering at the edge of the platform, Anne managed to stammer, "Oh, well thank you, Mr. Sanders."

"You remember Mr. Otis and Mr. Longstreet, don't you?"

Spying the two elegantly-attired men trailing behind him, Anne nodded a bewildered affirmation.

Mr. Sanders absentmindedly patted the shoulder of a young seamstress standing next to him. "Well, they were greatly impressed with the dress that you brought to Charleston, so they altered the dates of their business travels to make it to this here weddin' gown fittin' that Mr. Nesmith so graciously told us about."

Anne stared in wordless confusion.

"The gist of it is, Miss Brighton, that we are all tremendously impressed by your talent. I've had my eye on you ever since your family's Christmas party, when I had the opportunity to see those lovely chartreuse creations Mr. Mouzon raved so much about."

Anne's eyebrows knit in perplexity at the idea of Mr. Mouzon raving about anything at all, but Mr. Sanders waved at the wedding gown, oblivious to her look of incredulity.

"This dress has a touch of the Directoire style with that empire waist and collarless design, for all that you have a train."

"The Regency period, perhaps?" Mr. Otis stroked his chin.

"The flavor of it, but entirely her own," Mr. Sanders enthused as he turned back to Anne. "These gentlemen agree with me that we like your designs and want to hire you as a full-time designer."

"A designer?" Anne echoed.

"You would do much of your work here in Kingstree, so long as you're willin' to travel for shows and such."

"Shows?" Anne's brow crinkled.

"I would, of course, be attendin' as well," Mr. Sanders smoothed his graying moustache and averted his gaze back to Caroline's dress. "I would be more than happy to escort you."

Anne grasped Mr. Sanders' meaning in a rush of understanding that left her whirling, amazed with wonder at the opportunity. She was equally shocked at the depth of her misunderstanding. *Mr. Sanders has been courtin' me as a designer, not as a wife!*

As she stood speechless, Mr. Sanders explained, "Of course, you would no longer be sewin' within this factory. You'll have your own workshop. Here in Kingstree. Our firm is most happy to set you up. You'll be allotted funds for assistants, and I've no doubt your wage increase will be to your satisfaction."

The crowd parted like warm butter as Mr. Sanders stepped up to the stage. He took her hand, shaking it warmly. "I can't tell you how pleased I am that this has all worked out so well. I've been dreamin' of exposin' your talent, and that day has arrived at last." He beamed with satisfaction.

Warming in the clear affection he seemed to feel for her—or at least for her artistic talent—Anne finally found her tongue. "Thank you, Mr. Sanders. I am so honored." The simple words fell awkwardly from stiff lips. She bobbed then curtsied a bit more gracefully to Mr. Otis and Mr. Longstreet.

"May we call on you tomorrow to sign a contract?" asked Mr. Sanders.

A laugh caught in her throat. *At last he is to come callin' on me.*

Caroline glowed with pleasure at the recognition that Anne was receiving. She, too, had wondered at Mr. Sanders' failure to court Anne, and this revelation was a most pleasant, if somewhat less than romantic, explanation. She gazed in ecstasy at her beautiful wedding gown and slowly twirled once more. *I'm gonna marry my prince. My storybook, fantasy prince. In this fairytale gown. The very gown that is gonna transform my dearest friend's career as she becomes a brilliant new design talent. Life is sweet and pure and gloriously right.*

20• New Abodes

"SEE? WHAT DO YOU THINK?" Anne was going over sketches with Caroline at their usual picnic bench. A distinct vinegar aroma wafted from her forgotten cheese-and-pickle biscuit.

Caroline looked up from her magazine and raised an eyebrow. "I love the tiny pleats in the material, but she's shaped like a sack o' potatoes. How about a narrow sash? So you can see her figure?"

Pursing her lips, Anne examined the straight waist. "I kind of liked... but maybe that waist is too boxy. Hmm... perhaps..." Momentarily, Anne glanced up from her work. "Carrie, what are you readin'?"

With a sheepish smile, Caroline showed her the cover of *Good Housekeeping*.

"But you always say magazines are a waste o' money," Anne protested, "that they cost as much as one of your dime novels."

Caroline batted her eyelashes. "I just felt more like readin' this right now."

Anne laughed. "Anyhow, would you like to go with me tonight to my new workshop? I'm goin' straight there after we get off."

"Guess we better go while we can. There's that supper with Mary tomorrow evenin'. Can't believe it'll be your last day at the factory."

Anne glanced towards the hulking building and stowed her sketches. "Can't say I'm sorry."

After work, the friends walked together from the factory to the business district of town. Anne stopped on the brick pavement in front of a north-facing storefront with a large display window. She pulled out a brass key. "This is it."

Holding her breath, she unlocked the heavy glass-paned door. At the click, she pushed it open to reveal a large, airy front room. The smell of fresh wall-plaster hung in the air. Hardwood floors were dull except for dark, shiny areas where shelves had once formed lines down the room.

"Looks like you're gonna be busy for a while just tryin' to get this place ready," Caroline murmured. "Hope Mr. Sanders doesn't expect too much."

"He doesn't. In fact, I won't even have material for a while. Fletcher's gonna help me paint this space. It'll be the first entire week she's had away from the sewin' machines in over two years."

The young women wandered towards the back of the shop. A solitary, dusty desk sat in the corner of a smaller room in the rear of the workshop. Against the back wall, a broom leaned next to a staircase.

"Is the upstairs included with the shop?" Caroline asked.

Anne suppressed her elated smile for only a moment. "I'll have my apartment up there."

"You're gonna live here alone?" Caroline's eyes widened.

Anne gestured for Caroline to follow as she skipped up the stairs.

Bright light streamed into the rooms, pooling onto the floor. Whereas the downstairs side-walls were solid, here windows existed on three sides, casting setting rays over two spacious, equally-divided rooms. A large black stove occupied the back wall of the front room, but otherwise the space was barren.

Caroline could envision Anne in the apartment. The décor would be classy, to her superior taste. A sudden pang in Caroline's chest surprised her. *Anna's such a modern woman. Independent. Successful. Not bothered with men.* She gazed around the empty space, still unsettled. *Apparently she's not bothered about ghosts in empty buildings, either. I don't know…* "Anna, don't you wanna live at home?"

Anne wandered to the window overlooking the street and stared out blankly. "No, I think it's gettin' time for me to get my own place." Turning to face Caroline, she added,

"I'll be able to focus more on my work if I stay here. And it's safer. You know how I'm always walkin' alone late at night after work."

Caroline nodded ruefully. "But you do wear that extra-long hatpin."

"As if I could wield it. I can hardly see at all with that finger lamp, but I'm not gonna carry a big lantern back and forth—I'm already totin' too much."

"I'll miss you at home."

"You won't be there much longer. In fact, I can see Stephen's apartment from my window here, so it's almost like we're movin' out together. We'll be livin' quite close to each other. Come look."

Caroline peered out the window and down the street, towards Stephen's medical office. *Soon I'll be livin' here, too.*

"Truth be told," Anne said, quite near her ear, "I was hopin' you might like to work as my assistant once I get settled in." She smiled as Caroline turned towards her, mouth agape. "Mr. Mouzon's already agreed to relinquish Fletcher, but honestly, Carrie, I'm not gonna find anyone else with your stylistic sense and sewin' talents who can also model the dresses for me. Mr. Sanders did say I could have two assistants. Mouzon might not like losin' you, but he won't really have a choice. Do say you'll do it. Then my new job will be perfect."

"Oh, honey," Caroline laughed. "I doubt Mr. Mouzon would mind losin' me one iota. Did I tell you I figured it out? He hasn't fired me yet because he didn't wanna risk losin' you."

Smiling like the Cheshire cat, Anne waved an airy hand. "But what about workin' here with me? Will you?"

Caroline knit her brows. *Do I really wanna stop workin' altogether after my wedding? Sure, I expected to, but there's no pressin' reason, especially not right away, and this certainly isn't the factory. Couldn't I spend my days with Anne in her new shop while Stephen is at work? It would be so close. And interesting.* Caroline took a deep breath, elated with the newfound sense that she could have Anne's success and her company, too. "Well," she said with a grin, "I'll need Wednesday mornings off."

Anne rolled her eyes and squeezed her friend's hand.

Blinking away happy tears, Caroline looked out the window once again. "I've never actually been to Stephen's apartment, for all that he's been pesterin' me to stop by. He told me where he keeps the key. Wanna walk over with me?"

Anne shook her head. "I'd rather spend a while checkin' out the nooks and crannies here, but you go ahead. I'm sure you're dyin' to see it."

As Caroline left, Anne took a deep breath and gazed around her new apartment, marveling at the adventure hovering just before her. She was more than a little scared, but having Mr. Sanders to rely on would be a comfort. Besides, she wasn't going far. Her friends and family were nearby if she needed them.

Caroline crossed the street to Stephen's office, where Dr. Davis was just closing the account books. He stroked his fiery-red walrus moustache and told her that Stephen was on a house call.

Tentatively, she went back outside and opened the stairwell door leading up to his apartment. A knot of excitement formed in her stomach as her boots clacked up the stairs. *Stephen asked me to come by,* she reassured herself. *He wants to know if I'd like to change anythin'. To make it more of a home for us. This is gonna be our home. My home.* She could scarcely believe how much her world would be shifting so very soon. Uncertainly, she knocked on the closed door before reaching for the key he had told her was stowed above the stairway window.

After knocking once more to make sure she wouldn't surprise him, she unlocked the door to the apartment. It swung open smoothly. Gathering her courage, she tiptoed inside, feeling like an intruder. In a quick glance, she absorbed the simple elegance of the furnishings. Closing the door, she turned to better take in the room. Medical books lined an enclosed, glass-front bookcase. A few were strewn on a small table next to a blue-gray velvet sofa, along with the past week's *Kingstree County Record*. Otherwise Stephen's apartment seemed clear of evidence of a medical career. To her relief, it did not recall the sterile environment of his office.

An exquisite Oriental rug caught her attention. Lotus flowers and trailing vines entwined in a detailed yet muted pattern that cushioned the floor between the sofa and the fireplace. The Swanns had Persian carpets, but she'd never had one in her own dwelling. An unexpected thrill buzzed through her at the thought of sharing her fiancé's worldly goods. She approached the pale-blue velvet sofa and allowed her hands to run over the material. *This is it. This is where I'll be livin' in only one more month.*

She strode through the small apartment and looked out the window onto the street. *It's gonna be so different, livin' here in town. I'll be near Anne's shop and so many stores. Everythin' so close. Town life.* She hesitated. *But it's temporary. We're gonna build a house on his property. Soon. Not too far away, but further out in the country. Lots more room. Big stables. Stephen won't have to board his quarter-horses near the racetracks anymore. And I'll bring Julep.* She bit her lip and shifted uncomfortably. She still hadn't told Stephen about Julep. The guilt seemed never-ending—guilt at her deception and guilt for burdening Clayton. Anne didn't help matters. *I'll get it all straight when we've built our own place. Stephen will forgive me. But it'll be nice when it's figured out. Just me, Stephen, our horses, and maybe eventually...* Caroline glanced towards Stephen's bed, thinking of children. The crisp blue coverlet was spread smoothly, and a mahogany bedside table held a sturdy brass lamp. She stepped closer and fingered the coverlet. Its coolness penetrated her fingertips. Everything seemed so trim and immaculate in Stephen's apartment—so much so that Caroline felt like an actual intruder. *Am I gonna feel this way when we're married? It's all so... foreign.*

Ignoring the icy shiver that ran down her spine, Caroline forced herself to sink onto the bed. *This is why he asked me to come. He wants me to be comfortable here, to be happy here. I'm marryin' Stephen, not these things. I'll get used to them. And if I don't, I can change them.* Lying back, Caroline rested her head on the pillow and closed her eyes. When she noticed Stephen's familiar, lingering scent, the tension drained out of her like cobwebs being washed away in a cool rain. *It'll be alright.*

Stephen wearily entered his apartment, tired from a particularly long day of house-calls. He began to peel off the hot layers—his morning coat, waistcoat, tie, and finally his starched shirt, sticky with perspiration.

At the sound of his entrance, Caroline quickly arose, attempting to smooth the coverlet before he saw her. She stepped towards the main room and paused to watch, reluctant to announce her presence. At the sight of Stephen's lithe, muscular chest, however, she gave a small cough.

He looked up in surprise. "Carrie!"

"Hello, darlin'. I'm sorry. Didn't mean to startle you." She struggled to stifle her laughter.

He picked up his shirt and began to slip it back on, but she protested, "I'm about to leave. Don't worry about it." Quickly sidling closer, she slipped her arms around him for an opportunistic hug. She inhaled, memorizing his smell—castile soap laced with his natural scent. She brushed her lips against his chest, inspecting the light, v-shaped scattering of dark hairs.

"I'm glad to see you here, Carrie. How do you like my... our apartment?" Stephen drew back to see her expression, still holding her hand.

"I can't wait to move in with you. I'm sure it will feel like home if I'm with you. And I have a surprise." She bounced on her toes. "I'm gonna work for Anna. Right down the street."

He laughed at her enthusiasm. "Good. I was worried you might get bored up here, with me so busy seein' patients and all."

"Speakin' of busy, are you gonna be able to make it to Aunt Mary's tomorrow evenin'? It's a formal family supper, and she's insistin' we all be there." As she spoke, Caroline inched closer again, winding her fingers through wiry strands of chest hair.

"Of course." He sounded preoccupied as his arms encircled her once again. "Barring dire emergency. I had an elderly patient with some heart trouble today."

She frowned sympathetically, pressing her cheek against his chest. "Was there anythin' you could do?"

"I gave her a patent drug, but the best medicine would be a letter from her grandson. He's off fightin' in the Philippines, and she spends all her time worryin' about him. She raised him after his parents died a while back."

"Poor woman. Nothin' you can do about that."

"I s'pose not, but he's a good kid. I hope he gets through it." Stephen sighed. "They say there's a shortage of medics overseas. It's not just sickness. There are near-constant guerilla attacks. Seems wrong that we're gettin' an extra doctor in Kingstree when our soldiers don't have enough to go around."

She hugged him more tightly. "You can't take care of the whole world."

"Well, I suppose there's no need to worry about it right now." He kissed the top of her head. "His grandmother does enough of that."

"And you're done for the day."

He nodded slowly, distracted by the warm softness of Caroline in his arms. "It's so good to have you here. The place feels right—like you've brought your cottage with you."

Kissing his chest again, she allowed her fingers to run lightly over his collarbone then down his pectoral muscles. "Like this feels right?" She could taste the salt on his skin.

Stephen laughed and pulled her from him as though she were a naughty child. "Soon enough."

"How can you be so stolid? *Some* men seem to find me rather irresistible." She sighed, petulant but not surprised.

"Oh, really?" He grabbed his shirt and began pulling it on again.

"Why, yes." Caroline folded her arms.

He buttoned his shirt, not taking the time to align the buttonholes. "I'll just have to trust to your implacable character, then, to beat off those swarms of men."

"I don't know, honey." Caroline eyed the ill-buttoned armor he seemed to think necessary. "I may not be made of the same iron as you."

Secure in his shirt, Stephen now pulled her close again. He leaned to brush his lips against hers, whispering, "It will be worth the wait."

Caroline stood stiffly at first, but within moments she melted into his arms and was returning the kiss.

The next evening, they gathered together with the entire family and Reverend Scott for supper at the Swann house. Mary looked pretty in a peach-colored muslin with lawn ruffles, glowing with pleasure at the sight of her family all together.

The table was formally set with a white lace tablecloth, gold-rimmed china, and silver dinnerware. After the minister said grace, they sat down. The first course was oyster patties with dill-mustard sauce. Caroline was impressed with how fancy everything seemed to be. She gazed about in wonder at the house, which seemed to have been scoured from top to bottom.

As she took her first tangy bite, she eyed Mary's dress. *Uncle Sam has only been gone for a few months. You would never know it from lookin' at her.* Caroline frowned but bit her tongue. Mary's feelings would be hurt if she pointed out the lack of even a semblance of mourning. *But what on earth? I understand why she wouldn't want to stay in widow's weeds for the rest of her life, like they say Queen Victoria has done. I was happy when Mary went to purples and grays almost a year early. But I can't believe she's in peach now. She's supposed to be in mournin' another year or two or three, even.*

Her narrowed gaze shifted over to John. He was wearing an unfamiliar new dress coat and collar. Her frown deepened. *What about the clothes he inherited from Sam? And oh gracious, he had to have a double-breasted, ivory waistcoat, too? Since when has he become so extravagant?* "John, you look the dandy. Where did that coat come from?"

His face flushed. "The Sears-Roebuck catalog."

"Another one? But you just got all those—" At Stephen's light touch on her arm, her mouth snapped shut.

John's ears turned red, and Caroline realized she was still staring. With a shake of her head, she took a deep breath. "It's really nice. I was just surprised."

At John's nod, Caroline looked down at her plate being taken away. She'd upset him—and even before the first course was over—but she was still baffled. He was normally so practical.

A tureen of turtle soup was placed in the middle of the table and shallow bowls of steaming rice distributed. After everyone ladled their soup, Mary asked Anne about the types of clothing she would be making in her new space, and the conversation drifted in that direction. Unusually animated, Anne told them how Mr. Sanders would soon be delivering supplies to the shop, including two new Singer sewing machines—she'd have to get used to the regular foot-pedal kind, since she wouldn't have electricity anymore—and dress dummies as well as assorted cloth, lace, and ribbons. John promised to load the modest furniture in her bedroom into a wagon and bring it by whenever she was ready for her move into town. She thanked him then assured the girls that she would still be living at home for at least a couple more weeks, until the space was finished.

As the soup bowls were exchanged for tiny platters of Jerusalem artichoke pickles, each sprinkled with toasted pecans, Reverend Scott cleared his throat. "Anne's plannin' to live by herself?"

"We'll be a stone's throw away. No further than the cottage from here." Caroline motioned towards her little house. "And I'll be workin' with her most days, so I'll be over there all the time."

He sighed and murmured, "I declare, the notions young folks get nowadays..."

"Speakin' of young folks, what grades are you girls goin' into?" Stephen asked in a bright tone, addressing the youngest Swanns.

Caroline smiled at the not-so-subtle shift in conversation. His ploy worked, though—the girls responded enthusiastically, their conversation lasting throughout the main course. As everyone dug into roast venison with peach sauce, string beans, and red rice, Emma wondered if she might try school again. Then Lenora fretted over the lost spelling bee, vowing to take the crown from Owen Bodiford. By the time small dishes of spiced melon arrived, the adults were reminiscing about their own early years of school.

At last Ettie entered the dining room with the final course—a large, iced fruitcake. Her helper, Molly, carried a bottle of dessert wine.

John, Mary, and Reverend Scott were served. When Ettie set the cake aside, Caroline's eyes widened with confusion. She looked to Anne for clarification, but Anne was watching the proceedings raptly.

"Am I to gather that congratulations are in order?" Stephen asked, recognizing the old-fashioned tradition.

John stood, adjusted his wire-rimmed spectacles, then rang his newly-filled wine glass. He seemed more confident now. "Mary and I are honored to share this special evenin' with you all. We hope y'all will forgive us for not mentionin' sooner that this is our wedding ceremony." He paused at the audible gasps and looked around at each of them in turn, meeting their wide eyes earnestly. "I realize that this may come as a surprise, but I hope it's a welcome one... or at least will be."

A slow smile crept over Anne's face as she softly addressed the radiant couple. "I'm so glad."

Meanwhile, Caroline sat bewildered, struggling vainly to piece together how this could be. She was appalled that she had missed out on this development entirely. *Shouldn't I have guessed? He has been spendin' a lot of time with Mary. I knew that.* She bit her lip as she considered how often he had been staying nights at the main house. Her cheeks felt suddenly warm. *Good heavens… I was equally clueless about Mr. Sanders' intentions with Anne.* She shook her head in disbelief and glared at her brother for a moment, sure that he should have told her. At beholding his happy expression and shy smile, however, her vexation melted away.

John turned his attention to the younger girls, asking with a tentative air, "May I have your permission to marry your mother?"

"Yes! Yes!" Emma instantly squealed, but Lenora looked slowly from her mother to John.

She met his eyes and asked pensively, "Will we stay here, in our house? Will we all stay together, no matter what?"

Meeting her gaze, he answered in all solemnity, "I will do my best to keep the four of us together, no matter what. I don't know that I'll be able to manage this farm as well as your own papa, but I promise to do my best."

Lenora considered him for a long moment. "Well then, if it will make Momma happy, you can marry her."

John gave Lenora his heartfelt thanks as Caroline and Anne exchanged glances, wiping away unbidden tears. Then cake and dessert wine were served to the rest of the family, followed by a simple ceremony administered by Reverend Scott.

As the vows were pledged, Caroline slipped her hand into Stephen's, and he gave a light squeeze in anticipation of their own rapidly-approaching wedding day.

21• It's not the Horses...

IN THE DAWN HOURS of an already sweltering Wednesday morning, Caroline braced herself to face Mr. Keels again. With a quick step, she entered the Kingstree Feed & Seed to collect supplies for Julep. As she headed directly towards the oats, she was accosted by the preening shopkeeper.

"Good mornin', Mr. Keels," she tolerantly addressed him, trying not to sigh. She was resigned to their customary exchange.

"Why, good mornin' to you, Miss Corbett!"

Though she had assured him many times that she could collect and load her own feed supplies, Mr. Keels insisted he was there to serve, that he couldn't abide seeing her performing manual labor. He would heft the sack to his own thin back, sweat beading his brow, and follow her out to load Hurricane.

This morning, Mr. Keels wheedled, "Now, Miss Carrie, we still have those lovely new saddles on display, and if memory serves me right, you expressed an interest in them. Won't you come have a gander?"

Having put him off a great many times already, Caroline relented. She didn't want to appear overly anxious to be on her way.

Delighted, Mr. Keels led her with a springy step into an orderly room with shined-and-polished tack supplies gleaming on the walls. He drew in a big breath, his excitement bubbling as she ran her hands along the patterned leather that still smelled of the polish he'd applied the evening before. *Miss Carrie is a shy thing, to be sure. But here she is, though she can't have any real need for these trips to my store. For heaven's sakes, her brother is in here regularly and could get anythin' she wants—and he certainly buys enough horse feed.* Yes, they had a tacit understanding that she was there especially to see him. He had puffed up like a balloon the first time that she'd come in and asked him not to mention that she'd been there to anyone else.

He had, of course, been put off earlier in the year by her engagement with Dr. Stephen Connor, but he could see that she was getting tired of that dandy and wanted a real man, a smart businessman who was grounded and settled and could provide for her. Perhaps they had broken off their engagement by now. Feeling hopeful, he asked, "So, Miss Carrie, how about if I were to come callin' on you this evening?"

"But Mr. Keels..." Her finger stopped tracing the design on the seat of a saddle. "I thought you knew that I'm marryin' Dr. Connor."

He pursed his lips. "Now see here, Carrie. You two are completely unsuited. I thought you would have broken off with him by now. I'm quite impatient about this whole affair." *For the love of Pete, she's been comin' in here to see me secretly for weeks.*

Her brow wrinkled in consternation as she turned away from the saddle. "Mr. Keels! Why would you expect my engagement to be broken off? For goodness sakes, in what way are Stephen and I unsuited?"

"Look, Miss Carrie," he said staunchly, smoothing his goatie. "I am a hard-workin' businessman. I could take care of you in proper fashion, and I would be an honest, faithful husband—not runnin' off to those horse races all the time."

"And Stephen wouldn't? Besides, I love horses."

He stomped a foot on the well-waxed floor. "Land sakes almighty, it's not the horses I'm talkin' about—it's the whores! You think he'll stop with them just because you marry him?"

The room began to spin as though she'd been boxed in the ears.

He cocked his head proudly. "I know some women put up with all sorts of behavior, but you seem far too smart for that. *I* never have taken up with that sort."

Her stomach dropped, twisting into a pretzel. She turned and walked slowly out of the store, hearing Mr. Keels' reedy voice as if distantly.

"Miss Carrie, now Miss Carrie, I didn't mean to offend you. Look, come on back in here, and we'll just look at saddles. There's no need to run off."

Nauseated, Caroline headed towards home on Hurricane. Her head reeled like a sluggish top. *It can't be true. Stephen? My perfect Stephen, with that marvelous self-control and pure morals? My Prince Stephen, who makes fairytales real?*

She arrived home and went into her cottage, sinking to the sofa. After a while, she made a cup of chamomile tea to soothe both her nerves and her stomach. Stephen had been to the races the night before. In fact, he had slept over at the tavern there. He'd admitted to drinking at the track, and she had been glad that he would not be traveling home late at night while intoxicated. Far from feeling upset about the alcohol, she had thought it made him seem more human, no matter her mother's leanings towards the Temperance movement.

Caroline buried her face in her hands. *It can't be. No way on earth such a deeply moral and philosophical man would take up with whores. Why in the world am I listenin' to some snivelin', jealous rat? He's nothin' next to Stephen. I'm not gonna waste any more time on this.* Rising to her feet, Caroline walked to the sink with her cup and put away the chamomile tin. *Stephen will be here after a while. My life is just as it was. A pathetic little drudge like Robert Keels cannot destroy my world.*

Feeling marginally better, Caroline began tidying the cottage. Shortly, she settled down at the table to write out wedding invitations, enjoying the serene, reassuring look of their names together. She could think of no better way to soothe her insecurities. They were going to say their vows soon, and then she would dance with her husband while wearing her pristine white wedding gown.

That evening, Caroline strolled arm-in-arm with Stephen. He looked as handsome as ever, though somewhat tired from his night at the races. Even the dark circles under his eyes looked good on him. When they arrived at the stables, Caroline inhaled the comforting smell of hay and horses, then snuck her arms around Stephen, pressing her face to his chest and hugging him close.

He put his arms around her. "What is it, darlin'?"

"Oh, nothin'..." She sighed and buried her head into his chest, bursting out, "It's that awful man, Mr. Keels."

Gripping her shoulders in alarm, he stepped back from her. "What did he do?"

She smiled wanly, wiping a tear. "Oh, it's absurd."

"Tell me." His grip on her shoulders lessened, but his eyes still flashed.

"It's just... he said you sleep with whores at the races." She looked up at him, adding in a rush, "I'm an idiot for listenin' to him at all, because of course you'd never do such a thing."

His face had frozen.

"Stephen? It's a god-awful lie, right?"

He knit his brows and said carefully, "Carrie, you are everythin' to me. I would never intentionally hurt you."

A wave of nausea struck her again. She gripped the stable wall. "What do you mean? Have you been with whores?"

He looked agonized. "Carrie, I love you. I have never loved anyone else. I want to marry you. I want to be with you all my days."

She stepped back from him, a flush of horror and humiliation spreading throughout her body. He reached for her, but she ran out of the stables towards the cottage. Only a few steps into the yard, she crumpled to her knees, gagging fruitlessly. A sour taste filled her mouth, but the roiling contents of her stomach refused to come up. At the feel of his hand on her back, she spasmed once again, then spat on the ground and scrambled away.

"Carrie, wait," he pleaded as she rushed towards the cottage.

She turned back towards him, trembling with fury. "All this time? You never really wanted me? You prefer prostitutes? I'm not excitin' enough for you?" She gave him a look of pure loathing. "Get away from me, Stephen. Stay away from me."

His eyes were wet with tears, the first she had ever seen. Hardening her heart, she hurled, "If you need comfort, go find one of your whores. I despise you." Caroline ran into her cottage, bolted the door, and threw herself onto her bed, quivering with revulsion, rage, and tears.

Stephen stared at the closed door of the cottage, torn as to whether he should knock or leave her alone. He doubted any good could be salvaged from forcing a conversation right then. His own stomach was in knots, and he was stunned at the sickening turn of events.

He had never thought about Caroline being hurt in this matter. She was an exquisite, perfect light in his world. He had never dreamt of sullying her innocence, either by taking advantage of her or by exposing her to knowledge of that disreputable world. He did have visions of their wedding night, to be sure, when he would finally touch and explore her virginal body. He cherished hopes of her now-chaste womb bearing his children, and he would never in his lifetime tire of seeing her lovely face.

His thoughts of Caroline were pure, and he had taken care of less-noble urges elsewhere, as he had been doing for over a decade, ever since his school chums had first taken him to the horse races at the age of seventeen. Did Caroline think he had never been with a woman? Did she think he had lightly taken up lovers and discarded them?

Stephen turned to leave, scraping his heels, sick with worry. Caroline was his one true love, and his heart ached with apprehension.

Later that night, Caroline sat on the cream chintz sofa in the parlor of the main house. She lifted a pale, tear-stricken face to Mary. "Yes, I'm sure. I *never* wanna see him again."

Mary pursed her lips thoughtfully. "I know you're upset, honey. I can't believe Mr. Keels has put you through this."

Caroline blinked. "Mr. Keels? He has nothin' to do with this."

Placing her hands on her hips, Mary said angrily, "Why, he should stay out of others' private affairs. He is jeopardizin' your entire future."

"But... what he said was true. I'm grateful he told me, or I would have remained in utter ignorance. I feel like such a fool."

Mary paused and then sank onto the sofa next to Caroline, taking her hands more soothingly. "Honey, I believe that we aren't meant to know everythin'. Some things are too difficult for us to understand. What I do know is that Stephen loves you and wants to marry you."

Caroline pulled back as if she'd just been bitten. "So are you sayin' I shouldn't break off our engagement? What he's done is... disgustin'."

Sighing, Mary said, "Men are very different creatures from us, darlin'. They separate their hearts from their base urges more than we can understand. It's a shame that Stephen has made those choices, but they are not uncommon, and I don't think they were about you. It's clear that he adores you. He truly wants to be with you and loves you."

"But how? How? I am humiliated. He chose them instead of me. I would have slept with him, Mary, but he didn't want me. Why does he even bother with me?"

Mary persisted with mounting impatience, "Because he loves you. You need to stop thinkin' about this, Carrie. Stephen is a good man, but he is only a man. He respects you and has treated you like the lady you are. Now, you need to pull yourself together and *act* like a lady."

Standing abruptly, Mary straightened her skirts. When Caroline rose with her, she gave her a brisk hug. "Alright, darlin', go wash your face and do something to take your mind off of this. I hope you won't be willful and rash when Stephen returns. I have no doubt you'll be able to direct him away from any such pastimes once you are married. Men need our lovin' guidance."

Despairing, Caroline returned to her cottage. Mary's words sank into her like lead weights. The fairytale was over. Real life had hit her with its full force, and she had been woefully unprepared.

Stephen had been a fantasy figure from the beginning, and he had lived up to that ideal in every way, until now.

Caroline was devastated that she had wanted him so much, and yet he had been sharing his most sensual, intimate moments with other women. Her stomach heaved as she remembered that her Stephen had been with another woman only the night before.

As she realized the irony of calling him 'her Stephen', a hysterical laugh threatened to escape. He was not hers. He had never been hers. He had been the whores' Stephen.

The next evening, Stephen came to see Caroline at the tabby cottage. Pale and worried, he brought her a bouquet of asters and a simple golden angel pendant.

Caroline quietly accepted his gifts but refused to meet his gaze.

"May I?" He gestured at the pendant.

She mutely nodded, and he fastened the cold chain at the nape of her neck.

Returning to face her, he touched the pendant. "I chose this because it reminded me of you. You have always been an angel to me."

Her eyes filled with tears. "Perhaps that's the problem. Maybe if you saw me as a woman, you wouldn't have had to seek out other women."

He nodded slowly in an anguished admission. "Perhaps, Carrie. I don't know. I didn't want to treat you disrespectfully. I want my actions towards you to be worthy of you."

"Shouldn't you treat other women respectfully, too?"

"I—they—they're already in that profession. I try to be fair."

Caroline wiped at her tears. "I'm not an angel, Stephen. You knew that I wanted you." A fresh storm of tears began.

"But maybe you don't want me in that way? Am I not appealin' to you? Don't you want to take me to bed with you?"

He looked agonized. "I can't. It wouldn't be right."

"Why?"

Stephen shifted from foot to foot and looked away. "We're not married yet. I can't do that to you." Then his eyes turned to meet hers, piercing her heart. "But I'll stay away from the races at least until we're married. I swear it. I'll never again sleep with any other woman than you."

Listlessly, she nodded and moved towards the door to indicate that their evening was over. Her face turned away when he bent to kiss her farewell.

"Goodnight," he said, his voice cracking. "I love you, Carrie."

22• Jessie Visits Greeleyville

SWEAT TRICKLED DOWN JESSIE'S BACK and pooled in her undergarments. The coarse cotton dress chafed raw, tender skin at the seams under her arms, and her face was almost certainly blistering. The huge, hideous bonnet that Aunt Sally had told her to wear still hung on its peg by the door, but maybe next time she'd wear it just until they were almost there. It wouldn't matter in the end, however. Burns and chafes were hardly a bother if they meant she could see Clayton.

Sheriff Joe Bell was sitting next to her, considering shaving off his beard when he got back home from seeing his half-sister, Amarintha. He made a point of visiting her a couple of times per year, always bringing a supply of staples from town—sugar, flour, cornstarch, and the like. For the past couple of years he'd included a small, feminine present as well. Today it was a small ceramic jewel-box. She could keep the locket he had given her the year before in it.

Clayton had suggested the feminine presents when his uncle asked what Amarintha needed. Joe had seized on the idea, hoping that they might have a softening influence on Amarintha, whose manners could have shocked hardened sailors. It was unlikely, given her age, that she would change much, but he was an optimistic man and felt it couldn't hurt to try.

Amarintha had been dealt a hard hand in life, and Joe felt pity and responsibility for her. At the same time, her behavior repulsed him, so he tried to balance his lack of contact by bringing supplies semiannually.

He thanked the Lord for his nephew Clayton, the one bright spot in Amarintha's life. To be supportive, Joe routinely invited Clayton to come and stay with him in Kingstree for necessary respites.

Amarintha had been born out of wedlock over a half-century ago, a pattern she'd repeated with Clayton. She had been just a baby when their pretty, well-born mother had married Joseph Bell, Sr., out of necessity.

Regarded with a certain degree of resentment by both parents, Amarintha had sought companionship by catering to her half-brothers, especially Simms, and their coarse friends. They'd given her dubious attentions but kept her supplied in snuff and gossip.

When Amarintha became pregnant with Clayton, Joe had secretly wondered that it had not happened sooner. She never professed the father, though he presumed it was one of Simms' friends. Amarintha had no ambition, save that which she'd channeled to Joe, Simms' junior by four years. She, of all people, had steered young Joe clear of Simms and his friends. She would tuck him into his moss-stuffed bed at night and whisper, "You too smart and too good for dem hooligans. I'll whoop your hide if I find you wid 'em. You gonna stay away from 'em, y'hear?"

Though Amarintha would stay out late with Simms and his friends, she made sure little Joe got up on time for school, that he never played truant. She always asked about his schoolwork and crowed at every good mark, "You're not like us, Joey. You got all o' dat high-falootin' blood, and Simm's helpin', too. You gonna be somebody."

When Joe was old enough, Amarintha convinced their parents to let him stay with their mother's kinsfolk in Kingstree so that he could attend the more advanced school there. The town council had hired a strict disciplinarian, dour-faced Mr. Durand, who led the children through a rigorous three-year course reviewing Noah Webster's entire dictionary. Joe suffered from the stringent program, but his visits home made it all worthwhile. Amarintha's eyes would sparkle every time he used a word unfamiliar to her—and she never tired of listening to him read aloud. Proud tears overcame her on the day he was sworn into the public office of sheriff, but even while she glowed with exultation, she'd loudly declared herself his big sister, boasting about his hard work and noble blood, garnering pitying glances and a few jeers, both equally unbearable to the new sheriff.

Joe thoughtfully touched the butterfly engraved on the jewel-box. Amarintha never had this sort of thing as a girl, and he felt a mild sense of satisfaction in giving her a small token of appreciation. He could never hope to repay Amarintha's selfless affection, of course. It had been the least he could do to provide room and board when Clayton, in his turn, attended school in Kingstree. Now, Joe hoped to once again redeem himself by giving their young, strange niece sitting next to him a bit of the affection and positive direction that Amarintha had never received.

Gratified to see that Jessie was wearing one of her Christmas hair ribbons, he congratulated himself that he was not neglecting the child. She held more promise than Amarintha ever had. The girl seemed inordinately intelligent, and her manners and language skills were perfectly acceptable—leastways, they were when she chose to use them. She could be a great household help, as well, but he was determined not to relegate her to a common pauper's fate. He would bring her up to the best of his ability, as he wished someone had seen fit to do for Amarintha.

"Hey there, Uncle Joe, Jessie," Clayton called out as the wagon passed him working in the field. He quickly unhitched Button and brought her in.

Entering the house, he found them already seated at the table, sharing boiled peanuts with Amarintha.

"Looka here, Clay," announced his mother. She was wearing a worn dress with tomato stains down the front. Her apron was little better. She must've used it to carry the pots outside to wash, as she sometimes did. Amarintha was pointing at Jessie. "Joe done brought dis child wid 'im. It's 'bout time. I ain't seen da girl since she was a baby."

"Well, you oughta take advantage of the company while you have the chance, Mama." Clayton winked at Jessie, pleased that his mother was reining in her tongue, and then turned to his uncle. "How'd you like to take a stroll around the farm to see this year's crops? I'd like to pick your brain about puttin' up some fence."

Joe looked hesitantly at Jessie, not sure about leaving her with the strange older woman, but he was surprised to see her gazing curiously at Amarintha. He picked up a handful of peanuts and stood. "Alrighty, then. Come on and show me what you're talkin' about."

Jessie was, of course, fascinated at being inside Clayton's home for the first time, and she was uncharacteristically interested in the eccentric older woman, this woman who had brought Clayton into the world. Jessie wondered what it was like for her to live with him, to have him all to herself. She didn't even feel jealous, somehow. Perhaps Amarintha was just too unenviable.

Amarintha, for her part, was delighted to have a fresh ear on which to spew gossip. She was tickled at how Jessie seemed to hang on her every word, and she rewarded the child with the juiciest tidbits of her reclusive life.

"Your Uncle Joe brings da store to me, honey." She indicated the pile of goods and spat out a peanut shell. "But my brudder Simms gets me my white lightnin'. Yes, ma'am. I got it so good… Clay takes care o' me, and my brudders gives me alls I need."

Jessie silently absorbed Amarintha's garble until she finally asked longingly, "So, does Clay stay here all the time? He's always with you?"

"Dat's right." Amarintha gleefully grinned at the girl, revealing her decayed, twisted teeth. "Well, 'ceptin' when he's out gettin' supplies in town. He done got hisself a fine new horse, and he likes to go pick up feed and stuff fer it on Wednesdays. My, does he dote on dat beast. He sure ain't never looked at a woman like dat, but dat suits me jus' fine."

Jessie felt an instant, familiar clenching of her stomach. A sour taste arose in her mouth as she unconsciously stood and headed towards the door.

As she stepped outside, Amarintha called, "Where you goin', girl?"

The shed is the only place it could be, Jessie realized, scanning the fields vainly for the horse. She crossed the yard, swishing through itchy, overgrown grass, and entered the shed. The thoroughbred was in a fenced enclosure behind it. She stopped in momentary horror upon recognizing Mr. Swann's horse. She'd last seen him nuzzling the dead man. *How could his horse be here?*

Moments later, Clayton laid a solid hand on Jessie's shoulder, bringing her round. He had heard Amarintha calling to the girl out of the doorway. He'd hurried but was now quietly cursing himself. Taking Jessie's hand, he led her out the front of the shed to the shade of a copse of water oaks behind his house. She stared wordlessly at him as he pleaded, "Listen... I didn't mean for y'all to see that horse there. I'm takin' care of him for a friend, but we're keepin' it secret. Think you can keep your mouth shut 'bout it? I sure would appreciate it."

Her eyes narrowed. "Is it for that woman, Carrie?"

His mouth dropped open, and he grabbed her arm. "Jessie, swear not to tell a soul 'bout this. Unless you wanna get me in a heap o' trouble, you can't tell no one."

Jessie looked directly into his light blue eyes, shining as brilliantly as jewels, and nodded.

His shoulders slumped with relief. Then he gathered her into a bear hug.

Pressing her face into his neck, Jessie set her lips resolutely. She would do what she had to do to keep Clayton for herself.

23• A Choice at the Creek

AS SHE ARRIVED AT THE STREAM, Caroline waved hello to Clayton but made her way directly to Julep. Unusually subdued, she hugged the magnificent thoroughbred's neck for a long, comforting moment. Feeding him a carrot from her pocket, she glanced apologetically at Clayton. "I'll just groom him for a bit."

Clayton sat back on the picnic blanket and watched her fish a curry comb from her saddlebag then lead Julep into the shade, where she silently stroked his coat. After several minutes, he observed, "You seem down today, Carrie."

She smiled sadly. "Yeah, I s'pose so."

"What's the matter?"

"Life's not a fairytale?" She laughed weakly. "Stephen and I had our first fight."

Clayton whistled. "Only the first? Must've been one heck of a fight, the way you look. Wanna talk about it?" He waited, but she only shook her head and switched out her comb for a stiff-bristled brush. After a vigorous going-over, brushing off now-loose dirt and hair, she switched to a soft-bristled brush. He waited another quarter hour before interrupting her again. "Julep's been groomed plenty, don'tcha think? Sit down and have a little somethin' to eat."

She slid down onto the blanket and fingered a flaky piece of cornbread until she became aware of his gaze. His tender expression reminded her of how intensely he had looked at her not so very long ago, how he had once kissed her without the reservations Stephen maintained.

Feeling instantly guilty at the thought, she fidgeted with her skirt. *I'm bein' ridiculous. Why am I so hard on myself? A kiss is nothin' next to what Stephen's been doin'.*

Clayton laughed. "Wow, Carrie, your face is putting on quite the show."

She flushed. "I'm sorry. You've been so good to bring Julep. I'm bein' terribly ungracious."

"Oh, it's not entirely out of charity, y'know." He gave a half-smile and looked down at his cornbread.

Another immediate and all-too-familiar pang of guilt struck Caroline, and again she chided herself, *Stephen is sleepin' with other women, for heaven's sake.* Sighing, Caroline stood and started gathering her things to leave. Her heavy heart made her less likely company than ever.

Standing up, Clayton shoved his hands deep into the pockets of his overalls. "Sure you don't wanna wade a little? It's awful hot out."

"I should get back to work." She frowned at the thought of returning to that dingy factory without Anne. "I only have a couple more weeks there. Then I'm gonna be Anna's assistant."

"So does it really matter? That water is just callin'."

Caroline peered at the creek. It was murky, as usual. The sun was insufferable, though, and she had come prepared with a change of clothes—a precaution gleaned from their first afternoon at the stream.

Seeing her hesitation, Clayton chuckled. "Come on!"

Half an hour later, Caroline emerged from the stream laughing. Her worries had leeched out as if they were of no more concern than the tannins already staining the swampy water.

Clayton was grinning, delighted he had cheered her with his antics. They'd quickly escalated beyond their usual shallow wading. He'd belly-flopped into the deeper waters, danced a sluggish Irish jig half-obscured by sprays and splashes, and cheerfully belted out "If You Were Only Mine," leading her in an awkward, out-of-sync dance as their feet stuck in the creek mud. Afterwards, he tugged her playfully towards their picnic spot, where he pulled their blanket mostly from under the willow tree and then pointed. "Sit. This sun will dry us off in no time."

Shaking away her reservations, Caroline tumbled lightheartedly to the blanket, her riding habit thoroughly soaked. She lay back so that her head was in the shade of the tree, and Clayton sprawled onto his side next to her, propping himself up on his elbow.

"You know, there's an old story about this creek," he said.

"Do tell," she murmured, basking in the sun and Clayton's warm gaze.

"They say that long ago in Revolutionary days, a real pretty woman saw a group of British soldiers comin' down this road. She was alone and knew those men would steal anythin' of value if they got hold of her, after they'd had their way with her."

"Scoundrels," Caroline muttered, tutting.

"Yes, ma'am, some o' them were. Now, she was wearin' this ring of pure gold that the man she was gonna marry had given her, you see. It was set with a real shiny, expensive ruby. Well, she couldn't bear the thought of his ring bein' taken by those men, so she threw it in the creek before runnin' away from them soldiers, fast as she could."

"Did she get away?"

"Well, some say she hid in the trees until they were gone but that she never found her ring again." Clayton paused and began to finger the long, wet curls that splayed out towards him. "It's said that one day someone's gonna find it, somebody who has already found his true love to give it to."

A small shiver ran down Caroline's spine as she imagined the woman's ghost accompanying the ring to its new bearer and possessing her. She shook her head at the notion. "I wonder if anyone's ever found it?"

"Yeah, I think maybe someone did." Clayton paused and then added with shining eyes, "Cuz, Carrie, I'm pretty sure I'd have found it if they hadn't already. I've stayed to look for that ring every blessed time, siftin' through the muck, ever since you started meetin' me out here."

Caroline melted under his direct, open gaze.

He put a hand to her cheek and, in a voice full of emotion, asked, "How can I watch you marry someone else?"

Caroline's heart tugged towards him. She lifted a hand to touch his face, and he lowered his head towards hers, meeting her lips tentatively at first, then more passionately.

Within moments, a long-suppressed wave of desire released and coursed through her. Though Caroline's heart was in turmoil, her body responded to Clayton with a will of its own, her normal binds of constraint now too weak to rein her in.

As they kissed, he began to feel her breasts through her shirtwaist.

Helpless to stop herself, Caroline arched her back and moaned, consumed by the exquisite sensations she had so long craved.

Stephen helped Mrs. Kershaw to the door and saw her out. It was a bright, sunny morning, but he barely noticed. He was counting down the days until his wedding. The church reservation and invitations had not yet been cancelled, and he fervently prayed that Caroline would follow through with their marriage plans. Nothing had ever mattered so much in his life.

His heart ached at the recollection of her disillusioned, sad face, and he wished with every fiber of his being that he could undo his mistakes. *Why did I continue? I knew it was wrong. She's all that matters to me.* He closed his eyes and held tightly onto the door frame as he turned around to face his now-empty office. *I have to restore her faith in me.*

Something brushed behind him like a quick breath of wind. He shuddered and opened his eyes to find a small figure before him. Shifting under her disquieting gaze, he asked, "Aren't you the ward of the Bells? How can I help you?"

Jessie folded her hands in front of her, scrutinizing him for a moment before saying, "Carrie is meetin' with Clayton Bell this mornin'. I thought you might wanna know."

Stephen's eyes widened, but he quickly recovered his professional demeanor.

She stared back unflinchingly.

"Alright," he snapped. "What do you want with me?"

"I just thought you'd wanna know. She meets with him every Wednesday somewhere between here and Greeleyville." Jessie waved a hand vaguely in a southwesterly direction.

"And what does that have to do with me? Or you?"

"They're lovers," she said matter-of-factly.

"I've heard enough. Thank you." He opened the door wider and gestured for her to leave.

She dug in her heels. "She was his lover before she even met you, Dr. Connor. Didn't you know?"

He glared at her. "Get out of my office."

"Clay keeps the Swann's horse for her. He's prob'ly meetin' her with that horse right now, as we speak."

Stephen's face registered a sudden unwilling comprehension. The girl's words were uncomfortably informed and had an uncanny ring of truth to them. "Sounds like none of your business," he said gruffly.

"But it's yours. And it's not just business. Why do you think she asked him in the first place? I've seen them kissin' for myself. Did she even ask *you* to keep that horse, Dr. Connor?"

Grabbing her arm, Stephen flipped the sign to 'closed' and dragged her out of the office.

Jessie withdrew to the shadow of the awning as he locked up. She stayed there as he headed towards the town livery at a brisk pace, not sparing her a parting glance. When he broke into a run, she blew out a breath of relief. God willing, Dr. Connor would solve her problem for her.

As he urged Hermes out of Kingstree, Stephen brushed aside concerns about his remaining appointments of the day. Patients were used to his emergencies, although Dr. Davis usually covered for him now.

Applying his heels to Hermes' sides again, Stephen shifted his thoughts towards the tall, daunting farmer. The man had certainly been interested in Caroline, but Stephen had heard her turn him away.

She can't have been with him all this time—but it explains so much, damn it! His stomach churned as he remembered her taunt, 'Some men seem to find me rather irresistible.' *And wasn't she straightforward about not bein' made of iron?*

The thoughts sickened him, and a subdued anger boiled inside of him. He had been so careful with her. He cherished her purity, but other men might not prioritize her that way.

Would Carrie do this? He shook his head and rode faster, relentlessly hoping that the Bell girl had been wrong, had been lying. Caroline had been so upset with him, and he could hardly believe she could be such a hypocrite. After an hour of riding, Stephen was just beginning to feel more hopeful when he glimpsed a pair of horses grazing far ahead by a creek. His throat tightened as he recognized the chestnut thoroughbred. Quickly dismounting, he tied Hermes' reins to a nearby sycamore tree. His jacket was left tucked beneath the pommel of the saddle. He approached in his shirtsleeves, warily on foot. Soon he could see the couple on a dry patch of the bank. They were on a blanket, only partially hidden by the shade. Clayton was kissing Caroline and appeared to be removing her top.

Every muscle in Stephen's lithe frame tightened. Then, instinctively, he hurled himself towards the lovers.

Clayton lifted his head, suddenly alert, then scrambled to his own full height.

Stephen tackled the larger man with the agility of a panther, driven by velocity and savage emotion. The pair rolled into the creek before Caroline could gather herself.

Hastily buttoning her shirtwaist, she rushed towards the creek's edge, incredulous at the sight of Stephen on top of Clayton, forcing him underwater.

"Stop!" Caroline screamed, floundering into the stream. She threw herself on Stephen's back, desperately attempting to pull him off of the submerged man.

Ignoring her, Stephen focused all of his energies on keeping the large farmer pinioned, aware of his unlikely advantage. At last, Clayton ceased to struggle, and Stephen finally allowed Caroline to pull him away from the motionless form.

"No, no, no…" Caroline cried as she let go of Stephen and gripped Clayton's arm, trying to turn him over.

Stephen's eyes widened with panic. "Help me pull him out!"

They dragged him onto the bank, where Stephen deftly performed abdominal thrusts until Clayton began coughing up mouthfuls of brown water. Stephen then turned him to his side and supported his head as he vomited.

Caroline watched in shock, barely able to breathe.

Once Clayton began to regain consciousness, Stephen stepped away from him. Caroline rushed forward and knelt as the farmer blinked and looked dazedly up at her.

"I'd advise restin' here for a few minutes," Stephen brusquely directed. "You should take some Ayer's cherry pectoral when you get home for a couple of days to help cough out any residuals in your lungs." At this, he turned to Caroline with a cold glance. "Get your things and let's go."

Supporting Clayton as he sat up, Caroline said simply, "I can't leave him like this."

"I wasn't *asking* you. He'll be fine."

"No, Stephen."

Grabbing her wrist, he began to tug her towards the horses.

"Let me go!" Caroline tried to yank her arm from his grasp but stumbled forward as Stephen pulled her with a steely grip.

"I think Caroline said no." The husky, low voice came from beside them. Clayton now loomed next to her and put a protective arm around her shoulders.

Stephen's eyes widened as he saw them leaning into one another, and he falteringly released his grasp, asking in disbelief, "Are you choosin' *him*?"

Caroline looked between the two men. Stephen stood there with his beautiful dark hair and eyes, intensely staring at her. His white shirt and black slacks were disheveled and wet, but he somehow looked as sophisticated as ever. Images of their time together flickered through her mind: passionate kisses, long rides together, the planning of their future, his carefully controlled reserve and strict moral code… the pain and disillusionment, the shroud of mystery he wore, the cold worldliness and order of his life.

Then she glanced at Clayton's warm, rugged face and thought of his unbridled passion, his humor, his straightforward intentions, and his loving, unpretentious affection. He had willingly faced Stephen and had risked trouble with the law for her. Despite all this, he stood there pale and shaky, yet still bold and valorous. His light-blue eyes shone with sincerity; his dimpled chin set with steadfast clarity of purpose.

Looking Stephen in the eye, she replied in a shaky but firm voice, "Yeah, I'm gonna stay here with Clay."

Stephen stood for a moment in stunned silence, as though she'd slapped him.

Her heart wrenched as the color drained from his face.

With a final, anguished look, he turned to walk slowly towards Hermes.

Clayton stood quietly by her side as they watched him leave. Soon he was no more than a dusty speck in the road.

As if he'd been somehow waiting until Stephen was gone, coughs suddenly began to rack through Clayton's torso. When Caroline turned to him in alarm, he pulled her to his chest and held her close until the coughing subdued. Though soaked, and despite suffering through a terrible experience, he held Caroline with relief. He had not thought past spending time with her, hoping only that she would not marry Stephen. He had not thought past wanting to be with her.

Abruptly faced with the possible disruption of Caroline's marital plans, he now thought despairingly of his own worldly situation, of his own suitability as a husband. *How can I bring such a lady home to my mother? Our house is so small, almost as small as her cottage. Carrie is used to fine clothes and jewelry and all such. What do I have to offer her?* An emerging sense of desperation crept over him.

"Are you alright?" Caroline looked up at him. "You're shakin'. Here, let's sit you down a while. You've been through an awful ordeal." She found the picnic supplies and handed him the canteen of tea.

He sat down and sipped it slowly, swishing the sweet flavor around his mouth.

Caroline settled next to him in quiet thoughtfulness. After a while, she said, "We should get you home."

"Oh, I can get myself home alright."

"I'm worried about you."

Clayton shook his head. "It'll be easier if I don't have to explain the situation to my mother tonight. I'm honestly not up to it. I'd ruther just head home, wash up, and go to bed early." His chuckle turned into a cough. "Maybe I'll even listen to the good doctor's advice and take that cherry pectoral."

With a half-hearted smile, she rose to her feet, relieved at the thought of heading to her own quiet cottage for the evening. Too much was happening. She didn't want to cry in front of Clayton, but tears were already pricking her eyes.

24• Night of Sorrow

CAROLINE CAREFULLY AVOIDED CONVERSATIONS with her family for the next couple of days. She traversed to and from the sewing factory a solitary figure, now oddly relieved that Anne was no longer working there. Though she remained withdrawn throughout suppers, her kinfolk were so full of chatter that her reticence remained largely unnoticed. She dreaded telling them of the cancelled wedding, though she knew it must be done soon.

On a cloudy, blustery Friday evening, she sat alone in her cottage and stared at nothing, unable even to focus on her old, favorite dime novel. It was time to face her family at last and deliver the death-knell for her wedding.

Overcome by this sense of duty, Caroline reluctantly began her short journey towards the main house, full of introspective disregard for the forceful winds outside. The squall snatched at her clothing as if trying to pull her from her task, and when her outer skirt blew up over her head, she finally wondered at the weather's insistence to be noticed. The wind echoed and amplified her wish to avoid her plight.

Tempted to obey the lusty gales pressing against her, pushing her away from her undertaking, Caroline laughed and righted her skirts. As she did so, her cherished Libbey tale was snatched from her hand to fly helter-skelter across the lawn.

Exhilaration welled at the powerful forces, so congruent with her own feelings. Now grudgingly obedient to them, she began to chase after her book. It blew in the direction of the stables. After pursuing it halfway there, she shouted brazenly to the wind, "Alright, you win! I'm goin' for a ride!"

In the stalls, she stowed the book and outfitted Maritime with the side-saddle. When she mounted her at the block just outside, one hand stayed on her skirt, pinning it down against the strong breezes gusting from beneath. The intensity of the weather matched her mood precisely.

They set off. Each flick of hair stinging her face, each battering attempt of the wind to dislodge her from Maritime felt right. Caroline spurred the horse faster, laughing with relief at the thrilling precariousness of the ride and of her life.

Horse and rider melded as they flew past centuries-old forest with its host of creatures, each with its own timeless story. Her own troubles faded, however temporarily, to an inconsequential drop in the ocean of life, an insignificant ripple in the continuity of time.

At dusk, they finally arrived back at the stables, and she settled Maritime in with an easier heart, hugging her neck and kissing her velvety nose. Caroline ran back to her cottage with her novel and soon settled herself down for the night, falling asleep quickly and dreamlessly.

Caroline awoke to someone banging at the cottage door. Moonlight shone through the windows, illuminating the rooms as she approached the entrance, calling out, "Who is it?"

"It's me, let me in."

Recognizing Stephen's voice, Caroline deftly unbolted the door. She stood back as he stumbled inside. Closing the door behind him, Caroline took his kerosene lantern and asked with concern, "What are you doin' here? It's the middle of the night."

He gazed purposefully at her. As she considered his bleary eyes, stubble, and befuddled expression, she placed the lantern on the table.

He gestured broadly at it and had to catch himself on the wall. "You can put that out."

With dismay, she shook her head. "You look like you need to get back home. What are you doin' out like this?"

He regained his balance and smiled at her. "But this is exactly where I should be, isn't it? I understand now,

Carrie. I was wrong before, but I understand things way better now." He reached towards her. "It's all gonna be alright now."

"What are you talkin' about?" She took a step backwards.

"I thought about what you said..." He lurched forward in an instant and began stroking her tumbled hair. His gaze travelled slowly down her figure. He fingered the untied ribbon at the neck of her gown, "See? I didn't go to the races. I swore I'd never again touch any woman but you, Carrie, and I meant it."

Slowly she stepped away from him, again taken aback at the uncharacteristic gleam in his eyes. They were now riveted to the ill-concealed silhouette of her breasts.

"You told me you are a woman with desires, and I didn't understand. I was wrong. I'm here now, sweetheart. I'm here to give you what you want. What I want."

A choking sensation made Caroline realize that she was afraid—afraid of Stephen, of all people. She shook her head. "You're drunk. I'll get you some coffee."

He laughed and closed the space between them. "I've never been saner. It's all so simple, really. I'm sorry I didn't understand before."

Heedless of her protests, Stephen scooped her into his arms. He carried her to the bedroom and lowered her to the mattress, smoothly bracing himself over her.

Caroline fell silent, stricken with fear and confusion. The stench of liquor on his breath obscured the familiar scents of castile soap and even of Stephen himself. She could only stare at his determined countenance.

His eyes pierced her face as if searching for a sign. His brow furrowed as he murmured, "Shh, it's all gonna be fine. Finally jus' you and me, like it's s'posed to be."

Seamlessly, he pulled up her gown and unclasped his belt. Then he lowered himself to her, fastening his lips to hers with a bruising totality.

Caroline's heart pounded as she allowed him to continue. *Stephen wants me. He's here. He wants me.* Despite these thoughts, panic seized her when he began to enter her. Ambivalent emotions welled tumultuously, and she clung to him as if to a makeshift raft in the midst of a tempest.

A flash of pain interrupted her thoughts as he thrust himself fully into her, and her eyes brimmed with tears as he repeatedly drove into her. When he climaxed at last, he sank onto her for a moment before rolling to his side.

He lay there for a while and then sat to look at Caroline—only to wish that the moon weren't so bright out. Silent tears streamed down her face, abruptly awakening his conscience. *Isn't this what she wanted? Didn't she say she wanted me? I know she said as much. Not tonight, maybe, but she said it.* His certainty unraveled as he reflected on his drunken, forceful behavior, and a new thought struck him. *Oh God, did I hurt her? I didn't think I was hurtin' her.* Then his heart squeezed as yet another consideration occurred to him. Taking a deep breath, he bent his head to inspect the moonlit bedding. Dark crimson blood stained the white cotton of the sheets and her nightgown.

A sense of horror slowly engulfed him. *What have I done?* An agonized moan escaped him as he drew back and whispered with frenzied agitation, "I'm sorry, Carrie. I'm so sorry. I thought you had… I didn't know."

Her head swirled with hollow confusion. She wanted to reach for Stephen, but she was stunned and uncertain—and part of her was horrified.

Consumed with self-loathing, he withdrew from her bed and straightened his clothing before turning to her, rubbing his forearms. "Are you alright? Does it still hurt?"

She sat up and cast a long glance at the sheets, then waveringly answered, "I'm alright, I think, but…"

"Blood is normal your first time," Stephen said soothingly, hating himself even as he tried to reassure her. He took out his handkerchief from his pocket and carefully began to wipe the dampness from her face. His brow furrowed as he pleaded, "That's not how I intended our first time… your first time to be. It will never happen like that again. It won't hurt next time. I won't ever hurt you again."

Caroline placed a hand on his arm and replied more steadily, "I'm alright."

He gave a sigh of relief. "Don't worry, Carrie. Our wedding is almost here. You are still in every way that matters my perfect bride, but I am ashamed of my actions tonight." He paused and took another deep breath, then continued more hopefully, "Everythin' can still be alright. We'll just get married like we were goin' to, your honor intact. We can still have everythin' the way we've dreamt."

Caroline gazed at him in pained disbelief. His assumptions were so vastly disconnected from her own experience. She waved a faltering hand at the bed and answered tearfully, "I don't care about honor, Stephen. My dreams have been unravelin'. Our marriage can never be what my dreams were."

His heart seared with pain as he absorbed her words. He had no rebuttal. There was no medicine to heal this wound, and no logic could right what had occurred. He said softly, "I never meant to hurt you. I love you. I'll always love you." He hesitated and then added, "I can go away if that's what you want."

Caroline closed her eyes and nodded miserably.

Numbly, Stephen left the cottage. He rode Hermes towards his lonely apartment, wishing he could outrun his transgressions.

Weeping sporadically, Caroline spent the next hour washing at her porcelain pitcher and bowl, changing the soapy, pink-tinged water twice before turning her attentions to the blood stains on the sheets and feather-filled mattress. Though worried about Stephen, she felt a strange sense of relief about his departure as she scrubbed. She had always felt their relationship was somewhat forced, as though they were not naturally suited. However, an undeniable, even epic bond existed between them, and her heart was bound to him irrevocably.

She and Stephen did not truly understand one another. Their relationship had always felt new and unbidden—looming larger than life itself, powerful and monumental, a form of worship. The mystery of Stephen was irresistibly fascinating, and she ached with the thought that he was no longer the hero of her fantasies, that he was not going to be her husband.

Her grieving continued as she lay down to sleep on John's vacated bed. She clutched John's pillows, which felt secure and safe, but fell asleep only to dream of Stephen, waking with fresh tears on her face. The initial relief of freedom was gone, leaving only a vast void. Stephen had become central to her life.

It was almost noon before she finally arose. After dressing, she washed her face and forced down a cup of strong, hot tea that made her mouth pucker. Finally, even though her inscrutable, aching heart seemed to negate all rational thought, she convinced herself that she should head over to the main house. She slowly walked that way, unsure of her mission.

As she arrived, Mary and Anne came to greet her on the porch, visibly distressed. Caroline looked between them in desolate confusion.

"I just can't believe it." Mary wiped at her eyes. "I'm so sorry, my dear."

"I don't understand why he couldn't wait," Anne protested. "There will always be injured and sick people everywhere. He could have gone later."

Caroline stared at them in wide-eyed surprise.

Hugging her abruptly, Mary said, "I'm sure he won't stay there forever. The war will end. He'll come home."

"Stephen went to the Philippines?" Caroline whispered with a jolt of comprehension.

Anne's eyes flashed furiously. "Yes, he had his bags with him. With no warnin', and right before your wedding. He just came by this mornin' and explained everythin', leavin'—"

"Sweetie," Mary broke in gently, holding a palm towards Anne to stop her tirade as she addressed Caroline, "he explained that you were so upset with him that he didn't think he should disturb you again this mornin'. I'm sorry that you had to spend the night alone with that awful news."

Caroline's knees weakened as his words of the night before resounded in her mind: *I can go away if that's what you want.*

She'd only been thinking in-the-moment when she'd agreed, but Stephen had certainly simplified things. There was no longer any question of a wedding. He was truly gone, and she might never see him again. He could die in the Philippines. The guerillas didn't wait for engaged combat to attack—it wouldn't matter that he wasn't infantry. An image of Stephen's torn, bloody body lying mangled in a Filipino jungle flickered through Caroline's mind. Her knees buckled as she let out a wail of anguish.

Catching her, Anne helped her to the joggling board.

Mary waited for Caroline's cries to wane, then said matter-of-factly, "Now girls, we mustn't be selfish. We have to respect that he feels it's his duty.

"Like he said, our American soldiers are dyin' in great numbers from all the guerilla fightin', and they need more doctors. Just think how many lives he'll save over there." She paused before adding, "He's leavin' his practice in the hands of that new Dr. Davis, and Caroline is safe here with us. Surely we can wait. We should all be proud of his sacrifice."

The wedding was quietly cancelled as life resumed on the Swann plantation. Caroline began to work with Anne at her shop, which she found far more engrossing than those long, monotonous days at the sewing plant. Capable, reliable Fletcher took care of most of the heavy sewing, leaving her free to work on the finer details with Anne. She welcomed the diversion of engaging her mind with Anne's business and artistry.

Mr. Sanders arrived on a bright morning in late September to collect Anne's new fashions for a series of shows along the East Coast. He nodded approvingly as he surveyed the collection, then turned to Caroline with a reluctant request. "This may be in poor taste, but as wonderful as these new designs are, I feel that Anne's finest achievement to date has been your bridal gown. Given that the wedding has been indefinitely postponed and that the dress couldn't help but boost your friend's standin' among established designers, would you allow us to include it in our collection?"

Though Caroline should by now be accustomed to the familiar pain wrenching her heart, each reminder freshly exacerbated her grief. Forcing a cheery smile, Caroline assented, then watched with a heavy heart as Anne packed away her wedding dress. It seemed all evidence of Stephen was slowly disappearing, as if he had never been in her life at all.

25• Square Root

WHILE THE YOUNG WOMEN WERE FOCUSING on the new design shop, the young Swann girls began their fall semester at school.

Emma valiantly braved Mr. Wright and his switches, more confident knowing their intended targets. Mary had ordered a new tin bucket for Emma's school dinners, and now she proudly flashed the bright silver pail at other children on the way to school.

Lenora joined the advanced group for the Friday spelling match and was gratified to place first. As she took her seat, she cast a smug glance towards Owen Bodiford on the boys' side of the room and was surprised when Owen caught her eye and grinned. Her pulse raced when he mouthed, "Wait 'til the cipher down!"

Like an observant anole, Jessie sat quite still in her hard wooden seat, noting their interactions with intense curiosity—how Lenora's eyebrows rose at his challenge and her curls tossed as she looked away, back to her slate. Moments later, Lenora's hand reached down for her chatelaine and surreptitiously drew up a tiny memo pad. She scribbled in it then tore out the sheet, passing it down the row to Owen while pretending not to notice his pleased, lingering glance at her.

Jessie's skin grew clammy at their open display. She would never be so flagrant about trying to get a boy's attentions, and Lenora's flirtations showed her to be a coquette, like Caroline.

In contrast, Jessie was either withdrawn while at school or absent altogether. Mr. Wright rarely remarked on her absences anymore, unless she had to present for elocution and recitation. She dreaded those days.

In truth, Jessie's primary focus of classroom study was Lenora, who no longer wore mourning at all. If Jessie were like an anole, then Lenora was like a chameleon—always changing in response to her situation, ever resilient.

As Lenora settled back to her schoolwork, Jessie's thoughts drifted to Clayton. *He must still have that horse, and they say Dr. Connor left for the war. How can I keep Clay away from Carrie now?* Jessie gritted her teeth then forced her jaw to relax. *At least he doesn't know I told his secret to Dr. Connor. No way he'd have given me that box of lemon drops when he brought his crops to town if he'd had the slightest inklin'. He even winked when he gave them to me.* Jessie smiled and stretched her neck. *All I really have to do is keep things right with Clay… and with God. He showed me that horse. It was part of his plan. Now I have to show faith and patience. Besides, seems like Carrie's decided to wait for Dr. Connor, now that he's left for war and she's so sad.* Jessie nodded and leaned back in her seat, reasonably comfortable that she needn't worry about the peal of wedding bells anytime soon.

"Jessie! Jessie Bell!" A sharp voice cut through her reflections.

Her head snapped up.

"The classroom is waiting for your answer." Mr. Wright sighed. "As seldom as you show up for class, you could at least pay attention when you're here. Does anyone else know the answer?"

Lenora's hand shot up.

"Yes, Miss Swann?" Mr. Wright looked relieved.

"The square root of 144 is 12, sir."

"That's right." Mr. Wright beamed briefly at Lenora before scowling back at Jessie. "And can you tell me what the formula $2\pi r$ is used for, Miss Bell?"

Her mind scrambled, but she suspected this equation had been covered in yesterday's lesson, which she had missed—never a problem, as Mr. Wright held reviews before their quarterly exams during which she generally gleaned anything of importance. He was obviously just proving a point now.

"No, sir."

"Well then, please take your seat up here. Perhaps you'll feel more motivated to pay attention if you're wearing your thinking cap."

As Mr. Wright took the dusty dunce cap from its perch on the windowsill, she settled in the chair facing the class, coldly glaring at them all as he set the cap on her head.

"Mr. Wright!" Lenora's hand was again waving in the air. "Mr. Wright, I can let Jessie borrow my slate from yesterday—it still has the math problems. I think she missed them."

"Please mind your own work, Lenora, and let us proceed with class now."

Jessie dug her fingernails into her palms and threw an irritated glance at Lenora, who was not a logical creature, no matter how many math calculations she could perform or spelling matches she could win—spirited to a point, but emotional and empathetic to a nauseating degree. An iron taste sprang to Jessie's mouth as she saw the pitying look Lenora now cast her way. *So patronizin'. Lenora will get her comeuppance one day—and Carrie, too. I just have to bide my time until then.*

26• The Anvil

WHEN HE HEARD THE NEWS of Stephen's departure for the Philippines, Clayton felt himself grow light, as if an iron cage had been taken off his chest. He respected Caroline's sorrow by not pressuring her in any way. Instead, he continued to stew over how ill-prepared he was for a woman of her circumstances. For now, he was happy to simply be with Caroline during their weekly waterside trysts; when it was time to depart, he would hug her close and kiss her forehead, prolonging that one intimate moment.

Meanwhile, when not caring for his mother or spending quality time with Julep, Clayton was fully occupied with tending to his duties at the farm. He was satisfied at how his fields had progressed to maturity over the last weeks, yielding a bountiful new harvest of butter beans, cabbages, and pumpkins in addition to his cotton and other crops. Likewise, the seeds of intimacy he continued to sow with Caroline might one day bear fruit. Until then, he could at least enjoy their meetings.

About a month later, Mr. Sanders was surveying Anne's new day dress with an uncertain frown. She had created the pouter pigeon blouses, other functional shirtwaists, and skirts he had commissioned, but she had stepped back into her preference for elegant wear with this lingerie day dress. The frothy material billowed; tiny pintucks and passementerie gathered material at the neckline, elbows, and waist. The sleeve puffed below the elbow.

Since they already had the wedding gown for their special feature, he was annoyed that she had been spending such a large amount of her time on this production. Still, he could see that she had not neglected the skirts or shirtwaists. He had nothing but approval for the shortened lengths of walking skirts that would now stay clear of the ground, and he was particularly impressed with the fine, decorative stitching on the wrist cuffs of the shirtwaists. Such touches kept working attire feminine, but the tea gown was at another level entirely. Reluctantly, he asked Caroline to model the dress for him, in case they could use another highlight feature for their spring collection, after all.

Caroline obligingly headed upstairs, where the wood stove kept the apartment a comfortable temperature despite the late November chill outside. The gown had been fitted to Caroline's form, as were most of Anne's designs. She relished the softness of the material and was enamored with the liberating, romantic feel of the gown after so many practical, comparatively dull designs. Caroline undressed, removing her corset and then slipping on the dress. When Anne arrived and began fastening the hooks down the back, however, she paused and tugged at the rear closures.

"This isn't fittin'," Anne fretted. "I'm not sure what I've done. You weren't wearin' your corset when we fitted it, were you?"

"Of course not."

"It was fine a couple of weeks ago," Anne muttered. "Perhaps you can jus' show him the front of the dress? Or maybe you can put back on your corset? I'm afraid I'll damage the lace." Anne let go of the material and placed her hands on her hips.

"That might ruin the effect." Caroline bit her lip, then reasoned, "Perhaps the extra pintucks took more material than we estimated. Try it on, Anna. You're thinner than me. I know you're taller, but I think it's long enough."

Caroline slipped out of the gown. By the time she'd pulled back on her own garments, Anne had already donned the daydress, managing to fasten it on her own. Caroline's breath caught. "Oh, my gracious. You are exquisite." She pointed at the dressing-table chair. "Have a seat. Let me fix your hair differently. It'll just take a moment."

With a dubious frown, Anne patted her hair. "It's not gonna do anything else in a hurry. I used that bandoline dressing on it—the one with the resin and proof spirit we bought at the apothecary."

"And lavender. I can smell it." Inhaling the scent, Caroline tentatively touched the perfect coif. She'd wanted a softer look, but this hair was stiff as bread crust. Tapping her foot impatiently, Caroline teased out a few tendrils to frame Anne's face, working them until they released a fine white dust and softened. Brushing away the powder, she pronounced, "There. You're perfect."

Caroline watched with pride as her tall, elegant friend began to descend the steps. *If Mr. Sanders doesn't fall to his knees in adoration, then he's blind and daft. Knowin' him, though,* she laughed to herself, *he'll channel all that admiration towards the dress, never realizin' the treasure inside.* Caroline sighed good-naturedly. *It would take an anvil in the head to awaken that man, so perhaps I'd better go and be that anvil.*

As Anne descended the stairs in the lingerie day dress, Mr. Sanders watched in surprise. The way his breath caught at the lovely vision before him told him that, without a doubt, they had found a second spring design feature.

He clapped. "Miss Brighton, I hereby proclaim you the Muse of Design, and I shall no more question your judgment."

His reaction was precisely and infuriatingly what Caroline had expected. Upon her arrival downstairs, she saw that Anne was glowing with pleasure. Caroline rolled her eyes.

The small company fell silent as Anne slowly turned to allow him to examine the dress from all angles.

Moving to Mr. Sanders' side, Caroline whispered, "Isn't she beautiful? Can't you just envision Anna servin' tea in that dress? Imagine what it would be like to come home to such a lady."

Mr. Sanders nodded enthusiastically. "She does make a pleasin' picture in that gown. Miss Brighton, you're a wonder. I've seen all I need to for now. Thank you."

Smiling radiantly, Anne ascended the stairs to remove the dress.

Caroline did not immediately follow. Instead, she turned to face Mr. Sanders, speaking more directly. "And she would be such a gracious companion."

Mr. Sanders' gaze was still on the steps where Anne had stood a moment before. "Certainly. I greatly enjoyed her company in Charleston. I'm lookin' forward to our impendin' travels with her spring collection."

Caroline seized on the thought. "But Mr. Sanders, Anna can't accompany you without a chaperone. It wouldn't be seemly."

His brow creased, and he gave her an annoyed glance. "Of course she can. It was understood when she took the job. She has a contract."

"Well, perhaps so, but her reputation would be in question. Would you ask that of her?"

"You're bein' rather old-fashioned. It's perfectly acceptable for a woman to travel for work. What would you have me do? I need her with me."

"I'm sure you can think of somethin'. She wouldn't need a chaperone at all, of course, if she were married… but another man might not want her travelin' and workin' so much. Besides, it might be distractin' for her if she had to spend a lot of time caterin' to a husband."

His face blanched.

Then Caroline added with a nonchalant shrug, "Though if she married *you*, there wouldn't be a problem, I s'pose."

He blinked in astonishment.

Suppressing a laugh, Caroline realized that one anvil strike might not be enough. She would let it be for now, though.

"I'd best go help her with those fastenings," she called as she ran up the stairs.

27• Her Condition, His Purgatory

DRY, BRITTLE LEAVES BLEW ACROSS THE YARD in distinctive swirling patterns. Caroline listened to their playful passage as she sat in the upholstered armchair by her window, absentmindedly twisting the chain of the angel pendant at her throat. At last, she looked down at the garment in her hands, again contemplating the reason for her needlework. The christening gown was her first tangible admission of her condition.

She had not heard from Stephen since his departure for the Philippines. She'd checked in with Dr. Davis, who merely pulled at his red moustache and expressed his own dismay at receiving no word from him. John had tried to follow up with the nearest military offices, but they gave no firm information regarding Stephen's whereabouts since his departure from Charleston months ago, saying only that they'd deliver a letter, just to leave it with them.

Stephen was gone, and Caroline was pregnant with his child. They were unwed, and she could not be sure he would ever return. She clutched the christening gown as she realized, *If he dies at war, our child will be fatherless. A bastard.*

Her lips set in a determined line. After carefully laying down her needlework and smoothing the gown back out, she retrieved her sterling-silver dip pen, a bottle of rose-scented ink, and her sheaf of pale-pink writing paper. Sitting down at their small table, she gripped the cold metal of the pen and began to write. *He needs to know I want him to come home first. The pregnancy must wait.*

Moments later, Caroline re-read the short letter; she'd kept it to-the-point and would write more once they had established contact. She rolled the ink blotter over the painstakingly-crafted words before folding the letter and sliding it into an envelope. Glad to be doing something—anything—to salvage the situation, she changed into her riding habit and hurried to the stables, unaware that she was being observed.

Once in town, Caroline went directly to the post office to ask where she should address her letter. After sealing the envelope and adding postage stamps, Caroline held it to her chest for a long moment, the adhesive taste lingering on her tongue. Then she released it to the care of the postmaster.

It was more horrific than he could have imagined. American soldiers overwhelmed the medic tent in a relentless deluge. Victims of guerilla fighters and illness in equal numbers, they required administration of life-saving measures at all hours. Stephen was exhausted to his core.

When he had a moment to breathe, he would take a walk on the eastern periphery of the camp. The western side was unbearable. Beyond that edge lay a *reconcentrado,* a concentration camp for thousands of alleged Filipino guerilla sympathizers. He had once protested the camp's policies as inhumane, pointing out a suffering elderly woman only to have the commander of the camp order the prisoner shot along with the newly-captured Filipino guerilla soldiers.

Stephen worked tirelessly to save the lives of the American soldiers who had been wounded in the conflicts. Meanwhile, the dead were being hauled from the reconcentrado daily; the Filipinos were beyond his help, and Stephen closed his eyes to their miseries. He was too fatigued and overworked to write home, unsure whether Caroline would even want to hear from him. He had received a couple of letters from John and one from her; though she had asked him to come home, the brevity of the letter made him suspect that she had felt it a duty to write. He still considered penning a reply, but the hell surrounding him left him at a loss for what to say.

He was familiar with the Anti-Imperialist League's opposition to the Philippine-American war, sympathizing with Mark Twain's highly-publicized questioning of what America would gain from having the Philippine colonies. He had joined not in support of the war itself, but in support of the soldiers fighting the war. He hoped to make a difference for the young recruits, pawns of the American government's current whim to control yet another nation to extend its power and better satisfy its sweet tooth.

By day Stephen faced the horrors of the camp. By night Caroline's tear-stricken face and crimson-stained sheets flashed intermittently through dreams of mutilated American soldiers lying in congealed blood, of Filipino villages in cinders, heavy with the acrid smell of burnt flesh; echoes of Caroline's protests were punctuated by the unceasing, agonized cries from the concentration camp. Stephen lost track of the hours, and weeks turned into unbearable months of purgatory.

While Caroline was off mailing her letter, Jessie slipped into the vacant cottage, silent as a spectre. The girl frequently visited during Caroline's absences and while the others were at school, scouting for evidence of Clayton. She suspected they still met, but since he was not openly courting Caroline, she felt moderately secure for the time being.

Jessie approached the table and fingered the silver dip pen. Opening the box of writing paper, she sniffed its small rose sachet and nodded at the pink paper, wondering if Caroline had been writing Dr. Connor. Replacing the lid carefully, she wandered through the rest of the cottage, stopping to lift a small garment from a chair and to scrutinize the white needlepoint smocking. *Perhaps this is for Mrs. Swann. Make that Mrs. Corbett. She could be expectin' again. That would make sense.*

Despite this explanation, her stomach tightened at the thought that Caroline could be with child. *Would it be Clay's or Dr. Connor's?* Jessie pursed her lips. *She's engaged to Dr. Connor. I've seen those weddin' invitations.* Her head nodded slowly. *She's only met Clay in secret, so everyone would assume the child is Dr. Connor's. She'd have to marry him.* Mind whirling, Jessie slid back out of the tabby cottage like a shadow.

Week after week passed, but each time the postal wagon clattered down the dirt lane to the plantation, Caroline's heart plunged with the same sickening disappointment—a fleeting sense of hope eroding into grief. She no longer ran out to meet their aging, kindly mailman, hoping for word from Stephen. It was not coming. She tried to tell herself otherwise—that her tears were unreasonable, that the dread and certainty were prompted by her fears about her condition—but the feeling had taken hold with a relentless grip.

When the crunch of footsteps hastened towards the cottage only moments after the mail carrier left, Caroline braced herself. Her heart had leapt into her throat too many times—only for her to find out that the family was merely coming to check on her and sometimes share a newspaper headline. She closed her eyes, listening to the approach. As the footsteps broke into a run, her heart reluctantly began galloping along. Her eyes flashed open as John burst through the door, waving an envelope and clutching a rolled-up newspaper to his chest.

"It's a letter from Stephen—over a month old," he announced breathlessly, shoving it at her.

Without a word, Caroline reached out and took the bent envelope, staring at it as if it weren't quite real.

"Go on, open it." John's cheeks were flushed, his relief palpable. His anxiety wouldn't settle, however, until he heard that Stephen was alright. He'd wondered at the lack of mail, and he wasn't about to leave Caroline alone to discover the contents of the long-awaited letter.

Hesitantly, Caroline tore open the envelope and pulled out the enclosed papers. Slowly she unfolded and smoothed them out on the table. Her fingertips ran along the precise, neat script then separated the pages, lining them up one next to the other.

"Carrie? Are you alright? What does he say?"

"I'm not sure yet." She was staring at the papers and flattening them, inspecting Stephen's signature and the small inkblots without reading the words.

John laid a sympathetic hand on her arm. "Shall I read it to you?"

"No." Her voice was hollow. She traced the letters of Stephen's closing signature, and a tear trickled down her cheek. "He's dead, John. I can feel it."

He stared at her in consternation. "Good Lord, Carrie. Read the letter. For Christ's sake, it's right there in front of you."

"Have you checked the list of casualties yet?"

"I'm sure Carroll would have warned me. He reads those lists before deliverin' the mail, keepin' an eye out for all our families, you know. I ran over here as soon as I saw the letter."

"Check it first." Caroline indicated the weekly newspaper still in his grip.

As he incredulously unrolled and opened it, she lifted a sheet of paper and pressed the cool smoothness of Stephen's signature to her cheek.

"We've checked this list every week for—"

"He's in there. I know it."

"You're bein'—" John's voice broke off. Then he asked hesitantly, "Does his letter say which company he's in?"

She glanced at the return address on the envelope. "Company K."

John looked up from the newspaper to stare at the table.

"He's there, isn't he?" Caroline's voice was thin and distant, her expression wistful.

"I'm not sure. Oh God, Carrie."

"Show me."

John looked up at her with a stricken expression. "Maybe it isn't him."

"Let me see."

Unwillingly, he extended the paper to her and pointed to Company K's casualty list. It took only a moment for her eyes to alight on the name, *Steve Conyer*. It blurred as tears welled and began to pour down her cheeks, one after the other until John pulled the paper away from the hand that still pressed it to her cheek.

"You're gonna ruin his letter that way." His voice was soft and sorrowful.

She melted onto the table, folding her arms over the other pages of the letter, heedlessly allowing her tears to drench them.

John smoothed her hair while extricating the papers from under her arms. After setting them aside, he sank down and pulled her into his arms, letting her cry on his shoulder.

"It'll be okay, Carrie. We'll all get through this together." John shook his head to dispel the hopelessness that kept threatening to descend upon him, regardless of his increasingly important role in the family. The burden seemed too much, too overwhelming at times.

28• Proposal

CLAYTON WAITED ON THE BANK WITH JULEP, watching the waterfowl at their morning activities and listening to the soft trickle of the creek. It was a foggy Wednesday in January, the winter landscape brown and barren. The most-vivid songbirds had departed long ago for warmer climes. The blue herons, however, were breathtaking, stalwart nobles, indigo-stained Highlanders among birds. Clayton never tired of admiring them.

After a time, Hurricane's approach could be heard, and a heron spread his majestic wings, taking flight. Clayton turned to greet Caroline. The last couple of times that he'd seen her, she'd been consumed with grief over Stephen. This time, however, she waved cheerily, a brightness in her eyes despite the circles beneath them. He was glad to see her smile again.

"How you holdin' up?" he asked.

"Gettin' by somehow." She slipped off of Hurricane and secured Hurricane's harness to a tree. "Care to take a stroll? I've been sittin' far too long on that horse."

"Sure." His brows rose in surprise. Even on her worst days, she generally devoted the first portion of her visits to Julep. Then he shrugged, saying only, "If we walk up this way we might see a kingfisher. Its call was rattlin' out real loud jus' a minute ago."

She craned her neck to see down the stream as she gave Julep a brief pat. "Alright, I'll try to keep it down."

Linking arms, they paced in prolonged silence until he asked again, "How you been, really?"

"I'm, well, I'm…" She paused, staring across the water.

"I s'pose I needn't have asked. Jesus. I'm so sorry, Carrie. I wish I could help."

Her gaze came back to meet his concerned face. His love wound around her as tangibly as his arms once did, bringing light to her world. She gave a broken laugh, forcing herself back to earth. "There's somethin' else—somethin' I haven't told you yet."

"What is it?"

Her eyes lowered, staring at his chin cleft. "I'm with child."

"Stephen's child?" His voice was suddenly hoarse.

"Yes."

Clayton kicked a limb, splashing it into the stream. "Holy Christ, Carrie. Whatcha gonna do?"

"I don't know."

"John and Mary will help out, I guess." Clayton nodded and blew out a deep breath. "Lots o' family around. They're prob'ly already makin' plans."

"I haven't told anyone but you." She lifted her eyes to meet his. "I was waitin' to see."

His bewildered expression weakened her resolve, but still she managed to ask, "Would you marry me, Clayton Bell?"

He froze, not even blinking.

Caroline closed her own eyes. "I understand if you need some time to decide. It's a lot to think about."

"That's not it. It's just… are you sure that's what you want?"

When her eyes opened to regard his warm, caring face again, his expression brimmed with wonder, and she felt the rush of certainty. "Yes, Clay. You are good to me—good for me. You've always been real with me." She reached up to tenderly touch his cheek, laughing affectionately. "I put you out so much, but you never complain. I can see us together."

Pausing, she added, "But that's jus' what makes sense to me. I don't know if it makes sense for you, if it's what you want—especially with everythin' how it is. I know it's… not perfect."

"Carrie, I—"

She held up her hand. "Wait. Don't rush into anythin'. Think it through first. Maybe you should go home and sleep on it."

Clayton stared at her for a moment. *Do I want to raise someone else's child? Do I want to marry a woman pregnant with someone else's child?* As he gazed at her beautiful face, the face he had been in love with since she had first fallen into his arms, none of it seemed to make a difference. *Do I want to marry her? Yes.*

Cautiously, he suggested, "You should come to my house for a visit first. You've been straightforward with me, and I think you should know what you'd be getting yourself into. My home isn't what you're used to... and my mama ain't your typical lady. You've got a good place now, where you're at already."

She was smiling, the haunted look almost entirely gone. "So you want to marry me?"

"Carrie, did you hear what I said about my mama?" He rubbed his forehead.

Meeting his eyes resolutely, she reached for his hand. Pulling it away from his forehead, she threaded her fingers through his. "I don't need to see it. I know you, and that's what matters. You've taken care of Julep, and he looks as healthy and happy as I've ever seen him. Maybe I'll have to make a few adjustments, but I trust you'll keep us healthy and happy, too."

Clayton had no reply as he searched her earnest eyes. Then a cautious smile began to spread over his face. *Carrie will be my wife. No more worries about losin' her. No other suitors. She'll be with me always.*

"Well, then." He took a deep breath. "It's settled. Ain't nothin' else to think about." Reaching for her, he shook his head and laughed. As he drew her into his arms, his lips lowered to hers and found them soft and welcoming. The subdued reserve of the past months began to melt away, and when she moaned, his pulse began to pound. Her body melded against his, and he led her slowly back down the stream to the picnic blanket he'd laid out under the tree canopy, where they sealed their pact, uninterrupted.

Winter weather in the South Carolina Lowcountry is a capricious, flippant affair. Mary checked outside every morning before sending her girls off to school, attired in summer cottons one day and warm woolen hats and mittens the next. The unencumbered pair had just left when Caroline stopped by the next morning before making her way to Anne's workshop in town.

"Hey there, sleepyhead. Have a seat." Mary was clearing the breakfast dishes.

Caroline clasped her hands, trying vainly to remember the words she'd so carefully planned to say. "I'm not hungry. I was just wonderin' if you might have a moment."

"What's goin' on?" Absentmindedly, Mary scraped grits from a plate. In recent months she had encouraged Ettie to not come in until the afternoons.

"It's about Stephen."

"Oh..." Mary's face creased with sympathy. She waved towards the parlor, setting down the plate. "Let's have a seat. Dishes can wait."

Caroline sank onto the cream chintz sofa, and Mary came to join her, wiping her hands on a dishtowel. As she sat down, Mary patted Caroline's knee. "I know it's hard, honey. Especially since we can't be absolutely sure of anythin'."

Caroline sighed. "But I am sure. I already knew, somehow."

Her plaintive look begged Mary not to persist in the same vein, but Mary continued, "Those lines of communication are terrible. Sometimes it takes months for letters to get here. Don't give up hope. We don't know for sure that was him on the casualty list."

"He's not comin' back. I'm certain of it. We never married…" Caroline paused but then forced herself to continue, "…and I'm expectin' his child."

Mary sat back, stunned at the revelation. Her eyes scanned the young woman's rounder figure.

Caroline's cheeks began to burn, but she went on determinedly, "I've decided to marry Clayton Bell. He knows of my condition, and he's still willin' to wed me."

"Heavens," Mary finally said, her voice faint. "What if Stephen comes home?"

"I won't risk my child becomin' a bastard. I can't afford to wait any longer." Caroline indicated her thickened waist. "May we have the wedding here? I'd like for it to be within the next couple o' weeks, as I'm sure you can understand."

Mary shook her head. "You don't have to do this, honey. Everyone knows the weddin' was set to happen. We'll treat the child like one of our own while you wait."

"Stephen is gone. He's not comin' back, no matter what anyone might wish. I have to face reality, and Clay will be a good father and husband, I'm sure." Despite her firm words, she gazed at Mary beseechingly, as if her approval meant the world to her.

Mary set her jaw. "I think you're makin' a terrible mistake. You simply refuse to listen to the voice of prudence, though, don't you? There is no reason you couldn't wait a while longer, just to be sure. If Clayton is aware of your condition, a few more weeks won't make any real difference for that child's future—if Stephen is dead, as you believe. If he's not, then you'll have made a grave error."

Caroline paled. "Mary, please don't…"

"Oh, child." Mary gasped at the tears brimming in Caroline's eyes. She drew her into a hug. "If you must, I s'pose you may have the wedding service here—and a supper, if you wanna do it that way. Of course you may, so long as John approves of everythin'."

"Oh, Aunt Mary. Thank you. Thank you so much."

"I'm not happy with your decision, but you've already made up your mind. I can see that." Mary sighed and rose to her feet. "So stubborn, so rash—just like my Sam." She kissed the top of Caroline's head. "I guess I won't say nothin' else about it, as you won't listen to me—but I s'pose I do understand your reasonin'."

That evening, Caroline discussed the wedding plans with John, who deemed them wise. Unlike Mary, he was already convinced that Stephen would not be returning, and he preferred to keep Caroline's pregnant state unknown to their community until she was well-wed.

That night, however, Mary's biting words came back to haunt Caroline while she lay in bed. *Is Stephen still alive?* Caroline tossed and turned. *Am I wrong?*

Rising, she brewed a calming pot of chamomile tea, pacing the hallway as she waited for it to steep. When she finally returned to bed, she fell asleep reminding herself, *He's gone. I feel it. I knew it. John knows it. Clay loves me.* Caroline closed her hand around the angel pendant at her neck, willing the angels to watch over Stephen in the afterlife.

29• A New Family

THE WEDDING WAS TO BE A QUIET AFFAIR, much in the manner of John and Mary's nuptials. Caroline borrowed the lingerie day dress—Anne let it out by unstitching the pintucks—and Ettie simply repeated the supper menu and cake recipe so recently required by Mary and John.

When Amarintha arrived with Clayton at Swann plantation, she met Caroline for the first time in the foyer. Delightedly prodding Caroline's stomach with her protuberous, misshapen finger, she smacked her lips and pronounced all-too-loudly, "You got a good man now, sugar. Lucky girl, marryin' my Clay. He's right hon'rable, yessiree, an' he's gonna take good care o' his own."

Caroline flinched at her mouthful of twisted, blackened stumps as much as at the overt acknowledgment of her condition, which Amarintha clearly attributed to her son. Nonetheless, Caroline agreed wholeheartedly that she was lucky to be marrying Clayton.

The simple ceremony was attended by John, Mary, Anne, Amarintha, and the young girls. The guests were uncharacteristically solemn, excepting gleeful interjections of, "Dat's right," "Mmm-hmm," and "Hallelujah!" by Amarintha. These were mild in comparison with what Clayton had feared, and Reverend Scott even beamed at her. The young girls stared with large eyes, however, while Caroline just smiled at Amarintha's enthusiasm—and at her new husband.

Clayton tried to block out his mother's commentary, but as he looked into Caroline's laughing eyes, he soon found himself appreciating the spirit of it. He could not remember being happier.

After the service, John drove Amarintha to Sheriff Bell's house; she would spend a rare night there before being taken home by her brother the next day. On the way, Amarintha joked about the impending wedding night so lewdly that John's lips formed an unhappy line. The idea of Caroline living in close quarters with such an uncouth creature made his stomach churn, but it was too late for second thoughts. At least for the time being, the newly married couple would be staying at the cottage as a sort of honeymoon before heading back to Clayton's farm in Greeleyville. After those two weeks, John could only pray for his sister's welfare.

Caroline found contentment in the following fortnight. She was able to immerse herself in the beauty of her first days of married life with Clayton.

His warmth and friendliness soon won her family over completely, but the couple spent most of their time secluded in quiet retreat. Countless hours were spent planning, hoping, and dreaming about their future together. They would stroll over the estate, arm in arm, and take sweet pleasure in their intimate moments. A certain peace dwelled in Caroline's heart at last.

Jessie was profoundly stung by the news of Clayton's wedding. She had recently greeted the sharp cramps heralding the arrival of her monthlies with a satisfied joy, knowing she would soon be of marriageable age. She had been cautious but vigilant about his activities, and yet the marriage had sprung on her as if out of nowhere, as though Clayton and Caroline had intuitively planned to sidestep her.

After Amarintha's sudden appearance at her uncle's home, Jessie heard her aunt's gleeful rendition of events with abject horror. After a time, she slunk away unnoticed to spend hour after tormented hour in the bramble-filled thickets beyond Caroline's cottage.

The girl's jagged fingernails cut into the skin of her arms as she watched the couple walking together, stopping to lovingly kiss under the magnificent live oak trees—Clayton's hands gliding over his new wife while she pulled him ever closer. Once, he'd even taken her right against a tree, in full view. In the evenings, Jessie would sit under the screened windows of their bedroom and listen with revolted fascination to their rocking and moaning until she would quietly retch into the bushes. Then she'd lie there spent—as the couple would likewise eventually do.

Jessie whiled countless hours fruitlessly contemplating her failures and her future's possibilities. She vaguely hoped to understand what had gone wrong, though to what end she didn't know.

After days of observation, brutal honesty forced her to admit that Clayton simply wanted Caroline. He loved to look at her, to touch her, to be with her. He loved a blond, curvaceous beauty, not a thin, raven-haired girl. Jessie felt sick with despair.

She wondered if this were a punishment for her timidity, for expecting God's commands to be as clear as a burning bush—as though she were somehow as important as Moses. Collapsing to her knees, she began to pray in earnest, baring her helpless, desperate soul in hopes of some miracle of salvation.

At the end of the fortnight, Clayton and Caroline loaded a buggy with her few personal possessions and their wedding gifts of silver cutlery, then headed towards his home at last. She was not a little apprehensive about living in such tight quarters with Amarintha, but Clayton assured her that his mother had a generous and loving heart. Caroline nodded, trying her best to have faith.

Inside the small, dim house, crocheted afghans on the furniture showed up multi-colored against the white clapboard walls. The stench of tobacco permeated the structure, coating it with a sticky residue. Amarintha sat across from a thin, careworn man at the kitchen table, and the pair crowed with pleasure at the young couple's arrival.

Clayton greeted them, then presented the older man. "Carrie, I'd like you to meet my Uncle Simms. He comes by to look in on Mama when I'm not here. He's been tendin' to the farm—and Julep, too—while I been gone."

"Hang a cat if you ain't got yourself a looker, Clay," Simms wheezed. He cast a lecherous eye upon Caroline, who stepped closer to Clayton. "She'll make you some right smart young'uns. I see you done made sure she's a breeder afore hitchin' up with her, eh?" He nodded at the bulge at her waist and cackled at his own cleverness.

Amarintha joined in, "Yeah, he likes what's under dem skirts. Mmm-hmm. And it ain't fer you, Simms."

"Mama, come on now," Clayton chided, putting an arm around Caroline's shoulders. She'd pressed close to him like a scared child.

"Yeah, come on, Rintha," Simms laughed.

Amarintha grinned, then got up and began bustling around the kitchen. "I made some vittles. Here's some perlou and turnip greens."

"Dem biscuits ain't half bad, neither," put in Simms.

Following Clayton's lead, Caroline helped her plate and tentatively took her seat at the table, smiling half-heartedly as she slid into the chair next to Amarintha. After a few hesitant bites, she found the peppery rice palatable and ate with gusto.

Amarintha returned a garish smile, nodding approvingly at her plate. Then she narrowed her eyes knowingly. "Child, I'm thinkin' dat you gonna need some help figurin' out how to keep up dis place."

Caroline's heart plummeted at the realization that Amarintha expected her to take over the home duties. "I can't rightfully say I've ever cooked a whole meal by myself."

"Dat's what I figured. Don't you worry none. I been doin' deze here chores and da cookin' fer longer dan you been alive. I'll learn ya."

"I'd be honored to learn what I can from you, but I've never been much of a hand in the kitchen… so please don't expect too much."

Waving at her profile, Amarintha tutted, "You got all you need to figure it out."

"Clay done checked and made sure o' that," Simms put in.

"Ain't it da truth!" Cackling loudly, Amarintha added, "And now he done figured out how to have dat wet, warm somethin' in his bed all da time."

"Mama!" Clayton protested.

"I'm bein' nice. All I said was *somethin'*." Amarintha turned to Caroline, who was beet-red. "Betcha never made a baby afore, neither."

"Don't mean she ain't practiced a bit." Simms bobbed his eyebrows suggestively. "You like practicin', sugar?"

"Now jus' wait a cotton-pickin' minute," Clayton exploded.

Amarintha convulsed with laughter and slapped the table as Caroline stared speechlessly.

"Y'all stop." Clayton scowled, fists balled on the table. "Carrie ain't used to hearin' all that. I ain't havin' y'all upsettin' her."

"Better get used to it if she gonna live here," Simms murmured.

"Ain't made o' china," Amarintha added.

The rowdy siblings settled down, but the certainty Caroline had held about adjusting to Clayton's lifestyle was melting like so much lard in a hot skillet. *I'm gonna spend my life with these people? How will my child have any sort of decent upbringin' while livin' around these... crass, simply awful folks?*

Her lungs constricted as if they had just been swallowed by an enormous black serpent now coiled up in her chest cavity. She was still struggling to breathe when Amarintha patted her shoulder.

"Come on and help me clean up, sugar."

Nodding, Caroline tottered to her feet. She took the soapy dishes that Amarintha handed her and dipped them into a tub of clean water before setting them on cloths to dry. Her breaths came more easily by the time she went to put away leftovers, but then she stopped in bewilderment, perlou dish in hand. She glanced around for an icebox, knowing there wasn't a detached kitchen. When she noticed Amarintha eyeing her, she tried to swallow the lump in her throat and asked weakly, "What do I do with the leftovers?"

"Over derr's da slop bucket. We'll give it to da hogs in da mornin'. Just keep it covered up real good." Amarintha gestured at a wooden bucket near her feet with a board lying over the top. As Caroline continued to stand there uncertainly, Amarintha amended, "'Lessen you wanna eat some more in a little while. Den you can just leave 'em where dey is. Jus' put a towel over dem, but ain't no problem. You gotta eat healthy for da young'un. We gonna feed you 'fore we feed doze hogs, dat's for sure." She smiled kindly.

Caroline nodded, trying not to show how unsettled she felt. "I didn't even know y'all had hogs."

"Out past the field, in a fenced-in area of the woods," Clayton replied.

"Ain't nothin' to worry 'bout," crooned Amarintha, finally picking up on Caroline's anxiety. "Here, let's jus' sit down and relax."

As they sat with the men again, Amarintha lit her corncob pipe and offered Caroline a smoke, saying it would relax her. When Caroline declined, Amarintha shrugged. Soon she and Simms were filling the room with noxious clouds. When Caroline began to cough, Amarintha said congenially, "You'll get used to it, sugar. Never you mind."

Clayton glowered at her as Caroline continued hacking. Finally, he suggested they take a walk.

She gratefully accepted, stumbling out of the cottage after him, past the chicken coop and towards the shed. There, she inhaled the stable air as if it were a sea breeze. Meanwhile, she gazed at Julep, trying to settle her mind. More beautiful than ever in this humble setting, he seemed to still be thriving. *Just as we will thrive,* thought Caroline, as if willing would make it so.

Clayton stood tall and strong next to her. Comforted by his presence, she knew her world would somehow be bearable so long as he was with her.

And so the months passed. The slight bulge quickly grew to greater proportions, and Caroline learned to prepare Amarintha's country meals. She was grateful that the older woman remained patient with her, even though she was half-convinced that her mother-in-law purposely held back from correcting her just so she could have a few good cackles at her expense. To Caroline's relief, however, it seemed that the woman's foul mouth was at its worse when Simms was around, which turned out to be not all that often.

Clayton never lost the uncanny ability to make everything seem bearable, consistently showing his affection and brushing aside her faults. Fascinated by her ever-growing abdomen, he pressed his ear to it at night, listening for sounds of the child's heartbeat and laughing at every kick.

His first small trip into Greeleyville had gone far towards making her world a bit better. She'd asked him to pick up a small container of milk, but he came home with four glass quarts of milk instead. She burst into tears at the sight.

"What's the matter?" He instantly took her into his arms.

"The milk." Caroline waved a hand at it, unable to stop sniffling. "We can't drink it all before it spoils."

"Ain't you had clabbered milk before?"

Caroline buried her face in his shoulder. "No, and I don't want spoilt milk."

He laughed and patted her back. "Well, then, we can just stick it in the well. That'll keep it for a while. Longer if we make butter or cheese."

She stepped back and wiped her eyes. "The well?"

"Sure." He shrugged. "Ain't as good as an icebox, but it helps."

Caroline stared at him, eyes shining. "The well," she repeated. "I didn't think of that."

From then on, she eagerly anticipated his town trips, enjoying a few days of milk each time. Being large with child, she didn't travel into town herself or ever ride Julep these days, but the farmhouse kept her more than busy as she learned how to clean and cook; meanwhile, as Spring approached, Clayton was occupied with the outdoor work—breaking the earth and planting early peas.

Despite her relative contentment, she missed her family and friends, especially her work with Anne. Sighing, she looked down at the maternity dress she'd stitched from a bolt of blue cotton cloth with which Clayton had surprised her. She hadn't yet worn more than a single cotton petticoat underneath it. *I wouldn't even be wearin' a corset now if Anne hadn't ordered this maternity one for me while I was still in Kingstree.* She slid her hand over the supportive material, grateful for its removable panels and the adjustable cups for nursing. The rest of her clothing wouldn't be so easy to modify. She was dreading the number of alterations she'd have to make to her shifts, blouses, nightgowns, and dresses in preparation for breastfeeding her child. Just a few short weeks ago she'd been working for a fashion designer, and now fashion was the furthest thing from her mind.

Despite these gloomy thoughts, Caroline was comforted by Amarintha's reaction to the simple, button-down maternity dress. She had chortled, "You sure can sew. My ole eyes are only good fer makin' out yarn now, so you can take all da mendin' from now on."

Caroline for once had been excited at the notion of adding a duty, relieved that she was fully equipped to handle at least one household task already. Even though she couldn't sew basic garments at but a fraction of the rate she had on the machines, special touches and tailoring generally took not much longer by hand. Perhaps she could preserve the looks of her clothing, after all.

When Caroline finally sat down to write her parents and siblings, she realized just how much she missed John. He had been the one to write their parents about her wedding to Clayton, and now she wished he could be the one to tell them about the impending child. She eyed her letter unhappily. She hadn't mentioned a due date, but they would eventually guess that she'd conceived well before the wedding.

To her sister Vivian, Caroline penned another letter, including a hopeful note that she would relish any old dime novels more than ever, as she had neither spare pocket money nor convenient access to bookstands. Clayton, while ever attentive and vigilant to her needs, was none the wiser regarding her quiet craving for reading materials, and she hated to ask for more than he already worked day and night to provide.

Most of her time was consumed by the domestic responsibilities of the farm, anyhow. She struggled with unpleasant chores she had never before expected to do—nor been expected to do—but she tried to keep a can-do attitude as she scrubbed the table and swept floors, pumped water and washed dishes.

The worst chore by far was the weekly laundry. She had been braced for cleaning the woodstove and even for emptying the nightly chamberpots—pisspots, as Amarintha called them. After all, neither Ettie nor Molly had worked in the cottage. But Caroline had never washed laundry before—not beyond her undergarments. She didn't mind inspecting the clothes for stains or tears, sprinkling washing soda in the tub, and putting the clothes in to soak after they had their baths on Saturday evening. That was almost a pleasure.

She dreaded Mondays, though. Draining the tub and then hauling heated water to the washtub outside were difficult and exhausting. She wondered that the others expected her to lift so much while she was pregnant, but she supposed most rural farm wives did the same. In this way, entire Mondays were consumed with worry about upsetting her pregnancy as she toted heavy pots, churned the clothes, and scrubbed spots out.

The tasks were endless, and at night Caroline would collapse, huge and exhausted, into their moss-filled bed—a bed she had recently convinced Clayton they should re-stuff with cotton at the next harvest. She struggled to maintain a cheerful countenance. After all, Clayton did his painstaking best to keep her happy and contented. He worked from sun-up to sundown, openhandedly spent his time and earnings to support them. He produced tangible reminders of his commitment, such as the simple cradle he had built and sanded so carefully, ensuring an absolutely smooth finish for the infant's delicate skin. As the birth approached, she felt overwhelming gratitude for Clayton's steadfast devotion to her and the growing child.

30• Pie-in-the-Sky Offer

WEARING AN ELEGANT INDIGO EVENING GOWN of her own creation, Anne posed nervously, forcing her hands down by her sides as the photographers flashed their cameras.

"What can we expect from you next?"

"What inspired you to add a Watteau sash to the wedding dress?"

"Did you make the dress you're wearin'?"

Before her eyes could clearly make out the reporters, she found herself responding to their slew of questions as well as she could, unsure to whom she was addressing her remarks. She felt like a fraud, truly a shy, small-town girl only pretending to be a sophisticated designer.

After she'd been pummeled with questions for several excruciating minutes, a resonant, smooth masculine voice rang out, "No more questions for now. Miss Brighton requires a break. Thank you for your understanding." The gentleman placed his hand on her elbow and gently guided her away from the mob towards a small bistro table in the rear corner of the room, behind a stained-glass partition offering a semblance of seclusion. Anne sank gratefully onto a red-velvet, cushioned chair.

The polished stranger cast a charming smile, displaying an array of dazzling white teeth. "Miss Brighton, it is a pleasure to meet you. My name is Raymond Bryan, co-owner of Bryan Fashions." Fishing a silver case from his suit pocket, he opened it and handed her his card. "We are the primary sponsors of this gala event tonight. Can I get you a drink?"

Nodding, Anne was relieved that he didn't ask her to name a specific beverage. Mr. Sanders had blithely assured her that she 'would be just fine' if she bluffed her way through these society events, but he gave her no real guidelines, and she had determined by now that she would remain perpetually awkward. Even so, she basked in the praise heaped upon her during after-show receptions.

They'd already completed a whirlwind fashion tour of five cities when Mr. Sanders informed her at their last hotel that he'd just received a telephone call from his associates requiring her presence in Atlanta, even though her itinerary had not originally included this city. She had dreaded yet another stop, but she was being touted as the fresh, requisite design talent and could hardly resent being the toast of society.

Swiftly returning with two gin cocktails, Raymond gracefully took the seat opposite her. He took off his top hat and placed it on the chair next to him. "I am delighted to finally have the opportunity to speak with you, Miss Brighton. Your designs are impressive. May I ask where you studied?"

Nervously sipping her cocktail, she crossed her ankles before replying, "I've always been interested in fashion, Mr. Bryan, but I can't claim any formal trainin'."

"Come now. You had to have learned it somewhere," he insisted.

"Well, I may have been a bit obsessed with the pattern books that came through Mr. Sanders' sewin' plant in Kingstree. I'd take them home with me at night."

His jaw dropped. Gold fillings on his back teeth winked at her.

She blanched but continued, "And I learned sewin' from my mother and to embroider from my grandmother."

I should be able to do better than that, Anne thought desperately, regarding his gobsmacked expression. *Perhaps a little bluffin' really is in order next time someone asks.* She smiled uneasily and shrugged. "They were quite talented."

Raymond blinked and glanced around the room, gathering himself. He wasn't a man who often found himself at a loss for words, and his spiel wasn't affected by what she just told him, after all. "Well, however that may be, you have a superbly innovative and sophisticated sense of fashion which, I must admit, is a tremendous relief after that neverending, oh-so-conventional Gibson-girl phenomenon."

Pausing a moment for her reply, he settled for her half-nod of acknowledgment and a murmured, "No, I suppose that's not exactly my style."

"Indeed it's not. Your elegant lines are haute cuisine next to such common fare as that dreamt up by Charles Dana Gibson and his copycats. It's high time we move away from overdone pompadours and exaggerated curves." Leaning forward intently, Raymond met her eyes. "I'll come straight to the point, Miss Brighton. Your designs are precisely in sync with the styles of Bryan Fashions, with where our company is headed. We think you would be an asset to our company, and we are prepared to offer you a permanent position as a Bryan designer here in Atlanta. You would produce creations for international fashion shows and patterns for the latest trends in ready-made dresses. We're prepared to offer you a full-time designer's salary of two thousand dollars annually plus our company's carriages and drivers available on demand."

She nearly dropped her glass. "I… I do have a contract."

Shaking his head, he continued dismissively, "I won't take no for an answer. We insist that you join us, and we'll pay the penalties for the broken contract. We'd like for you to start next week. Your household furnishings can be shipped here at our expense. We'll set you up on a company tab at the Peachtree Hotel until you've found other accommodations."

Uncertainly, she explained, "Mr. Bryan, this is so far from my home. I'm not sure I'm ready to make that kind of move. I'll need to think on it."

With an impressed smile, he put up a palm. "Alright, Miss Brighton, we'll raise it to twenty-four hundred if that's what it takes. I can't imagine that you're going to find a better offer anywhere else."

"Mr. Bryan! I'm not bargainin' here, truly. It's just… such a surprise. I haven't considered this yet."

Leaning in more closely, he confided, "I realize you're new in this industry, but you must understand that to reach the pinnacle of your profession, you really are going to have to join a top-notch design company in a major metropolitan area. I'm sure you know ours is one of the five largest fashion companies in the nation."

Anne absorbed his words. A top-notch designer. A few months ago, she had not the slightest notion of working professionally as a fashion designer. Now, gilt-edged success was being handed to her, but Anne still felt uncomfortably as though she were being manipulated—a sensation not helped by her inexperience.

Trying to exude confidence, Anne drew in a deep breath. She would bluff, per Mr. Sanders' orders. Waving a hand airily, she said, "I appreciate the offer, Mr. Bryan. I should be in town until next Friday, so I will think on this over the next few days. Perhaps I can visit your offices tomorrow?"

Sighing, he replied with resignation, "Very well, Miss Brighton. Our driver will pick you up at ten o'clock if that works for you." He stood and reached to shake her hand. "It has been a pleasure meeting you, and I look forward to seeing you tomorrow."

"Goodnight, Mr. Bryan."

The next morning, Anne joined Mr. Sanders for breakfast in the hotel restaurant. It was decorated in shades of blue. Even the boy in the corner, who was playing popular tunes on a phonograph, wore a blue-striped suit; his hair was parted straight in the middle, slicked down on either side, and he was taking requests, efficiently changing wax cylinders after each song. Navy tablecloths were bedecked with daisies in white vases, fresh pineapple juice in small glasses, and sunny-side-up eggs that, taken altogether, made the tables seem to glow like constellations scattered throughout the room.

When the 'Laughing Song' came on the player, Anne smiled and told Mr. Sanders about the offer she had received.

He scowled. "But obviously you won't accept."

"You don't think I should?" Anne sipped on Java coffee and pierced slices of banana onto her fork, still marveling at the year-round tropical fruit imports of the bigger cities.

"Of course not. You are already doing quite well with us. You wouldn't want to break your contract or join that high-paced, fast lifestyle. This is a pie-in-the-sky type of offer. Best stay with us. You're already a success. Sellin' your patterns individually to Bryan amongst other companies is workin' out beautifully."

Anne stared at his lapel as 'A Bird in a Gilded Cage' began to play. She was just beginning to recognize surprising new threads of resentment towards Mr. Sanders.

Soon after breakfast, Anne was promptly delivered to the stately, colonnaded headquarters of Bryan Fashions. Beatrice, a sophisticated young designer in a smartly-tailored two-piece dress, met Anne, explaining that Mr. Bryan was preoccupied with business and wouldn't be meeting with her. Then she led Anne on a tour of the six-story building, including numerous trips on the creaky elevator—an experience that always gave Anne gooseflesh, no matter how safe they assured her all the mechanical groans were.

Early in the tour, she was paraded through the future location of her own private office on the fourth floor, as if her acceptance were a foregone conclusion. Large windows revealed a breathtaking view of the Atlanta skyline. She'd never had a view that extended so far; the tips of buildings fanned across the city, touching the clouds—almost unreal, like a child's paper cutouts and cottonballs had been stuck to the windows.

The bright, spacious office was across the hall from workrooms where entire teams of assistants were busy carrying out the designers' instructions. In nearby offices, future colleagues were in various stages of completion with their creations.

Her neighbor Herbert had drawings strewn about his floor; as soon as he spotted Beatrice, he begged in a high, lispy voice to hear which designs they preferred for a gala event, and in which colors. The women tiptoed precariously between sketches in order to see them all. Anne bit her lip to keep from giggling with excitement as she selected her favorite, a racy, bare-shouldered scarlet gown meant to go with a white feather boa. She instantly sobered when Herbert gasped and pointed to the heel of Beatrice's boot on one of his colorful drawings. "You brute! Get off my designs."

"Get off my back," Beatrice retorted, hopping forward as Anne picked up the crinkled paper and tried to rub off the indelible mark.

"His own fault." Beatrice pushed Anne towards the door, sticking out a playful tongue at Herbert and saying a little too loudly, "Herbert thinks he's a bigshot, that nothin' should ever happen to him, but he'll be okay." Dropping her voice, she added, "He's pretty swell, actually."

"You're going to redraw this for me," he called after them, waving the paper.

Another designer had so many bolts of cloth propped in the hallway that they had to clamber over them. "It's Marion," Beatrice explained. "He always does this. Says he needs to see the material to know how it will drape, though why he needs them all helter-skelter in our way, I just don't know."

Anne's excitement escalated to even greater heights when they reached the small-scale production rooms full of completed designs and a runway. With starry eyes and light feet, she followed Beatrice back to the elevator and down to the street, only realizing the tour was over after they stepped into a nearby restaurant, where they were led to a table. To Anne's elation, the waiters in tails didn't seem in the least fazed by their lack of male escorts. While they were eating, Beatrice attested with wide-eyed sincerity to the critical importance of working for a magnate such as Raymond Bryan in order to achieve true career success in the fashion industry. Then she enthusiastically related her own transition from small-town life to the global world of fashion, albeit with a period of study in Paris in between. As they returned to the offices, she leaned close to Anne's ear and whispered,

"Between you and me, you'd have to be off your trolley not to take the job."

By the time Anne arrived back at the hotel, her head was whirling somewhere amongst the Atlanta skyline's clouds, and she was buoyantly convinced of her new destiny. At supper, Anne resolutely informed Mr. Sanders that she was going to take the position with Bryan Fashions.

"Don't be a fool." Frowning, he dipped a sliver of asparagus loaf into a creamy béchamel sauce. "I suppose they turned your head with talk of Raymond Bryan's wealth. Mind you, those are *his* riches, and that's how he wants it to stay."

"Actually, he's made an impressive offer and is prepared to pay you handsomely for the broken contract," she countered. "I'd be a fool to walk away from such an opportunity."

"You can't go," he said simply, spreading out his palms. "We have plans. I won't give you up."

Anne sipped her red wine, savoring the flavor before saying, "I don't believe it's your decision."

"Well, it's your own damn funeral!" sputtered a red-faced Mr. Sanders, throwing down his napkin and leaving her to finish her meal alone.

The following morning, Anne dressed smartly, noting on her agenda to order a pattern for a two-pieced tailored suit. As she buttoned her kitten-heel boots, she recollected Mr. Sanders' angry face, and her jaw set. She was all-too-eager to accept Mr. Bryan's offer.

Shouldn't I feel guilty about not stayin' loyal to Mr. Sanders? He did get me started, after all. I owe all of this to him.

Her stomach twisted as she realized that she was accepting the offer in part to spite him, though he had only brought her success and wonderful new experiences. Her shoulders stiffened. *I am grateful, but he doesn't own me.*

At breakfast, both she and Mr. Sanders were tight-lipped and terse, despite the tropical fruits and sunny table. As they rose to leave, he asked, "Have you absolutely decided to accept their offer?"

"Yes, sir. I'm headed there now."

"I'm disappointed, Miss Brighton."

Good, she thought to her own dismay, but she only said, "I understand. Have a good day, Mr. Sanders."

With a tight feeling in his chest, he watched her stride away. He had pinned so many hopes and dreams on Anne, and she was just walking away with them. He sank slowly back into his seat, an emergent, surprising sense of desperation rising to the base of his throat and settling there like glue.

It made little sense. After all, he'd seen designers come and go for years and kept a vigilant eye for new ones. Whenever he lost a particularly-talented designer, he'd shrug and consider himself well-placated with broken-contract fees, from which a substantial portion of his wealth had been derived. He even sometimes referred to himself as a head hunter for the entire fashion industry, designing contracts for this very inevitability.

Mr. Sanders had never felt this way about losing a designer before. He had great plans for Anne, and this time he wanted the designer for himself. Struck by the realization, he considered more slowly, *I want her for myself.* Caroline's startling words, *If she married you, there wouldn't be a problem,* sprang to mind. He had mused over the statement many times but had never dreamt of following through on it.

Mr. Sanders drummed his fingers, his pragmatic mind racing. *If I propose to Anne, she'll stay with me. With my company.* In a moment, he'd gathered his sack coat and dashed out of the restaurant lobby, hailing a cabbie to transport him to Bryan Fashions.

Arriving just as Anne approached the imposing double front doors with a little more jaunt to her step than was usual, Mr. Sanders called to her from his carriage window. "Miss Brighton! Wait, Anne!"

At the sound of her name, she turned to see him stumble out of the cab. His top hat fell into the gutter unheeded. She watched with astonishment as he shoved money at the driver and hurried towards her.

Out of breath, he gasped, "Marry me."

"What did you say?" Anne put a hand to her throat.

"Marry me, Miss Brighton. Don't take this position."

A cool breeze tickled her neck. "Am I to understand that you are proposin' marriage to me?"

He nodded.

"So I won't go to work for Bryan Fashions?" she asked incredulously.

Flustered, he touched his head as if finally missing his hat. "Well, yes."

Glowering, she waved a hand at his head. "You must have bats in your belfry. Good day to you, sir."

His stomach quivered like aspic as she pivoted on her heel and began to march again towards the front door. "Wait! Stop, Anne!"

She turned, angry determination written across her face. "I have had enough, Mr. Sanders. If my life is to be about my career, then I'm gonna focus on my career. I certainly will not marry you simply so that you can deprive me of this position."

Mr. Sanders shook his head, murmuring, "No, that's not…" Realizing he would have to try harder to be persuasive, he gazed at her earnestly. "Do you realize that I don't eat, sleep, or breathe without thinkin' about you? I have been gloryin' in our days together, and I've been content for the first time since… since Eleanor died. I can't bear the thought of losin' you."

A confounding rush of elation made her dizzy. Still, she shook her head. "Dress designs are one thing, Mr. Sanders. Marriage is somethin' entirely different."

His earnest face broke into a smile. "Oh, but it wouldn't be so different for us. You thrive on this. We could spend our lives together, focused on our designs."

With dismay, she replied, "But what about love? What about children?"

"Do you doubt I love you? I adore you."

Again, she asked dubiously, "What about children?"

Mr. Sanders waved a dismissive hand. "We'll hire nannies to travel with us, if we must."

Anne stood warily, searching vainly for crucial questions, but logic seemed to evade her. She could only remember the hopes and dreams that she'd held so long. Her new opportunity for career advancement paled to nothing as he stood before her, waiting hopefully. Her face creased with annoyance at the mercurial nature of her own decisions as she said impatiently, "Oh, alright, Mr. Sanders. I'll marry you."

"Very good, my dear Miss Brighton." At this, Mr. Sanders breathed a sigh of relief and offered Anne his arm. "Let's go back to the hotel now, why don't we?"

Anne tutted at the pleased expression on Mr. Sanders' face—it was one he often wore after a successful business transaction. Still, she smiled, marveling at their interlinked arms, at the entwined future they had just agreed to.

When they reached the hotel, Mr. Sanders bid her a good day and kissed her cheek awkwardly. Once securely within her room, Anne sighed with a strange relief and settled onto the chaise lounge. She closed her eyes and attempted to envision a wedding, from elegant clothing to exchanges of wedding vows, but paused at the unbidden thought, *What on earth is Mr. Sanders' given name?*

31• The Birth

CAROLINE WOKE WITH A CINCHING SENSATION around her vast middle, as if she were going to be sick. Minutes later, more abdominal muscles tightened in unison. Her breath rushed out as if squeezed by bellows.

She reached across the quilt to wake Clayton, touching his shoulder and shaking him gently.

"Honey, I think it's time," she whispered, her voice catching.

He blinked and gazed at her dazedly.

"Clay, wake up. My labor has started."

Bolting upright from the bed, he quickly dressed. "What do you need?"

As the squeeze died down, Caroline laughed, "Well, a midwife, for one thing."

"Let me get Mama."

Moments later, Amarintha entered the bedroom and felt Caroline's abdomen, her touch brusque but efficient. She pressed her ear against Caroline's stomach and listened for the baby's heartbeat. Patting her arm, she reassured the young woman, "Don't you worry none. I done helped birth lots o' babies. You in good hands. I heard dat Dr. Davis don't know nothin' 'bout birthin', an' I wouldn't count on him fer deliverin' my sow's babies. "

Amarintha felt the baby's position once more. "Dat baby's head is down where it's s'posed to be." She cast a keen eye at Caroline. "Still, dis is most likely gonna take a long time, girl. You oughta come eat somethin' and walk 'round 'tween doze pains."

Through that morning and afternoon, the contractions began to arrive more and more frequently, gradually increasing in severity. Throughout, Amarintha brought Caroline drinks of water and bites of food, insisting that she needed to keep up her energy.

After several hours, Amarintha suggested, "Now, honey, let's see if dat baby's comin' out soon."

Making her way to the bedroom, Caroline laid back. As Amarintha peered between her legs, Caroline closed her eyes, not as mortified as she would have expected. The overwhelming urge to give birth to her child was all-consuming, and her reservations fell aside like so many cornhusks.

"You 'bout ready. When you feel dat baby comin', you jus' push!" Amarintha crowed.

Caroline heard Amarintha as if from a distance, the intensity of a new contraction was so great, so consuming. When she began to sob, Amarintha held her hand and commanded, "Look at me, sugar. One, two, three..." She counted through Caroline's moans until they quieted, and somehow the distraction helped. When Amarintha left to relieve herself, Caroline's moans escalated to hysterical cries, and Amarintha rushed back, saying, "I ain't gotta go dat bad."

At last, Caroline began to nod off between contractions, which eventually came to a standstill. She lay dozing, her brow slick with sweat.

Amarintha nodded with satisfaction at the labor's progress. Soothingly, she murmured, "Soon, real soon," before finally slipping away to the outhouse.

She was back twenty minutes later when an excruciating contraction woke Caroline—not just a squeeze, but her body's unified effort to expel the baby. The pushing continued through several contractions, until Amarintha's worried face puckered. "Dis baby's a stubborn one," she muttered.

After another twenty minutes, Amarintha said to a barely cognizant Caroline, "I gonna send for dat Dr. Davis, Carrie. Dis baby don't wanna come out."

Caroline woke in sudden lucidity and clutched Amarintha's hand. "No, not Dr. Davis... get Dr. Thomas."

Amarintha furrowed her brow and muttered, "Root doctor or know-nothin' city doctor. Guess it don't much matter." She hobbled to the door of the cottage and sent Clayton for Dr. Thomas, telling him, "You need to fly on dat fancy horse o' yours."

Heart in throat, Clayton was thankful for the thoroughbred as he hastily saddled Julep and set off at full gallop in the direction of Kingstree.

Hurrying back to Caroline, Amarintha urged, "Now, girl, dis baby thinks it's more hard-headed dan you. You gotta push."

Caroline felt no control over her body's independent will to expel the baby. The contractions were more powerful than anything she'd ever experienced or could imagine willing, regardless of Amarintha's directive. They continued agonizingly for the next couple of hours, convincing her that Stephen's baby was ripping her body apart. She would fall unconscious, only to be awakened time and again by her own unbridled screams at the tearing pains.

Dr. Thomas, a surprisingly youthful mulatto man, arrived with his box of tinctures only minutes before the baby emerged. Clayton had given him the thoroughbred to ride and was following as quickly as possible on Dr. Thomas's own mount.

Amarintha lifted the baby and placed it on the spent mother, occupied with tending to the blood that gushed freely from the birth canal. She pressed handcloths firmly against the cavity, attempting to staunch the flow as Dr. Thomas mixed blue cohosh and shepherd's purse tinctures, administering dropperfuls into Caroline's mouth, commanding her to "Swallow!"

She gulped the bitter concoction without thought as the room flickered and faded around her. Within moments, she drifted away.

Meanwhile, Clayton let himself into the room. Amarintha ordered him to stand back as she released pressure and deftly delivered the placenta.

Dr. Thomas shook his head at the growing pool of blood between Caroline's legs. He woke her up enough to give her another dose of the hemostatic herbs, then helped to apply pressure to stop the hemorrhaging.

Clayton fretted in the corner, consumed by helplessness as Caroline lay there, no longer fully conscious, in a stupor from blood loss and pain. Blood drenched the sheets and almost completely coated both Amarintha and the baby lying on Caroline's chest.

After a couple of heart-stopping minutes, Amarintha looked up. "She ain't bleedin' no more. I ain't never seen so much blood."

Dr. Thomas grasped Caroline's wrist. After a moment, he said, "Her pulse is weak, but there."

Lifting the cyanotic infant, Amarintha presented her to Clayton. "You got yo'self a baby girl!"

Clayton blinked, watching the blood-streaked, bluish newborn wave about in front of him. "Is she breathin'?" he gasped.

Amarintha folded the baby into a blanket and began to vigorously rub with her gnarled hands. The infant's skin turned pink, and a small wail arose from her. Amarintha turned triumphantly to Clayton. "Yessir, she is!"

32• Meeting Vivian

CAROLINE GAZED DOWN AT THE INFANT nursing in her arms. The baby smelled sweetly of breastmilk and was cushioned in a cream-colored cotton baby blanket knitted by Amarintha. "Hello, little Vivian," she cooed.

The name held a new appreciation for her now that she'd developed the habit of repeating it aloud, emphasizing each syllable with a gentle touch to the tiny nose. Caroline glanced gratefully at the crate of books that her sister Vivian had recently sent. She would have plenty to read while holding and rocking the baby during the long months ahead.

She still felt weak from the birth, but every day was an improvement. Clayton would spend hours holding and carrying Vivian, allowing Caroline time to take care of personal needs and a few household tasks. Amarintha had resumed most of the chores, to Caroline's infinite gratitude—she felt blessed to be allowed to rest with her baby throughout the days. Vivian woke every hour or two to nurse, and Caroline lightly dozed with her through half the day, never sleeping deeply except on those occasions when Clayton or Amarintha would take the infant for a spell.

Clayton was as in love with their daughter as she was. He would frequently take a break from his outdoor work just to come and peek at his little girl. Her fair, delicate skin was as soft as rose petals, and he feared his rough hands would scratch her. A bit of dark fuzz served for her hair, and her blue eyes shone like the surface of a lake.

After two months, Caroline felt almost fully recovered from the birth, and she resumed her long, frequent rides on Julep for the first time since she had brought him to stay on the farm. Her affection for the horse was now gilded by Clayton's insistence that Julep had saved her life as she had once saved his. She would brush Julep's flanks and murmur, "Evened-up, hmm?" as though it were a joke between them.

Stephen had left for the Philippines only a year ago, but so much had changed. She had been through grieving, pregnancy, marriage, a traumatic birth, and a period of recuperation. She thought of Stephen often, but the warmth and joy she took in her marriage and family were constant validation of the decision she had made to be with Clayton.

Life was full, and the months passed quickly. On their quiet farm, they heard little from the outside. Only the most shocking news made its way to them, such as the assassination of President McKinley in far-off New York and his replacement by Teddy Roosevelt, now the youngest American president ever. Instead, their attentions dwelt on each other and on Vivian, who was growing to be a delightful and engaging baby, securely beloved in her own little world.

Mary and John came twice to see them, bearing all manner of practical supplies such as paper, ink, and soaps from town; on both occasions, Clayton took his mother and Julep to Simms' house until the guests were gone. They brought news and shared stories of the family—Lenora had decided to prepare for teaching exams, and Eli had left their parents' home after all, not for the Klondike but in hopes of staking a homestead claim in Oklahoma.

At last, Anne came to visit, bringing baby outfits in different sizes that she had been buying on her tours. Children were not her area of expertise, so she had prepared thoroughly.

With six-month-old Vivian perched on her lap, Caroline gaped at the array of clothes. "Why, Anna, you've brought enough clothes for all the tots in Greeleyville combined. She's gonna outgrow half o' these before she has a chance to wear them. And we live in the middle of nowhere—no one is gonna see these gorgeous frocks."

"Listen at you, when those little pleats she has on are as adorable as anythin' I've brought with me. But I hope you like 'em. I wasn't sure what she would need, so I included lots o' different sizes. The world of children's apparel is a different creature entirely." Anne sighed, smiling as she mused, "Besides, we should dress for our own pleasure. Every little girl wants to be a princess and have fancy clothes, whether or not she needs them."

"If you say so…" Caroline looked skeptically at Vivian, who was at that moment leaning from her arms in an attempt to mouth the strap of Anne's tote bag. The tea kettle began to whistle, and Caroline thrust the baby unceremoniously at Anne. "Here, why don't you hold the little princess for a minute?"

Anne started as the warm body was deposited in her lap. Dutifully, she folded awkward arms around Vivian, staring at her with wide eyes as if waiting for her to cry. Instead, Vivian clutched a fistful of hair—loose locks that Anne had arranged over her shoulder—and tugged with a steely grip, laughing delightedly as Anne winced. When Anne finally managed to pry the chubby fingers off of her hair, the baby grabbed her lower lip and promptly clamped her own mouth to it, sucking with such vigor that Anne made a guttural sound of alarm.

Caroline rushed back, inserting a finger at the corner of Vivian's mouth to break her seal. "Vivian! Stop that! You're gonna scare Aunt Anna off, and look how long it already took her to come see us." Caroline continued to scold as she perched the squirming infant on one hip and used the opposite hand to serve the tea, held at arms-length to avoid the child's reach.

Soon enough, Anne felt more at ease with the mischievous baby. Before long, Anne was competently wresting hair tendrils from her daunting grip and playing peek-a-boo with her.

Later, Anne listened with fascination and horror as Caroline described the birth at length. Then Anne shared the details of her engagement, cautioning that her career was so consuming that they were planning to wait for some time before having the wedding itself. She wanted to make her own gown, but there were two seasons of designs to create first. Then, of course, there would be tours of the accompanying shows.

Caroline laughed. "So you jus' don't have time to get married—too much of a hassle to bother with right now?"

"I just want it to be absolutely perfect," Anne assured her.

Shaking her head in wonder, Caroline hugged her friend, again admiring the successful, professional woman Anne had become.

During Anne's visit to the farm, Caroline eagerly demonstrated the simplicity of their daily life—sure that Anne would consider it as novel as she had. At first, she stuck with more pleasant activities, such as gathering eggs and walking through the fields to hand-select summer squash for supper.

Within a couple of days, however, Anne was changing diapers and burping Vivian despite her protests that she preferred to change the baby's outfits and rock her to sleep. She teased, "I'd better go now, before you have me scourin' floors and scrubbin' clothes!"

Not until Clayton brought his mother back from Simms' house, however, did Anne realize it was truly time to depart. Sufficiently warned about Amarintha's mouth, she at first tried to keep up a smile through the anticipated inappropriate remarks. She managed well enough that when Clayton and Caroline rebuked the older woman, Amarintha just laughed, "She ain't da one havin' a conniption fit, now is she?"

Anne might have been able to tolerate the woman's behavior better if Vivian had not been present, but she cringed each time the baby's snaggle-toothed grandmother held her.

Despite the crass woman, Anne grudgingly admitted that what mattered most to Caroline was not her surroundings, but intangibles such as Vivian's smile and Clayton's warm attentions. Even Amarintha seemed to have found a niche in her affections. Anne could see that Caroline was content with this simple life.

When Anne finally bid them farewell and drove her handsome carriage away from the happy family and farm, she wistfully recognized a vague emptiness about her own life, as though her priorities were topsy-turvy.

At the thought, Anne looked down at her fine linen dress and smart carriage then shook her head at her own folly. *I can have fine things and a wonderful marriage and children, soon enough.* As bucolic as Caroline's country life might seem, Anne knew that her own well-thought-out path suited her best.

Vivian's first word was 'Da-da', which prompted Clayton to hop with joy. She quickly learned to walk and soon expanded her vocabulary. Before long she was a busy toddler with her hands into everything.

Even with all eyes upon her, she managed to escape detection at times, thinking it a clever game to hide from her caregivers. At first she would just pull the woven mat from the kitchen floor over her head and delight at Caroline's pretend, "Where is Vivian? Where did she go?" The game quickly escalated, however, and soon a more anxious Caroline was finding the impenitent child behind chairs and under beds.

Once when Vivian was two years old, she disappeared while Caroline was hanging linens on the line to dry. Caroline searched the coop, the house, and the shed. After a while she became so frantic that Clayton and Amarintha joined in the hunt. Panic mounted until at last Clayton spied her under the house. She was stroking the black-and-white tomcat, Pepper, and humming to herself, seemingly oblivious to the shouts of the worried adults.

Repeat scoldings only served to validate Vivian's delight at the prank, especially since they all-too-often laughed with exasperation when they found her. On the rare occasions when they didn't seek her out, she would inevitably show herself or call for mama when she tired of the trick, but Caroline sighed with frustration at the girl's incorrigible game, wondering how she was going to manage Vivian now that she was expecting her second child.

Caroline was once more in her maternity corset by the time she took a trip into Kingstree with Vivian. The two of them bundled up and joined Clayton as he took a load of produce into town to sell. Caroline was looking forward to staying with John and Mary for a few days, to seeing a play in the new theatre, and to dining at the Kingstree hotel again. Soon the trip would be too uncomfortable and risky, and she was determined to enjoy it before being overcome with the inevitable girth of this pregnancy and the subsequent all-too-familiar baby duties.

They arrived at the Swann plantation on a Wednesday afternoon, Clayton staying only long enough to say his hellos. Caroline was weary from the journey and glad when Vivian was swept into the house by Emma. The pair held hands at first. Then Emma simply picked her up, carrying her into the nursery where she eagerly showed her the dolls and toys, things Lenora had long since grown too old for.

After only a few perfunctory greetings to the family, Caroline made her way to the cottage, where John had stoked a fire in the woodstove. Reveling in the comfort and familiarity, she fell into her old bed.

"It's been ages!" sang Anne the next morning, running out to meet Caroline and her bleary-eyed little girl in front of the shop, where John had dropped the pair off, along with a couple of bushel baskets. After holding Vivian at arm's length and marveling at how she had changed, Anne gathered the child into her arms. "Sorry, Carrie. I'll hug you later."

"I understand," Caroline laughed.

"What are you doin' with those bushel baskets?"

"Last crops of the season. Winter vegetables. You've got collards, beets, and rutabagas here," Caroline swung one basket forward then stared down at the other one with a bemused expression. "This one is s'posed to be full o' canned tomatoes, but I think maybe someone filled it with bricks instead."

Anne put Vivian down to help Caroline bring in the baskets, setting them just inside the door. "Thank you for the produce and especially for the bricks. Tell Clay I appreciate it, won't you? He's quite the farmer. He still does all this and cotton?"

Caroline shrugged. "Cotton's still his main crop, but he plants a variety—'specially corn. We couldn't get by without it."

When they entered the shop, the whirr of the sewing machine ended abruptly. Fletcher stood up from her work station at the rear of the room and called out, "Well, if it ain't Carrie Corbett." Glancing at the little girl with Caroline, she chuckled and amended, "I guess it ain't! You done got married and left me all alone to help poor Anna here."

Anne laughed as she opened the new, small downstairs stove, adding wood to the incandescent ashes. "Hardly poor Anna. We have plenty of help. Don't let her give you a hard time."

Proceeding to kiss mother and daughter soundly on their cheeks, Anne took on a serious air and stood back, tapping her chin as if studying their garments. Clucking in mock disapproval, Anne failed to control an irrepressible smile as she said, "Those clothes will never do. You're in town now. I suppose you'll have to change into some of my things while you're here." At this, Anne turned to two emerald-green dresses that hung on the rack behind her. "Hmm, I s'pose these might do for you." Trying to hide her excitement, she presented the frocks.

"You have maternity dresses and children's sizes in your current collection?" Caroline's eyes grew large with appreciation.

"Oh, no. They're from my personal closet. I don't know what I was thinkin'. Preparin' for every eventuality, I reckon. You can keep them. I can't imagine when I'll be able to use them." Anne sighed and shrugged, eyes twinkling merrily.

In no time, Caroline and Vivian were outfitted in the matching attire. Caroline wore a muslin day dress with an empire waist and satin trim, while Vivian bore a dress of the same material at knee length with black cotton stockings.

"You didn't have to do this, Anna," Caroline protested, feeling overwhelmed and overdressed. "We don't need all this. Our lives are simple now."

"I'm just glad to clear some space here," Anne said, still enjoying the pretense. "Now hold still and let me finish." Once satisfied with a few minor alterations, she began to style their hair while Fletcher sewed the adjustments. Caroline's blond curls were piled in a classic upsweep, and Vivian's dark locks were soon tied back with a green ribbon. Once they were situated to her satisfaction, Anne added a final touch—she presented Caroline with a matching parasol and the picturesque child with a new stuffed bear.

"Oh, Anne, it's too much!" Caroline twirled the parasol. "Vivian, say thank you to Aunt Anna."

The girl stared at the bear and then back at Anne. "It's mine?"

"Yes, it's yours. One of those teddy bears, named after our president," Anne said warmly, her heart full. "Now, have a good day, and I want to see you ladies in these dresses when we go to the show this weekend." She followed them to the door and watched as they began their exploration of town hand-in-hand. Anne sighed and re-entered her shop, intending to diligently apply herself to finishing her current project. There was still much work to complete before the weekend, some of which had accumulated due to her preoccupation with the muslins. *It was worth it,* she mused. *As much for me as for them. I can't wait to show Carrie the newest parts of town life—in style.*

Elated with her fine wear, Caroline felt vibrant as she showed Vivian the shops, keeping a tight grip on the one free hand of her recently-turned-three-year-old. Horses and buggies rattled by, presenting more of a hazard than she'd ever realized before having a child. Not only that, but a bevy of temptations existed for a little one with a penchant for hiding—countless mysterious doors to enter and stairs ascending to unknown worlds.

Caroline's sprightly steps slowed as they passed the bakery with its aroma of warm, fresh bread. She allowed Vivian to pull her inside, and soon they were savoring a tart, crumbly lemon-poppyseed muffin. As they left the bakery, Caroline glanced wistfully at Stephen's old office. To her surprise, she noticed that Stephen's name was still displayed on the door alongside that of Dr. Davis.

Giving Vivian's hand a light squeeze, she asked, "Honey, do you wanna see a real doctor's office?"

Vivian's mouth was full as she garbled out something that sounded like, "Yes, ma'am!"

"You'll have to be quiet in there, okay?"

At Vivian's nod, Caroline split the last morsel of the muffin between them. Then she picked her up and entered the vacant office. The door bell jangled as they stepped inside. Taking a seat in the waiting room, she settled her daughter on her lap and gazed around, remembering the days when Stephen would come out of the door to the exam room looking so handsome and serious.

Within moments, the door to the exam room did open, and an elderly patient made his way out. Caroline glimpsed the white doctor's coat following him. She stood to greet Dr. Davis, but her words fell away when the physician appeared. The tall, dark-haired man who entered the room was Stephen.

Caroline sank slowly back into her seat, suddenly uncertain on her legs.

Stephen stopped in his tracks at the sight of the woman he had once planned to marry.

The door bell clanged again as the patient left, and they were alone. Feeling faint, Caroline continued to stare wordlessly. Time and space suspended once more as she absorbed his presence, drinking in the sight of his clean-shaven face and those dark eyes she had never expected to see again.

"Stephen…" A confusion of emotions welled in a flurry as she regarded him, struggling to comprehend. She whispered softly, almost inaudibly, "I didn't know you were alive."

He couldn't answer. He had paled but stood transfixed, still enmeshed in the surprise of being in her presence.

The two remained frozen, bound in their silent communication until Vivian cried, "Mama! Down!" and pushed against her mother's chest.

Only then did Stephen become aware of the child in Caroline's arms. He approached slowly, his eyes swiveling between Caroline and Vivian, a question in the furrow of his brow.

As Vivian again demanded her freedom, Caroline tightened her arms around both the squirming child and fluffy stuffed animal. She drew in a deep breath. Then, in a wavering voice, she said, "This is Vivian."

"Is she...?"

She answered him carefully, softly. "Oh, Stephen. Clay is her daddy. He's always been her daddy… but yes."

Stephen stared in awe at the beautiful child.

In a more controlled, motherly tone, Caroline prompted, "Sweetie, this is Dr. Connor. Can you say hello?"

The girl looked up at him and then burrowed her face in her mother's shoulder.

At last Stephen's trance was broken. He smiled slowly. In a tender, husky voice, he said, "It's so nice to meet you, Vivian. I like your bear."

Caroline noticed that Stephen's eyes were sadder, more thoughtful. New lines creased his brow. Her heart ached anew, her old grief awakening and morphing into guilt. The thought of his suffering, that he could not raise his own child, caused her throat to close, her chest to constrict. Painfully, she managed to say, "I'd like for us to talk. Perhaps we can meet at the plantation? I'm stayin' in the old tabby cottage with Vivian."

He nodded, finding it difficult to speak.

"This evenin', then? Would you come by after supper?" As she spoke, her eyes begged for his understanding and forgiveness.

Just then the office door opened, and a large family marched in. Stephen gave a quick, confirmatory nod before turning to greet them.

Dazedly, Caroline carried Vivian from the office, an ache of regret and anticipation consuming her heart.

After supper, Caroline took Vivian through her nighttime routine and put her to bed a little earlier than usual. While tucking her in, she discovered a children's book placed conveniently next to the bed. With gratitude and delight, she read aloud the tale, written by a Miss Beatrix Potter. Vivian nodded off at just about the point where Peter Rabbit finished his chamomile tea and grew sleepy, but

Caroline continued reading the story until a knock sounded at the door. She folded the book closed and took a deep breath. *Stephen is here.*

When she ushered him into the cottage and invited him to have a seat, he greeted her in a halting, low tone. "Hey, Carrie. Hope you're doin' well."

Her heart took no time at all about lodging itself into her throat. She choked out, "Yes, I'm well. I… I can't imagine what you've been through these past couple of years."

"It all seems a bit like a dream," he admitted as he sat on the loveseat. "I'm honestly not sure if this is the dream or if that hell in the Phillipines was just an unrelentin' nightmare." He shook his head. "But it got better after Taft became governor. Taft and Chaffee weren't so bad."

Tears pricked her eyes at the hollow tone of his voice. She sat down and turned to face him, confessing, "I thought you were dead. Mary didn't think so, but I felt so sure, and we thought we saw your name on the casualty list. But it wasn't your name, obviously. I don't understand why I was so sure…"

Stephen shook his head slowly. "I was dead, in a way. The hell of war almost killed me—spiritually, emotionally."

"It felt like you were gone." She hugged a peacock-adorned pillow to her chest.

"I couldn't feel myself. I didn't think I could take it anymore. Somethin' happened, though, one night that made it more bearable somehow."

Caroline's eyes glistened. "What was it?"

His fingers pressed into the textured material of the sofa, and he stared at his knees. "My nightmares had been an ongoin' hell. If I wasn't awake and in the desolation that surrounded me there, I was tortured in my dreams with guilt about the soldiers I couldn't save and the victims at the camp—and about our last time together."

"Oh, Stephen."

"Then, one night, I was havin' the same awful dream. I was enterin' the cottage—leavin' the horrors of the camp and comin' straight into this very cottage. I was bracing myself for your cries, for the entire regrettable experience, but it didn't happen."

Caroline leaned towards him and touched his arm, willing him to continue despite the tears her other hand was brushing from her eyes. "What happened?"

Stephen paused and looked up at her. His eyes transfixed on her face with a look of wonderment. "You were there, Carrie, but you weren't scared. It was entirely different. You told me everythin' was gonna be alright. We sat down at your little table and had tea and talked. I held your hand. That's what we did every night after that. The nightmares went away. That's how I got through the rest of my tour of duty."

"We had tea? That's what we did every night?" She smiled through her tears.

He nodded. "Yes, that's what we did. You were my angel. Those hours saved me."

"And then you came back here only to find—" Her voice broke off, the impact of what she had done engulfing her with sadness. "I'm so, so sorry." The words were barely a whisper.

Shrugging, he brusquely wiped his eyes. "Life takes its own course, I s'pose. I understand."

Her face crumpled. "Maybe I knew you might come back, but I was afraid you wouldn't. Perhaps I just told myself those things. I'm so sorry, Stephen."

He sat silently for a moment as she began to sob, then moved to embrace her. Holding her gently, he asked hoarsely, "Are you really happy with Clay? He's good to you?"

Caroline nodded and spoke into his neckline, nearly overcome by his familiar, castile-soap scent. Through stabbing pangs of remorse, she admitted the truth. "Of course. Clay is wonderful, and he's devoted to Vivian completely… and I'm expectin' his child now. As far as everyone is concerned, this is his second child. We're a family."

Stephen nodded. He wanted to be glad that they were well, that Clayton had taken care of them.

"May I look in on her?"

"Of course you may." Relieved to have even a small way to help, Caroline mopped at her face and walked him to the door of the moonlit bedroom.

Stephen approached his daughter. Gently, he touched the sleeping child's cheek. He stood quite still for some time.

Stepping back into the dark hall, he murmured softly, "Carrie, I understand that I have no real place in your life or in Vivian's life now. I haven't earned that right. However, I want you to know there is nothin' I wouldn't do for you—or for her. I love you. I'll always love you."

Her throat constricted as Stephen wrapped his arms around her, savoring his last moments with her. He planted a gentle kiss on her forehead and reluctantly released her.

Caroline managed to let him go, holding herself perfectly still. Only when the door clicked softly behind him did she move, opening it to watch him mount Hermes. As he began to ride away, leaving her and his child once again to their lives without him, a desperate, insistent ache swelled up, and Caroline impulsively ran after him, calling, "Wait, don't go!"

Reining in Hermes, Stephen turned his sad, anguished gaze upon her.

Rejecting her inner voice of caution, Caroline pleaded heedlessly, "Wait… please come back inside. This isn't right. I want to tell you about your daughter. You should know about her. Please come back in. Let's… have tea."

"Tea?" He blinked at her, his face transforming with astonishment. Finally, his mouth closed, and he smiled ever-so-slightly. With shaking hands, he dismounted and fastened Hermes' reins to the post before following her back into the cottage.

There, Caroline resolutely avoided his eyes as she fixed the tea and began telling him matter-of-factly about Vivian. Once they were settled at the table, she relaxed, sharing about everything from the pregnancy and birth to Vivian's first words and incorrigible games.

To his amazement, Stephen felt his grief lessening as he became drawn into the stories. He listened with growing fascination to his daughter's impish ways, and as Caroline became more animated, his enjoyment grew.

At his sudden laughter, her own sorrowful heart surged with a ray of pure happiness. Stephen could not be Vivian's daddy, but he could share in the stories of their lives. A peculiar euphoria overcame her as she continued to regale him with more tales of his daughter. When he took her hand, the years seemed to melt away, and she reveled in this magical land of happy, carefree conversation with her long-lost prince.

Finally, Caroline forced herself back to the small cottage and reality. More soberly, she asked, "Do you want to tell me about the war?"

Stephen shook his head. "I try to think about other things. Thank you for tellin' me about Vivian. Meetin' her and talkin' with you tonight have been the best medicine I could've hoped for."

Nodding, Caroline told him, "I won't be able to come back to town for a long time, I'm afraid. I wish there were some way for you to see Vivian, for me to tell you about her more often. I see you in her. You are a precious part of her, and you should know her one day."

Squeezing her hand, Stephen replied intently, "Listen, you have nothin' to feel badly about, Carrie." He grimaced. "I was the one who… and then I left. I understand why..."

Caroline stared at him helplessly, unsure if she should speak the words of comfort and love that ached to pour from her lips.

Stephen again felt the rising tide of an urgent, too-pressing desire to take her into his arms. He stood abruptly, releasing her hand. "I should go now."

Mutely, Caroline nodded and rose to her feet as well. The thought of his departure seared her heart. She couldn't bear to see him ride away again, couldn't bear to see his beautiful face so sad, so alone. Reaching out a trembling hand to touch his arm, she whispered, "Stay, don't go."

Stephen closed his eyes, overcome with wanting to take her into his arms, to finally love her as he had always hoped to, planned to. His pulse pounded throughout his body as he struggled with the idea of making love to her at last, the way he should have the first time. Thoughts of why he should go, why he needed to leave paled next to his need for her. As he agonized, the soft touch of her hand slid up to the nape of his neck, and the warmth of her body pressed against him. When his lips touched hers, all thoughts were forgotten. The bliss of uniting with her, of being with her again consumed him.

As his kisses began to trail down her neck, Caroline tugged him towards her bedroom.

Stephen let her guide him, delirious with the joy of being with her, with the sense that this would finally be right—perfect love and unity with his beloved. As he stumbled with her in an inexorably, ecstatically slow journey to her room, however, his eyes were drawn by the moonlight that coursed through the lacy curtains of the window over Vivian's bed. The child's face was alight in the soft glow, and he found himself halting. "Hold on, Carrie," he breathed.

She allowed him to pull her into the small room, where he drew her in front of him, wrapping his arms around her from behind. "Look at her. Just look at her."

They gazed down at the cherubic face. Vivian's skin seemed radiant, dark strands of hair curling in tendrils around her soft cheeks and under her chin. As Caroline regarded their child, the passion that coursed through her began to settle into a sense of awe.

"She's beautiful," Stephen whispered reverently. "We made her. She's part of this world now. She's a central part of our world now."

Caroline nodded, still gazing at the girl.

His hands slipped down over Caroline's abdomen, and he cradled them there for a moment. "You've got another little one to think about, too."

Her hands slid on top of his, then lifted them to her lips. Closing her eyes, she kissed his fingers one by one before turning to burrow her head into his shoulder. "I know. I know. But I love you."

"And I love you. We'll always have that. Always."

With a shaky breath, Caroline glanced at the still-sleeping little girl and smiled weakly. "But you'd better go now if you mean it. I think I'm past the tea stage for tonight."

They embraced once again by the front door and stood together for a minute—and then another, neither willing to let go. Stephen's desire for her flooded through him again, but he only allowed himself to dwell on the ecstasy of just holding her. Caroline could feel his heart pounding through his chest, and she wrapped her arms around him more tightly, willing him to stay with her.

At last, he kissed her on the forehead and withdrew. She followed him outside and stayed there for several moments after he had ridden away. Despite the longing, despite the guilt, she felt a renewed gratitude for his idealism, his constant determination to hold his loved ones as sacred. She felt blessed to know him, blessed by his love.

Caroline fingered the pendant that she always wore and knew that he'd meant every bit of what he'd ever told her, that she was to him forever angelic and pure. *He is still my prince, after all.*

33• Anne's Wedding

GAYNELLE BLINKED BRIGHT BLUE EYES and gurgled up at the affectionate face of her mother, a face that would come to fade from her memories completely.

As the newborn nuzzled against her mother's warm bosom in search of milk, Caroline cradled and rocked her on the porch. Letters flapped in her hand, but she was contentedly distracted with this delightful bundle of humanity.

Her second daughter's birth had occurred on a bright June morning—quick and intense, but uncomplicated and fairly bloodless. She'd slid out as easily as a pea from its shell—at least in comparison to Vivian. *This little one's birth was so easy and straightforward*, Caroline mused, *just like my relationship with Clay, whereas Vivian's birth like to killed me...*

Caroline hadn't been able to stop thinking and worrying about Stephen. Life was simple and good with Clayton, but a sentimental portion of her heart longed to be with Stephen, to soothe his worried brow and kiss away the haunted expression from his eyes.

She sighed and stroked her infant's soft skin. Looking out at Vivian playing with the pullets and hens in the yard, she reminded herself, *These children are my priority. If anyone needs me, it's them—Stephen was right.* She shifted in the rocking chair. *I suppose that's why no one bothered to tell me he was back. Must've thought it'd be better if we didn't even know. Maybe they were right, too. I am married to Clay, after all. And I love him. One woman can only be and do so much.*

Caroline gazed at her newborn's face. *Her father's chin.* She appreciated its perfect, dimpled shape in the same way that she wistfully ran her fingers through Vivian's dark hair. *This hair, though, is definitely from me*. Caroline touched the wispy blond curls with a sense of joy.

As the wind rustled the papers in her hand, her attention turned back to her letter from Anne, for whom wedding bells had yet to peal. She continued to stay busy with her designs and travels, never ceasing to obsess over her latest wedding gown. Cream-colored gauze and silk charmeuse were featured this time, with a high waistline but a fitted shape, the letter told Caroline. The charmeuse would form the outer skirt in a bias cut to accentuate Anne's slender hips. Gauze and lace would flow underneath more loosely to her feet, and the skirt would gather in the rear to form the train.

Caroline inspected the sketch Anne had included in her letter. The dress would undoubtedly be exquisite, but she wondered if Anne would actually be the one to wear it this time—Anne had already given up one stunning creation to meet work deadlines. *If she does that again, I'm gonna have to go down there and march her straight over to the ready-made racks,* Caroline mused. *Otherwise she might never get married. Clock's tickin' for old Sanders.*

Caroline giggled at the thought, imagining Anne's indignation. Then she sighed, knowing she would probably never be with Anne enough to tease her like that again. Still, Anne's letter said that the couple had finally agreed to a wedding date only six months away, right in Kingstree, and Caroline couldn't wait.

Clayton brought Caroline and the girls to stay in the Swann cottage on a sunny, dry morning three full weeks prior to the wedding. They'd scheduled out Gaynelle's infant baptism and Caroline's dress fittings well in advance to make the most of their time in Kingstree.

As Mary and John escorted the small family to the small tabby cottage that evening, Caroline failed to stifle a yawn. With a small laugh, she batted her lashes at them. "Whew… Need my beauty sleep. Gotta get up tomorrow for my first fittin' with that amazin' fashion designer." With Gaynelle still in one arm, she tossed her head back, striking a pose, and then twirled about.

Vivian giggled and twirled around, too.

"Look at the ballerinas!" Mary exclaimed.

Vivian twirled again, even faster.

With a sleepy smile, Caroline said, "See how giddy we are 'bout seein' y'all? And… I've been meanin' to tell y'all how excited and grateful we are to have this second home to come stay in. It's like a dream, the way y'all keep the place so tidy and welcomin' for us."

"Sure is," Clayton added, scooping Vivian up as they reached the cottage door.

Mary turned towards them, her face puckering into a frown. "I s'pose we should mention that we let some… other folks stay here these last few weeks."

Caroline looked from Mary to John. He appeared unhappy, even uncomfortable. She waved an awkward hand. "Of course you have. We don't expect it to sit here empty when guests come visitin'. Not really. I was jus' puttin' on airs."

"I haven't even checked on it," Mary admitted. "Only thing at all I've done is send over some fresh linens."

"Mary's been fund-raisin'," John put in. "Tryin' to raise money to buy more textbooks for the school for colored children."

"Well, isn't that jus' the finest thing I ever did hear!" Caroline exclaimed. "Didn't know you were so community-minded as all that. You must be awful proud o' your wife, John."

"Oh, he's been busy, too," Mary interjected, sounding strangely dismal. "Been spendin' his free time helpin' to build a new house down on the workers' lane—and puttin' additions onto some o' the old ones."

Caroline beamed proudly at her brother. "Always takin' care of everyone."

"Even been endin' the farm work early each day so they could finish up 'fore y'all got here," Mary said, a little less dismally.

"You didn't have to do that, John," Caroline protested. "We don't expect you to hold our hands the whole time we're here. You got work to do, and it'd jus' be settin' us a real good example if you did that sort o' thing while we're around."

Letting Vivian wriggle back out of his arms, Clayton murmured, "I think Mary meant he did it so's we can stay here in the cottage, so it would be open."

"Oh!" Caroline fell silent, finally comprehending the air of anxiety that had been expanding with the seeming fragility of a soap bubble. "What happened? Who'd y'all have stayin' here?"

"There was some unrest a couple o' months ago," John began in a reluctant tone. "About a dozen folks turned up out-o'-the-blue. Relatives of some of our workers."

"Desperate," Mary chimed in.

"What in the world?" Caroline muttered.

"Came up from a town called Statesboro, down in Georgia. Sounds like near every Negro in the town deserted with 'em."

"Well, you can't let 'em *all* stay here. You don't have room for jus' anyone who takes a notion to live here. It's your land," Caroline protested.

"Their families live here, too," Mary chided.

"I s'pose we've got room for those that are already here," John added. "They're helpin' out with the farmwork."

"What if more come floodin' up here?" Caroline insisted.

Clayton soothed, "Jus' as likely they'll wanna go back home after a while."

"Doubt it." John adjusted his glasses as he cast a concerned glance at Vivian, but she wasn't paying attention to their conversation. She was twirling once again, touching Mary's skirt each time she made a revolution to make sure Mary noticed. His voice dropped. "Couple o' Negroes were dragged from the Statesboro courthouse. Burnt alive by a mob."

"From the courthouse?" Caroline gasped. "They get off from committin' a crime or somethin'?"

"That's the thing." John frowned. "It was done *after* they were convicted. They were already scheduled to be hanged."

"My Lord, what'd they do?"

"Seems they were part of a gang that murdered a farm family of five. Two about the size o' your own children."

"You're lettin' them come here?" Caroline's voice rose sharply, and Gaynelle started to cry in her arms. Vivian stopped twirling, looking curiously towards them.

"These folks weren't the ones who did it," John snapped. "They're scared. Seems the paper printed pictures o' the family's remains, and that mob went a bit crazy. Shot one o' our people's cousins, along with a couple o' his friends."

Caroline scowled, ignoring her crying baby. "Maybe cuz that cousin and his friends were part o' that murderin' gang?"

"Maybe!" John blew out a frustrated breath. "But like I said, these folks here were jus' scared senseless and didn't feel safe in Statesboro no more."

"And do you feel safe here? Now that they're all here?"

"Carrie," Clayton interjected. "From what I've heard, they'll beat folks, especially colored folks, into makin' confessions, 'specially when folks is riled up. I s'pect no one really knows if any of 'em were ever really guilty."

"But there's no question what that mob did," John added, running a hand through his hair. "Look, I couldn't've said no even if I wanted to. You ain't never seen our people worked up quite like when they heard what happened. Even ole Ettie didn't come up to the main house for days."

"They needed her more than we did," Mary put in mildly.

"Yeah... but she didn't even send word to let us know," John muttered. "Jus'... somethin' was in the air. Field workers glarin' at me like we were the ones who killed their cousin."

Caroline shuddered, envisioning the murdered farm family in Statesboro and vaguely recalling other stories of butchered plantation families.

"Things gettin' any better?" Clayton asked with concern.

"I think so." John nodded. "They seemed real grateful by the time we got the new house built."

"Sounds like you handled it 'bout the best you could."

"I didn't really mind helpin'." John turned to open the door to the cottage. "Fact is, felt good to be doin' somethin' more for them. I always mean to, but I prob'ly should make it more of a priority."

The cottage had been left in perfect order, but Caroline had trouble falling asleep, reflecting on who might have occupied the bed before her. At first she was afraid, wondering if it was safe to have her children at the plantation, but soon her thoughts turned to how awful it must have been to flee like that, what misery those folks' lives must've been those past few weeks.

Curiosity along with a substantial element of fear prompted her to keep an eye out more than usual for the plantation's new residents, especially once Clayton left for Greeleyville, but life seemed not much different from before. Everything remained pleasant. On their very first weekend in town, while Clayton was still with them, Gaynelle had been baptized in the same christening gown that Vivian had worn three years earlier.

Later, back in the cottage, Caroline had thoughtfully stroked the arm of the chair she'd sat in while making the precious dress—when she had hoped so desperately for Stephen's return, before she had decided to marry Clayton. Since then someone else had sat in the chair, someone with far worse problems than she had. The realization should have put her own problems in perspective, but guilt nagged at her. It'd been more than a year, and she still hadn't told Clayton about seeing Stephen. Now her husband had left her here once more, and again she harbored hopes of meeting up with her former fiancé. *Perhaps we'll see Stephen at the wedding and get it straightened out...*

The guilt was double-edged. Despite her family obligations, Caroline felt a separate duty to Stephen, a pressing need to share the joy of his daughter's life with him. This preyed on her mind as she busied herself with helping Mary canvas for donations for the school and then hold a clothing drive. Her babe-in-arms made people all the more friendly and willing to help out. After she'd traversed the town with her bright little bundle several times, passing back and forth in front of the doctors' office without going in, she finally opened the door to its familiar chime.

He warmly greeted her, then asked her up for tea. "Dr. Davis can cover for me," he said. "We've got this down pat."

"I can't stay long." She touched her hat, flustered but pleased at the invite. "I'm on my way over to Anna's workshop for a second fitting of my matron-of-honor gown, but Gaynelle fell asleep, and it seemed like a good opportunity for us to speak without her makin' a fuss."

"A fittin' won't take long, will it?"

"Well, then I'm plannin' to spend the rest o' the afternoon gettin' in Fletcher's way."

He laughed as he led her out to the stairwell. "Not in Anna's way?"

"Oh no, that's Gaynelle's job." Caroline kissed the baby's soft cheek, then hiked up the stairs after him to his apartment. "I'm gonna try to mend some o' the clothes we collected in the clothin' drive, if I can get to the sewin' machine."

Soon she was sinking onto his plush velvet sofa with relief, holding a teacup in one hand while cradling Gaynelle in her other arm, totes and diaper bag at her feet. A soft cacophony drifted through the open windows—clapping hoofbeats, carriage wheels rolling, strident voices calling out, the occasional jangle of the office door bell, and every now and then the cooing of a pigeon that had settled above the window. It all helped to distract her from the guilty twinge she felt over her family not knowing she was there in his apartment. A palpable sense of relief washed over her, however, as she began to relate the pent-up list of anecdotes about Vivian that she hadn't even known she was keeping.

Stephen absorbed these snippets of his daughter's life, laughing until tears ran down his face at a tale of Vivian in the coop nesting box.

"So then, Li'l Miss Priss was hidin' in there, pretendin' to be a chicken layin' an egg." Caroline had long since placed her teacup in its saucer on the end table and was gesticulating with her free hand. "When I found her, she began cluckin' away. Next thing I knew, she was holdin' out a cracked egg for me, proud as anythin'!"

Stephen laughed again.

With an exaggerated scowl, Caroline growled, "I told that stinker, '*You're* the cracked egg.' And do you know when I hauled that child out from that itty-bitty space, she squawked the whole time? She does beat all."

Chuckling, he said, "You sound so different, Carrie."

Her smile faded as she reflected on the words she'd used, the country way she'd just sounded—almost Amarintha-worthy. Picking at her calico skirt, she replied quietly, "Well, I do live out in the country now. And I ain't been readin' as much as I used to."

"That's not what I meant. It's just that you're… you're a mama now. Your children are your focus." He smiled. "It's nice seein' you like this. And our daughter… who knows what she'll do with herself? The world is openin' up for women. It'll soon be Vivian's egg to crack."

Her head cocked to the side. "Openin' up more than it has been? Ever-so-many amazin' women are out there and have been for ages—writers and explorers. Lots of 'em English," she added, wanting to sound at least somewhat intelligent. "Seems to me it was good for women over there, 'specially, while Victoria was on the throne."

He nodded. "Over sixty years."

"But now a man's on their throne again, and men have always ruled over here, and women still can't even vote." Her head shook pessimistically. "I really jus' don't see it gettin' better for us ladyfolk anytime soon."

"Yet a woman just received the Nobel Prize for the very first time," he pointed out. "She discovered a highly radioactive element. Quite remarkable."

"Anne was tellin' me about her." Caroline waved a hand dismissively. "Said Madame Curie received the prize alongside her husband, or it never would've happened."

Stephen shrugged. "Maybe not."

"But you told me yourself that Florence Nightingale single-handedly brought hygiene into the hospitals, savin' thousands upon thousands of lives. That was decades ago. Madame Curie doesn't begin to compare."

He laughed. "Alright, alright. I can't argue with that. But our daughter sounds like she'll be a clever one. I'm sure she'll make the most of her opportunities."

"Her daddy's a farmer," Caroline reminded him, "but maybe at least a few opportunities will present themselves—to her *and* to Gaynelle." She tried to smile, still subdued at the realization that he didn't see her in the same way as before. Of course he didn't. She'd changed. The toes of her boots dug into his Persian carpet, and she wondered if they were dirty. Sighing, she figured it was time to leave. Instead of rising to her feet, however, she picked up her teacup and held it aloft, regarding the clear, garnet-colored liquid. "What is this, anyhow?"

"Sassafras tea. Used to be real popular—a major export from the American colonies. Cleanses the blood."

She sipped, exploring the fragrant, astringent taste again. "Not bad—and so pretty."

"Sure doesn't look like that in root beer."

"It is in root beer, isn't it? What made you think to make it into tea?"

Stephen shifted and turned his attention to his own cup. "I've been spendin' time with Dr. Thomas, actually. He told me how. Grows everywhere around here. Just boil the roots." He looked up. "Sassafras was a common tea, once upon a time. Street vendors sold it in the cities."

"Wonder why they don't anymore? Might jus' have to make some myself." Caroline glanced at him curiously, wondering if he'd grown closer to the root doctor since learning of Vivian's delivery. He hadn't yet spoken much this visit, but she'd been telling him about his child, after all. Now she asked, "And how about you? How you been?"

"Keepin' busy with patients." He paused as if reluctant to say more, but then added, "I work with my quarter horses some, and I have a promisin' new foal."

"Congratulations." She lifted her teacup. "Not about to get into those automobiles, are you?"

He shook his head.

"Saw one in town the other day," she shared. "Quite the rage, aren't they? For rich folk, anyhow."

Stephen grimaced. "Certainly the future, but I'm holdin' out. Hard to care about a hunk o' metal, not that I can afford one."

"Julep's better than any ole car," she said with a wry expression.

"Heard tell that Vanderbilt heir hit 92 miles per hour in a Mercedes down in Florida."

Caroline's face screwed up in confusion.

"Over twice as fast as the fastest Julep could ever go," he clarified. "No horse can compare with speeds like that. I don't like to think about it."

"Does sound dangerous."

As Gaynelle started to fuss and stretch in her sleep, Caroline stood up to bounce her back and forth across the carpet.

He gestured towards the babe. "You haven't told me about Gaynelle yet. How did her birth go?"

"Amazin' how different two births can be," she said in a sing-song voice, trying to soothe Gaynelle back to sleep.

"Jus' sorta popped right out. Like squeezin' a scuppernong." She grinned but then shook her head and sighed. "Been spendin' too much time with my mother-in-law. Soundin' jus' like her. But anyhow, those afterpains were dreadful this time."

Stephen smiled sympathetically. "Yes, ma'am. Worse with each child, in general. The labor and birth are often easier, whereas the afterpains grow more severe with each subsequent delivery."

"How awful, Dr. Connor," Caroline laughed. "That's the worst news I've had all day."

The return of this medical bent of conversation was oddly comforting, a good note to end on. Caroline was all too aware of the hour and a suddenly-pressing need to feed Gaynelle. Relieved at the comparative ease of this visit, she urged, "Please say you'll be at Anna's wedding. John will be there. Y'all can talk all about Panama and whether we should dig a canal or not."

"We have already," he chuckled, rising to his feet.

"And Vivian will be there."

Gaynelle fidgeted in her sleep, starting to pull at Caroline's dress.

"She'll be wearin' a precious lavender dress that Anna's made to look like mine. You might even get to speak with her again, if we can find the right moment."

Stephen's brows furrowed as he gathered her bags together. "Not sure I'm up for a wedding, but I'd like to see Vivian again. And you."

"Can't wait to see her in that little gown. Her hair is growin' longer and thicker. Looks just like yours." Caroline raised a hand, giving in to the irresistible temptation to run her fingers through his hair.

When his eyes closed, she laughed. "I do that to Vivian every single day, and I'm always reminded of you."

He sighed. "I'm glad she has you. In some strange way, it feels like a part of me is with you, too. It's comfortin'."

Caroline's knees felt suddenly unsteady, but she managed to quip, "Gonna melt me into a puddle, talkin' like dat," purposely exaggerating her Amarintha accent as she jiggled Gaynelle. Her eyes were still soft, however, as she added more gently, "I felt that way from the moment I suspected I was pregnant with her. You were gone, but a special part o' you stayed with me, and I've always been grateful for that."

Stephen couldn't find the words to respond. Despite the lingering memories that haunted him, he could detect no reproach in her wide gray eyes. The tightly-coiled ball of regret and reproof that had taken up permanent residence in his gut loosened a little in that moment. He wrapped an arm around Caroline and closed his eyes, breathing in her rosemary-scented hair, feeling the smooth skin of her face against his neck as she leaned into him.

Enveloped in his tenderness, Caroline knew her pleasure at their visit was now impossibly complete. As she inhaled his comforting soap-scent and reveled for that extended moment in his embrace, Gaynelle began pulling more vigorously at her mother's dress. Laughing, Caroline drew away at last. Her visit with Stephen had been perfect, and it was time to leave—anything more would be problematic and anything less would have been inadequate. Wiping away an unbidden tear, she bade Stephen farewell with a wistful smile.

Dashing through a throng of pedestrians and between slow-moving carriages to get to Anne's workshop, Caroline waved away her friend's offer to take Gaynelle.

Briskly making her way into the dressing room, she dropped her bags and settled onto a stool while fumbling with her buttons and flaps. As her milk let down and her infant settled against her, she exhaled with relief, then wondered why she hadn't wanted to nurse her baby in front of Stephen, in particular. He was a physician, after all. With a bemused smile, she gazed at the gown she'd try on for its last fitting. That wouldn't take long, and then she'd get to work sewing—just after changing Gaynelle's overdue diaper. There was so much to do. She shook her head, marveling at how life carried on as it did. *But I'm glad that Stephen and I are comin' to terms with our past. We're forgin' a new path—an acceptin', lovin' way forward. It's the only way I can see.*

At last, Anne's wedding day arrived. It was set to be the finest, most memorable wedding the town of Kingstree had ever seen. White camellias with baby's breath and lavender tulle adorned the ends of the pews, the altar, and the windows. The church was full of murmuring townsfolk, their contagious enthusiasm buoyed by the languid, rich string harmonies of a chamber ensemble Mr. Sanders had brought in all the way from Charleston.

Reverend Scott, Mr. Sanders, and the groomsmen—including a ruddy-cheeked, self-satisfied Mr. Nesmith—took their places at the front of the church. The resonant voices of the string instruments grew louder, evoking an uplifting yet serene atmosphere. Preludes included Handel's 'Largo' and Bach's 'Jesu, Joy of Man's Desiring'. When Pachelbel's 'Canon in D Major' began, the congregation turned expectant eyes towards the aisle, eager to see the procession at such an opulent ceremony.

Less accustomed than ever to finery and crowds, Caroline led the procession, striving to hold her chin high and match the music with her step-pauses, even more awkward because of how her torso jutted forward in the new S-line corset Anne had insisted upon. As she passed by, Clayton's eyes met hers, and Vivian reached out to touch her skirt, still technically obeying their admonition to remain absolutely quiet for the ceremony.

Lenora followed, glowing with pleasure at being in her aunt's wedding. She smiled at her young students, who peppered the congregation and gazed at her with wide, interested eyes, having only ever seen her in teacher's attire. Her lavender gown and soft, elegant hairstyle made her look as though she'd been peeled right off of a fashion plate.

Immediately after Lenora, Emma came down the aisle at the pace of a millipede, so absorbed in her task of strewing flower petals that she didn't look up at all. Her hair was down, and she wore a white muslin gown with a lavender sash.

When she reached the front of the church, the music fell silent for a moment. Then a vibrant, familiar sequence carried throughout the sanctuary: triplet, long note, triplet, long note. As it repeated, a harmonic third was added and then a full chord. The congregants craned their necks to see the bride, and their collective gasp of appreciation carried all the way to the vestry. She was a vision. From the classical high chignon down to the pointed tips of ivory satin shoes peeking from beneath silk charmeuse, Anne radiated class and refinement in her slim gown and fine lace veil.

Carrying a bouquet of white camellias, Anne stepped in time to Mendelssohn's 'Bridal March' from *A*

Midsummer Night's Dream. As she approached the front of the church, she looked unwaveringly forward to the somewhat less decorous, but unfailingly debonair figure of Mr. Sanders. *Here is the man with whom I have worked and traveled for these past several years. Here is my best friend and soon-to-be lover. I've waited so long for this day to arrive, and now here it is. Everything has fallen into place.*

Arriving at the front of the church, Anne turned to face her groom, who wore a matching white-camellia boutonniere. The couple gazed at one another while reciting their vows. When at last they turned to face the guests, Reverend Scott enthusiastically pronounced, "I now present to you Mr. and Mrs. Bertram Sanders."

Anne glanced sideways at her groom, taking careful note of his given name.

34• Caroline's Fate

SUMPTUOUS STRAINS OF STRING MUSIC continued to swell over the reception guests that evening. Paraffin oil lamps flickered soft white light upon the glass ornaments, and more lavender tulle and white camellias decorated the outdoor tables. After posing for photographs insisted upon by Mr. Nesmith, who blustered about with his Kodak Brownie camera, the wedding party mingled and danced with the guests, drinking Ettie's creamy syllabub and enjoying a rare night of feasting and revelry.

Caroline leaned against a magnolia tree, taking a moment's respite from the gaiety of the evening. The air was growing brisk, but she didn't yet feel the need to don her wrap. She glowed with celebratory wonder, still enamored with how the slim elegance of her lavender dress reflected so harmoniously with the bride's gown. Beloved couples danced past her, circling the yard and bobbing up and down in time with the music a bit like horses on a carousel. Charming, tall Owen and lovely Lenora were so engrossed in one another that they might as well have been off in the clouds in one of the Wright brothers' new aircraft. John and Mary, on the other hand, nodded and spoke pleasantly each time their path crossed hers. Caroline laughed when she noticed Mr. Mouzon sitting at a table nearby, checking his watch. This was a celebration to remember, every minute of it precious, and Caroline was grateful that her friends and family were all together.

She had already danced through several songs with Clayton, who had playfully swooped upon her much as he had their first night together. When they passed near to Anne and Mr. Sanders, they stole covert glances at the pair, chuckling at the sight of this business couple behaving as lovers at long last. Caroline had half-expected them to continue with their work-like manner, but she was pleased to see tender glances and touches—and Anne flashing her wedding ring at anyone who would admire it.

Stephen had attended, after all. He'd kept a polite distance but now appeared at the magnolia as if her thoughts had conjured him. His eyes crinkled warmly as he asked her for a dance. She beamed, happily accepting, certain that her evening was about to be impossibly complete.

Clayton felt dizzy when he saw his wife in the arms of her former lover, of this ghost from their past—his little girl's birth father. Caroline was radiant. Clayton scowled with confused dismay at the pleasure and lack of surprise on her face. Their familiarity nearly doubled him over with angst. A burning, uncharacteristically volatile reaction threatened to overcome him, even as he argued with himself, his thoughts racing pell-mell. *I'm sure there's nothin' to get worked up about. Disturbin' this reception would be plain wrong, and I don't wanna bother anyone with my overreactin'. I'd best take a walk 'til I calm down—or get to the river, whichever comes first. Then I can throw myself in if needs be.* With a final bewildered glance at Caroline and Stephen, he managed to mutter his congratulations to Anne and Mr. Sanders before striding away.

Oblivious to her husband's reaction, Caroline had been transported once again to her fairytale land while waltzing with Stephen. Regardless of her reality, the timeless fantasy remained. It felt harmless now—magically pure and sweet.

As the dance came to an end, her fingers unconsciously tightened around his. Tentatively, she suggested, "I was hopin' you and Clay might say hello."

Stephen had glimpsed Clayton's face as they whirled past him, however. He shook his head. "Not tonight. At least, not right now. He might need a little time to adjust."

She sighed. "Alright, but meet me by the tulip tree over there in a couple o' minutes. I'll go get Vivian and bring *her* to you to say hello."

He nodded and smiled with relief. "Now that sounds like a nice idea."

Caroline absentmindedly scanned the crowd of children for Vivian. As her eyes sifted through the throng of smaller guests, the chamber orchestra struck up another waltz, and her mind replayed the one she'd just danced with Stephen. She hummed to the ongoing music and milled through the crowd, swishing back and forth, remembering the light pressure of his hand at her waist and the smooth feel of his palm against hers. She expected a flash of lavender or dark hair to grasp her attention at any moment, but eventually she encircled the entire reception area without a single glimpse of Vivian.

Mild alarm ran through her, banishing more fanciful thoughts, and she began to focus more intently on the subject of her search. Her eyes flitted across the guests until she noticed John. She hurried over to him. "Have you seen Vivian?"

"Not since we first arrived. Why?" John straightened his tuxedo jacket and stood at attention.

"I've lost track of her. Maybe she's with Clay. Have you by chance seen him?"

"Well, I saw him speakin' with Mr. and Mrs. Sanders a few minutes ago." His face puckered like a prune as he said Anne's new name. "Do you think that'll ever sound right? Mrs. Sanders?"

She gave a feeble smile. "Sure it will. Thanks, John."

"I'll keep an eye out for her," he assured her.

When she found Anne, she asked, "Do you know where Clay or Vivian is?"

"Clay said goodbye a few moments ago. Did he leave without you?"

Caroline's heart plunged. "I don't know. Did he take Vivian with him, perhaps?"

Anne shook her head. "No, I'm sure he didn't. I saw him headin' down the road alone."

"You know, he might have had some indigestion, now that I think about it. Don't worry about it. I'm just lookin' for Vivian, really." The last part was certainly true. She could deal with Clayton's feelings afterwards, but Vivian's whereabouts were her pressing concern.

Several minutes later, a distraught Caroline arrived at the tulip tree where Stephen was already waiting. Trying to hide her worry, she laughed half-heartedly, "I'm afraid the little imp is hidin' again." She held her hand to her forehead, dreading the thought of searching yet another go-round through the crowd for Vivian.

Stephen chuckled as he made the association. "Don't worry, Carrie. You're used to this. Look, I'll head right into the thick of the party to search for your little Houdini, and you can stroll around the periphery. Here, why don't you take this lantern?" He paused and reached for a copper kerosene lantern hanging by its handle from a post near the periphery of the celebration. "You'll be able to see her better in this dark with a light. We'll find her in no time. I'm sure she's fine."

His eyes were bright as he patted Caroline's shoulder soothingly, then undertook his very first parental task.

"Are you lookin' for a little girl?" The orange glow of the lantern revealed a young, thin woman with raven-colored hair pulled back tautly. Her eyes were wide and luminescent in the lantern-light.

"I am. Have you seen her?" Caroline asked breathlessly, pressing her hands against her chest.

The young woman pointed across the neighboring field. "I saw a little girl with a dress like yours go into that house over there jus' a minute ago. I was thinkin' 'bout goin' in after her."

Caroline regarded the two-story ramshackle dwelling with dismay. The porch sagged, and broken windows leered like jagged teeth that had consumed her child. A chill seized her, but she nodded her thanks and dashed towards the menacing structure.

Jessie patted her bun and slowly followed Caroline. The worried mother climbed the precarious porch and opened the front door, calling out for Vivian as she entered the dilapidated house. Tracing her path across the porch, Jessie hesitated on the threshold. The child's answering cry from above was followed by the unmistakable clatter of footsteps up the stairs.

A sudden, loud crack was immediately followed by a crash. Jessie gasped in surprise. She waited but heard no more movement. When she gingerly stepped inside the house, she saw that Caroline had fallen through to the floor. She was unconscious. A heavy wooden joist from the collapsed stairs lay across her.

Jessie stood for an interminable moment, observing the motionless body with quiet regard. The lavender skirt clung to the blond woman, and her fair locks fanned outward as though she'd been placed there with care, laid out as if she were a corpse.

As she stared, Jessie realized that Caroline wasn't going to get up. Jessie's heart began to race. Her rival, a woman she could never hope to surpass, was lying still as death—perhaps even still with death.

God's merciful hands were opening the path for her own future happiness. *Clay's had his time with Carrie, but maybe now it's over.* She took a deep breath. *It's time for him to be with me.*

I'll comfort him. Love him faithfully. Not make a cuckold out of him like she does. Like she did. A flush of triumph rushed over her—a feeling she had not known since before Caroline had dashed her hopes and nearly destroyed her future. Jessie was dizzy with ecstasy and relief. *Tonight, God's smilin' upon me. I was faithless, foolish to think that my life was ruint. God had a plan. He always did. The Lord's protectin' Clay. He heard my pleas. He looked and saw her sin, and now he's answerin' my prayers.*

Consumed with wonder, Jessie approached Caroline and sank to her knees. With fascination, she laid a hand on Caroline's chest then closed her eyes to give a solemn prayer of thanks, as though it were a thousand years ago and Caroline were a sacrifice. Just as she began her thanksgiving, however, she perceived faint movements under her hand—the almost imperceptible beating of a heart. Jessie's eyes flew open, and she lowered her cheek to Caroline's mouth. A soft brush of air caressed her face.

Bolting upright, Jessie withdrew her hand. *Not quite dead.* A sick, giddy realization made her dizzy. *Sacrifices aren't already dead. They have to be made. The Lord is demandin' this sacrifice of me. I have to prove I am his servant. God's waitin' for me to show my obedience.*

Jessie rocked back and forth on her heels. *If I don't follow through, He'll punish me, punish Clay for my lack of faith—he'll be stuck carin' for an invalid the rest o' his days. It'd be my fault. All I have to do is trust in God, act when He shows me how. He provides the answers. He always provides the answers.* She scanned the room, hoping for guidance. The orange glow of the kerosene lantern beckoned. It was lying on its side, flames flickering wildly as though it were her burning bush. She could doom both herself and Clayton to lives of misery by not obeying, but if she only followed God's lead, she would manifest the destiny always meant to be hers.

Like an acolyte preparing to light a funeral pyre, Jessie approached the lantern. Reaching reverently for its handle, she lifted it and straightened the glass before ceremoniously removing it. She circled the room, lighting heavy, faded curtains one by one. Her sense of serenity grew with each solemn step. The curtains flared around the room like a circle of immense candle tapers on a vast advent wreath. Brittle, loose papers on a wooden table seemed to snatch at the lantern's flames, and fabric covering an old sofa acted like fatlighter for the central, final candle of the wreath pattern.

Carefully setting the lantern's glass cover back in place, Jessie stood still, watching the flames grow into a life of their own, readily consuming the kindling and spreading to the aged wood of the building itself.

It's done. So simple, yet He will reward me for my faith. From her innermost recesses, a slow thrill began to slide its way to the surface, expanding into a distinctly familiar surge of power that had so long lain dormant, repressed securely in wait for this fateful evening when she once again channeled God's power—a remarkable feeling. He alone controlled destiny, and she was his vassal. Having resurrected itself with a new majesty, this power spread throughout her with a ferocity mirrored by the fire. Triumph swelled inside her as she realized what her final step should be, the single action that would cement her link to Clayton and solidify her importance to his life. God had prepared it all.

Carefully, she began to ascend the broken stairs, picking her way up on fragments of broken boards, clinging to the remaining rail.

"Vivian?" she called out, rolling the name on her tongue. It felt strange there, as though holding power for the one who spoke it—as if she were taking possession of the child merely by calling her name. Jessie waited, listening for a response before resuming her search. At last she heard a muffled voice. The girl was sitting in a closet, clutching an old rag doll.

Vivian looked up in surprised speechlessness at the stranger but didn't protest when Jessie whispered, "It's time to go," and leaned to pick her up.

As Jessie cautiously descended the remnants of the stairs, she explained in an even tone of voice, "The house is on fire. Shut your eyes until we get outside so the smoke won't bother them."

Jessie tossed the lantern in Caroline's direction and heard a gratifying shatter—proof of the cause of the fire. Acrid smoke was beginning to billow around them, and Jessie coughed as she grasped the searing handle of the front door. Flames licked at her singed dress, flaring in patches, but she beat them out once she and Vivian were safely away from the old building.

"It's a fire!" Vivian's eyes were huge as she stood next to the strange woman.

"Yes," Jessie agreed, once again scooping the girl into her arms. Staring at the house, she stroked Vivian's hair. An oddly tender sensation came over Jessie as she realized, *Vivian's my daughter now. I called her name, and so God is truly blessin' me.*

Smoke poured from the windows of the house, and flames lit the night sky. Black clouds hung over the field like a canopy, spreading out towards the wedding reception.

By the time that other guests started to notice the house fire, Jessie was serene again. Their murmuring voices approached. Then shouts rang out. Before long, a small crowd began to form around her.

Stephen stepped forward, his eyes narrowing as he identified the young woman with the lost child in her arms. "I'll take Vivian," he said. "I've been looking for her."

Fear surged through Jessie at the recognition flashing in his eyes. Instantly, she chided herself for her momentary weakness. *I have to deserve God's reward,* she reminded herself, tightening her arms around Vivian.

With a deep frown, she replied, "Dr. Connor, I managed to get Vivian outta there, but the stairs fell on top of her mother."

His eyes widened with horror. Turning on his heel, he rushed towards the collapsing structure, disregarding calls for him to stop. As he entered the house, he immediately discerned Caroline's form through the smoke. She lay motionless underneath a beam, her dress ablaze. Frantically, he attempted to pull the massive, burning wood off of her body. As he inhaled the scorching air, heat scalded his lungs. Desperation drove him to ignore logic, to disregard the falling building and suffocating smoke until he, too, collapsed, unable to continue.

Overcome, Stephen dazedly opened his eyes for a last moment to gaze at his beloved Caroline. He reached out a hand to touch her angelic face. The pain seemed distant as he willed his spirit to join hers in their journey to the afterlife, into Caroline's oft-mentioned fairytale land. He smiled faintly as his consciousness faded away.

35• Ruins

THE CANOPY OF SMOKE DREW THE LAST GUESTS from the reception just as Clayton arrived. He was sopping from head to foot and had been wandering alone just beyond the outskirts of the reception, aware that he wasn't presentable but not ready to leave entirely. Now, though, he followed the stragglers, soon making his way to the front of the crowd of spectators.

Heat radiated from the house. It was careening as though preparing for a glorious collapse. Scanning the crowd for his family, Clayton soon spied Jessie holding Vivian.

"What's goin' on?" he demanded.

"Fire!" Vivian answered.

Jessie said nothing, shifting Vivian from one hip to the other as she noticed that he was clad in only the slacks and shirtsleeves now plastered to his skin.

"What's goin' on, Jessie?" he repeated.

Reluctantly, she admitted, "Carrie and Dr. Connor are in there."

Clayton tore towards the burning structure, ignoring cries of dismay and protest, including Jessie's own.

His weight splintered the rotten wood of the porch, but he was scrambling onwards in mere moments, his slacks torn and his leg dripping blood. His imposing figure was framed in brilliant orange as he burst into the building. Flames seared him with their heat. He fell onto his hands and knees and moved forward, desperately seeking his wife.

The smoke-obscured spectacle was surreal, but within moments Clayton discovered Stephen. He looked as though he were merely sleeping, his face turned in the direction of a collapsed, flaming pile. The stench of burnt hair and flesh stung Clayton's nostrils, and the roiling air scorched his lungs when he gasped at the sight of Caroline's body. It was hardly recognizable, alight in sections. Other areas were already charred, clearly beyond recovery. In despair, the brawny farmer grasped the doctor's leg and pulled him roughly towards the door. Blistering heat burnt his chest with each inhalation as he crawled out of the building, towing Stephen behind him.

Onlookers rushed towards the porch and pulled both men onto the field, away from the blazing, teetering building. Clayton coughed and rolled on the grass, a deep anguish seizing him. His wife was in that moment burning to ashes.

Stephen lay unconscious. Dr. Davis rushed to his side and began moving his arms in turns above his head and then back to his chest to assist his respirations. Mary and John hurried to help the red-headed young doctor, and eventually Stephen began to cough. Within a few more moments, he regained consciousness. As clarity slowly returned, he drew in ragged, painful breaths and stared hopelessly at the relentless fire. It was somehow burning without him. He had been kept on earth by fate's cruel whim.

Nearby, Anne fell on the grass next to Clayton, heedless of her wedding dress. She placed a hand helplessly on the large farmer's shoulder. He coughed and moaned, and her own tears spilled onto her ruint gown.

Cries and laments arose from the crowd of onlookers as word spread of Caroline's death. They witnessed with awe the formidable power of nature before them. The house was now a leaning skeleton, black against the orange-and-crimson flames, gray smoke obscuring the roof. As the fire expanded, a group of men and women circled the house, stomping and beating out any fire that strayed into the yard.

When the house roared to the ground, a vast emptiness overtook Stephen's soul. He barely perceived Dr. Davis directing guests to lift and transport him to his own medical office.

Meanwhile, Clayton was guided away from the scene by John and Mary, whose aching hearts throbbed in unison with each shudder that racked his body. Jessie's silent accompaniment with Vivian only seemed a matter of course.

The following dawn, Stephen made his painstaking way to the ruins, solemnly intent on finding Caroline's remains. An overpowering need to find her last physical traces propelled him, if only so he could sit with them in quiet mourning. As he came within sight of the blackened remains of the house, his lungs constricted, a visceral recollection of the smoke so recently inhaled. Stephen paused in his tracks to catch his breath.

After adjusting the bandage on his hand, he picked his way over the singed sections of the remaining wall, bracing himself for the sight of her. Heaps of burnt rubble lay where he knew her body had been. Carefully avoiding glass shards from broken windows and the iron nails that now littered the site, Stephen wound through the hazardous wreckage near to where the stairs had once stood. Studying the debris with a critical eye, he painstakingly unearthed skeletal fragments, staring at them for a long while but failing to recognize Caroline in their charred, jagged contours. No semblance of her sweet smile or bright spirit remained here for him; she was entirely gone.

Scalding dregs of tears felt like iodine in his dry eyes. His throat seemed to sear closed, and he began to turn away from the pointless, agonizing mission. As he wrenched his gaze away from the residual pieces of her charred skeleton, an inexplicable compulsion gripped him, forcing him to look back at her paltry remains. As if guided by an unseen hand, he bent towards a jutting clavicle, a solitary vestige of Caroline's alabaster throat and neckline. Upon that defiant, persistent remnant was an inconspicuous, sooty projection. Gingerly, he leaned forward to examine it, gasping roughly when he saw that it was attached to a broken, slender chain. Slowly, he lifted the blackened but intact angel pendant.

His heart wrenched as he collected the memento of his beloved and clasped it to his chest. Everything that connected him to her had remained behind. Even this necklace he had given her, this charm she had faithfully worn, was somehow left behind in the end. While he could be glad that their daughter was still alive, he couldn't think to dispute the role of being her father with the man who had raised her, who had saved his life, even—not that he could reconcile his own continued presence on the planet. No, he was still here, alone, without her entirely. In the end, Caroline had gone, taking nothing of Stephen with her.

36• Assuming the Mantle

THE WHINE OF A CHILD ROSE PIERCINGLY, and chickens pecked at her bare ankles as Jessie collected their eggs. The monotonous, creaking voice of the rocking chair droned on endlessly.

Jessie tried to ignore both the hens and the older woman sitting lazily on the porch, the evidence of a greasy breakfast on her dress. Humming to herself, Jessie selected another smooth, pale oval from the nesting box and placed it into her basket. A jutting piece of wicker scratched her skin, but she disregarded it. Minor nuisances mattered little, and she derived profound satisfaction in possessing these small golden treasures, destined by God to be taken from their mother's nests and used to feed her family.

The shock of Caroline's death was passing with excruciating slowness for Clayton, but Jessie, of all people, well knew the value of patience—now more than ever. She had accompanied the family to their farm, having managed to convince Uncle Joe and Aunt Sally without too much hassle that she should go with Clayton to help with the girls. Since then, concerned inquirers had breathed a collective sigh of relief that the children would be looked after by a capable young woman. Jessie had been the obvious solution to the family's gaping need as she could be directed in childcare duties by her aunt. Before leaving Kingstree, she was taught how to prepare a 'percentage-method' condensed-milk formula, thus equipping her to fulfill vital motherly duties. Content to tend the children's needs, she quietly bided her time by becoming an integral, even essential member of the family.

After the passing of a complete cycle of the seasons, Clayton had grown used to Jessie. For a time she barely seemed to exist at all. Then, as his grief lessened and he became aware of her constant gaze upon him, his thoughts gravitated towards her. She was unique, like no one he had ever known—but no longer that brazen, troublesome child. She was a woman now, more attractive than one realized at first. She worked hard, too. As time passed, he appreciated her help more and grew accustomed to her watchful eye. She began to edge her way into his thoughts during long days in the fields.

One dark night he awoke, sensing her presence. He wasn't alarmed, as she often hovered by the door like that. He shook his head, but instead of rolling over and ignoring her as he usually did, he hesitated. After a long moment, he murmured hoarsely, "Come here."

Quietly, Jessie slipped between the sheets—Clayton's words had been as clear as God's messages had ever been. She lay perfectly still, hardly daring to breathe as he cupped a small, taut breast. *This is God's plan. God's plan. Clay needs to know me. As his wife.* He waited so long that she finally wriggled her gown up and pulled him to her. Once he was braced over her, she welcomed him—his heavy breathing, the pressure as he entered her, and the unexpected sharp pain that surprised her. She was still glad, joyfully glad. As he glided back and forth, her thoughts repeated chaotically, in bursts punctuated by small, rhythmic breaths. *He needs to know me. He couldn't see it. He was blinded. By his memories. By that other woman. But now I'm with him. Me. Just me. And him. Where I'm supposed to be. I have faith.* He paused deep inside her, and then a warm, pulsing sensation surrounded her womb. Triumph surged through her. *I am one with Clay.*

Every night after that, Jessie clambered into bed with Clayton at her normal bedtime, transitioning as naturally as if she had nothing to be ashamed of. It passed unremarked for a couple of weeks, until Amarintha told Clayton in a matter-of-fact tone, "You oughta marry dat girl. You done ruint her."

Jessie froze over the mixing bowl she was holding, hardly daring to breathe on the thick cornbread batter. A thunderous conviction that God was speaking through her aunt, taking care of her and bringing His will to pass, made her hands shake and her heart thrill.

When Clayton agreed to take Jessie to the courthouse, she had to excuse herself, leaving the mixing bowl with the spoon sticking straight up. Trembling, she knelt by their bed and repeated her thanks to God until Vivian came to tell her the baby was crying.

Jessie understood God's power, and she understood patience. Others ignored His power or tried to wield it themselves, but they were too often impatient, clumsy, and fainthearted. God would never reward such uncertainty and faithlessness.

As monarchs have done for centuries, Jessie had acted as God's vassal to eliminate her predecessor. For her steadfastness, she would now wear the mantle of Mrs. Clayton Bell.

Epilogue

AS TIME PASSED, Jessie's influence on Clayton became pervasive. She followed God's will in all things, and the Almighty, in return, rewarded both her and her loved ones. When she heard there was money in tobacco, she heeded this message and urged Clayton to farm tobacco. When he brought in the expected profits and the Lord sent the landlord by for a visit, she advised Clayton to buy the land they'd been renting that very afternoon.

Her satisfaction was nearly complete. Clayton was hers at last, a reward for carrying out God's will. She had listened and made the necessary choices. She had proven her faith and would continue to do so. Gratified that her sacrifices had yielded the desired fruit, she held little patience for indulgences such as regret—for regret would mock the Lord's decisions. She was happy to be Clayton's wife, to wipe clean the tarnished relationship in his past. Clayton had deserved better. God had listened to his vassal's prayers and acted through her.

Jessie tolerated her coarse aunt well enough, like an old mutt not expected to last much longer, whereas she found herself oddly uplifted by Vivian. The child's dark hair and intense nature—indeed, even her tendency to hide away—triggered a maternal, resonant chord. Jessie could easily pretend the child was hers—a lovely, sanguine version of herself.

Gaynelle, however, was a trial from God. An unrelenting presence, she was the base seed of the unholy union between Clayton and Caroline—a union born out of lust, rooted in coquetry and seduction. Dealing with Gaynelle was a ceaseless strain. She was often unable to soothe the child, and her own impatience was at times intolerable.

Assuming the baby's basic needs were met, even Vivian could soothe Gaynelle better than Jessie. The curly-haired toddler trailed her sister throughout the long days, much to Jessie's relief and consternation. Glad as she was to have Gaynelle off her hands, she was concerned about Vivian spending all her time with the corrupting influence. Nevertheless, God had placed this burden in their midst, and she would raise the child until she no longer had to.

Gaynelle's dimpled chin and curly blond hair were deceptively innocent-looking. In reality, they were a constant, nagging reminder of the bond between Clayton and his deceased wife. Though Jessie's most fervent desire was for her husband to forget Caroline altogether, she felt a stabbing certainty that he thought of her each time he looked at his youngest daughter.

Her soft, full lips and ready smile indicated a pleasant, sweet nature—a nature Jessie had little regard for, being painfully familiar with how it could ensnare others.

As she grew, Gaynelle intuitively averted her stepmother's hidden loathing. Like a child born at sea, she was accustomed to gusts and waves. The greater the occasional hostility, the more she clung to the masts of the ship—her father, sister, and grandmother. She found security in their unwavering warmth and love, and her bright blue eyes followed them with trust and affection. An internal compass steered her clear of ill-will, somehow deflecting the bulk of Jessie's wrath.

In time, as the child became more obedient, Jessie grew used to her. Her own dominion assured, Jessie grudgingly accepted the gentle, resilient spirit that inhabited Gaynelle's small body. While the small creature would always be the spawn of Caroline, Jessie recognized elements of Clayton in her as well. If she could corral the child's worst tendencies, perhaps Gaynelle would turn out alright, after all. Certainly she could manage that, if it be God's will.

Thus Jessie did not recognize her match in either of Caroline's indomitable children. She would eventually, but that juncture was still many years away.

Acknowledgments

I WOULD FIRST LIKE TO THANK my wonderful husband Michael for supporting me through this entire writing process. He patiently participated or stood back as needed; he encouraged, worked, cooked, and watched the children for me while I obsessed. He also listened to me read aloud, proofread, and gave much helpful feedback. I love you, sweetheart!

My sister Stephenie sat on the phone and listened to me ponder and agonize over fates of characters for countless hours throughout the drafting of the trilogy. Much love to her for taking it all with a grain of salt and being incredibly patient with me.

A dear local friend, Virginia, was *Silk*'s first reader. Her thrilled enthusiastic support, which included a show of prickly gooseflesh, gave me an author's dream reaction—which really couldn't have come at a more needed time.

My BFF, Laura Landstrom, was *Silk*'s first editor. She made innumerable suggestions to help flow and consistency; every chapter of the book bears her mark. Laura also first edited Sam Landstrom's sci-fi novel, *Metagame*—the reading of which inspired me to finally try my own hand at writing. They generously shared their expertise and tips on publishing with me.

My genealogical inquiries unearthed much of the inspiration for the characters in these novels, though all are fictional and many are fabricated entirely independently of that source. I am immensely grateful to those who have made genealogical resources widely available, and in particular for the posthumous publications of *Remembering Kingstree: The Collected Writings of Bessie Swann Britton* and Samuel Davis McGill's *Narrative of Reminiscences in Williamsburg County.* Bessie's and Sam's personal, regional anecdotes of so long ago fueled my imagination as I created this mostly-fictional saga.

A debt of gratitude is owed to my writing groups, other friends, and family who were helpful and supportive at various points throughout the writing process—especially Kelly and Jennifer. My children, Alex and Fiona, were intermittently impatient with the process, but they were unfailingly positive and encouraging when I faltered;

when my daughter was finally old enough to read the manuscript, she proved to be an invaluable content editor. Many friends inspired me along this journey with supportive words and gestures—so often we don't realize how much a few simple words can encourage our dear ones to shoot for their dreams.

Much love to Mom & Dad for their tolerance of my love affair with novels from a very young age. Mom has also been a reliable, consistent beta-reader, catching mistakes here and there—and more important, expressing unflagging interest. They are my constant rock, and I am grateful for them.

Keep reading for a preview of Silk's sequel:

Tapestry

A Lowcountry Rapunzel

SOPHIA ALEXANDER

ONALEX BOOKS

Savannah, GA

1• Gaynelle's Time

January 1918, Greeleyville, SC

WHEN GAYNELLE SNATCHED HER TOES from the hard, freezing floor, her breath caught—not so much from the cold as from the bed's squeak of protest. Shivering, she fished out a scratchy woolen sock from under the mound of covers. Socks were like cats, always wandering off at night.

"No, please no…" the lumpy mound whined. "It's so cold."

A few clumsy pats revealed that the quilts had shifted off of the ice blocks that were her sister's feet. The second stray was curled up next to them.

"Sorry," Gaynelle whispered, putting the quilts back in place.

Padding into the kitchen, she blew the cookstove embers and lit the kerosene lamp, taking care not to smudge her sleeves with soot. After layering a coat, hat, and boots over her nightgown, she hurried into the bracing chill of the early morning air, thrilled to be free for at least a little while. When her boot slid on the porch, she gave a short, elated gasp. Her exhalation was a cloudy puff in the swinging lamplight.

As usual, Gaynelle was the first to rise. No matter the weather, this was her favorite time of day, when the world belonged to her alone. Mama generally stayed up at night until she was sure everyone was asleep in their beds, so earlier and earlier bedtimes had led to the discovery of this hour or so for herself. It was so peaceful that she could hardly believe a war was going on across the ocean, a Great War that didn't have a blessed thing to do with her, seeing as how her daddy was too old to have to register for the draft.

Crunching across icy grass to the stable, Gaynelle let herself into Julep's stall. He nuzzled her hand.

"Just a minute." She reached into a burlap sack for a handful of oats. His lips tickled her palm. She hugged him close, enveloped by his warm horse breath. She patted his sleek chestnut coat.

After feeding Julep and the mules, Gaynelle climbed up a narrow wooden ladder to her perch in Julep's stall, where she hung the lantern on its hook; its orange light illuminated the small space and part of the stall with a tangerine glow, leaving the other half in shadow.

Daddy had built the perch for her after he found her reading in the straw on the floor of Julep's stall. Novels upset Mama even more than schoolbooks, so he'd fashioned a cubbyhole under the seat that allowed her to stow her books where Mama wouldn't see them. Since Mama didn't much like Julep either, Gaynelle imagined she might not even know about this spot. Each morning, after the family clattered awake,

Gaynelle would stow her book and complete the outside morning chores.

For now, though, she settled onto her perch and pulled out *Rebecca of Sunnybrook Farm,* a gift from Aunt Anna. Gaynelle seldom saw their old family friend, but Daddy would sometimes stop by her place when he took his produce into Kingstree to sell. Occasionally he brought back presents from her for his girls—usually novels or new clothes. Daddy would stash the rectangular packages that meant books directly in her cubbyhole.

When Gaynelle finished a story, she'd see if Vivian wanted to read it. If not—and it had been a while since Vivian had shown any interest in reading—she'd send it with Daddy back to Aunt Anna's for safekeeping, where big oak bookshelves waited like a far-off horde of hidden treasure.

Mama didn't approve of books and clutter. In fact, Mama didn't approve of much anything Gaynelle liked. She'd find fault with whatever caught her attention. Even the stable was resented for being sturdier than their house—never mind that Daddy could only do but one thing at a time, and the stable had been built long after the old house. It was true, maybe, that if it weren't for the kitchen cookstove, the stable would be warmer than the house during the winter. Even now, the animals' body heat kept the stable almost cozy. But Mama's resentment would no doubt multiply if she took the trouble to discover Gaynelle's perch, a hardwood construction sanded perfectly smooth with such obvious care.

Shaking her head, Gaynelle shifted, trying to get comfortable on her cushion. She'd sewn it herself from one of her prettiest outgrown dresses—one that Aunt Anna had given her. Lace and buttons had been salvaged from the dress to decorate the cushion, and it was stuffed with leftover cotton from the field; she'd picked the neps from the bolls by hand. If she had to do it over again, however, she might leave off the buttons—not because Mama was right in her scorn for unnecessary ornamentation, but because they poked her bottom. It was like sitting on rocks, almost.

Gaynelle's favorite clothes used to come straight from Aunt Anna, but they hadn't received anything new in a long time. Now her best dresses were hand-me-downs from Vivian. If Mama bought Gaynelle anything, it was certain to be ugly. Serviceable, Mama called it. She'd always been more indulgent towards the strong-willed older daughter—or previously strong-willed, since Vivian was only a pale reflection of her exuberant self these days.

To drown such thoughts, Gaynelle sniffed at the ink-print of her book. It smelled heavenly, though the story wasn't as thrilling as her last read, *The Turn of the Screw*. Still, Gaynelle identified with poor, plain Rebecca. She could imagine leaving their meager conditions at home to stay with her aunt—only living with Aunt Anna would be worlds better, as Aunt Anna wasn't much like the spinster aunts in the story. In fact, she wasn't even technically their aunt. She'd been the best friend of their birth mother, Caroline.

A widowed fashion designer, Aunt Anna was not only successful, but she'd married into money. She used to visit them on occasion—until Mama told her not to. It wasn't fair, but Daddy always insisted that they do whatever Mama wanted. He wouldn't tolerate complaints, cutting his girls short every time, saying they'd have been lost without Jessie—and that Gaynelle owed her respect and obedience. He knew how unfair it was, though—Gaynelle was certain of it.

She sometimes wondered what Caroline had been like, what her own life would have been like if Caroline hadn't died. Even Vivian didn't remember her.

Daddy rarely mentioned his first wife, but he once told Gaynelle that she had Caroline's blond, curly hair. That suggestion had burrowed into Gaynelle's consciousness like a wood-tick under her skin—or at least Mama would deem it just that pernicious. Mama preferred Vivian's smooth, dark tresses.

Even though Vivian was pretty much already a grown woman—and had recently begun wearing her hair up like one—Mama had taken to brushing it every night. Vivian just let her.

Mama didn't brush Gaynelle's unruly locks in that same gentle way. If Gaynelle didn't fix her own hair in the morning, Mama would yank the brush through unmercifully. Braids were safest. Gaynelle had asked Daddy how Caroline wore her hair, but he didn't want to talk about it.

Hair was only one small way that Mama preferred sixteen-year-old Vivian. The best Gaynelle could manage was to do her chores and stay out from underfoot. She wished it were just the staying-out-from-underfoot part, because then she'd sit and read all day long, but all too soon the stable door was creaking open.

Daddy's voice called out, "Mornin', Gaynelle. Time to get to it."

Gaynelle flicked the book's ribbon into place and slid it into the cubby. Out of the stall in seconds, she caught up with him before he'd headed too far towards the new field—a field he'd been steadily clearing for the past month. She tackled him from behind, wrapping her arms around him. He laughed and spun around, sending her hat flying. She screamed with mock indignation. Early morning was not only *her* special time, it was *their* special time, if only for a few moments. It had been for a couple of years now.

When her feet were again safely on the still-crunchy grass, she snatched up her hat and took off for the chicken coop, calling back over her shoulder, "The chickens are waitin'!"

Indeed, Ivanhoe and Old Dom were crowing majestically as she headed over to let them out of their coop. "Here, chick,

chick, chick," she piped in the cheery, high-pitched voice she reserved for critters. Ivanhoe, the handsome young rooster, was always the first one out; he strutted confidently, lifting his bright red comb high in the air and showing off well-preened feathers. Old Dom, the patriarch of the black-and-white-barred flock, stayed with the hens, more concerned with keeping order. Gaynelle threw down scratch-feed for them, then lugged some firewood into the house.

After depositing the wood, she began to pull off her coat but immediately realized the house was practically an icebox. Vivian was sitting by the inert wood stove, rubbing her arms as Mama tucked a blanket around her. Gaynelle bit her lip. *I forgot to get the stove goin' this mornin'. Again.*

Mama scowled at her. "Well, it's about time. Your sister's gonna catch her death. Don't dawdle. You need to fix breakfast, too. I swear, child."

"Sorry, Mama." Gaynelle stoked the fire, equal shares of guilt and resentment igniting at once. With a sigh, she snapped up the kettle to fill at the pump. When she returned, she set it on the stove with a small clatter. As she prepared the breakfast, she periodically cast her mama a glance that said, *You could do it yourself.*

Finally, Mama's steely hand seized her arm. "I've had 'bout enough outta you. You're this close to a lickin'."

Gaynelle stumbled over her own feet as she was hauled to Vivian's side.

Mama's short fingernails bit into her flesh. When she let go, it was to clamp Vivian's pale hand against the nape of Gaynelle's neck. "Feel this. You jus' feel this."

Gaynelle gave an icy shudder.

"Don't give a second thought to your sister, do you? Only thinkin' 'bout yourself, but you ain't cold like her."

The hand wasn't growing any warmer. The cold seemed to sting Vivian with a ferocity that evaded the rest of them.

Her lips were tinged blue, her extremities those of an ice maiden.

Gaynelle peered anxiously into Vivian's pale, drawn face. A disinterested glance flicked upwards; then the glazed, empty stare found its way back out the kitchen window, unsettling Gaynelle more than anything Mama could say. With a queasy stomach, Gaynelle regarded the dark hollows surrounding Vivian's blue eyes—hollows which bespoke sadness, dark winter, and disquieted, tormented thoughts. A chill that had nothing to do with the icy hand on her neck trickled down Gaynelle's spine. When the tea kettle whistled, breaking the spell, she shook herself. *Too many ghost stories.*

Mama poured the steaming water over a cotton drawstring bag that contained a mixture of dried herbs and roots. Handing the ceramic cup to Vivian, she murmured, "Hold this to warm your hands first, then drink all of it."

As Gaynelle inhaled the aroma of mint, she imagined the warmth thawing Vivian's hands. Her own body began to slump with relief.

Nodding absently, Vivian obeyed Mama's instructions. This had been the routine for some time, ever since the weather had grown cold.

Ain't nothin' to worry about. She's not in any real danger if she can pull herself together like that. Despite the vacant stare, Vivian had at least been tidy as usual this morning, hair pinned neatly back.

Gaynelle poured some hot water in a pitcher for her own morning wash. Taking it to their bedroom, she stood on the rag rug and scrubbed beneath her nightgown as fast as she could. Peeking back out at Vivian, she dried off, reassured. Her sister looked perfectly normal sipping on her tea. Gaynelle had just sighed with relief when she noticed Mama slipping Vivian's boot onto her foot.

As Mama tied it for her, Gaynelle froze, stunned at the sight of Vivian being dressed. Swallowing the lump in her throat, Gaynelle knew that she would have to leave for school alone, once again. Vivian hadn't felt well enough to attend school nor church for some time, but Gaynelle hadn't been overly concerned until now. After all, she could practically still hear Mama's clear voice repeating those words she'd said so often these past months—"Vivian already has 'bout as much learnin' as a girl could want."

At this rate, Gaynelle hoped she was right.

2• Rosa's Secret

CLAMBERING DOWN FROM THE SCHOOL WAGON, Gaynelle could hardly feel the rough wooden side planks, her fingers were so numb. She hurried into the Greeleyville schoolhouse, where it was blessedly warm, and slid into her seat next to Rosa Pack.

Gaynelle straightened with pride, ignoring the sharp prickles as her fingers began to thaw. Carefully she set her books and slate on the shared table. Sultry, voluptuous Rosa was allowing her the privilege of sitting there during Vivian's absence. Gaynelle glanced admiringly at Rosa's thick red shawl draped over one shoulder and drooping to the opposite elbow.

"Hey," Gaynelle murmured shyly, putting her hands under the table to stretch and clench the tingling away.

Rosa drum-rolled her own fingers as she cast dark, frustrated eyes her way. "Isn't Vivian ever comin' back to school?"

"I dunno. Maybe not." Lengthening her back to seem as tall as possible, Gaynelle asked, "Whatcha itchin' so bad to tell her 'bout?"

Rosa pursed full lips, considering the earnest face before her. "I ever tell you that you look like the girl on the Jell-o ad, only without the big blue hair bow?"

"I'll wear one tomorrow." Gaynelle tossed a braid, elation fluttering in her chest. "You know, *I* can tell Vivian whatever it is you wanna tell her."

Rosa regarded Gaynelle for a long moment. "You hafta keep it a secret. You can only tell Vivian."

Gaynelle's heart pattered with excitement. She bent close. Rosa smelled like fig preserves.

"I went to a party with my ma at Rennie's place," Rosa whispered with relish. "You remember my sis and her husband, Zingle, right?"

Holding her breath, Gaynelle nodded, though she only remembered hearing their names.

"Well... while Ma and Rennie were busy dancin' and showin' off, I started talkin' with Henry." Her dark-brown eyes glowed. "He ain't never even looked my way before, but this time he shared his drink with me. I was pretty much walkin' on a slant by the time we made out behind the barn." Her voice rose to a squeak, and she cupped her hand over her mouth.

Eyes round as marbles, Gaynelle gasped, "Henry Timmons?"

"What? No!" Rosa cast a horrified glance at their classmate, then replied in a whisper, "No, silly. I'm not dilly-dallyin' with little boys. Henry is Zingle's brother. *My* Henry is a man." She batted her eyelashes. "A full-grown man. One old enough to get married."

"Or go off to war," Gaynelle said flatly. "Bet he had to register for the draft."

Her eyes flashed. "Better not. Figures I'd finally meet someone and him be sent off straight-away to die. So much for Wilson keepin' us outta the war."

"That liar," Gaynelle agreed. Waving a dismissive hand, she leaned in closer, wanting to hear more. Pretty much anything Rosa chose to do was instantly fascinating, even if all the boys Gaynelle knew were imbeciles. In a whisper, she asked, "Did you really kiss him?"

Rosa's frown softened into a smirk. "Ain't you ever kissed no one?"

Heat rose in Gaynelle's cheeks. "Not a big grown man. Not like that."

Rosa tossed her head. "Every fella is different. Henry knows what he's doin'. He don't flail about like no drownin' fish." She bit her lip as if to stop from saying too much. Turning back to her slate, she murmured with a sideways glance, "I'm gonna tell Vivian the rest myself."

Her heart full, Gaynelle gazed at the older girl. Rosa Pack was, for sure, the wildest friend they had. It was her Injun blood, that Injun blood they weren't supposed to talk about. Rosa's ma had a reputation for throwing parties and dancing, and everyone chalked her behavior up to the fact that she was part-Injun—just in whispers, of course. Rosa's pa was off hunting or out of town with his sales business half the time, leaving his family to their own devices. The rest of the time he was there, joining in.

Turning to her own slate, Gaynelle started to copy sums from the board until Rosa breathed in her ear, "We been meetin' on the sly, and not even my ma knows."

Gaynelle looked up into eyes twinkling with mischief. "Would she be mad?"

Rosa's lips curled. "Prob'ly not, but it wouldn't be so much fun, then, now would it? 'Sides, Ma's always stealin' my thunder. Talks Henry's head off whenever she's 'round him. Don't give a chicken's gizzard that she's takin' his attention from *me*."

Gaynelle nodded sympathetically.

"Anyhow, could be we get married. Then if they make him register for the draft, he can try for an exemption."

"Would they give it jus' cuz he's married?"

"Maybe… 'specially if we have a baby."

"A baby?" Gaynelle gasped.

Rosa laughed, preening under the girl's gaze. She might be only three years older than Gaynelle Bell, but anyone with two eyes could see that she was a woman ready for a family, worlds different than the pinafored child seated next to her. Rosa wore a ladies' two-piece dress, and her black hair was coiled into a large bun. Not to mention all her feminine accomplishments. Her jelly rolls were now in demand at each and every church function, and her singing voice was near loud enough to drown out the pump organ she played tolerably well. No one had had to teach it to her, neither. Her pa had just brought it home one day. He was so proud of her for learning to play it that he'd toted it around ever since, wherever they moved—and they moved fairly often. Some folks had to depend on sheet music, but Rosa played by ear and didn't need it. She patted her bun, sublimely self-satisfied.

Just then, the morning bell rang. The schoolteacher rapped on her desk for their attention, and they stood for the pledge of allegiance, reciting by rote, "I pledge allegiance to my flag and to the republic for which it stands, one nation, indivisible, with liberty and justice for all."

Gaynelle touched her own hair self-consciously. Maybe she'd wear a bow tomorrow, but it wouldn't help her seem any older—and she'd never given much thought to actual boys at all, much less grown men. Gaynelle frowned. She was excited to be included by the older girl, but she wouldn't officially turn into a teenager for another half-year, and she'd really still rather think about animals and books than boys. *Even earthworms are more interestin' than the boys around here*—at least, that's what she and the rest of the girls told each other at recess, where the boys stuck with the boys and the girls with the girls. That had always worked for Gaynelle until now, but if she was going to be Rosa's friend, then the few older students would expect her to start behaving more like them.

Sliding a hand down her still-relatively-flat chest, Gaynelle reminded herself that Vivian was nowhere near as voluptuous as Rosa, either. Nor was Vivian even talking much about boys yet, for all that she had been fascinated by that scandal about Mata Hari and was getting near old enough to marry.

The thought struck Gaynelle like a mule-kick. Bad enough that Vivian was so sickly. If she got better, romance could then steal her away, assuming Rosa's shenanigans were anything to go by. Gaynelle thought about it a moment longer, then sadly shook her head. *Vivian can't meet no one while she's sick at home. That's the last thing I have to worry about—and marriage to some draft dodger ain't the worst thing that could happen to her, not by far.*

3• Jessie's Flower Garden

WITH INFINITE CARE, Jessie patted the crumbly, cool earth around the newly-planted bulb. Red camellias bloomed nearby. The scraggly remnants of mint so recently crushed underfoot invigorated the air with an aromatic scent. Between patches of green, the dry ground was uniformly barren in shades of brown—the blackish-brown of the earth, the dull brown of the grass and dead stems, and the copper-brown of pine straw heaped over flower beds. Twining, thorny rose briars, overdue for a pruning, haphazardly graced the fence.

During the past several years, Jessie had developed this herb and flower garden in front of the clapboard house, looking forward most especially to seeing the lilies rise in the spring. Comfrey, mint, and chamomile all had their set places in the garden, but Vivian's disarmingly lovely attendants, the lilies-of-the-valley, had spread with relatively little assistance—their rhizomes ever finding new, fertile soil in which to propagate, long before Jessie had any inkling she would have such need of them.

Vivian was lying down for a rest in the house as Jessie weeded the garden and mulled over the young woman's dosage. Vivian was again refusing her food. *Perhaps I'll give her less for a spell*, Jessie decided, though she normally waited until Vivian took to complaining about her vision before reducing her measure of the *Convallaria* tea.

Her skin was cold as death this mornin', Jessie fretted. *S'pose I'll just have to substitute plain mint again for a while. No point keepin' the child safe at home if she dies on me,* she determined grudgingly. She pulled up a briar growing under the camellia, wincing as a thorn pricked her hand. Her job was difficult and thankless, but as Vivian grew older, it was imperative to protect her from the dangers presented by society in general and one man in particular.

Jessie still shuddered at the memory of Dr. Stephen Connor approaching them nearly a year ago. She'd always fretted about the ongoing presence of the Kingstree family physician, Vivian's blood father, and time had eventually proven her right. He'd left them alone for so long, though, not bothering them once in all the years since Caroline's death. Then out of the clear blue, he'd startled them with that audacious offer.

Clayton had actually been enthused; he'd been *excited* at the suggestion that Vivian be sent off to live at some secondary school for young women far away from them in the big city of Charleston. He'd dismissed Jessie's arguments like so much hot air. To tell the truth, her faith in Clayton's devotion to his family had been undermined that day. *How could he? How could he consider sendin' Vivian away?* Of course he preferred his own flesh-and-blood daughter, Gaynelle, but Jessie had never expected him to send away her own favorite. *Thinks I'm ignorant to the fact that Vivian isn't his blood-child, no matter that she looks so much like Dr. Connor—but that jus' makes it all the more shameful that he's set on sendin' her away*. Stabbing her spade into the earth, Jessie pried at an invading root.

Clayton had referred to Vivian as *nearly a grown woman* and *independent*. Maybe he'd been right on those counts, but Jessie had swiftly taken care of that independent streak and had done so ever since with the assistance of her flowering helpers. Vivian would stay home where she belonged. No conniving, manipulative man was going to take her away from her loving mama's arms. Dr. Connor had certainly not raised the girl, and Jessie had spent far more time tending to the child than Clayton had. She clenched her lips together, vowing, *Vivian is my very own soul child, given into my keepin' by the Lord Almighty himself, and no one on earth will tear us asunder.*

Nevertheless, a few days of vibrant health would hardly persuade anyone that Vivian was well enough even to return to her local school, no matter how much Clayton might wish it. Jessie smiled slightly and patted another bulb. *If they do insist, well, my faithful lily attendants will swirl and steep to perform their sacred duty, as always.*

The Silk Trilogy continues in

TAPESTRY

A LOWCOUNTRY RAPUNZEL

If your stepmother were a sociopath, how would you know? And who would you turn to?

Life is not as ordinary as it seems for Gaynelle and Vivian, who only understand that the woman they now call 'Mama' is complicated and difficult to please.

Is the romantic love that Gaynelle finds at a too-tender age going to last? And will Vivian uncover the truth about her parentage while recovering from a strange illness?

Rural South Carolina meets the Roaring 20's in this tale of two sisters who face separation and trauma with the resilience of the young and find their way, despite everything.

Don't miss The Silk Trilogy's thrilling conclusion:

HOMESPUN

Meet Zingle Caddell, who doesn't regret the destruction left in his wake so much as he is annoyed by it.

Figuring no man can continue to have such bad luck, Zingle is waiting for his fortunes to improve. He knows what he likes—alcohol, women, and family, in about that order—and he'll continue on with them as before.

That is, until he's surprised by a violent encounter with his match, Jessie Bell, when her stepdaughter doesn't come home as expected.

Bad blood is rampant between the Bells and the Caddells by the time Jessie's daughter and Zingle's nephew unwittingly fall in love. Forbidden to see one another, the couple must decide how much they're willing to risk. Is it worth being ostracized from their families? Destitution? Their very lives?

About the Author

I, Sophia Alexander, am the mother of two college-age children and a number of manuscripts. As a naturopathic-doctor-turned-writer, I used to feel sheepish about the huge swing in my career; more recently, however, I've learned that some of my favorite novelists also have science backgrounds, so I'm in outstanding company that way. My family resides on the outskirts of the beautiful city of Savannah, Georgia, where my husband was born. We studied at the College of Charleston in the even-more-beautiful city where *I* was born, then at Bastyr University in the magnificent Pacific Northwest, where our children were born. My time is now divided between our Savannah home and my grandparents' old home in rural South Carolina, near my folks. There, most of my hours are spent in a spacious writing study that used to be the parlor I was once forbidden from entering. I sometimes wonder what my granny and granddaddy would think of this, and if I'm actually being ornery...

The Silk Trilogy is my debut work, aside from a few award-winning short stories in local anthologies. I hope you enjoy reading it. If so, you can hear my musings and receive updates on my publications by signing up for my newsletter at authorsophiaalexander.blogspot.com and by following me on social media:

www.facebook.com/authorsophiaalexander
Instagram: authorsophiaalexander
Twitter: @authorsophiaa

Made in the USA
Columbia, SC
17 March 2023

14b02108-f3aa-4ac5-84f4-c063cdc07e3aR01